# BONE BOXES

## THREE MYSTERIOUS FIGURES RISE FROM THE DEAD AND APPEAR IN JERUSALEM

### SKIP BALL

*BONE BOXES*
*Three mysterious figures rise from the dead and appear in Jerusalem*
by Skip Ball

Printed in the United States of America.

ISBN 9781498493710

www.xulonpress.com

# FOREWORD

One of the most curious passages in the New Testament that has perplexed commentators for centuries is found in Matthew 27:52-53. There we read that at the time of Jesus' crucifixion, *"The tombs broke open and the bodies of many holy people who had died were raised to life. They came out of the tombs, and after Jesus' resurrection they went into the holy city and appeared to many people."* In this highly engaging work, *Bone Boxes*, we have a fascinating fictional story woven around the mystery found within these verses.

Author Skip Ball has created three engaging characters. First, there is Adam, a child murdered during "the slaughter of the innocents." There is Anna, a woman who was caught in adultery. And finally, Democritus, a former demoniac who lived his life as a prisoner, bound by chains in a cave. Each of these died before Yeshua's death, and are raised to life at his crucifixion. These bold witnesses seek to accomplish their mission of proclaiming Yeshua and his resurrection, and ultimately find their stories culminating in Rome's notorious amphitheater.

The author has sought to stay true to history with his facts and dates, but has woven into it an engaging fictional story. This is a one-of-a-kind historical novel that delves deeply into the issue of Christian persecution that is happening around the world today. Touching also on the pertinent topics of the death of a child, adultery, forgiveness, demonic possession, prostitution, self-mutilation, insanity, molestation, cancer, suicide, and the occult, Skip has written a story that many believers and unbelievers alike will find both fascinating and compelling. It is my great pleasure to recommend *Bone Boxes* by Skip Ball.

**Joel Richardson is a New York Times best-selling author of** *Mideast Beast, The Islamic Antichrist, When a Jew Rules the World, Mystery Babylon* **and Producer of** *End Times Eyewitness Documentary.*

"An engaging novel, tightly woven with Biblical and historical facts. *Bone Boxes* is a story of hope and redemption amidst 1st Century persecution that in many ways resonates with what some are facing today."

**Bill Myers best-selling author of** *Eli, The Face of God, Angel of Wrath, Fire of Heaven.* **He is an award-winning filmmaker. His combined books and videos have sold over 8 million copies.**

*"He who believes in Me, though he may die, he shall live."* Jn. 11:25 NKJ

Skip Ball has drawn on his own life experiences and zeroed in on the critical mindset required of the end-time Church: not loving our lives even when faced with death. The last generation of Christians must parallel the first in their unflinching devotion to following the Lamb, even if it means following Him to martyrdom. I highly recommend *Bone Boxes* to all believers because it will inform, touch and inspire as it begins where our story will ultimately end - the resurrection awaits!

**Christopher Mantei, Managing Director, WingsOfTheEagle.com**

———————•———————

Captivating!! Ancient History mixed with absolutely riveting stories, *Bone Boxes'* characters will leave an indelible mark upon your soul. Yahweh's mysteries, shattered hearts, and ultimate redemption that may change your life forever!

**Valerie McCabe Rose, author of** *"Did the Bible Predict . . ."*
**by Son Catchers Publishing © 2005**

# INTRODUCTION

The creation of *Bone Boxes* has been inspired by a mysterious text from Matthew's account of the crucifixion of Jesus. Consider these verses from Matthew 27:50–53, *"And when Jesus had cried out again in a loud voice, he gave up his spirit. At that moment, the curtain of the temple was ripped in two from top to bottom. The earth shook and the rocks split. The tombs broke open and the bodies of many holy people who had died were raised to life. They came out of the tombs, and after Jesus' resurrection they went into the holy city and appeared to many people."* Each one of these events was catastrophic in nature, yet they were merely a forerunner of something so grand that the course of humanity's hope would change forever. They were pointing to the ultimate sacrifice of Yeshua's death and resurrection, which overshadows all of mankind's attempts at self-redemption found in every civilization and culture up to today. All the historic events prior to Yeshua's crucifixion were pointing to the One Man who offered his life so completely and who called his disciples to follow him toward their own cross as they embraced his death and resurrection power.

How did this story unfold? It began with two guys who like to eat, chat and debate theological issues. One sunny California day as I sat with Preston Curtis in a corner of Weiler's Deli in the San Fernando Valley, we were discussing aspects of the resurrection. Preston suddenly said, "I've been thinking, you should write a historical novel based on the people who were resurrected." That was an exciting challenge. We wondered what happened to the saints who were resurrected from their graves after Jesus' crucifixion. Who were they and where did they go? Preston rattled off several suggestions. We realized that neither of us had heard a single sermon or Bible study on this topic. In fact, few commentaries offered sufficient explanation of this passage. And yet, since the Gospels are true, this account is part of that magnificent story. We might only have part of the story but we know it's purpose.

With that planted in my mind my imagination took hold. A passion grew as the story unfolded and blossomed on paper. I felt God's Spirit bring inspiration. So, I give special credit to my friend Preston Curtis for his rare perspective on what Scripture teaches about life itself. In the spiritual realm, his analytical skills are largely innate—coming to his mind in a moment of inspiration.

This story has been written in layers. As characters began to come alive, Deb Timinskis offered to be my preliminary editor. She laid down some ground rules for grammar and layout. As her role at a private family foundation became more demanding, Deb carved out a sacrificial niche of coveted time to help get *Bone Boxes* off the ground and on the road to success. Deb, I'm forever grateful for the hours you invested.

Then along came John Fraley, my brother and encourager. What a guy! This brother took me under his wing and made this book his pet project. He took my words and clarified each line's meaning. He provided editorial content, proof reading and finally gave stylistic editing to the story. After eight cover to cover edits, over a period of more than two years, John corrected and edited my writing until a beautiful story emerged that gives glory to God through his Son, Yeshua. John, you have blessed me with your faithfulness throughout this project.

Yeshua shines through you. When I became weary, you lifted me up, every time. Thank you brother.

Finally, my son, Chris, has added his natural and highly trained expertise to the design and covers of *Bone Boxes*. Chris poured himself into this project. He did layer upon layer of highly professional work that went above and beyond my expectations. He took my ideas and made them come alive. His wife, Katie, modeled one of the characters for the front cover, and together have made this a magnificent work of art. Chris, I'm so proud of you and Katie.

With a host of family and friends, we've bathed this story in prayer and truly sensed the Spirit's inspiration as truth emerged. I believe many can identify with Adam, Anna and Democritus, feel their pain and rejoice in their victories. You'll see through Malchus and Artamos how sin grips the human heart, how demons seek to conquer and divide and how the vilest person can find hope in Yeshua. *Bone Boxes* is packed with contemporary issues we question every day like depression, cancer, demon possession, fear, poverty, suicide, loss of a child, broken families, prostitution, dementia, terrorism and mass-murderers.

*Bone Boxes* is written from an Israeli perspective. Yeshua, the Hebrew name for Jesus, was an Israeli; he lived in Judea, walked the streets of Jerusalem and died and rose outside the city walls. His disciples were all Jewish. Much research on the Judean culture and the Roman Empire has been incorporated into this book. Scientific, historical, cultural and Biblical references are footnoted to guide you to the source material. All biblical references come from the New International Version, 1985 edition.

While our characters are fictional, Scripture declares that bodies that had once died were made alive in an instant and burst from the grave to become witnesses by the power of Yeshua's resurrection. This story is a type, or shadow, of that great day of resurrection when all saints will be resurrected to be with Yeshua for eternity. Saul, who hunted Christians until he surrendered to Yeshua's love, wrote, *"I want to know Christ and the power of his resurrection and the fellowship of sharing in his sufferings, becoming like him in his death.* (Phil. 3:10.) Still today, Yeshua's enemies are relentless, his followers persecuted. Yet we have hope. That ancient resurrection power is still available for you and me.

In an effort to remain factual in telling a historical narrative within the life of Yeshua, the author has investigated numerous historical documents from both Christian and non-Christian texts such as Jewish and Greco-Roman sources along with Biblical references of historical figures such as Herod the Great and Emperor Tiberius. While there are various opinions among scholars, I've used dates they have generally agreed upon in their historical analyses of the life, death and resurrection of Yeshua. Virtually all modern historians agree that Jesus did exist, taught a life-changing message and was crucified. Therefore we can assume approximate ranges of dates for these events. Based on dates that correlate with contemporary Roman rulers, most scholars assume a date of Yeshua's birth to be between 6 and 4 BC. He taught for at least three years. Many scholars calculate his death as having taken place between AD 30 and 36. *"Astronomical scholars Colin Humphreys and W. Graeme Waddington therefore suggest a scenario where Jesus was crucified and died at 3pm on 3 April AD 33, followed by a red partial lunar eclipse at moonrise at 6:20pm observed by the Jewish population, and that Peter recalls this event when preaching the resurrection to the Jews (Acts of the Apostles 2:14-21)."*[1] The 14th of Nisan in the Jewish Calendar, as written in John's Gospel, equates to Friday, 3 April, AD 33.

For those who love history, I would encourage you to research the non-biblical historians Tacitus and Josephus as well as many other resources on the life, death and resurrection

---

[1] "The date of the Crucifixion" Colin Humphreys and W. Graeme Waddington, March 1985. American Scientific Affiliation website. Retrieved 17 January 2014.

of Yeshua, the Jewish Messiah. To begin, you can find a "Chronology of Jesus" in Wikipedia.

I hope this story blesses and inspires you to believe on his name. As John says, *"But these are written that you may believe that Yeshua is the Christ, the Son of God, and that by believing you may have life in his name."*[2]

---

[2] Jn. 20:31

Chapter One

# "The Blossom of Martyrdom," Prudentius

**Beit Jala, Judea, 4 B.C.**

The night was black with churning clouds that roiled across the horizon. The little village below lay asleep. A chilling breeze whisked leaves into the blackness and dropped them indiscriminately. Somewhere a dove cooed. A baby snuggled closer in his mother's arms. Within another house a child laughed in her sleep. For centuries Beit Jala had remained unchanged: a village of peasants filled with children's laughter in its streets without fear of Rome's suppression.

Without warning, a scream shattered the calm followed by trilling wails that sent shivers into the heart of the earth. A second scream was heard . . . and a third . . . until pandemonium exploded from doorway to doorway. A hideous evil had been unleashed. This night would be unlike any other. Evil was pillaging the most guiltless of sleepers: infants. The Prince of Darkness had orchestrated this hunt for the Child of Promise eons before the sun cast its first rays upon the earth's horizons. This night would fulfill a prophetic nightmare exposing the wantonness of Death to hunt down the Author of Life and destroy God's plan for human redemption. Tonight, a flower would blossom red as the first martyrs are taken in the name of Yeshua.

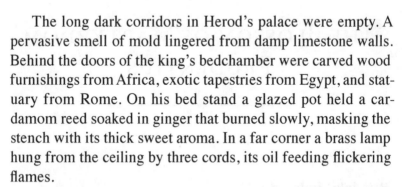

The long dark corridors in Herod's palace were empty. A pervasive smell of mold lingered from damp limestone walls. Behind the doors of the king's bedchamber were carved wood furnishings from Africa, exotic tapestries from Egypt, and statuary from Rome. On his bed stand a glazed pot held a cardamom reed soaked in ginger that burned slowly, masking the stench with its thick sweet aroma. In a far corner a brass lamp hung from the ceiling by three cords, its oil feeding flickering flames.

The king pulled back a heavy curtain of coppery brocade that concealed a small window overlooking the Judean countryside. In his hand he held a fragment of parchment he'd torn from the *Tanakh*, the ancient Hebrew Scriptures. He had obsessed over the two-line inscription for months. His fingers traced the raised letters over and over as if to extract something tangible from the mysterious text, or perhaps to rub out its revealing truth. *"I see him, but not now; I behold him, but not near."* It was babble. *"A star will come out of Jacob; a scepter will rise out of Israel."*[3] It was nothing more than an old scribe's delusional rants . . . but the star . . . he'd seen it . . . and it haunted him.

Tonight, Herod's face was drawn, his expression brooding. He suddenly shivered as he studied the night sky. Something was wrong. Where was the star, the sign? Even on the stormiest of nights, its radiance made the clouds luminescent. Like a cosmic signal, nothing had hidden its brilliance. It was either a

---

[3] Nu. 24:17

portent or . . . a beacon, but tonight Yerushalayim's[4] skies were draped in black. He needed that star tonight and it was gone. He suddenly felt afraid.

Above Beit Jala, intermittent clouds shrouded the moon's face. In the shadows, a soldier emerged from a low doorway. He was panting with a wild-eyed rage, as his thirst for blood was still unquenched. His armored body nearly spanned the door's width. Pools of crimson lay at his feet. The assassin had slaughtered another family, leaving a woman rocking insanely in a corner. Butchered as they slept, a husband and two sons lay on the floor, their sightless eyes peering into nothingness. Blood on the door lintel offered no protection tonight. From within the hovel, the woman's unearthly wail rose upward, filling the room with inexplicable human anguish.

"Ohhh, God, why?" she pleaded. "Why my son?" But no answer came.

The soldier pulled the door shut and disappeared into the darkness away from the woman's cries. Artamos studied the shadowy streets and alleyways of Beit Jala. Behind him was destruction; before him trembling fear. No windows or doorways were lit. The night hung like a leaden curtain. Leaves quivered as a bitter wind pushed its way down crooked streets then flowed out into the expanse of the desert. The moon's faint glow cast a pale blue shadow that draped across the rooftops like a satin shroud.

*Where are you?* He scanned the Heavens, hoping it would betray the whereabouts of a promised child-savior. But the star's brilliance was waning and the soldier could not distinguish any guiding rays.

---

[4] "Yerushalayim" is the Hebrew form of "Jerusalem" found in the Tanakh, the Hebrew Bible, meaning "the city of He who is Perfect."

The man's thirsty craze grew and churned in his gut. No battle he had ever fought held such terror as tonight. He felt driven . . . goaded, and he struggled to maintain sanity.

*Herod is obsessed with this invisible enemy of his.* "Herod the Great!" The mocking words hissed into the wind. "I've trained Rome's best men. I taught them courage and justice," he muttered. "Now I'm just an assassin." Artamos walked toward the village.

Behind each door, in every earthen hovel, families huddled and prayed. They'd awakened to the sounds of terror and sensed the hideous presence that stalked their streets. They were defenseless tillers of the earth. They could do nothing but pray and wait for the inevitable evil to come. Fathers fought panic, mothers wept in silent terror and infants whimpered.

"Hush my babies. Hush. God help us," they pleaded, unable to comprehend the cost of redemption. God himself was groaning under the weight of the hunt for his beloved Son, who even this night lay sleeping in his mother's arms. The enemy was very close. God alone would pay the price for the redemption of the world. Humanity's only hope lay sleeping in Bethlehem merely a few miles from Beit Jala. A Redeemer was born and, already, a relentless pursuit was underway to find and destroy him.

Artamos was suddenly startled. His eyes twitched. He stared down at his bloodied hands. The moon's pale light turned the blood to black. The soldier wiped his hands on his tunic. *Still there!* He smeared them on the ground. *Still bloody!* Panic clutched his throat. Blood had never bothered him before. The soldier hurried toward the village square where the well stood. It had been visited by every mother and daughter in Beit Jala for centuries. Hastily he lowered the bucket. After he drew water, Artamos placed the bucket on the stone edge and thrust his hands into the liquid. Blood from infants, fathers, mothers and older sons mingled as one. He watched as curls of black crimson spiraled into the clear liquid until all had turned guilty red.

Clouds had shifted and the moon's face gazed at him in silence: he felt exposed. As he turned to go, the bucket toppled, spilling the blood into the well, now forever polluted. There the tainted waters would cry out for justice. The assassin cursed.

Artamos hurried down a tangled street that led to his next victim. No homes were barricaded. No one resisted. The soldier pulled a tattered sheet of parchment from his belt. A census had been issued that held the identities of every family living in Beit Jala. With the tip of his blade he'd scratched out the names of thirty-seven infant boys and their families. Any one of them might have been the promised child. He glanced at the final family name on the list—Ben-Asher.

*Perhaps this is the one.* His eyes stopped briefly on Herod's great seal. Artamos headed toward the house.

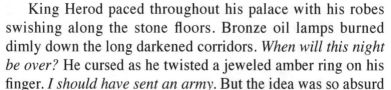

King Herod paced throughout his palace with his robes swishing along the stone floors. Bronze oil lamps burned dimly down the long darkened corridors. *When will this night be over?* He cursed as he twisted a jeweled amber ring on his finger. *I should have sent an army.* But the idea was so absurd he laughed nervously. *Sending an army to kill a bunch of peasants would make me the laughing stock of Rome.*

Inflamed by obsession for power, Herod was certain one of these male babies was the prophesied *HaMashiach*, the Hebrew Messiah the astrologers had foretold. The king stopped pacing and leaned his forehead against a stone column. Pressure pumped through his skull and drilled down his neck. "Where is Artamos?" he bellowed at the walls.

Herod was gripped by fears. He feared the observations of stargazers, the bones of dead men and the predictions of prophets. He'd already murdered his wife, three sons, mother-in-law, brother-in-law and uncle. If a peasant's child was a potential threat to his throne, he must destroy him as well. A handful of babies meant nothing to him. Wiping out the sons of these villagers was little in his eyes if he could only be certain the usurper was dead. Herod stopped at a window and studied the moon. The star was gone. Perhaps Artamos had found the child king. He must be patient.

A wind had risen in Beit Jala and doors swung uselessly where bodies lay slaughtered. The soldier eyed the dwelling of Ben-Asher. From there he would head to Bethlehem and finally home. Artamos had children of his own. His wife, Claudia, would be asleep with their two young children in the village of Beit Rahel. His three-year-old son and five-year-old daughter were safe. He had fathered a bastard son somewhere; the boy meant nothing to him.

The clouds shifted in restless patterns as he stole down the narrow lane. The soldier suddenly realized a sound was growing in the night air. Its incessant rhythm throbbed. He cocked his head against the wind. The night was groaning. Voices cried and wailed everywhere he turned. It merged into a universal lament rising up into the ears of God to ask the eternal question:

*"Why God? Why death? Why my child?"*

Artamos clamped his hands over his ears as he rushed through the streets like a madman. "Stop. You don't understand. Stop!" Artamos bellowed. "You must listen. If I fail, *my* wife and children will be slaughtered! I have no choice!" But his voice was swallowed up in the cacophony of the night.

An evil spirit rippled through the soldier. Instantly, his pupils dilated and his eyes went black. His jaw tightened. He moved down the final street in Beit Jala and headed for the last house in the village where an infant boy lay sleeping. He was trained to kill without mercy.

The tiny house was wedged between two larger dwellings, their fronts connected by crooked walls and an uneven roof line. The walls made of mud and straw were weathered and colorless. No trees were on this street, only an earthen pot with the faint scent of rosemary. Its alpine scent flowed down the lane along with the cold wind, and was gone.

Inside, Ben-Asher and his wife Rachel huddled in the semi-darkness. To sleep was futile. A clay lamp on a rough wooden table held a single flame creating shadows that danced across the walls.

Rachel comforted Adam as she rubbed his tiny back trying to calm her son's troubled dreams. She touched the heart-shaped birthmark on the nap of his neck with tender affection. Her own heart trembled. The child had slept restlessly for the past hour. He wakened at every scream and fretted until sleep closed in again. Rachel knew her son sensed the nearness of evil: so foreign and now so present. She felt his tiny limbs stiffen at the sounds. She held him tight but still he trembled.

Outside, the sounds grew louder, closer. Rachel looked fearfully at her husband then toward the door. He was here. Death was imminent. The child cried helplessly. The trilling wails across the village chilled Rachel's heart. Adam awoke, fear etched his tiny face. Round eyes questioned his mother, but she could only comfort . . . she could promise little except her undying love.

"Okay, my baby. Quiet now. Quiet." Rachel rocked her son. Adam's troubled cries roused the room's silence. "Quiet, little one. I'm with you. God is near." His breathing was labored.

An armored fist hit the door. An iron hinge snapped. Rachel screamed, then buried her face and the baby's in Ben-Asher's embrace. The child cried and trembled in her arms. Ben-Asher had no weapon. He was not a fighter.

"Who is it?" His voice wavered and cracked.

"In the name of King Herod, open up."

"It's the middle of the night and we're all in bed. Please leave us alone."

Rachel's eyes were wild with fear. She held Adam so tight she feared she might crush him. The room seemed to dim around them as darkness approached. There was no place to hide.

"Open this door or I'll smash it like the others!" his voice roared. The soldier banged and kicked the slatted door; it didn't resist. A glint of metal pierced the wood.

The family crouched back against the wall, Ben-Asher standing in front, his arms protectively outstretched. A beast had been let loose and Beit Jala was weeping.

"Please leave us alone. Haven't you done enough destruction to our village?" Ben-Asher pleaded. "The blood of our sons is on your hands already. Don't do any more killing. Perhaps God will forgive you."

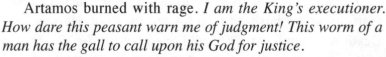

Artamos burned with rage. *I am the King's executioner. How dare this peasant warn me of judgment! This worm of a man has the gall to call upon his God for justice.*

With a heavy thud, his body hit the spindly wooden door. Riveted armor tore into soft pine. Splinters jettisoned across the room. Rachel screamed and the family flattened against the opposite wall in sheer terror.

Ben-Asher could do nothing but pray. He cried out, "God of Abraham, Isaac and Jacob, save us!"

A second hit caused the door to explode sending flying debris into every corner of the room. Rachel screamed again. A spike of wood slashed Ben-Asher's forehead and blood gushed down his face. Instinctively, he raised his arm while his body continued to hide his wife and son from the beast. As the soldier tore through the opening, his size overpowered the tiny room.

"Don't! In the name of Jehovah God, don't harm . . ." Ben-Asher shielded his family as the blade swung, slicing through tissue and muscle, leaving a gaping wound across his chest. An inch closer and his throat would have been torn open. Rachel screamed and Adam cried as his father slid to the floor in agony.

Ben-Asher's wound was deep. He pressed against the opening as blood oozed between his fingers. He felt light-headed and his legs went weak. Through a spiraling fog, Ben-Asher struggled to pull himself up. The soldier tried a direct lance to his throat. As the blade flashed, Ben-Asher slid sideways and it lodged in the plaster, spraying fragments in the air. The dagger twanged.

"I'll kill all of you. You're nothing but swine to the king!" Artamos cursed as he yanked the blade free from the wall.

Ben-Asher was losing blood and the room began to spin. He wiped blood from his eyes and tried to stand, but the soldier slammed his boot against Ben-Asher's chest. He kicked him aside and moved toward Rachel.

Ben-Asher grabbed at the soldier's ankle causing him to stumble. He snatched an empty jug and threw it into the soldier's face. Shards and dust covered the soldier, but he quickly shook it away. Before the beast could stand, Ben-Asher lunged forward and threw himself on top of the soldier, causing his own blood to spray across the walls. He pummeled the soldier's face with his fists. Artamos shoved him aside and with a single move pinned the peasant on his back. He slashed Ben-Asher's face with his studded cuff. Finally, he stood and laughed.

Ben-Asher had no more strength. He crawled across the dirt toward his family, leaving a bloody trail behind him. "God will defeat you even if I can't," he gasped.

Artamos moved toward Rachel and the boy.

Rachel's face blistered red with terror. Tightness choked air from her lungs as her world tumbled into chaos.

She cried, "Don't kill my baby! Herod's a madman! The king is a coward and a fool! Don't kill my son!"

Artamos closed the gap between his face and hers. He grabbed her arm and pulled her toward himself.

"Treason!" His breath was hot and putrid. "You speak treason against Caesar and against King Herod!" His eyes were like black holes staring without mercy.

"What purpose is there in all this killing?" Rachel questioned.

"To fulfill the king's command," his voice danced. Artamos peered at the child in her arms for a chilling moment. The assassin studied the tiny face. *Perhaps this is the hunted one the king fears. If he is the one, then I alone have found him. But, if he really is the Jewish Messiah and I destroy him then I am damned forever.*

The child had become silent in the face of death. Pools of golden brown liquid stared innocently into his killer's eyes. A single glance from the child questioned evil's senseless rampage. In that split second, confusion washed over the soldier's face . . . then, like a dream, vanished. Cold riveting eyes glared back at the child's innocent gaze. The soldier raised his arms high. Rachel screamed, shoving herself into the corner of the room. The blade hung in the air, its tip stained and ready to tear life from the living. With one swift move, the tip pierced the smooth unblemished skin of Adam without mercy. The child's eyes glazed over in seconds. His body went flaccid in his mother's arms, his mouth still open in a silent death scream.

Rachel screamed in terror. She'd felt Adam's life dissipate like a vapor. He was gone.

Ben-Asher had not reached his son in time. He'd crawled within two feet of his tiny body before he lay dead. The father had done everything to stop this murderer but failed to do so.

Rachel slid down the wall still holding her lifeless baby, his life blood soaking in a pool in her lap and seeping onto the floor. Adam's blood splattered against her cheek. She pressed her hand against the wound in Adam's chest, fruitlessly trying to stop the bleeding. It gushed from his chest until the body was white and cold. She sobbed uncontrollably. Her world suddenly seemed senseless.

Ben-Asher crawled toward them and wrapped his broken family in an embrace. Shameless tears burned his cheeks. His son was gone. He held them until his wife collapsed into unconsciousness.

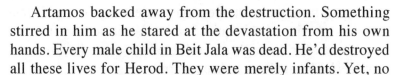

Artamos backed away from the destruction. Something stirred in him as he stared at the devastation from his own hands. Every male child in Beit Jala was dead. He'd destroyed all these lives for Herod. They were merely infants. Yet, no power on earth could bring them back to life.

Slowly, the assassin staggered backward until his shoulders hit the wall. The flame from the clay lamp flickered. The tiny room was airless, suffocating. His shadow loomed large for a moment and then shrunk as the flame withered and died. The oil of life was gone, the flame extinguished.

Still facing his victims, Artamos moved through the broken door frame, stumbling into the street. He turned the corner, heaved bile, then staggered into the night and disappeared.

"I must find him. I must find him."

# Chapter Two

# BETHLEHEM, JUDEA, 4 B.C.

Cavernous shadows lingered deep in Bethlehem. The night's silence was interrupted only by a hush as mothers sang lullabies in the darkness. An owl hooted softly. But from the west, the same restless sky over Beit Jala was now moving to this quiet hamlet. Unsuspecting families were in bed for the night. A chill blew through the streets as families huddled closer to keep warm.

All at once from within one dwelling a light blazed with a blistering radiance. The unearthly brilliance pierced the house. Light seeped outward from every crack in the simple abode. The phenomenon lasted mere earth seconds and then was gone. An arc of light then seared across the black horizon, leaving a ripple in the atmosphere like heat waves in the desert.

The cottage lay in darkness once again, but the inhabitants were now stirring. Low voices spoke in urgent tones. Something fell to the floor. A lamp was lit. Voices gave way to anxious movements that only Heaven observed.

An hour later, a donkey was laden with bedding, food and drink for a long journey into the heart of Egypt. The mother glanced at her child and marveled. Their urgent movements hadn't disturbed him, but *her* face was lined with concern.

Before the midnight hour, their shadows emerged from the darkness of Bethlehem heading into the barren desert toward the great tombs of the kings. Mary's heart was heavy. She studied Yosef's face, remembering the words of the old man, Simeon: *"This child is destined to cause the falling and rising of many in Israel, and to be a sign that will be spoken against, so that the thoughts of many hearts will be revealed. And a sword will pierce your own soul too.*[5]*"*

Was this just the beginning? Mary had learned to trust God without hesitation. But not even she could possibly fathom the relentless hunt that would scatter her people into exile. She could not comprehend that her son would be the target of hatred by a people yet to be. Religions not yet created would one day rise up, twisting truth into a sword of destruction to hunt and slaughter God's chosen ones. The history of barbaric acts against those who bore the name of Yeshua would be unleashed across the planet until the blood-soaked ground would cry out for justice. History's final page would be written in the blood of martyrs.

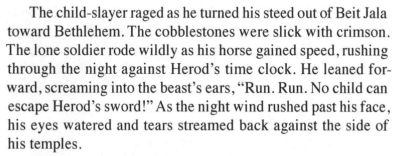

The child-slayer raged as he turned his steed out of Beit Jala toward Bethlehem. The cobblestones were slick with crimson. The lone soldier rode wildly as his horse gained speed, rushing through the night against Herod's time clock. He leaned forward, screaming into the beast's ears, "Run. Run. No child can escape Herod's sword!" As the night wind rushed past his face, his eyes watered and tears streamed back against the side of his temples.

*I'm covered in blood. But not a drop is my own. What have I done?* His victims had not resisted. Where did this savage lust for blood come from? Why couldn't he stop it? Grinding

---

[5] Lu. 2:34-35

his teeth, he pushed the horse harder. The stallion lowered its head, flattened its ears and raced into the blackness. Artamos could only hear the rhythm of hoofs pounding the earth and the heavy breathing of the war horse beneath him.

Out in the desert, the sky was velvet black with pinpricks of light hung high overhead. A shooting star seared through the night, beyond the escaping family, and vanished on the horizon. The donkey's plodding steps were silent in the sand—only its steady breathing could be heard. The deep silence was weighted by what Mary was certain she could hear. Behind them was the sound of despair rising from the village of Bethlehem—faint, but unmistakable. Mary's eyes locked on Yosef's face. He, too, heard the cries but could only shake his head. Mary wept for those who had no warning. They were dear friends and neighbors. Huddled into a solitary shadow, the family moved over the dunes into the unknown.

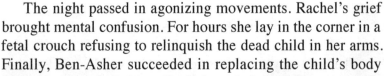

The night passed in agonizing movements. Rachel's grief brought mental confusion. For hours she lay in the corner in a fetal crouch refusing to relinquish the dead child in her arms. Finally, Ben-Asher succeeded in replacing the child's body with a bundle of clothing. Rachel needed something to caress. His heart was ripped apart, too, but grief would have to wait.

Ben-Asher's own gash oozed with a dulling pain he refused to think about. He had tied long strips of cloth around his chest in a feeble attempt to slow the blood flow. He wrapped another strip of cloth around his forehead; it was immediately saturated with blood. He then carried the body of his son into the kitchen and carefully laid him out on the rough wooden table. He looked one last time into little Adam's eyes. The fire had gone out. He touched the lids tenderly and closed them. Life in this world promised much, but gave him very little. Now there was nothing more to offer.

Gently he peeled away the bloody clothes that wrapped his son's body. His skin was cool and smooth. Ben-Asher ran his fingers along the child's arms down to his fingertips. His dreams of the muscular son who would work the fields would never be. Those fingers that clutched at a ball of twine, those eyes that laughed at the playfulness of a kitten, those little feet that were so eager to always run instead of walk lay deadly still . . . forever.

Deep loss and sorrow replaced the terror. Ben-Asher felt faint as the adrenaline flow ceased. His hands trembled as he prepared his tiny son for his last journey to Yerushalayim, the city of peace. Inside, his own stomach ached with a new brokenness never before experienced.

Adam's body had quickly turned ashen gray, his lips pallid and blue. Death wasted no time claiming its prey. Ben-Asher sponged the body with clean water and was especially meticulous around the gash in his chest. Then he took a bottle of ointment containing jasmine and frankincense. He removed the clay stopper from the jar and immediately its sweet fragrance wafted through the room like an offering of brokenness.

*Why must life be so hard?* Death was the one unavoidable stone that all humans eventually stumble upon, and from which they never recover.

Ben-Asher left the house just after dawn. The sky was somber with a pewter gray that hugged the ground. Thirty miles over low hills and bleak stretches of barren earth sat the city of Yerushalayim. There he knew a Roman stonemason, Hermes. As he walked beside his graying donkey, he recalled taking this trip last year. That journey was to purchase a sarcophagus for his mother's body. Today his son lay wrapped in a bundle across the back of the donkey. He caressed the bundle. Although Adam was no longer there, Ben-Asher's heart did not want to let go. He still wanted to protect his precious offspring. The journey would be strenuous.

Rachel remained in a catatonic state. Her sister, Susanna, had helped Ben-Asher carry her to bed where she numbly lay in a curled position, refusing to eat or drink and unable to speak coherently. Susanna would help to bear the grief of her younger sister while Ben-Asher buried little Adam.

The donkey's hoofs crunched on the rocky ground as it carried death's burden. The morning was still cool. This journey would take two days. Maybe the rigorous trip would give Ben-Asher time to accept something that he could not change. The tiny bundle clung like a cocoon to the donkey's back.

"You did not deserve this, my son." Tears erupted. "I had such great hopes for you, Adam. Your brightness amazed the village," he spoke in sobs. "Everyone loved you. But evil happens. The history of our people is full of atrocities. I just never thought . . . I just never dreamed it could happen to us . . . to you." Adam's body rocked gently as they plodded down the dirt road. The dry dust kicked up by the lonely travelers hung in the air.

Perhaps Rachel would never recover from Adam's death. Perhaps they would never bear another child. How does anyone prepare for such a tragedy? He had heard of Rome's meaningless cruelty many times. *First they conquer Judea to plunder our resources. Now they kill our sons and leave us to suffer and die. But God gave Israel a choice. ". . . I have set before you life and death, blessings and curses. Now choose life, so that you and your children may live and that you may love the Lord your God . . . for the Lord is your life . . ."*[6]

"Oh God, how can this be?" Ben-Asher let out an anguished wail and stumbled to his knees. The donkey startled and bolted. Ben-Asher's grief tore at his soul. Grabbing handfuls of dirt, he threw it on his head. The unthinkable had been done and his precious son was gone—his only son.

"Why God? Why?" Ben Asher cried. "Why?" he wept bitterly. "Did you not hear all my prayers of protection for this life you entrusted to me? What's the point of life if it only ends like this? My son is gone forever." How could he trust God now?

Ben Asher's words were so familiar, the agony so real. In ancient history a mighty king had faced these emotions. King David had pleaded for his infant son to live. When the child died, the king said, *"Can I bring him back again? I will go to him, but he will not return to me."*[7] Somehow the king recovered and still trusted God.

Time filtered past his grief until the sun stood directly overhead. He had fallen into an exhausted sleep. He woke with a sudden start, his grief melding into anger. Ben-Asher raked his fingers through his hair in desperation and finally lifted himself from the ground. His body ached as his wounds tightened. Blood seeped through his makeshift bandaging.

"I must go on, too."

His donkey stood grazing, still bearing death's burden. Ben-Asher must hurry. He had no time to debate with God. *Either I believe it all or I believe nothing.* With every dream stolen, Ben-Asher still called out for help. "God, help me to get to the city in time." Death could not wait. Weary and in great pain, Ben-Asher moved with purpose toward Yerushalayim where

---

[6] De. 30:19,20; given to Israel from Moses; Israel was given a choice as to how they should live; life or death.

[7] 2 Sam. 12:23

his son would rest alongside the humble and great on the Mount of Olives.

"*HaMashiach*, come quickly. This life is too painful for us to be on our own."

Dawn broke as the calloused soldier returned from his carnage in Beit Jala and Bethlehem. Herod was enraged. He was certain the Messiah child still lived. His sorcerer's potions, bones and amulets gave confusing signs. His astrologers witnessed a shooting brilliance in the night sky that carried an ominous sign.

Artamos knew he was not strong enough to fight the king's phantom enemy. No soldier could satisfy this paranoid ruler. The blood of newborns was on Artamos' hands, the stains indelible. His career was in ruins . . . his life over.

"I gave you a simple order." His stale breath blasted Artamos' face. "You alone were to kill all the male infants in two insignificant villages." The king's hands shook with rage. "You know why I ordered this, because we must be certain that the One Child was found and slaughtered."

His high-pitched voice squealed and whined. "That's all I asked. A simple task! You fool, you incompetent fool. My enemy is defenseless, and yet, you can't find him." His voice became erratic, wavering out of control until he was screaming again. He paced in circles; his robe billowed wildly.

"I did as you commanded, O king." Artamos bowed his head in deference to Herod. "Every male baby aged three and under was slaughtered." Artamos' left eye began to twitch. His mouth quivered. He was bewildered at the king's response. He tried to remain at attention, but his feet backed away. He realized his shoulders were slumped in defeat. He made a vain attempt to stand tall . . . like a commander.

"Every male child? No one escaped? No one was missing?" The king's eyes studied him. He moved closer, eye to eye. Herod circled the soldier three times. He didn't say a word, just circled the pitiful man who called himself a commander. The king turned to a guard. "Strip his armor."

Two guards tore off Artamos' armor, boots and straps. They unbuckled him, ripped and pulled every scrap of metal from his body until he stood there before the king in his tunic. With his head hung low and body defeated, he waited for the king.

"Look at you! You're a pathetic excuse of a soldier." Herod waltzed around the soldier laughing in mockery. "I used to think you were a real man . . . but now look at you." The king traced Artamos' face with a long, manicured finger. "What a waste." He shook his head. "But now I see you're just a maggot."

Herod stopped in front of the doomed man. He studied Artamos' eyes.

"You . . . failed . . . me!" he shrieked in his face, leaving spittle dripping from Artamos' beard. Every soldier in the room was startled at the outburst. "A house was empty, a family missing." Herod's pupils narrowed into black holes. "I sent two spies to follow you. Do you think I trusted your word alone?"

"Y-your Majesty . . . there was . . . a carpenter's house, but no one was there. It could have been empty for weeks. I . . . I left no male infant alive . . . sir . . . none." The king was shaking. His face darkened. "You failed, Artamos. I have no use for you anymore."

"Guards!" he shouted. Immediately, the clatter of running soldiers brought fifteen guards to Herod's side. They rushed Artamos, encircling him with spears. "Get him out of my sight. Throw him into the dungeons . . . at Masada. Keep him alive for now."

He turned back to Artamos, studying him up and down. "Perhaps . . . oh . . . eighteen months might do you a world of good, commander." He laughed again. "Forget about your family. I'll come up with some devious story of how you died."

Artamos had a single thought as he was dragged away from the king's presence. *"Where were all these soldiers last night in Beit Jala?"*

The dungeon was carved deep into the mountainside of one of Herod's palaces. The room was small with a single shaft that brought in a meager exchange of stale air and only a spear of light. The smell of mildew, feces and urine stung his nostrils. Artamos realized he was not alone. Dark shadows moved about in the hole, preparing for his torture. Instinctively he backed away from his tormentors. Someone was behind him.

Something shook his skull so hard it made his teeth grind. Sparks pierced his vision. A pain throbbed in his head, then all went dark. When Artamos awoke, his arms were stretched out from side to side. Chains held him suspended in midair. His legs were splayed wide with three-inch manacles and chains stretching him like a roasted pig across the center of a black hole. A four-inch iron collar encircled his neck with a chain embedded in the back wall.

Two tormentors took turns lashing his back and chest with whips until their arms were exhausted. Artamos fought to maintain his sanity. He thought about his children and wondered if he would ever see them again. He thought about Claudia, but her image dimmed as consciousness fled. He had never needed anyone before. The king believed in this messiah and feared him. Where was he? Just before blacking out Artamos whispered hoarsely, "Where are you, Messiah?"

Eighteen months of flogging and torture wasted the commander to mere pulp. His concern for life faded as he was beaten, stretched, hung upside down, and savaged by a dog. His limbs shook, his left hand withered. His eyesight had dimmed and the scarring on his back and chest was a mass of webbing. His hair and beard had become a tangle of gray.

When Artamos was released he was a broken man—he was useless. Recurring dreams left him incapacitated, unable to function during the day. Every night he would wake screaming from some unimaginable nightmare. They were always the same; the innocent faces of babies, the terror-stricken parents. Claudia and the children shunned him and finally abandoned him.

Day after day, Artamos sat at the gates outside Yerushalayim, his eyes fixed on the road leading to the walled city. *Perhaps the Messiah will come today. Perhaps today fate will bless me.* He would wait for the child he had failed to find.

In the ever-unfolding drama of human history time never stands still. The promised God-Child successfully escaped Herod's grasp. Night after night, shrouded in the darkness of the barren desert, the lone family traveled, their solitary shadow plodding into the unknown at the obedience of a beneficent command. There was no star, no pillar of fire, only confidence in a divine plan. Finally, they reached the safety of Egypt's borders. Their concealment was so perfect: only history kept the secret of the Messiah's whereabouts. Perhaps hidden in one of the bustling cities of Alexandria, Memphis or Thebes, strangers sustained and nurtured the exiled family.

Although the infant Yeshua remained safely concealed from Herod, the expanding Roman Empire seeped into Egypt's burgeoning cities through traders and merchants generating international commerce. Day after day, the family inevitably mingled and rubbed shoulders with cultures from Mesopotamia, Hispania, Gallia, Italia, Africa, Noricum and as far away as Germania. All the while, the child was being prepared for a task no human had ever undertaken; he was born to bear the weight of humanity's sins upon his shoulders. It would ultimately crush him to death. But death itself could not hold him. The God-Man would rise, conquering humanity's greatest enemy, and provide an offering of forgiveness to every culture and to all who called upon his name.

# Chapter Three

# YERUSHALAYIM, 29 A.D.

The room was small, lit only by two clay oil lamps casting shadows that distorted the watcher's vision. He stood hunched outside, cloaked in darkness, with one eye peering through a tiny slit in the back door. Blinking to focus, he watched the shadows. One slender form moved gracefully across the room with elegance: the other, a massive shadow, stood still, waiting. The eyes peered to either side straining to extend his peripheral vision. Clothes had been thrown on a chair. The man grunted, demanding that she hurry.

"Don't make me wait all night, woman. I'm paying good money."

*That voice!* The peering eyes widened. *I know that voice.* Then the huge form moved into the light. The light was dim but bright enough to catch the glimmer of drool that ran down his double chin. It was enough to expose the face. Shock stunned the voyeur and he cursed under his breath. Hidden in darkness, the eyes blinked again.

*That swine. Why has he let himself be lured into this woman's bed?* The priest's eyes were riveted as the shadows moved. His heart beat fast, but he could not resist. Then the priest chided himself. He should turn his head away. He should walk away from this scene, but something pulled him to stay. His own senses stirred as he watched the shadows move.

*What a reckless thing to do, the Temple high priest . . . visiting a harlot.* The onlooker shuddered. There lay his superior like a swine in the mud. The priest crept away under the heavy cloak of darkness, his passions stinging him like a swarm of bees . . . shame, anger, wantonness.

Rage rose up like a fire in his chest. *How could this happen? It was the woman's fault—that sensuous beautiful woman who lured unsuspecting innocent men into her viper's nest.* He tried to shake the image out of his head as he rushed hastily into the night.

The man was obese. He lay beside the slender beauty like a beached whale. Suddenly he rolled onto his side, grunted a couple of times, and soon snored a steady roar. Anna lay silent next to the huge form, clutching the sheets tight around her face. Her eyes were wild like a frightened rabbit. Even with so many years of men using and abusing her to the frenzy of their animal passions, Anna still ached inside. It never got easier contrary to her father's promise. He often told her, "You'll get used to it, little Anna. It's like any other job—you do what needs to be done; take the money and leave. Don't think about it; think about the money."

Four years had passed since her father forced Anna into feathering his nest. He got rich while Anna's heart shattered like porcelain, broken into a million pieces every day. Only one man had come close to loving her: a Roman soldier from Puteoli, Italy. He treated her with kindness, but no, that wasn't love. It couldn't have been. Alexander was married.

The man stirred. His movement brought a wave of pungent body odor and stale garlic. Anna covered her mouth to keep from gagging. She slipped from the bed holding the sheet close to her body, grabbed her scarlet tunic and wrapped it around herself. Then with practiced stealth, Anna picked up the pouch that lay on the table. It only contained two coins, meager earnings for selling her soul.

Her father would be angry, but they both knew that men in the Temple were often the stingiest of all creatures. Anna felt the coins between her fingers. The worn relief of Caesar's face felt contemptible.

*Whose offerings were these?* She glanced one more time at the old snoring priest and made a calculated move toward his clothes strewn on a mat. She grabbed them and slipped out of the house, tossing them into a muddy ditch before heading down the cobbled lane. *What will they say at the Temple tomorrow when the priest arrives naked?* Her bare feet stirred little currents of dust as she walked with determined steps toward the public baths.

Thankfully they were empty. Plastered walls encircled the pool that warmed during the day. Anna walked down a pathway and into the entrance. The walls closed in around her leaving only the sky above. She looked up at the starry night. It felt like a canopy covering her—a canopy of deep blue sprinkled with glistening diamonds. Canopies reminded her of Jewish marriage vows, something she feared she would never experience. How she had hoped for that canopy of protection found in marriage, the strength of a husband, and the pleasure of children laughing and clutching at her clothing.

"But that will never be," she spoke aloud. The hushed sounds touched the walls gently and then escaped into the night air like a vapor. Anna slipped her clothes from her shoulders and stepped into the pool. The water was colder than she had anticipated—she gasped and caught her breath. Cold or not, she must cleanse herself. She plunged into the pool, immersing her entire body. Coming up for air, Anna threw her head back and splashed water onto her face and neck. She wanted to rid herself of the smell, the touch, the words of the dirty priest.

*How could a man be holy one moment and filthy the next? How could a priest do such deeds of evil in darkness and proclaim blessings of light upon the people in the day?*

Water trickled over her shoulders, down her breasts and back into the pool. The feelings of filth lingered as Anna plunged her shivering body back beneath the surface. She allowed only her face to emerge above the water until she calmed. The stars threw a spray of diamonds across the Heavens while the luminous moon brushed each ripple with liquid silver.

Repeatedly, Anna plunged beneath the surface. But the anguish of so many men using and abusing her would not wash away. It never did. Her guilt and shame were a part of her soul. Fate had misled her into a world of misery. She imagined Alexander's arms around her, his lips near hers. Anna shivered as she recalled her foolish dreams. That's all they were. No one loved her. Not really.

*No matter what my future may be, my past will always haunt me. I can't get rid of the sins of my past. I hate these men who do such filthy things to me. I hate myself for living like this. I hate my father for forcing me to live like . . . a harlot . . . If only he would love me as his daughter instead of . . .* She wouldn't allow herself to think the truth about her father. *If only . . .* But Anna knew there were no answers awaiting her questions. She believed that beyond the blue velvet midnight the Heavens were as hard as brass. No one heard her pleas for help.

She looked up into the night sky and suddenly realized the salty water she tasted was her own tears. How many nights had Anna pleaded with tears to a God she could not understand and who obviously seemed not to care about her wretched life?

Anna stepped out of the water. The moon's light cast a pale glow against her skin. Shivering with the cold, she wrapped the scarlet robe around her wet body and walked away from the bathhouse still carrying with her the sin stains of her broken life.

The morning began with a slight breeze that brought relief from the sun's penetrating glare. Anna rose early enough to prepare herself for being in public. Her eyes were swollen. Crying oneself to sleep was never recommended as a potion for beauty rest. Last night's dream brought Alexander out of the darkness and swept her off her feet, and together they rode away from her cursed slavery of prostitution. When Anna awoke, her tears were as real as the day. Her dream quickly faded into the pit of her stomach, like gnawing hunger when there is no food.

Anna glanced at the table. The two coins were gone. "Oh papa," she cried in defeat. "I needed that for food today." But her father was also gone. She knew he was probably already sitting under a shady tree drinking ale and talking with friends. Sadness overwhelmed her. She wondered if life was worth all the heartache.

After washing, Anna sifted through her clothes until she found some brightly colored tunics. A royal blue tunic reminded her of the night sky. She slid it over her head and tied a soft green belt around her waist. Over her shoulder Anna threw a head cover of green silk. Once outside, she would cover her head and face, allowing only her piercing eyes to be exposed.

For a moment, the bright colors made her feel better. She stood in front of the mirror and surveyed her appearance. She felt that sickening shame—betrayed by her own reflection. Using a small brush, Anna painted her eyelashes with Egyptian make-up, lining her eyes to hide her sadness.

She headed for the market with what few coins her father had not found. She needed fresh vegetables and fish. The sky was warm and felt good against her skin. The smells of the market place, the sound of vendors mixed with children's laughter, brought momentary pleasure to her soul. She remembered playing in these same streets . . . sneaking a crust of bread from the baker when he glanced away. She remembered laughing with friends. But that was before she lost her soul and her innocence. That was before her father had touched her.

A plump mother moved among the stalls with a trail of children. Anna smiled as she followed the little family, somehow longing for what could have been. The mother bought a piece of smoked fish and handed it to the girl behind her.

"Share," demanded the mother. The daughter picked off a piece of flesh, popped it into her mouth and passed the remainder behind. Finally, after all were satisfied they pranced along behind their mother—just a trail of children, filled with laughter, fish and contentment. Anna simply ached.

A stall filled with the colors of Egypt caught Anna's eye. They were rich and luxurious. The vendor shouted, "Dress like the Queen of Sheba. Buy exotic Egyptian linen and silk for a price only Jews would dare to haggle over!"

Anna moved closer. The colors seemed to shimmer in the sunlight. She smiled.

From beneath the canopy, the vendor's eyes wandered until he spotted Anna. With teeth missing and two day's stubble, the vendor moved close enough to grab her arm.

"Ah, we have a woman of the street, and a beautiful one I might add."

Anna yanked her arm loose and turned her back. She felt heat rise in her face.

"Oh my. Such a temper." He stroked the material Anna had been eying. "I see you have a taste for the expensive. Certainly you have a rich man who takes care of such a beauty as you." He shoved it into her hands.

She dropped the bolt of material. "Leave me alone." Anna began to walk away.

"Come now, you must be used to rough men." He undressed her with his eyes.

Anna pulled the veil over her face and turned away. Her hands began to shake. Suddenly she had become the center of attention. A cluster of women had heard the merchant's remarks. They moved closer to listen. When they spotted Anna, someone shouted, "The marriage breaker herself! She has enough gall to show herself in public!"

"How did you like my man last week? Did he treat you the way he treats me?" The woman lifted her veil to show a bruise on her face.

A third woman cackled loudly, "Oh, did you hear the High Priest Phinehas rushed through the village this morning, stark naked? No doubt, he had a busy night."

Anna's face seared with shame. Under the cover of her veil, her dark eyes glared into the faces of the women. Frightened, she looked around her, desperate to escape. Crowds grew and the taunting swelled. Someone threw a tomato at her. The blood of the fruit splattered her face.

The merchant shouted, "Get out of here! I've got a business to run!" He shoved her into the crowd causing others to push her away. She stumbled.

The mother had returned with her trail of children. As they entered the chaos, they too joined in the ridicule. One child grabbed an egg and threw it in Anna's face. Her eye liner ran down her cheeks mingled with egg yolk and tears. Anna tried to flee, but the crowds surrounded her and barred her from retreat. She slipped on the splattered eggs but caught herself. Someone yanked her veil from her head. The crowd laughed. They mocked her, throwing whatever was in reach. Moments earlier, this crowd seemed happy and content—now they swarmed like vultures.

Anna finally collapsed in exhaustion. The crowd cheered and closed ranks. Then a trio of priests pushed through the hecklers. Anna's hair was tangled with broken eggshells and splattered tomatoes, her face smeared with egg whites and make-up. Shame poured into her soul like an unquenchable fire. As she started to lift herself up, a foot slapped against the ground trapping her clothing beneath it—she couldn't move. She looked up into the face of a Temple priest. Eyes lined with smoky cataracts glared with judgment beneath great bushy brows. His condemning words were laced with poison.

"Whore. You're nothing but a cheap whore. I saw you last night. You took Phinehas the high priest into your bed. You're corrupting Yerushalayim and now the Temple priests with your prostitution."

Anna tried to lift herself, but the priest held his foot down tight. Her veil was nowhere in sight. Another priest's foot pinned down her long hair. Unable to turn her head away, she was forced to face her jury in shame.

"You're a cheap whore."

She was trapped, condemned, and sentenced. With united judgment the crowd closed in like a net, hands raised no longer with tomatoes, but with stones, large deadly stones. Anna's heart thumped loudly in her ears. Death loomed heavy in the brilliance of the day as everything had turned sour in a reckless moment of condemnation.

The voices rose higher. "Whore! Stone the whore! Stone the whore!"

"Yes. Stone the whore!" The crowd seemed to be waiting for a priest or self-appointed judge to give the order. Anna stared into their faces. Even the children's faces were filled with contempt. Tears splashed across her cheeks.

Anna wanted to die. The people's judgment was correct. She was a whore that polluted this holy city. She didn't deserve to live. But the empty ache in her heart loomed larger than her shame. She did not want to take either emptiness or shame to her grave.

Suddenly, a movement stirred the crowd to silence. Anna lay there quivering—like a bird with a broken wing. The faces of her accusers were shadowed by the sun's glare, their arms still raised high, each ready to throw a stone. Someone had entered the arena. A murmur rippled through the crowd . . . a nervous cough. Without a word spoken, people stepped back to make a path for the newcomer. Anna's neck ached from being pinned down. Still the men had not released her. She saw shadows parting, sandals stepping back. Then she saw a pair of strong feet wrapped in leather moving toward her. *This isn't Phinehas the high priest. No, this man's step is light and steady, not plodding. Perhaps it's a Pharisee coming to throw the first stone.* Anna trembled in fear. Then she wondered, *Could it be Papa?* Her heart ached, nearly beating out of her chest.

*Oh, Papa, please come and take me home. Please Papa.* But she knew her pleading was futile. It was only the cry of a frightened little girl. She watched as the feet took steady steps toward her. She saw the lower hem of his robe, a raw earthy-white. The man was tanned and strong, possessing a gentle boldness. Who was he? What power enabled him to have such sway over this herd of evil doers?

The priest that pinned her down reluctantly shifted and stepped away. The stranger came closer. Anna looked up. Like a solar eclipse, she saw his shadow haloed by the sun's brilliance. His shoulders were broad, his hair ruffled by a breeze, his face obscured in shadows. Whoever this man was, he'd entered her circle of shame. He turned and stared at the people for a long unnerving moment. Anna trembled.

The man studied the crowd, studied the eyes of each accuser as if he were reading their hearts. *Murderers. Adulterers. Liars. Thieves. Hypocrites.* His authority came from somewhere inside. When he spoke, the marketplace suddenly went silent. It seemed even earth was listening. With a single sweep of his arm he pointed to each person in the crowd; every heckler, every jealous woman, every self-righteous judge, every taunting child.

Then he gave the command, "Go ahead. Kill her. You who have never sinned, go ahead, throw the first stone. You, or you!" He pointed and moved closer. "Or any of you jealous, hate-filled women, strike the first blow." He looked into the eyes of a boy. "You're so young to be full of hate. Who taught you to hate like that?" He looked at his mother and then back at him, "Are you sure you want to murder this woman?" His stare was electrifying. Every accuser visibly shrank from his gaze. The circle of judges backed away.

With dull thuds, the deadly weapons dropped. The circle widened. Religious rulers scuttled away quickly, robes wrapped tightly around them. Women covered their faces. Children hid behind their mother's skirts. Finally, the most arrogant accusers bowed their heads in shame from this man who challenged their authority. Only two people remained, Anna and this stranger.

The street was now empty. A breeze blew and Anna could smell the freshness of a spring morning. Her senses began to return. Gently, the man reached down to lift her to her feet. Anna, covered in the filth of her sin, reached up and took hold of his strong grip. He must not know who she was, otherwise he would recoil like the others.

Anna was weeping. She kept her head bowed low, unable to look into his eyes. His very presence felt holy and pure . . . and she turned her head away.

"Anna." His voice was forgiving, cleansing. He reached out and lifted her face toward him. She hesitated then looked up. One look into his eyes and she knew she was forgiven. His presence was unlike any other. His eyes spoke peace—melting shame and offering purity. She couldn't turn away from the face of Yeshua. She was captivated by his presence.

"Go home, Anna. I forgive you. Go home and leave this life of sin."

Tears of remorse coursed down her stained face, but the stain in her heart was gone. Anna felt free. She was free from performing for her father. She felt hope for the first time ever. Yeshua smiled and nodded. She really was free. Anna knelt at his feet and worshipped him.[8]

---

[8] This account is based on John 8:2-11.

Chapter Four

# GERASENE, SYRIA, 29 A.D.

The cave stretched low into the damp limestone ground.
It extended down, zigzagging into squat crawl spaces
that always made the man panic as he squeezed through.
His panic eased only after he reached the high cavernous room
that had become his prison. The constant acrid smell ate at the
lining of his nose and throat. Various recesses in the limestone
walls held wrapped bones of the dead. Diablo had given them
all a nickname to keep him company. At his back, the prisoner
heard only constant trickling of water as it seeped into a pool
just out of reach. In front of him loomed silence, except for the
daily scraping of a stone dish left hastily by his caretaker. The
only way to reach his food was to drag his chain and painfully
inch his way through the wormhole. Each day brought a new
dread of claustrophobia overcome only by the driving hunger
for food.

Diablo's world was almost ink-black. The cave's three-
foot-wide entrance was so far removed from his inner chamber
that no light could penetrate the threshold of his world. His
eyes had adjusted to recognize shapes and shadows. In brief
moments of sanity Diablo wondered about the world outside.
He remembered tombs, white tombs tightly lined beside each

other. He had hid among them at night. But that seemed like another lifetime. He longed to be free from the confines of blackness, yet he feared the unknown.

This fear wreaked havoc in his thoughts. Thinking of freedom made him tremble. As fear took over, his breathing was constricted. When he could stand it no longer, he would scream for the demons to return and take those fearful thoughts away. Empty of fear, Diablo's thoughts became a whirlwind of confusion until he lost touch with reality. And *fear* was the only reality he knew. The demons numbed the man into a narcotic trance-like state, easing the irrational fears they had implanted.

Loneliness, like the shroud of a bereaved lover, consumed his existence, and left no memories of love. The only time he felt companionship was during storms. They invariably brought a family of jackals or foxes that sheltered in the cave entrance. Diablo listened to the whimpering cubs and heard the mother nudging them into safety. For an hour or two, tranquility took over as the little family waited out the storm. Diablo's mind returned to another time in his past when he felt nurtured and comforted from storms, but he could not remember the mother or her cub. Whenever he attempted to recall distant memories, the voices would start calling him . . . clanging voices like chains of torture.

Diablo sat naked against the cave wall. His matted hair hung down to his shoulders and met his beard like a blanket of black wool. Dark tendrils hung over his left eye. He shoved his fist toward his brow using his thumb to move the hair away. The hair annoyed him. He would shove it away only to have it fall back against his forehead. Anger stirred. He felt a burning inside his chest that grew with the thought of annoyance.

The constant dripping of water echoed throughout the cave. It was incessant and disturbing. The monotonous sound agitated him. The clump of hair fell back onto his face. The burning in his chest got hotter and rose up his neck. His face flushed with rage. He shoved the hair away again and it fell back down.

Diablo suddenly shrieked like a crazed animal using wild sounds without syllables.

Spittle sprayed into the air and dribbled down into his beard. With both hands the man tore at the clump of hair. His muscles rippled as his fists tightened. He tore handfuls of hair from his scalp, leaving bleeding gaps in the matted crown of filth that clung to his head. Fresh raw skin was exposed to the grime of his prison. It would soon fester.

The clump of hair no longer annoyed him. Rage calmed in his chest. He leaned his head back against the stone and banged it in a rocking rhythm. The beat calmed his spirit as rivulets of blood trickled down his brow, each tracing a troubled furrow. The blood seeped into the corners of his eyes, but he didn't care. He saw nothing but darkness. Diablo was at peace for a fleeting moment. He slept.

A scraping sound awoke him. His empty stomach growled at the familiar noise. Food. He crawled past three sets of bones.

"Ahab, sorry pal, chow time."

"None for you, Zerubbabel." He kept crawling.

"Sorry, Methuselah, don't have time to chat."

He shrugged apologetically at the third set of bones and kept moving. He came to the narrow tunnel and stopped for a second. He took a deep breath. Like always, Diablo inched through the wormhole, dragging his heavy leg iron until the chain was taut. Today, like every other day, he stretched for the plate of food scraps until his festering leg bled. The plate was always just far enough away for him to risk pain to get the food. It was worth the effort though, because he would eat for one more day. He had no conscious thought of wondering where the food came from. He survived on minimum levels of thought.

The man had aged beyond his twenty-seven years. His body, mind, and spirit had been ravaged by demons. The utter presence of darkness, mingled with the tirade of demanding voices in his head, formed a recipe of pure torment. He no longer spoke words of Arabic, his mother tongue. Sometimes words came in a stuttered phrase. He seldom thought with reason, for reason had fled. Instead, he grunted and moaned like an animal.

As he stuffed food into his mouth, he growled like a savage beast. He finished his food and licked the plate empty. Diablo roared for more, but there was none. In anger he threw the stone plate into the darkness. It struck against the wall and splintered into shards across the cave floor. He lumbered back to the wormhole, scraped through its tortuous length, then entered the recesses of the cave on all four limbs. His chain dragged by his side. The man's naked body, scarred with self-inflicted pain, searched in the blackness for the still warm space where he sat, day in and day out, waiting. Waiting for what? He knew not, but somewhere inside hope flickered for release.

Finding his spot, he sat and began to gently bang his head against the wall, like a child whose emptiness longed for some comforting embrace. He drifted in momentary thought. The rhythm slowed and images emerged into his mind; images of his life before demons swarmed his waking moments. Diablo slowed his movements to a stop. For a short-lived moment he sat there, still and silent.

He remembered something good. Hope. Hot tears streamed down his face seeking refuge in his crushing sorrow. For a brief moment, reason was reborn and the demon-ravaged man remembered and longed for release.

Deep in the recesses of his memory came a thought; something his mother had told him as a child. She had mentioned a messiah - a savior; one who would rescue people under oppression. *Was this true? Could he help me, a goiim[9]?*

*Messiah, if you are there . . . if you are real . . . come. Please . . . come. Please come soon.*

Then reason fled. Five seconds of sanity. Only five seconds, but it was long enough for Yeshua to hear. Diablo resumed his banging rhythm as the demons feared eviction and clouded his

---

[9]  Goiim; גוי, Hebrew word for Gentile

senses once again. They knew that the presence of the Messiah was very near . . . and they trembled.

Diablo had drifted into his netherworld of dreams; dark dreams of terror, mixed with confusion and despair. A flash of brilliant color and light caused him to startle, but when he woke all he remembered was his world of darkness and fear. He could not recall color or love or peace.

"Back off! Back off!" Diablo awoke to his voices screaming in high-pitched volumes of terror. He covered his ears, but it didn't help.

"Get away from me. Back off. You are too near. We know who you are."

Diablo felt the demons screaming inside him. They pummeled his stomach muscles and grabbed his intestines in terror. They raced up and down his trachea screeching curses. Outside the cave a jackal heard and began to howl. The legion of darkness tore at Diablo's body and consciousness.

"Crawl back, crawl further back into the cave." Diablo obediently slithered on his stomach into the recesses of darkness. His body quivered against the damp floor.

"Back . . . further back." The chain went taut. The man grew angry. He screamed and roared at the chain.

"Break the chain! Break the chain, Diablo," the demons demanded.

"BREAK THE CHAIN!" A legion of voices screamed into every sensor of his body. He shook, he raged, he howled and tore his hair.

"BREAK THE CHAIN NOW!"

Diablo reached down and grabbed the cold iron. He roared as he held it in his hands. He shook with rage.

"BREAK THE CHAIN, DIABLO! HIDE US! DO IT . . . NOW!" Suddenly he let out a terrifying scream as power tore through his body. His chest heaved. His forearms rippled with superhuman power. The chain snapped like a branch from a withered tree.

*I am free,* he suddenly thought. In that brief instant, sanity emerged.

"NO!!" A howling screech resonated off the walls. Chills ran down Diablo's spine. The multiple voices grew fierce. "You belong to us. You'll never be free. Hide us now."

The demons trembled as the man awakened to thoughts of his own; thoughts of freedom! Thoughts of hope! The Messiah! Against the demanding voices, he began slithering through the wormhole, groping with his fingernails to pull himself through the suffocating space before the voices could stop him.

Yeshua trailed his fingertips in the water as the small fishing boat glided to shore. He smiled as he watched a silvery shoal of fish just beneath the surface. They followed his fingertips as the boat moved across the lake. As they approached land, his eyes grew serious. He focused upon some distant point ahead. He seemed deep in thought. Sometimes he had appeared distant to his friends, although never rude, only melancholy. Yeshua knew Peter and John had noticed something stirring, for their hearts were like an open book. Sometimes silence was Yeshua's greatest ally.

Yeshua was resolute in heading into Gerasene country, specifically to the town of Gadara. Peter shuddered. He had never stepped foot in this region before—pig country, Gentile scum. He heard too many stories: *snout soup, pig's feet tenderloins, pork belly chowder. Unthinkable!*

Peter refocused on his task and guided the boat to shore. He jumped out into knee-deep water and pulled the boat up against a protruding root, tying it securely. Before Peter turned around, Yeshua had jumped out of the boat and splashed toward shore. He definitely had an agenda. Peter would follow, but he had questions. John, too, was puzzled as he followed Yeshua out of the boat. Both were committed to their leader, regardless of his unusual actions. Always his reasons were correct. Always!

For a brief moment the three men stood knee deep in water. Yeshua saw the puzzled look on their faces and suddenly grinned. As John came out of the lake, Yeshua bent down and flicked water into his face. John jerked his head with a startled reaction. He saw the twinkle in Yeshua's eyes and flicked water back. Droplets sparkled across their master's face like beads of sunlight. Then Peter joined in. Before long, Yeshua and John had grabbed Peter and threatened to dunk him. For a few moments, they played like three overgrown kids until Yeshua pulled Peter out of the water and slapped him on his dripping wet back. He looked into his eyes.

"Trust me. This visit won't hurt as bad as you might think. You might even like this guy. He needs me."

He headed up the bank toward a clump of cypress trees ten yards from the lake shore. His friends followed. Yeshua took off his outer robe and tunic, then spread them out across a few branches to dry in the sun. John and Peter just sat down beneath a tree in their wet clothes. Yeshua leaned his bare back against the tree trunk, his smooth muscular chest heaving with breathlessness. Slowly he ran his fingers through his hair and raised his face toward the sun. As his breathing relaxed, he spoke to his friends. He understood their confusion. His voice was low and smooth.

"When an evil spirit comes out of a man, it goes through arid places seeking rest and sometimes does not find it." Yeshua leaned forward and rested his elbows on his knees. Peter copied his actions without thought.

"We have seen you drive out demons many times, Yeshua. You have brought peace to many people and set them free."

"I do it by the finger of God." The men nodded in agreement.

John leaned forward and grabbed a blade of grass. "So . . .?" He waited for the next point.

"When they find no other place to go, they return to their host and bring more dark spirits to join them. A man or woman, or even a child, may be hosting more demons than you two have ever imagined. These spirits are powerful."

Yeshua's pupils narrowed as he studied their eyes for a moment. They needed to understand. "If a man is under the power of such a strong man, he no longer has control of his own life. He is controlled by the strong man." Peter and John were beginning to understand.

Yeshua continued, "Satan is the strong man. He is fully armed and he guards his own house, or the spirit of a person he possesses. When someone stronger attacks and overpowers him, Satan's armor, in which the man trusted, is taken away. The new owner divides the spoil."

"I don't understand. Who are you talking about, Yeshua?"

"Satan seeks to control and destroy any person who allows him in. Without my help, that person's life will ultimately be destroyed by darkness. No one can free himself of demons without my help. My power is greater than you can comprehend right now. No matter how powerful Satan is, I am greater. Where he comes to destroy, I come to bring light. I've come to bring people out of darkness and show them the Light of Life." He paused briefly. "My life."

Peter rubbed his chin that now showed several days' growth. A few gray hairs peppered his cheeks. His hair was disheveled, still dripping with water. Suddenly, Yeshua looked back over his shoulder. They followed his gaze, but saw nothing. Then Yeshua turned back to their conversation and spoke more earnestly. His voice grew softer. "This man needs me. He has called for my help. The Father has great plans for him, but he must first be released." Yeshua paused and listened again. Cocking his head sideways, he stated simply,

"He's coming now."

"Who's coming? I don't hear anyone."

Peter and John were startled when a naked man appeared from behind a tree. He stood bent like an animal ready to spring, and looked more animal than human. His body had open cuts and dark scars. His eyes were haunted. The creature leaped in a single bound and landed three feet from the men. Peter and John bolted up and stumbled over each other.

"Don't be afraid, men. I know this man. He has called for my help. Don't be afraid. I'm with you. Greater am I than the spirits that rage in this man's soul."

Diablo's eyes darted around like a cornered beast. Half squatting, he waited—muscles coiled, limbs poised for flight. He hissed and arched his back.

Peter and John moved behind Yeshua who remained calm and in control. He showed no fear as the man moved forward.

"It's a beast." Peter's whisper was hoarse and low. "It can't be human."

Yeshua stepped closer to the man. He reached out his hand toward him, but Diablo recoiled and snarled. Yeshua didn't flinch. The man's fingers began to claw the air as his body leaped up and landed within inches of Yeshua. The Master made no move. Diablo gave a hideous laugh and cursed. Then a force threw him to the ground. He curled into a fetal position and whimpered.

Horrified, Peter put his hand over his mouth. John stood paralyzed.

In that fragile state, the man's voice suddenly called out, "*HaMashiach*, help me." The voice was human, full of fear and pleading.

"I've come to release you," Yeshua declared.

In an instant, with a glazed look in his eyes, the man sprang to his feet and flew toward them. Yeshua's words stopped him in mid-air, and he plummeted to the ground.

"Stop. This man is mine," Yeshua demanded.

The man landed on his feet and stood coiled—knees bent and arms out. He opened his mouth and a rush of hot wind exploded. Sounds like a million whispers cried out in some strange dialect.

"*имеют вас, котор нужно сделать с нами?*" "What have you to do with us, Master?"

Yeshua replied, "*Вы не имеете никакую силу над им. Пойдите.*" "You have no power over him."

The voices tried to resist. "We've been invited to live in this host. This is our home. Get away from us . . . Master. We know you are the Christ."

As the words ripped through the air in gasping acknowledgment, the scene grew calm, the trees settled. In spite of their protests, the demons were forced to concede that Yeshua's authority over them was invincible. They trembled.

"You have no right to this man's soul." Yeshua spoke with such commanding authority that Peter and John rose to their full height. They'd cowered at the spectral's demands, but now, drawing from their Master's authority, they wanted to face the tormentor and fight. Yeshua glanced their way and shook his head. Then he turned back to the man and confronted the demonic hosts.

"I demand you to leave. He has called upon my name for help. I will not fail him. He does not belong to you."

"Please . . ." a million voices pleaded, moaned and begged.

"Be muzzled."

The voices were jumbled, spluttering to speak. "P. . . ., pleease, send us somewhere else, anywhere b-but the Abyss.[10]" The man remained motionless as the demons whined and begged. Different voices quarreled in a myriad of dialects. Peter shuddered at the eeriness of the scene before him. A cloud had

---

[10] 2 Pe.2:4 refers to a place where angels who sinned are reserved in chains of darkness for judgment; Re.9:5, "a reserved place for demonic prisoners who hate humanity and seek to destroy them."

swept across the sun's gaze and shadows lay somber tones upon the hillside. Although it was warm, Peter shivered.

Not far from this group of men, a servant was herding about a hundred swine down the pathway toward a farmyard. The servant was unaware of the event taking place so close to him. He was so busy pushing and prodding that the grunts and oinks were drowning out all other commotion.

One demon's voice shrieked in desperation, "Pigs . . . w-we want p-pigs! Send us into the pigs, M-Master . . . p-please."

Yeshua looked at the herd of swine, then he turned his head toward Peter and John. They were horrified at all the commotion. The animals had come closer and now weaved in and out around their feet while the smells, sights, and sounds caused Peter and John to become nauseous. The men sensed intense evil in their presence. The disciples drew back. What had they gotten themselves into? Peter eyed the boat as an escape. He gagged.

Yeshua understood their inner turmoil and gave them a reassuring smile. He said, "Watch me. I want you to learn from this. You will see the finger of God over darkness." Then his eyes turned and became riveted upon the broken man now hunched before him—waiting, hoping, and longing to be set free. Yeshua's eyes grew sad, for he could see the deep emptiness of Diablo's wretched life.

"Legion, I command you to leave this man immediately. I send you into the swine NOW!"

Diablo's body went limp and collapsed to the ground. Peter studied the figure. Had he died? From within the man a rushing noise swelled, rose up his windpipe, and finally forced its way out through his mouth like a million voices all screaming in terror. The man's body was lifted by sheer force as the darkness was expelled from his spirit. The swarm of spirits squealed, wheezed, roared, and barked as they were thrust out of the broken man. The specter appeared agitated by the presence of pure light. The legion howled as it raced into the herd of pigs.

Instantly, the pigs stirred. Their eyes went dark, snouts distorted, and limbs went wild. They snorted like wild boars, ran into each other, squealed and growled, and began racing down the hillside. The servant did his best to corral them, but it was impossible. The animals ran, stumbling over logs and ramming into trees. Some got caught in bushes and squealed . . . others ran straight into the lake . . . while still others butted heads in their confusion. The servant screamed and ran away from the overwhelming chaos. As he ran, stumbling up the hill, he looked toward Yeshua and shrieked.

"Get away. Get away, magician. You've ruined me. I've lost my master's pigs. He'll send me to prison until I pay him back!"

The disciples watched until the man was out of sight, his voice trailing off into the distance in a tirade of curses.

The last of the pigs limped while others dragged their back legs feverishly until they reached the water. They splashed into the lake where they immediately drowned. Within minutes, already-bloated carcasses were floating upside down with their stubby legs reaching skyward. The demons could not live in a dead carcass; pig or human. The legion of demons was hopelessly swept away into the outer darkness of the Abyss. They would never infest life again. Only a few escaped by entering into the servant as he cursed Yeshua and ran from his presence. There, they would fester and multiply.

---

Diablo sat naked on a rock, reason steadily descending into his mind and heart. Sunlight had streaked through the trees and danced across his face. Like a man waking from a dream, understanding brought with it unsurpassed peace upon his countenance. His face brightened, but the rest of his body remained feral-looking and fearsome.

Peter and John marveled at all they had seen. This creature had suddenly become sane, yet he looked wretched and wild.

Certainly, Yeshua wouldn't add him to the band of disciples. Despite Peter's doubts, Yeshua had not made a wrong choice yet. Everything their Master had done was motivated by something higher than the disciples could comprehend. Peter mused, *He drew me in . . . a smelly fisherman.*

After resting awhile, Diablo became uneasy. He seemed to suddenly be self-conscious of his appearance. He was naked, smelly, and dirty. He had a ten-year growth of hair and beard. Timid, he stood and walked down into the lake where he submerged himself. He came up gasping as water poured from his head and dripped down his face. He dipped again, and carefully began to wash away years of grim and sweat. Meticulously he washed crusted stains and dried blood from his wounds, until finally his body was clean. Yet, the scars and crooked bones stood out in severe contrast. His body had wasted away, leaving him little more than skin and bones.

"John, come over here please." Yeshua nodded for John's help. "You've got a blade of bronze don't you?" John nodded. "Come help us make this friend look civil."

John understood and gladly helped. They trimmed his beard and hair. Within a short time, Diablo's appearance became more human.

Yeshua reached for his cloak that had dried in the warm sun. This day he had worn a deep crimson outer garment. Keeping only his tunic, Yeshua gathered his cloak and put it over Diablo's shoulders. In servant fashion, Yeshua slid Diablo's arms through the openings, then wrapped a band of cloth around the man's waist and tied it. Diablo, the demon-possessed man, was wearing the Messiah's robe.

The contrast in Diablo's life was so profound he staggered at the disparity. His former masters, the demons of darkness, wanted nothing but absolute control and ultimate destruction of his very soul. They'd nearly succeeded. Yeshua gave his own robe to give him dignity—to cover his wounds, to hide his scars. Yeshua was strong, forgiving, and yet humble enough to offer his own possessions to care for the wretched man. Diablo would never forget this moment. Such a gesture of mercy would burn into his memory like a branding iron. It would carry him through battles and into prisons for the sake of his new Master, Yeshua.

Tears erupted and spilled down Diablo's face. "Master, I'll live and die for you. How did you know where to find me?"

Yeshua replied, "You found me. I heard you call out to me and I recognized your voice." Yeshua looked into his eyes. "Your new name will be Democritus, 'a judge of the people.' You will be given eyes to see the hearts of men and women who have also lived in darkness. I'm sending you to them. I will come to anyone who calls after me regardless of their past sin. Democritus, you will be my messenger. You will release them by my authority."

"But why me? I'm the worst of the worst."

"But little is much when I am in it. If a religious man thinks he can offer God so much because he feels he is qualified by his own standards, then I can't use him."

"We don't understand." Peter and John had puzzled expressions.

"Because he is so consumed with himself, there is no room for me to work. I work best in empty vessels. I fill empty vessels with a spiritual power that draws people to me."

Yeshua studied Democritus for a moment. "I want you to follow me."

Peter and John had drawn closer, their eyes wide with wonder. This man resembled in no way the demon-crazed man they had just seen. Wearing Yeshua's crimson robe, clean from head to toe, his dark curly hair falling over his shoulders—this man looked almost royal.

"A day is coming when I will be lifted up. Each of you will know then why I have chosen you. Democritus, I've pulled you from the fire of destruction for all eternity."

"I'll go anywhere with you."

As Yeshua's hand held firmly on Democritus' shoulder, something unexpected began happening to his body — an intense heat from Yeshua's fingertips radiated from limb to limb, head to foot. A broken femur that had never been set, caused him constant pain and left his leg dragging — now, it snapped into place. Muscles aligned themselves proportionally. Democritus stood straight.

Peter stepped back in astonishment. This man was now taller than he was. New hair had sprouted on his forehead and curled down in ringlets. Torn flesh was restored and regained its natural color. The heat from Yeshua's hand penetrated down to his toes. The scarred ankle from the leg iron was now new, unblemished. The darkness in his face vanished. Shattered teeth were made new in the presence of the Holy One. Democritus felt the gentle stirring of restoration from head to toe. Muscles strengthened, skin tightened. He would follow him to the ends of the earth.

"I want you to go to the pagan cities of Decapolis and tell them all the things you have seen and heard. Tell them about me. It will be difficult, but you are chosen to do this for my glory. I'm preparing you to be my warrior."

"I'm ready now. I won't ever leave your side." He glanced at the two disciples that stood at a distance. "Can't I follow you like them?"

"You mustn't fear loneliness. God's presence will go with you. Your fight against the demons has trained you to work as a lone soldier. I need you to go behind enemy lines and represent me in a pagan land. You will have eyes to see the enemy, to distinguish between battles of the flesh and battles of the spirit-world. This is a training ground. Fighting spiritual warfare takes intuitive training. You will be equipped to wage war on a spiritual battlefield. How you fight determines how you win."

As the sun settled low against the hilltops and twilight took on an ethereal glow, intense colors radiated across the landscape. Democritus sat in front of the fire and listened. John had prepared a catch of fish and filleted each piece. He rubbed the white flesh with crushed herbs of rosemary, a handful of scallions, and a sprinkle of salt. Then he let it roast over the open fire until it sizzled, filling the night with a rich aroma. Democritus had eaten nothing but gruel for ten years. This food, prepared with love, was a banquet beyond his dreams. As the four men feasted together, Democritus realized that such intimacy of friendship was as close to Heaven as he could imagine.

For most of his life, his companions had been dark and deadly. Yeshua had brought light into his life for the first time since early childhood. The contrast was breathtaking. He said little, but sat in silence listening intently to the conversation. Their discussion was full of hope and love for others. They spoke with deep respect for one another and mostly for Yeshua himself. To be in the presence of absolute godliness overwhelmed his emotions. Did these men fully realize who sat amongst them?

His thirsty heart drank in every drop of communion. John reached toward the flame, speared the last piece of fish, and offered it to Democritus. "Take this, Democritus, my new brother. I've saved this piece for you." John's eyes sparkled. Democritus accepted the gift with gratitude. Such kindness was foreign to anything he'd ever known. Although Democritus enjoyed the companionship of Peter and John, he was in awe of being so close to Divinity. Each word had a profound significance, not a syllable wasted. Yeshua's words were compelling and Democritus wanted to remain in this circle for eternity.

Yeshua spoke about catching men from the seas of destruction. He first looked at Peter and then directed his gaze at Democritus. Democritus was transfixed by those eyes, so full of sadness for a world that would soon reject the King of Glory. Yet, the love he saw was deeper still.

Silently the purple night weaved its spell of slumber and settled like a blanket. The voices slowed to intermittent phrases of blessings upon one another. Sleep was upon them. Democritus lay back onto the soft grass. His Master's cloak felt comforting against his clean skin and he pulled it tightly around him. Gingerly he reached down and touched his ankle, marveling at its smoothness. In the darkness he touched his brow—it, too, was like a baby's. Swathed in contentment, Democritus slept. His dreams took him to far away cities with strange names and faces.[11]

---

[11] The story of Democritus is based on Lu. 8:26-39

## Chapter Five

# PUTEOLI, ITALY, 29 A.D.

Alexander stirred just as dawn tiptoed over the Italian landscape. The breeze floated through his open window, shuffled the parchment pages on his desk, fluttered a rose blossom in a vase, then moved toward the sleeping soldier, ruffling his rusty-red hair. Alexander's eyes popped opened instantly. Pushing back the covers, he sat up, slapped his feet on the marbled floor and waited there for a moment until his mind could match his body's discipline to wake. His green eyes blinked the sleep away.

His usual habit was to meet the sunrise on the veranda in solitude, but today he was late. Already a gray light stretched across the horizon. He jumped to his feet as the first light crept through the window. He was angry with himself for his lack of discipline.

Alexander needed these moments of solitude to discipline his mind, but he had not been his usual self recently. His troubled heart wreaked havoc with the restraints of military life. In the instant of waking, he knew that very soon his *solitude* would be introduced to its partner *loneliness,* and the latter could reduce that coveted seclusion to depression and self-pity.

This left him with an uncomfortable queasiness in his stomach. Soon, grieving would not give him a moment's peace.

Alexander was a high-ranking officer, a captain in Caesar's army in command of a thousand foot soldiers. His disciplined life impressed the caesars, and he was revered as each successive emperor came into power. He wanted justice in all things. Consequently, he was growing weary of the power hungry emperors of Rome, their constant bickering with the senate, the conniving plans of evil men.

Justice was a jewel among Alexander's prized longings but always seemed so elusive in the life of Rome. Few shared his passion for truth, even among the gods. He wondered if any of them cared enough about Rome's inhabitants to guide them into peace instead of further conquest and bloodshed.

The soldier's strength was loyalty, both to the Caesar and Rome. Against creeping doubts he remained loyal to the Roman gods whose temples adorned the great cities of the Empire. If they did not have the answer to peace, then who would?

A great longing of Alexander was that Lucia should bear him a child. After ten years, however, his wife remained barren. The goddess, Diana, promised fertility for those who participated in temple prostitute rituals. Alexander often prayed for a child and visited the temple prostitutes, but Lucia remained childless. Alexander's faith was wavering. He finally turned to Zeus, the god of the Heavens and supreme being of all.

Alexander's white linen toga was folded neatly beside his bed. After splashing water on his face and grooming his thick hair, he slipped on his toga, the emblem of freedom for every true Roman citizen. This distinguished him from the foreigners who were saturating the city. The Roman Empire grew as they conquered more lands, soon wrapping itself around the great Mediterranean Sea. The customs and religions of these new cultures were being absorbed into the fabric of the Empire.

Migrants were coming from Judea and Syria, from Corinth and Mesopotamia. Alexander was not particularly bothered about their many gods. Rome was already full of them. It gave the crowds more choices. But each culture also brought its own traditions and customs. Eating habits, hygiene and family disciplines clashed with their neighbor's customs. In addition, many immigrants left the poverty of their homelands in a mistaken optimism of finding riches in Rome. As the population expanded, however, fewer jobs were available and swathes of unemployment created idleness which led to drinking, riots and lawlessness. Caesar inaugurated citywide games as a form of entertainment for the people. Alexander found the games a waste of time, but he obliged Caesar to please him.

The tall soldier padded his way from his bedchamber down the long hallway toward the veranda. A life-size statue of Zeus stood silent against a column. Alexander nodded to it in respect then patted its head.

"Let's see what you've brought us today. I hope not a thunderstorm. I've got a lot of work ahead of me." He paused for a moment, looking at the statue, staring at it up and down. "We've got to get a toga for you. Your indecency shocks my servants. Of course you know all that, don't you. You're the god of the universe. I don't need to tell you a thing. Still, you should do something about that." He grinned at his own wit and continued toward the veranda.

A young Jewish maid curtseyed as she passed him in the corridor. In Alexander's gruff morning voice he said, "Good morning, Deborah. I'll have some tea and warm bread on the veranda as usual." She curtseyed again, slipping away to the kitchen to prepare his breakfast.

"Oh, Deborah," Alexander called. "How was Lucia through the night? You didn't wake me. It must have been a better night."

"I'm afraid not. She moaned much in her sleep, tried to get out of bed several times and almost fell. She became difficult when I offered to help her. I couldn't understand her mumblings in the midst of her delirium. With my singing I was able to comfort her to sleep. I fear she's slipping fast into another world. Let's hope that it's a better one than this."

His face darkened. "Deborah, I've told you before. You must always wake me if that happens. I want to be there. She needs me. She's very fragile. You can't handle that alone. Do you understand?"

The maid's face blushed and she nodded. "I didn't want to disturb you, sir. You've had so much on your mind recently. I'm sorry. I'll do as you ask." She quickly slipped into the kitchen away from his frown.

His anger subsided as his face suddenly tensed in worry. "There's not much time left," he whispered to himself. "I must finish my preparations immediately."

His bare feet padded further down the hall and out onto the veranda. The breeze brushed his face with a morning coolness that woke his senses. He could smell the rich earth, the herbs beneath his veranda, and the freshness of wheat fields in the distance. His mind soon calmed and, as always, he sensed the greatness of the world around him. *Whose world is it though? Who does it belong to?* His constant questions never had answers. He was growing bolder in his philosophical questioning day by day. Pain seemed to force a person into such challenging questions. He needed to know.

From the veranda Alexander's world spread across the horizon. The vista always inspired him. This morning he stood silent. He watched as the deep silken sheet of purple was pulled silently from the hills. A new day was born. Like slender flags unfurling, pink and orange streaks spread across the sky. The colors grew brighter, deeper. Then the celebration acquiesced to an expanse of azure blue, the sun giving color to every living thing on the face of the earth. Life was one glorious surprise after another.

Deborah arrived and set the tea and warm bread on the table next to him. She paused beside him just a moment and surveyed the beauty. "God is good to us."

"Some god is. I'm not quite sure which one though. There are so many gods and goddesses—most of them are more concerned with bloodshed and the human appetite. Which one do you suppose made all this, Apollo? Atlas . . .?"

Deborah blushed at his comment and replied in earnest, "I believe Jehovah God made all that we see and know."

"Oh, that's right. You believe in only one god. How unfortunate."

"It makes so much sense, one God as Creator of the entire universe." The servant girl spoke with confidence.

Alexander glowered at her. Deborah shriveled under his glare, but was resolute.

"I believe this beautiful day was created by . . . probably Zeus since he is so powerful."

The maid realized she had no place denying her master's strange religions. But she knew what she believed and kept it quietly in her heart.

Alexander rambled on. "Zeus . . . oh, I don't know. Maybe he did. Maybe he didn't." Then he added flatly, "He needs a toga."

"Pardon?" Deborah was surprised at her master's comment.

"Oh nothing. It's a joke between Zeus and me."

"You've talked to him?"

"Oh, in a manner of sorts." He winked at her and grinned.

Deborah gave a puzzled smile, relaxed slightly, then headed back to the kitchen.

Alexander turned back to watch the horizon continue its transformation. As the sun rose high in the sky, the hills terraced with tall slender cypress trees began to show their true colors, a rich emerald green. To the east were vineyards. A harvest was ready to yield its fruit. He could almost taste the sweetness of the grapes—their aroma was rich. The wheat fields in the distance waved like a sea rolling into a gentle swell.

Alexander sat at the round tiled table and took a sip of tea. He tore a piece of bread glistening with butter and ate. Musing at the expanse of the skyline, he wondered what was beyond the world he knew. He marveled that the gods could create such beauty and then encourage bloodshed. He was growing weary of the emperor's games in the amphitheaters. The gladiators were trained to compete, but they were no longer games. Too many were being slaughtered. The emperor would also put criminals in the arena just to amuse himself as the lions tore them limb from limb. Most of the criminals were merely itinerant peasants who didn't fit into the scheme of Rome's glory.

Alexander finished eating and licked his fingers. He reflected on his own rise to power. He came from a military family first serving under Augustus, later followed by Tiberius. He belonged to an influential group. He had built this elaborate villa in Puteoli because his family, and their family, and their family before them had grown up in this small Italian village.

As a child, Alexander had played through the winding streets weaving up and down the hillsides. He knew where he could find the best Italian breads and cheeses. He also knew the best places to climb fruit trees and pick the juiciest Mirabelle plums, stuffing his pockets full until the juice squeezed through his clothes, all the while knowing that his mother would be furious.

"Deborah, bring me another cup of tea and some fruit please." Soon she appeared with the tea and a plate of plums and grapes. "Ah, Mirabelles. The best plums this side of Heaven. Deborah, why don't you make jam from some of these. That would be good for winter days."

"Yes, master. I'll do that today." She stood there only for a moment waiting his approval.

Just as she was about to leave, her master said, "Deborah. Such a strange sounding name! How did you get it?"

Deborah straightened her posture, proud to speak of her heritage, faith, and her people.

"Deborah was the only woman judge of Israel before the time of the kings. She was wise and could see beyond what others could see."

"She was a witch?"

"Oh no, master. She was God's anointed prophetess as well as judge of the people. She risked her life to lead them into freedom." The maid looked out toward the skyline and watched the colors change before her eyes. In a wistful tone she added, "She wrote songs of victory and, ever since, the people of Israel have sung songs about her and her faith in Jehovah."

"Hmm . . . I see." He sipped his tea. "Well, I hope the gods will give us good weather. I have some more traveling to do. I'll be heading to your part of the world, Judea, soon."

Deborah's eyes brightened. "I long to return. Someday I hope to go see my family again."

Deborah had been here for Alexander throughout his wife's illness. She nursed her and sat beside her in the night. Lucia was becoming critically ill with little hope of recovery. Soon Alexander would be alone.

Deborah stepped back into the kitchen, Lucia's favorite place. Lucia loved life. She was vibrant. She laughed often. Then the lumps came in her stomach. They brought so much pain. The doctors gave her many kinds of herbs to no avail. They decided to get rid of the disease by bleeding, but this only weakened her. Finally, the doctors could only prescribe medication that would ease the pain. Her prognosis was not good.

Alexander stirred a few drops of honey into his tea. Taking a sip, he reflected on the choices he had made in light of his success. He had served Tiberius faithfully although the emperor was seldom in Rome these days. The man was a harsh ruler, but Alexander's training had forced him to be compliant in spite of his personal differences. When at work he was determined, fierce, and conformed to all the emperor's decisions. He had watched Rome change. In spite of its grandeur, the populace was becoming more and more bloodthirsty. Justice was hard to find. The Roman senate tried desperately to maintain control, but the imperial throne wielded such uncontainable power that it invariably turned ordinary men into tyrants.

Out in the open field a wild stallion had been grazing, its sleek coat shining in the sun. Something had startled it. It reared its head in alarm then raced toward the forest of trees in the distance.

Alexander often reflected on Rome and its military conquests. He looked at the powerful animal racing across the field. There were no reins, just a wild stallion running at will. Rome was like a chariot being pulled by two strong horses, both wild and reckless. One horse drove the chariot to conquer; the other drove the chariot toward a thirst for killing.

*Why does power change human nature? What is in man that makes him want total control? What benefit is there to kill people for sport? No single man or woman can win against the fierceness of a lion or a bear. So there is no real game. The results are already decided. The beast wins and the man loses. How is that entertaining?*

"But the people lust after it and the emperors give them their desires," he spoke out loud, completing his thoughts for the morning. He had few answers. Was it in himself to discover the answers or should he talk directly to Zeus? He shook his head as he walked back into the house, passing the god's stone face without a glance.

Alexander headed to Lucia's room. He opened the door quietly. The slender woman lay flat on her back with her eyes wide open, staring up at the ceiling. His heart beat wildly. Had she left this world? Then he saw a flicker in her eye and breathed a sigh of relief. Her once beautiful auburn hair was now thin with streaks of gray.

"Lucia, my sweet, how are you today?" He bent over and kissed her forehead.

Her eyes were sunken with blue-gray circles. Her cheekbones were gaunt. Sharp edges now replaced her once graceful lines. She had withered like a dried leaf in autumn. Her arms were like brittle branches without life. Slowly she turned her head toward his voice, but she was not looking at him. After a moment a faint recognition came to her face.

"Oh, Alexander! You're home. When did you arrive?"

"Lucia, I've been home. I sat right here by your side for hours yesterday. Don't you remember? I returned from Rome two days ago. Has the pain lessened at all?"

She turned her head away. "Never mind, Alex . . . never mind. Life is full of pain. I'm just sorry . . . sorry that I failed you." The trace of a tear trickled down onto her neck and into her bedclothes.

"You have never failed me, Lucia my love. Never."

"But I did. I could bear you no son or daughter. You so badly wanted a . . ."

Alexander interrupted her. He slipped his arms under her body and pulled her to himself. His heart ached as he realized how frail she was. Lucia was no more than a skeleton held together by a delicate membrane of flesh. He held her close and brushed her forehead with his cheek. He put his finger to her lips.

"Shhhhh, Lucia. You know better than to talk like that. It's you I love with or without a child. I'm just grieved that you're suffering so much. I'm frustrated that the doctors can't find a cure for your illness. I'm angry at the gods for making you suffer." He wanted to keep holding her but feared she'd break. Her pain left him with few words with which to comfort. She groaned; pain etched across her brow then moved like a shadow down into her eyes, finally enfolding her entire body in its grip. Alexander gently lowered her back onto the bed.

"We all suffer in this life. I don't understand why, but we do, Alex. I wish I knew a better way, whom to pray to, whom to have hope in, but I don't. Without hope there is no sense to this world. I've given up hoping." Lucia suddenly raised her voice in emotion. "I've come to believe that all the gods are just creations of our own longings. I know I've created a god in my mind . . . but he doesn't exist."

Alexander raised his eyebrows in surprise. "Tell me about your god. What is it you wish in a god?"

Lucia's eyes drifted through the walls of her room and peered into space. For a moment Alexander saw a glimmer of energy in her delicate face. "I dream of a god of . . . peace and compassion. At night, I sometimes dream that a great presence comes to me and whispers words of comfort, promises of hope. In those dreams it's like there is a god in the Heavens who really cares about me and my suffering." Her eyes sparkled as tears pooled at the corners. She continued to peer through the frescoed walls into another dimension.

"Who might that be, Lucia? Eros or Aphrodite? Do they visit you?"

"Eros? Aphrodite?" She turned her head away in disdain. "Eros is no goddess of love, only *lust*. Eros only breaks hearts, tears lives apart. Aphrodite makes people insane with craving sex."

Lucia looked around her and held up her spindly arms. A thin transparent film of flesh sagged from her bones. She gazed around the bedroom. Richly colored tapestries hung from one wall. A slender statue of Venus stood in the corner, her face in deep shadows. Lucia's bed was ornate with satin pillows and spreads in emerald green. The headboard was a rich mahogany imported from Africa. The floors were covered in warm brown granite. Surrounding the room was a thin diamond pattern in pink vein marble. Lucia's eyes surveyed the room and she shook her head.

"This is it, Alex. This is all we get. It means nothing in the end."

"No, Lucia. There must be more. I've heard of a healer in Judea."

"No, Alexander. No." Her voice rose with a strength that surprised him. "I've given up on healers and magicians. If there are gods, they're determined to make us suffer for whatever reason. They roll the dice, play the games, and look down on us to see what pleasure they can get out of our suffering."

As Lucia wept, Alexander noticed bitterness in her stare that he'd never observed before. "I love you, Alex, but there's nothing more to say. Goodbye, my darling . . . I'm so very tired right now." She turned her head away, and Alexander knew that the conversation was over.

The soldier stood, then walked hesitantly out of Lucia's bed-chamber. He turned and looked in one more time. He feared that she might not last the month. "I love you too, Lucia," he said softly and stepped into the hall.

The hallway was lined with fine paintings, lush ferns in Grecian urns and ornate gilded concave moldings against vaulted ceilings. But Alexander saw nothing as he headed back to his chamber. His world, too, had gone gray.

The soldier entered his room and closed the door. He leaned his forehead against the door and softly beat his fist against the wood. "Why . . . Why, Lucia?"

Raising his head and taking a deep breath, he walked to the table where the parchments lay. He held the top page up to the light. His own etchings were rough, some scratched out; others had texts beneath. A stack of bound parchments lay beside his work. Alexander had studied them, finding designs he liked and others he didn't. He picked up another page. On it was a com-pleted design, carefully drawn with ink. Each line was labeled and each figure titled with names. The next page was another completed drawing of the top of Lucia's sarcophagus. Her face was drawn with a devotion that accurately depicted her happy days. The legend in the corner included all the exact dimensions and textures, including an ornate plinth in polished red granite. Lucia's dwelling after death would honor her life with glory, beauty, and peacefulness.

Two months earlier, Alexander had arranged with Hermes, the greatest stonemason in the entire Mediterranean world, to carve the basin of Lucia's sarcophagus. Word was returned last week that it was complete. He could not discuss these trips with Lucia. It took all the effort he could muster to plan and execute the task. To prepare her tomb was admitting defeat. Lucia was dying and nothing could stop the horrible force growing within her. Her life was slipping away.

As Alexander packed for yet another trip to Judea, panic rose in his heart. It swelled upward, constricting his breathing. His powerful world was crumbling. Now it loomed dark and fearful. His questions only drove him to despair. *Will Lucia be gone before I return? If she is still alive will she remember me? Should I tell her I'm preparing her sarcophagus for burial? Will she forgive me for being away so long . . . in her sickest hours?* The soldier was fighting a losing battle. He breathed a prayer to the gods. "Mighty gods of Rome, masters of the Heavens, ancient powers that control all life, I beg you to keep Lucia alive until I return. I beg you. I will do whatever you ask, only keep her alive until I return."

As Alexander collected his finished diagrams, the sun's glare streaked across his desk casting light through the parchment. The sketches that took so much thought and work now looked fragile and faded under the sun's brilliant force.

"Nothing lasts forever," his trembling voice whispered. Alexander rolled and secured the parchments with a cord, then put them in his bag. He picked up a leather pouch that contained enough gold coins to pay the slaves, pay Hermes for his work and secure his passage for the journey.

Alexander stopped and straightened his back as he finished packing. His body was weary. This whole battle with life and death, loving and losing, took its toll. Alexander suddenly realized there was still one item to be packed—a gift. He walked to a tall chest near his bed. Opening the top drawer, he shuffled through some clothes until his hands touched a small ivory box. He pulled it out and looked at it with pleasure. It was delicate with intricate carvings on all four sides. He lifted the lid to inspect the contents, then closed it quickly and packed it beside his pouch of coins. These were his most precious items for the journey.

Before the sun rose tomorrow, he would be on horseback heading toward the boats where a ship awaited him to set sail for Judea. A quarried block of red granite from the Italian hills had already been delivered to Hermes. His initial sketches were also with Hermes, but he would deliver the final details in person—the artist's intricate drawings of Lucia's beautiful face.

With much pain and effort, Lucia rolled over to face the wall. Something terrible was happening inside her body causing insufferable pain, turning her skin a yellow-gray. Her face was gaunt with sunken cheeks and parchment-thin skin. Whatever was growing inside her was not life, but death. Why was this world so cruel? What wrong had she done that she should deserve this? Nausea rose up in her stomach and she retched. She fell back on her bed exhausted. Each movement took every ounce of her energy. She had just discovered that Alexander was going on yet another journey to Judea. She would be alone—alone perhaps for the rest of eternity!

A miniature idol of Diana stood by her bedside. "I trusted you to send me life, to give me a baby, but you refused. I sent Alexander to your temple prostitutes so that I would bear a child, but instead you let evil grow inside my body. You're sending me to my death. Why have you done this, Diana? I cannot trust you any longer. You've deceived me."

Teeth clenched, she grabbed the idol and flung it across the room where it hit the wall and shattered into pieces. She moaned bitterly, "I have no use for you, Diana. You just bring me pain. You don't care about human suffering. You taunt us by giving us longings that can't be fulfilled. You ravage our bodies with pain and then delight in seeing us suffer." Her weakened voice rose in anger. "Isn't there a god somewhere who cares?" Her small fists beat the bed covers.

She wept until she drifted off into a world of delirium and dreams, bringing a temporary relief from her body's debilitating pain.

*Darkness swirled around like a mist. She felt alone. Lucia called out in the darkness, "Who is out there? Is anyone there who can help me?" The mist swirled tighter around her until she felt she was wrapped in an embrace. She called out again. Lucia saw no face. The arms cradled her frail body and began to rock her. Then she heard a song.*

*"Yahweh is compassionate and gracious, slow to anger, abounding in love. He will not always accuse, nor will he harbor his anger forever; he does not treat us as our sins deserve or repay us according to our iniquities. For as high as the Heavens are above the earth, so great is his love for those who fear him; as far as the east is from the west, so far has he removed our transgressions from us. As a father has compassion on his children, so Yahweh has compassion on those who fear him."* Lucia drifted as the singer repeated the refrain, *"So Yahweh has compassion on those who fear him.*[12]*"* The voice slipped away into the distance.

Lucia's eyes opened as the rocking stopped and called out, "No, don't go. Don't leave me." She tried to get out of bed, but her legs were twisted in the blankets. "No, please don't go! Please don't leave me!" She lunged forward in an attempt to follow the song, but instead she fell onto the cold stone floor. "Please don't leave . . ."

Deborah was right by her side, but Lucia pushed her away.

"Don't! I want to find the song. I want to see the singer's face."

"Mistress Lucia, it's me, Deborah. You've fallen out of bed. Let me help you back in."

---

[12] Ps. 103:8-13

Lucia was exhausted. Without resistance she let Deborah lift her up and slip her beneath the covers. She stared at the ceiling for the longest time, confused, searching for something she couldn't see. Then her mind went into a deep blackness. Caressing her brow, Deborah continued reciting Scripture as she lay silent.

Hermes, the stonemason, stared at the sketches before him. The sun blazed directly above. Although sweat stains had splotched the parchment, most of the diagram was clearly defined—only the face remained a mystery.

The stonemason's back was bronzed, his hands calloused, the creases of his skin filled with the dust of newly hewn stone. As his eyes squinted over the diagrams, he effortlessly added up measurements, subtracted for wall thicknesses, multiplied to calculate the layers of the three-dimensional relief on the lid. More drops of sweat fell from his forehead onto the parchment.

The lid of the sarcophagus was designed to have a life-size image of a woman reclining at a banquet table laden with a feast. Like a blank sheet of parchment waiting for the scribe's first strokes, a three-ton block of red granite stood waiting behind the sculptor's hand for his hammer to strike. He stared long at the block of stone, as though hidden beneath its rough surface a beautiful woman lay in repose—he had only to find her. The base stood silently in the shadows of his shop, gleaming with polished surfaces and intricate carvings of seashells and garlands.

Hermes' workspace was crammed between two streets. On one side of his yard, a row of bone boxes was lined up along an irregular boundary line. They were of different sizes with simple rough-hewn surfaces all made of limestone. In one corner a bone box had been stacked on top of another. Half a dozen lids were stacked in another corner beside broken pieces and cracked boxes. In the far right side of the yard, a white marbled box was complete with scenes of battles and victory. The marble was veined in black that streaked across the stone's face like lightning.

Hermes laid the diagrams to one side and wiped his brow with the back of his arm causing a dark streak to stick to his forehead. Damp tendrils of peppered hair fell against his brow and down the back of his neck. The heat was merciless and the air as motionless as his statuary. He had no breeze to cool his face.

In the shade of his roof, a bucket stood half filled with water. First, the stonemason took a long drink, splashed water on his face, then poured a cup of it over his head. For a brief moment he felt refreshed. He pulled out a folded page that had accompanied the parchments from Alexander of Puteoli. The letter was addressed to him. Hermes studied the text carefully.

*To Hermes, the stonemason, greetings in the name of Caesar! As to date, your work has been flawless for my Lucia. She is growing weaker by the day, and I fear there is not much time left. I will arrive in Yerushalayim within the next three weeks. I look forward to your progress on the lid, the most significant feature of this masterpiece. When I arrive, I will pay you for all your work rendered. I ask one favor. Please give Anna the Harlot my greetings and let her know that I will be arriving soon. The gods have not listened to my pleas for a child. Instead they have sent death to my beloved Lucia. I would greatly appreciate speaking with her regarding Lucia. Her house is in the lower city, not far from the Serpent's Pool. You'll find the familiar red marking on her doorpost.*

*Faithfully,*
*Alexander of Puteoli*
*Commander of the Imperial Guard*

Hermes folded the letter back into its original pattern, squinted at the brilliant horizon, and shoved the paper into his waistband. He would begin this piece before sunrise tomorrow. He wondered if he could complete the work in time and how close he could match the sketches of Lucia. His mind, however, wandered to thinking about Anna, the harlot.

## Chapter Six

# YERUSHALAYIM, NEAR THE SERPENT'S POOL, 29 A.D.

The silence of night flowed into Yerushalayim, replacing the babble and jangle of commerce with a transfusion of evening calm. The market vendors were gone, leaving the remains of their long day in corners and beneath eaves. Earthy smells of wheat fields, myrtle blossoms, golden marguerites, and corn poppies replaced the smells of sweat and grime, of strange Arabic spices, Idumaean vinegar, and strong foreign beers.

Shops were locked up tight. Their merchants—flax spinners, wool combers, shoemakers, carpenters, and stonemasons—were home with their families; everyone was with those they loved.

Alexander had felt an expected despondency as he passed from the upper city with its stately mansions of wealthy merchants and princes, their villas and exquisite gardens, down to the small winding streets of the lower quarter. Here were the two opposite spectrums of society: the excessive luxuries of opulence, and the corresponding cheapness of bare necessities. Yerushalayim was a city with two faces. The soldier wandered alone through the empty streets, up one cobbled street and down another dusty lane, all the while brooding over the barrenness of his life.

*How long will Lucia live? Why have the gods ravaged her? Why have they destroyed her beauty and health? How will I live without her? Why are we childless? Why is life so unfair? Why, why, why?*

He felt very lonely. Then he thought of Anna the harlot and pushed onward. Alexander wandered down several unfamiliar lanes. Studying the engravings on a wall, he recognized a landmark, a stone inscription leading to the Serpent's Pool. He was heading toward the lower part of the city where the denizens huddled in small squat dwellings. Turning a dark corner, Alexander recognized the tiny crooked house at the end. As odd as it may be, the dwelling was always clean and fresh. He knew it well, but tonight something was different about this place. Something had changed.

Alexander banged on the door. It sounded so loud and demanding. He didn't want to stir the neighborhood, only rouse the woman inside. The tall redheaded man felt conspicuous as he stood waiting, watching for the sign of life behind the door. Houses in the poorer sector of the city where crammed so closely they were almost stacked on top of one another.

An old woman peeked from behind a curtain across the way, her stare lingering uncomfortably. A dog began to bark; voices could be heard in the distance, but there was no response from inside Anna's house. He glanced to the night sky in thought.

The night was lit with a full moon draped by a thin cloud covering. It scattered the reflected light across the lower horizon of the sky. High above, stars glittered in a profusion of grandeur. No expense was spared on its beauty.

Alexander looked back at the door. Why wasn't she answering? Then he realized what was different—the customary red mark of the harlot's house on the door frame was gone. *This was Anna's house!* His mind raced. *Has she moved?*

*Maybe she's in trouble.* He tapped one more time, listening for a sound.

With his face flush to the door, he whispered, "Anna? It's Alexander of Puteoli. Can you open the door?"

A flame flickered behind the slats in the door. There was a rustle of sound. He sighed with relief. His heart beat fast with hope and expectation. He glanced behind him. The old woman was still watching, her rounded silhouette unmoving. Alexander thought about waving, but decided against it. He turned back toward the door. Someone was coming.

"Anna?"

An iron latch lifted and the door opened only a crack. The room was in darkness. Only the small flame from a clay lamp lit the woman's face. Alexander recognized Anna's round dark eyes even in the dim light of the oil lamp. He was relieved to see her. Before, her eyes always had a longing in them, but tonight they were brighter, more peaceful, a deeper blue.

"Anna. It's me, Alexander. Can I come in?"

Recognition slowly emerged and she smiled. "Alexander, I heard you were coming. But I am no longer . . . no longer . . . offering my services." She raked her slender fingers through her hair. "Many things have changed in my life over the past three months, and it would take too long to tell you tonight."

"Changed? Anna, I didn't know. You no longer are . . . are . . . a . . ." He hesitated.

"No, Alexander, I'm not a prostitute any longer. That's in my past." She sensed his surprise.

"Well . . . well . . ." he stammered. "It's been so long since I've seen you, Anna. I've missed you." He paused again, selecting his words nervously. "I really came because . . . because I wanted to talk to you about Lucia. Can we at least talk?"

There was a long unnerving pause. Alexander looked at the ground for a moment, then stared straight into her blue eyes.

"Not tonight. Not here. Of course I want to know how Lucia is, but we can't talk tonight. It's not appropriate anymore."

Alexander was puzzled. "This is important . . . and I've come a long way."

"I understand, but I cannot meet with you tonight . . . here . . . like this." She hesitated and looked across toward the eyes behind the curtains. "You can come by tomorrow morning."

The puzzled look slowly gave way to an accepting smile. "Yes, of course. Tomorrow morning. I'll come at dawn. I'm sorry to have disturbed you, Anna, but I've missed you and have much to tell you." The moon's glow cast a radiance upon Anna's hair.

"And I have much to tell you, Alexander. I've met a man who has changed my life forever. I will tell you more in the morning. Good night, Alexander."

Alexander stood there stunned by her words. But Anna gave a warm smile, nothing sensuous, nothing with motives, just a reassurance of her friendship. With that, she closed the door and was gone. Alexander stood for a long moment looking at the flimsy wooden door. It felt like a stone wall had suddenly blocked him from beautiful Anna. Shoulders slumped, he headed toward the inn.

*A man in her life?* He was staggered. Alexander pondered her statement. He was puzzled. He was curious. He also was angry. He was equally surprised at his own emotions; a streak of jealously that fluttered like a bat flapping against the walls of his heart. His emotions confused him.

*Anna was only a prostitute. Was she any different than the temple prostitutes of Diana or Aphrodite? My gods not only give their approval to temple prostitution, but they demand it as a fertility rite.* Somewhere in Alexander's heart, a struggle had begun to grow in his conscience. That struggle intensified when he met Anna a year ago. She had nothing to do with fertility rites; he sought out this woman to meet his own human desires. And because of that, he had let Anna into his heart.

Alexander quickly walked away from Anna's house feeling the sting of rejection. The night was so quiet, yet it had a thousand eyes. At least no one could hear the thoughts of his heart, he hoped. Troubled, he turned west and headed toward the upper city.

Alexander walked along a path that led him beside the city wall. He ducked his head as he passed under a low hanging eucalyptus branch. A hidden web brushed across his face. Somewhere in the darkness a dove cooed. The lone soldier didn't notice. He followed the winding lane that took him between several inns and taverns. Even the smell of strong ale and roasted lamb that came from the inn where he'd book a night's stay didn't interest him. His stomach had turned sour. Not caring anymore about much of anything, his pace quickened. Those words of Anna hit him like a slap in the face. He had made himself vulnerable.

*But how could that be? I am deeply in love with my wife, Lucia.* New unsettling thoughts struggled for attention and demanded consideration. Every god of Rome he had trusted would have applauded his attempts. Why was he feeling so guilty? The more the Roman struggled with his conflicting thoughts, the more quickly his steps took him to the inn. He was angry with himself. His emotions had betrayed him. He felt out of control.

The soldier reached the door of the inn and shoved it open. It was low with one step down into a dimly lit room. Alexander hunched his shoulders and dipped his head as he entered. There were only a few men sitting around the room, some drinking, others talking in noisy tones. Two men in a corner were debating politics. The smell of roasted lamb and onions lingered. As he closed the door behind him, everyone turned and stared in loathsome silence. Alexander was not feeling very tolerant tonight. Would there be a brawl?

Alexander's size and training gave him an advantage over all these men. Some were old, the younger untrained, most were fearful, but all filled with hate. A deep unfiltered hatred could, if provoked, overpower him with enough strength to kill. He'd experienced it on the battlefield many times. He hesitated, then instinctively thought like a commander. Instead of a ready blade, he gave a slight diplomatic nod.

One man gave a clipped acknowledgment; the others merely glared, their faces darkened with palpable hatred. The room was extremely hot and stuffy with the stale odor of ale and sweat, but the reception was definitely laced with ice. Alexander expected no less.

After making their feelings known without a word, they slowly turned and resumed their conversations. A young man with black curly hair sat alone at a corner table. He held a drink in front of him and watched the air of antagonism with indifference. His presence in the room seemed detached from the surroundings. For the briefest second his eyes met Alexander's stare, then he looked away.

Tonight in this room, Alexander represented the lowest of the low. He was an outsider, a pagan, uncircumcised; therefore, he was absolute swine. Romans were pagans who believed in many gods and lived as though there were none. That's what the Jews thought and Alexander knew it was quite true. Furthermore, Judea was under Roman occupation, successfully building a wall of inbred hatred from one generation to the next.

The contrasts between Rome and Judea were staggering. Rome's buildings and entertainment arenas were crowned with opulence paid for by the Jewish taxes. Judea was a poor country with little to speak of except sheep and a rich Temple built by Herod the Great. Rome was magnificent, rich in wealth, with not a respectable shepherd among them.

As Alexander walked across the room toward the counter, he felt hostility hit the walls. His pulse was racing, his anger rising to a boiling point. He was tempted to tighten his fist around the handle of his blade.

"Rough night, huh soldier?"

Alexander swiveled around in a flash, his hand tight on the knife's handle.

"You got a problem with me being here?" Alexander questioned.

A stool scuffed and the big man stood. He took a couple steps toward Alexander and tightened his jaw.

"Yeah, we do. We don't like Roman swine very much. They make too much stink wherever they go." He stepped closer to the soldier.

"You got a pretty bad attitude, shepherd, or are you a sheep?" he smirked. "I can't always tell the difference; they both smell the same." At that, a couple of men stood, anger simmering. The beer-bellied man lunged forward. The next step brought him face to face with Alexander. The soldier slid the blade free from its sheath and held it up. The bulky man staggered, his eyes rolling. Suddenly, he swung a fist toward Alexander's jaw. It missed, but his knuckle grazed the soldier's right eye leaving a thin cut.

Alexander swiveled, held up the blade, pulled the man's arm tight against his back and swung the blade up against his throat. He let the sharpness slide across the tender skin and a trickle of blood oozed from the cut.

"You'd be wise to keep to yourself, old goat. You could find yourself in bad company, locked up tight." Alexander shoved the man away from him. He stumbled, bumping into a stool.

Suddenly the silent man in the corner spoke up. "Simon, calm down. You've had too much wine, that's all. This man is a guest here, and he's done nothing to provoke you. Calm down." The curly haired man stood, speaking as if he were talking to a child. "Simon, it's okay." He reached out and took hold of Simon's shoulder. Simon yanked it away and stared long and hard at Alexander, then finally pulled away from the group and left the inn.

"Dim-witted Romans," Simon muttered under his breath just as he pulled the door closed. Alexander burned inside. He leaped to the door. Out in the street the burly man staggered toward a doorway four houses down. Alexander heard him mumble but all his words were now strung together making no sense at all. He was just drunk.

Alexander breathed deeply until his emotions ebbed. He walked back through the door. No one looked at him except the curly-haired man in the corner.

"Please forgive Simon, sir. His drinking gets the best of him most often. I'm afraid he's a habitual drunk."

Alexander slowly calmed down. "Men like him are only fools. I think one of your own poets spoke about the mockery of too much wine."

"You're right, sir. One of our, . . . kings. But for some of us, the lessons are hard to learn."

Alexander walked to the counter. Slowly repressing his anger, he ordered a flask of black ale from the innkeeper, climbed the steps to his room, pushed the door open and shut it with a quick flick of his heel. It banged loudly.

His night had not turned out as he had planned. He looked about him. The room was scant; bare floorboards, a simple bed in one corner, a rough wooden stand beside it with a basin and jug of water. The wool blankets smelled musty. The only light came from the moon's glow that had followed him from Anna's house to the inn. He sat on the edge of the bed and took a long drink of ale. It burned as it slid down his throat and scorched the pit of his stomach. He shuddered. He bent down and unlaced his sandals, kicking one off after the other. Looking out the window, he took another long drink and winced. The soldier spilled some on the floor, but didn't care. He stood, removed his wide leather belt and tossed it in a corner. Punching the pillows a couple of times, he slumped down on the bed.

Alexander thought about Lucia. He pictured the pain in her face which had gradually hidden the face he'd fallen in love with. He winced and took another drink. He would do anything to see her well again, but he knew it was too late. She was no longer available to meet his needs. *His needs.* She was too weak to care for herself. In his mind, they were no longer man and wife. He was her caretaker. His once beautiful wife had faded into a pale sickly woman. He'd wept because she suffered so much. He couldn't stay in her presence for any length of time. The pain was unbearable—his conscience pricked.

*Lucia, my beautiful Lucia.* His eyes were getting watery, and he slouched forward. *I love my Lucia. Why have the gods taken her away from me?* He raised his fist up at the sky. *My Lucia is almost gone, almost faded from this world into . . .* He paused to think where she might go. His mind was becoming confused . . . he thought about Anna. He took another drink, a long one, wiping his mouth with the back of his hand.

*Anna! She was the only one I could talk with about life. She was the only one who cared enough to listen to my pain. But who was this man of whom she spoke? Does this mean she's married . . .? Nobody marries a harlot. No one . . . not even a Roman swine!*

Finishing the ale, Alexander eased his head onto the pillow. His face was flushed with sweat beading on his forehead. He rolled on his side, faced the open window, and stared out into the night sky. The clouds had dissipated and the moon was crystal clear, suspended like a glass orb. He reached out toward the globe of light but couldn't touch it, hold it in his grasp. Just like so many other things in his life, it seemed too elusive. He stared at the moon until it began to spin. The room swirled. He drifted into a troublesome sleep.

---

Lucia closed her eyes. The heavy weight of sickness in her stomach rolled across her abdomen like a stone. Somehow it was growing, not with life—but death. She clutched her stomach and turned onto her side. The pain brought tears that lingered at the corner of her eyelids. The stone seemed to be growing upward toward her chest. Her breathing was getting tighter, thinner. It was happening.

"Deborah?" she rasped.

"I'm right here, mistress. I'll not leave your side until you're asleep." Deborah wiped Lucia's brow with a gentle stroke. Her care for Lucia was like a daughter's devotion.

"Deborah, you're so good to me. Who taught you to be so caring?"

"It's easy to care for you. You're like my own mother." She smiled into Lucia's face. "You have been so kind and generous, allowing me to work under your roof, treating me with respect, and . . . making me feel loved." She kissed Lucia's forehead, then held her cheek against Lucia's face for a long tender moment.

"I love you, Mistress Lucia." Deborah smiled gently and tucked a curl behind Lucia's ear. "You are such a beautiful woman."

"And you are like a daughter to me, Deborah. Yes . . .," she paused thoughtfully as if the thought had only just occurred to her. "You say I'm beautiful? I haven't looked into a mirror for a year now. I wouldn't recognize myself. I must look like the mask of death. I can feel my face withered and bony. I've lost all beauty, my child." The word *child* had slipped out unconsciously and Lucia's face clouded.

Deborah smiled. "Your beauty is more than skin deep. I admire your courage to live with such pain without bitterness."

"But I am bitter, Deborah. I'm bitter that the gods cannot help me. I'm bitter that they promised me something they could not provide, a child, and instead gave me a stone of death." She rolled toward the wall so that Deborah would not see her tears.

"But Mistress Lucia, my God cares about your life." Deborah hesitated, fearing offense. "He sent me to care for you." She tucked a blanket around Lucia's shoulders. "What can I do for you, my mistress?"

"Nothing, Deborah, nothing. Just stay near me. Alexander is gone, isn't he?"

"Yes he is, mistress. But he will return . . . he loves you very much."

"He's in love with who I was, not who I am now. No man could love a woman who looks the way I do. I only feel his pity."

"He doesn't sleep well these days, mistress. He's so troubled about your health. I know he loves you. I've seen it in his eyes. I've heard him speak it." Deborah stared directly into Lucia's eyes, watching her emotions, feeling her pain, reassuring her with attentiveness.

"Shall I sing for you?"

"Please sing me a song from your country." Lucia's steel gray eyes looked up at Deborah hopefully as she rested her head back down on the pillow. She silently prayed to any god who might listen. She prayed for sleep to come. She longed for a visit from the One who offered her peace. *Whoever you might be, please comfort me tonight. Rock me in your arms. Show me your face.*

Deborah began to sing gently as though lulling a baby with a soft Arabic melody. Her voice was lilting, and her face took on a faraway look as she sang.

*"I will praise you, Yahweh, with all my heart; before the 'gods' I will sing your praise. I will bow down toward your holy temple and will praise your name for your unfailing love and your faithfulness, for you have exalted above all things your name and your word. When I called, you answered me . . ."*[13]

Lucia's eyes were closed. Outside, gentle rain began to fall. Drops splattered on the broad green leaves just beyond her window. A smell of freshness rose up from the earth wafting into Lucia's bedroom. She drifted off to sleep hoping to meet a friend.

---

[13] Ps. 138:1-3a

Deborah could finally hear the slow breathing of her mistress. Her melody turned into a prayer—without missing a beat, her voice became more somber . . . *"May all the kings of the earth praise you, Yahweh, when they hear the words of your mouth. May they sing of the ways of Yahweh, for the glory of Yahweh is great! Though Yahweh is exalted, he looks kindly on the lowly . . . Though I walk in the midst of trouble, you preserve my life . . . Yahweh will fulfill his purpose for me; your love, Yahweh, endures forever . . ."*[14] Deborah caressed Lucia's thinning hair. She stroked her forehead, then lowered to kiss her brow.

"Rest peacefully . . . mother," she whispered softly. Deborah, the servant girl, left her mistress' room leaving a single oil lamp burning.

Anna lay awake in the darkness of her tiny room. The sodden walls were rough and had been crudely plastered many years ago. Soot marked the place where once had been a wall-mounted lamp. The oil of her lamp had gone dry, the flame flickering out without a sound. She listened to the rustle of leaves as a breeze whisked past her window.

Anna pondered the recent choice she'd made to follow Yeshua. Her past transgressions were forever banished—the raging flame of sin extinguished; the smudge wiped clean. She could never explain the depth of freedom that forgiveness had brought to her soul. Of course, no one knew how dark her past had been. No one but Yeshua knew the terror of living with her father, the wicked demands, the rage, and now the rejection. How could she explain this to Alexander? He was a pagan, but actually no more than she was only three months prior.

---

[14] Ps 138:4-8

Anna tossed in her bed. She rolled onto her side and her soft raven hair fell across her cheek, curling into the hollow of her neck. She closed her eyes, remembering the words that brought release. It was like Yeshua had opened a floodgate that had been dammed up all her life—all her childhood . . . ever since she could remember . . . ever since her father had touched her.

That day in the market place as her accusers dropped their stones and walked away, Yeshua had reached down and lifted Anna to her feet. He'd whispered in her ear, "Anna, they're gone—not only your accusers, but your sins. I forgive you. As far as the east is from the west, so far have your sins been removed from you. The past is forgiven forever. Go and sin no more."

The judgment of gossiping women and cursing priests could not change what Yeshua had done for her that day. Although her neighbors chose to still condemn her, to treat her with disdain, she knew the past was gone. Before, she was judged for being a prostitute. Now she was scorned for following Yeshua. Even her own father disowned her. He hated the One who spoke out against sin, his sin. He knew that whatever this man, Yeshua, had said to his daughter destroyed all his coveted profits.

Anna's faith in Yeshua had brought enormous joy and freedom such as she had never known before. It had also made a substantial change in her personal income. Without a husband or father to care for her, she was left penniless. What would it take to provide for herself? Anna's life could only be stitched together by courage to face the future with God's help and a willingness to choose another lifestyle. Making a living as a seamstress was difficult in the city where the women despised her, but they brought her business. They seemed to take pleasure in giving her the most demeaning of tasks; repairing their husbands' undergarments. Soon Anna had more work than she could handle as the wives brought the filthiest of garments for bleaching, washing and repairs. Still the joke of the town, Anna was grateful for every garment she repaired. Her joy was centered not in her work but in Yeshua who forgave her and now gave her purpose. No one could take that joy from her.

Anna nestled her head into the pillow. The wind whispered outside her window. She thought again about Alexander. She had not anticipated his visit. She had not thought of him since Yeshua had entered her life. Alexander had never been her typical client. He was different than the rest of the men she had known. She had cared about him.

*I have no right to even think about Alexander. He's a married man. Lucia, his dear wife, is dying. Am I foolish to even talk with him tomorrow? Perhaps Alexander will accept Yeshua when he sees the change in my life. Or perhaps he will reject me, too. What will Alexander do when he knows about me? Yeshua, show me the way.*

A restless uncertainty stirred in her heart for the first time since she had turned from sin. Emotions wriggled into her thoughts unbidden, along with flashing memories, long talks, and words shared in the night. She tossed in her bed until she focused again on the words of Yeshua, "Your sins are forgiven, Anna. Go and sin no more."

Slowly, like a mist gathering itself around the moon, Anna's mind rested in the One who had brought her forgiveness. She closed her eyes and slept. She would face tomorrow, tomorrow.

Anna woke just as the sun touched the horizon with a thin show of colors. Within minutes, flaming light burst through the grayness as it rose over the hills. Precious light burst through the darkness into every house, window and doorway.

Through Anna's window the sun threw a beam of light against the wall on the opposite side of the room. It quickly moved across the room as the sun rose until it lit on Anna's shoulder. She smiled and finally stretched.

Immediately Anna remembered Alexander's words, "I'll be there at dawn." She bolted upright in bed and felt a flash of dizziness. After sitting silent for a moment, allowing her body to adjust, she slowly stood to her feet. The birds were singing. Alexander was late which was most unusual, but she was glad. It would give her time to freshen up before he arrived. She walked to the jug and poured fresh water into the basin. After splashing water on her face and neck she dried and looked into the mirror.

"I look a mess . . . my hair . . . what am I going to do with my hair?" She raked her fingers through her long black hair. Shuffling through her clothes, she found only a couple of halugs, or tunics, that fit her; something loose. She found a light blue halug and tried it on.

"I look horrible in this. It makes my face pale." She tried on a red one.

"This makes me look like a woman of the street." She tossed it on her bed trying to remember why she ever kept it. Then she found an emerald green halug that suited her well. Brushing her hair felt good. She would let it hang down and tuck it back behind her ears. Picking up a deep blue silk scarf, she threw it over her shoulder. Small gold rings adorned her ears, but she wore no other shimmering bangles. That was no longer a part of her world. She loved color, but her dress was now modest and appropriate for her world of business.

There was a heavy knock on the door. Anna's heart raced in surprise.

She felt apprehensive. Steadying herself, she paused and breathed a prayer. "Lord, help me remember that I have nothing to fear. You, the Judge of all judges, have forgiven my past for all time." As Anna walked to the door, she pictured the face of Yeshua in her mind. She remembered his eyes of forgiveness as they pierced her darkest secrets, then banished them forever. Anna raised her head, lifted the latch and opened the door.

## Chapter Seven

# Yerushalayim, Anna's House Near the Serpent's Pool, 29 A.D.

Alexander watched the door. A drop of sweat trickled from his neck down the deep ridge of his back and sank into the clothing around his waist. He was anxious. The back of his red tunic clung to his skin in the early heat of the day. His wide leather belt squeaked as he moved about restlessly. The door opened and Anna's face appeared. Her smile was as radiant as ever, but with tranquility he had never imagined. She stepped out into the sunshine.

"Hello, Alexander. I've thought many times what I'd say if you should come."

Alexander was speechless. He opened his mouth, but nothing came out. His heart was pounding like a racehorse.

"Anna . . . Anna . . . I . . . I didn't know." His face turned a blushed red.

She smiled shyly. "I understand, Alexander. I didn't know for a long time either. I thought something was wrong."

He stuttered for words, looked about him for help. His eyes lingered on her eyes, but then without control they moved down the length of her body. "Who . . . but who . . . I mean . . . are you . . . are you . . .?"

Anna's smile was so confident and settling. She finished his thoughts aloud. "Yes, Alexander. I'm probably about six months pregnant, and no, sadly, I don't know who the father is. I only know that my responsibility is to nurture this child and love it with all my heart. I want to give this baby the love I never had as a child—the love I longed for my whole life." She looked him squarely in the eye. "If you are ashamed to be seen with me that's perfectly fine. Shame is nothing new to me."

"No, Anna. No. I'm just so surprised. So . . . you're not . . ."

". . . married? No. I'm no longer a harlot either. I've met the Messiah. He has forgiven me, Alex—forgiven my sins, every one of them. I'm a new person. This pregnancy happened before I met Yeshua. Somehow, however, it seems a blessing in disguise."

Confusion washed over the Roman's face. His recent blush now turned pale, his expression blank. For a moment he stood, then shook his head as if to knock cobwebs from his brain.

"Anna. This has taken me by such surprise. You are more radiant now . . .," he glanced at her from head to toe, "in . . . this . . . condition, than I've ever seen you." As if he had finally recovered his manners, he leaned over and gave her a slight kiss on each cheek. Anna did not flinch, nor did she respond. She simply smiled.

Anna pointed toward the west wall. "Why don't we take a short walk so we can talk? I want to hear about your dear Lucia and your great conquests in Gaul." Alexander followed without question. As they moved, a cooling breeze followed them toward the arch that would lead out of the city and into the countryside. A bird sang them several tunes as it flitted from one branch to another. The air was fragrant with jasmine.

Alexander walked an even pace with his hands grasped behind his back. With grace and dignity, Anna walked beside him, her green halug matching the green of the soldier's flashing eyes. Alexander contemplated this new woman as they walked side by side. He felt more attracted to her now than ever. *Anna has such a confidence about herself. The tranquility that surrounds her is almost otherworldly.* Alexander tried not to stare, but he found his eyes lingering her way when she wasn't looking.

"Tell me about Lucia." Anna's eyes focused on his face.

"Lucia has very little time left. She's in such pain and the doctors only offer herbal remedies that provide little relief." His face clouded as he spoke.

"You love her very much, Alex, don't you?"

"I did, but she's gone now. She's just skin and bones, unable to contribute anything to our relationship." They passed beneath the arch. An old beggar sat to one side of the gate. He asked for nothing, but his eyes were fixed on a distant point beyond the horizon. Anna smiled down at him. From the folds of her tunic she produced a single coin. She bent down and placed it between the old man's fingers. The man broke his stare and looked up into Anna's face, then down at the coin in his hand.

"The Messiah. I'm looking for him. He might come today." His eyes drifted back toward the horizon.

"Old man, the Messiah has already come. He's here now. His name is . . ."

The man broke in. "The child will come soon. I won't miss him this time."

Anna smiled knowingly. As she passed she leaned close and whispered in his ear, "His name is Yeshua." The filthy condition of the beggar didn't seem to bother the beautiful woman walking beside Alexander.

They resumed their walk beyond the gate and headed out into the open countryside. Alexander seemed puzzled. He grabbed a blade of grass and studied it as they walked. Anna continued their discussion like it had never been interrupted.

"Alexander. Love doesn't stop when human frailty is gripped by disease. That's when love is seen at its best. Real love rises to the occasion of pain."

"Yes. I do still love her, but not like it used to be. Not like . . .," he hesitated.

"Ours was never love, Alexander. Human passion outside of God's laws is only that, a lustful passion. It fills emptiness for a fleeting moment, but in the end it crushes the spirit. Real love does not crush the spirit."

"You never used to think like that before, Anna. What's made you change?"

"I had never met Yeshua before."

Alexander's voice tightened. "Who is this . . . this Yeshua, another Jewish magician? They seem prolific in this region."

Anna looked surprised at the rise of sarcasm in his voice. "Yeshua is the One we've all been waiting for. All I know is that when he looked into my eyes, my pain became his pain. I knew he had forgiven me. In him I saw my sins forgiven."

"But what did you have to be forgiven for, and how could a man forgive?"

"Infidelity, fornication, destroying families, causing men to lust and stealing people's reputations. I hated myself and was jealous of others around me who seemed happy. I found myself using people for my own benefit . . . shall I go on?"

"I think you're being too hard on yourself, Anna. You're a beautiful person . . . caring, and gentle." Alexander had torn the blade of grass into shreds and reached out for another longer stalk.

"My father trained me in the ancient craft of harlotry, but meeting Yeshua helped me see what I was really like inside." Her eyes peered into the emerald green of his stare, and then looked down.

They had reached a rise in the hill. The grass was lush and windswept to the north. Birds flitted into the tall grasses then back out again. A small bird swooped down from a tree and landed nearby. It chirped a tuneless song. Anna smiled and focused on the bird.

"Do you hear that bird?"

"What?" The soldier looked around, confused. "What are you talking about?"

"There. Listen. It's a wren. It just chirps without a tune."

"Interesting, but what does that have to do with us?"

"It's like the way I used to be when we first knew each other. I had nothing in my life that was beautiful or pure. I did what I was told. I smiled, I enticed, I sinned. But when I met Yeshua, the Messiah, he took that all away. He gave me a song of freedom. I'm forgiven." She looked at her stomach and held her hands around it. "This child is a result of my past, but I'm forgiven. Now the child will be a blessing that I never dreamed could happen to me."

Anna needed to stop and rest. She sat down on the grass. Alexander's mind was reeling. He remained standing for a minute, then finally sat. He shook his head in confusion. "How do you know this religious man is for real? Maybe he's just another joker trying to get a following."

"I believe he's more than a man. He sees right through people and into their hearts. He exposed not just my sin, but everyone else's in the crowd that day. He speaks with authority." Anna recounted the day she met Yeshua, from the condemnation of the townspeople to the moment he spoke to her. "No ordinary man could do that."

"You were just doing your job. A harlot is like . . . like a politician or tax collector."

"No, Alexander. We both know that's wrong. It's written in our hearts. Adultery is sin. It tears marriages apart. It goes against God's intended purpose." Anna could see confusion and anger in his face. He did not want to hear this.

"But how can a man forgive sin?" Alexander was struggling.

"How can a stone idol hear your prayers?" Anna's steady gaze was intense. "How can a cupid give you love? All I know is that he has changed my life. He's more than a rabbi. I know rabbis. A rabbi cannot see into my heart. He's more than a prophet, because he not only showed me my sin but also forgave me and took away my shame. He saved me. Alex, he looked right into my heart and saw everything—even my childhood and the touching . . ."

"Touching? What are you speaking of? I know nothing about that."

"It doesn't matter now, Alex. Yeshua knew everything about me from the moment he walked into my circle. Once, I was blinded by the sins I committed, but now I'm free. You have no idea what my profession was doing to me inside. Every time a man wanted me, it shattered my soul. But now I'm forgiven and I know God is pleased."

"Which god? There are hundreds."

"Are you being sarcastic again or do you really believe that?"

"Rome is full of gods. We have temples and statues everywhere."

"I've never been to Rome."

"I'll tell you, it's a mad world out there. Most Romans don't know what they believe or whom they should believe in. So we pray to them all and do as we please." He hesitated. "I just wonder sometimes . . . is . . . anyone listening?" He studied the sky for a minute as though searching for a sign. "What a waste in the end, if there were no one out there and we're just talking to ourselves."

Anna wanted to take Alex's hand, but she hesitated. Instead she whispered, "The ancient scriptures say, *'Of what value is an idol, since a man has carved it? Or an image that teaches lies? For he who makes it trusts in his own creation; he makes idols that cannot speak. Woe to him who says to wood, 'Come to life!' Or to lifeless stone, 'Wake up!' Can it give guidance?*

*It is covered with gold and silver; there is no breath in it. But Yahweh is in his holy temple; let all the earth be silent before him.'"[15]*

Anna knew Alex was confused and yet thoughtful. She knew that only Alex alone could find his way through the maze of beliefs he had inherited from his ancestors. She knew he would have to find the true Messiah on his own. There was a long silence. Anna let herself relax, her eyes focusing on the cloud patterns overhead.

Alexander's voice broke through her thoughts. "How are you going to take care of the child? He or she will be born in the winter. Where are you going to get money to pay for food and shelter?"

"I'm trusting God for that. I don't know yet. I'm taking in some sewing to earn a few pennies . . . but the neighbors aren't especially kind to me. Of course I can understand."

"Pennies!" Alexander's voice boomed. "Trusting your God for pennies? Is that all he can provide? Look at Rome compared to this barren place. Rome's gods offer us wealth, victories, prosperity, good living. Your Hebrew God gives you pennies. You and this baby of yours won't last the winter."

Anna turned her head toward the hills. She studied them, letting her thoughts weave through the scriptures. Alexander's words hurt. Finally, she turned back to him and stared. She remembered phrases from Psalm 50. Quietly she repeated them.

*"I am God, your God . . . every animal of the forest is mine, and the cattle on a thousand hills. I know every bird in the mountains and the creatures of the field are mine . . . the world is mine, and all that is in it . . . call upon me in the day of trouble; I will deliver you, and you will honor me."[16]*

Alexander's face became blistered with rage. "This is all a bunch of rubbish. Why have you become so . . . so pious? Is

---

[15] Hab. 2:18-20

[16] Ps. 50:7-15

it because of this baby of yours, or maybe because you've lost your edge in the trade of prostitution?"

His words stung as if she'd been slapped. Tears welled up, and Alexander knew that he had gone too far. He'd struck his opponent like a soldier, quick and deep in the heart. He felt instant shame.

"I'm so sorry, Anna." His emotions wavered from anger to shame, then back to love for this woman who did not belong to him. Anna's eyes were wet with tears. "I had no right to say such terrible things." He paused. "I don't know what's wrong with me."

Anna was crying but didn't retaliate. She looked down into her lap, avoiding his eyes. Finally, she spoke.

"I know you don't understand the changes you see in me. It's confusing to me at times, too, but I know that what I was and what I am today are not the same. I hate who I was, and for the first time in my life I feel free and good."

"I see that too, Anna. I . . . I just don't understand the whole religious thing. This man . . . Yeshua; it's too much for me to understand." Still uncomfortable, Alexander and Anna sat in the tall grass and stared out toward Yerushalayim's walls in silence. Finally, he reached into an inner pocket in his tunic. Awkwardly, he pulled the box out and offered it to Anna."I've brought you a gift from Rome. I'd like you to have this."

Anna sat up straighter and stared down at the tiny box. It was beautiful. She'd never seen anything like it. The entire box was made of ivory with roses and vines carved into the sides and draping over the lid. "It's for you, Anna. It's been passed down through my family for three generations."

Anna was stunned. She was speechless. She wanted desperately to touch it, to hold it in her hands, to feel the carved blossoms. Finally, she looked up into his pleading eyes. "I can't accept that, Alex." She pulled back slightly.

"I know . . . I know this is hard. But Anna, you mean so much to me. Let me show you what it is. Look." He lifted the delicate lid and inside was a richly-ornamented gold ring. Its face had the Roman seal of Caesar. Alexander held it up with pride. "This ring was given to my grandfather by the great Julius Caesar for bravery in combat—one of the treasures of Rome. I've had a goldsmith resize it to fit you. It's never gone outside our family in Puteoli before . . ."

Anna was overwhelmed with many emotions; this gift, this man, this moment.

"Alexander, I can't . . . no . . . no. I can't accept this gift. I have no right to take it. Please don't." Anna rose from the ground.

Alexander took hold of her arm and pulled her back down. "Anna, please." His grip was strong.

Anna pulled away and tried to get free. "Alex, don't do this." Tears streamed down her cheeks. "Let go of me, Alex. You're hurting me."

Alex pulled his hands away, raising them high, suddenly aware of what he was doing. "I'm sorry, Anna. I didn't mean to . . . I didn't mean to hurt you."

Anna's emotions were suddenly stripped bare. Her arm had quickly turned red and her scarf had fallen to the ground. Sobbing, she wrapped her arms around herself.

Alex picked up her scarf and put it around her shoulders. "I'm so sorry, Anna. That was so wrong of me. I just . . . I love you so much and want you to have this ring."

Anna lowered her eyes and wiped them with the scarf. She was bewildered by her conflicting emotions. Her first love and loyalty was Yeshua. She and Alexander were worlds apart. Accepting this gift felt like she was compromising her devotion to Yeshua, not to mention that Alex was married to Lucia and she alone should be wearing this band of gold.

"I can't take that, Alexander. You are married to Lucia. Please. You're making this so difficult for me. This is a terrible mistake." She rose and took a couple of steps to distance herself as he stood. The soldier's strength drained from his face.

"I care so much for you, but this is wrong. I could not accept such a valuable gift as this. I just can't."

"Please accept this, Anna. I love you."

"Alexander, don't. This is wrong and we both know it. You are married to Lucia. She needs you now. Please go." She began to walk away from him back toward the city. Alexander watched her dark hair flash in the morning sun. Her movements were so delicate. The breeze rippled her clothing as she rushed away from him. He could tell she was crying. His world was crashing down around him.

"Anna, don't leave," he called out, already knowing it made no difference. She was right. This relationship was flawed from the start.

The soldier placed the ring back in its box and put it inside the folds of his tunic. A feeling of loss smothered by rejection weighed on him.

## Chapter Eight

# YERUSHALAYIM, DUNG GATE, 29 A.D.

T he once virulent soldier who had fought in Rome's fiercest armies, won accolades for bravery and was ordered by King Herod to destroy little boys and babies in Bethlehem, now lay by the roadside in Yerushalayim's dusty streets begging for his supper. Unable to satisfy Herod's demands, he endured eighteen months of inhuman torture until he was considered worthless to anyone. The shell of a man remembered nothing but violence, heinous images that wouldn't let him go. Year by year, decade after decade, Artamos existed, hoping for death but clinging to life. Three decades plus one, the soldier was a mere shadow to all who passed by.

Artamos leaned back against the wall, his hair a confusion of wiry gray masses. His beard, like barbed wire, crowded his chin. The clothes he wore were the remains of someone's cast-aways, now stained with his sweat and earth's red dust. The creases of his face were deeply scored road-maps leading to nowhere. The man's eyes were vacant, exposing the doorway to his soul. His uncompromising stare riveted him to a task he had set for himself. He would watch for the *HaMashiach* to come. If he were that important to King Herod, then he would watch until he arrived. Without him, the demons of the night would ultimately destroy him. A woman rushed past him, then through the gate. The green of her tunic flashed in front of him and then was gone. Artamos continued to watch the horizon—waiting, hoping.

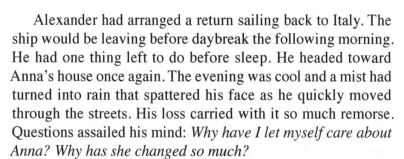

Alexander had arranged a return sailing back to Italy. The ship would be leaving before daybreak the following morning. He had one thing left to do before sleep. He headed toward Anna's house once again. The evening was cool and a mist had turned into rain that spattered his face as he quickly moved through the streets. His loss carried with it so much remorse. Questions assailed his mind: *Why have I let myself care about Anna? Why has she changed so much?*

The more he thought about the changes in Anna, the more he realized what was hidden deep within his heart. Her new faith made his character look shabby. He hated that. Alexander arrived at Anna's house. The rain slanted against her front door. His ginger hair matted flat against his head. He knocked hard.

Within seconds, Anna opened the door and stood there in silence. Her eyes were red and puffy. A deep sadness had engulfed her.

"Anna, I'm leaving for Puteoli tomorrow morning. I probably won't see you again. Since your Messiah only gives you pennies, my gods have supplied me with enough to share with you. You will need it for the baby." He held out a pouch heavy with Roman coins.

She just stared into his eyes with sadness so deep Alex turned his head away.

"Alexander." But words could not be found for her mixed emotions. She felt anger at his sarcasm and rejection of her new-found faith. But she also knew this Roman soldier could not be a part of her life. He was blinded to the truth she had found. Of all the emotions Anna felt today, the least was pity for Alex's sense of rejection.

"Take this, if not for you, then take it for your child, Anna." He tossed it onto the floor. A hardened look squared his features. Shoulders no longer proud like a commander, he trudged through the street away from Anna's house.

"Alex . . ." but her words were lost in the rain. Sadly, she closed the door.

"Alexander, Alexander." Her voice was weak and trembling, hardly audible. Lucia's eyes were sunk so deeply into their sockets Deborah could hardly bear to look upon such suffering, but the love for her mistress overcame her emotions. The servant rushed silently to Lucia's side.

"Mistress Lucia, I'm right here. It's Deborah, your servant."

"Where is Alexander?" Lucia seemed to look right through Deborah into another world.

"Mistress Lucia . . ." She knelt down so that her face was close to Lucia's. "I'm here for you. Alexander is still in Judea. He should be back soon, very soon."

"I want to see the stars." Deborah's mind rushed. What was she talking about?

"Why do you want to see the stars, mistress?" Suddenly, Lucia looked directly into Deborah's eyes and Deborah knew exactly what she wanted.

"Please take me up to the rooftop. I want to see the stars before I die. Please, Deborah."

"Yes, mistress. But you aren't going to die tonight. I won't let you go. You're too precious to me."

"I know I'm going to die, Deborah, please help me." She tried to lift herself up from the bed. "Please help me." Deborah found a robe and helped wrap it around Lucia. Deborah became anxious and her heart raced. She knew time was short.

*Lord, help Lucia to know you before she dies. Jehovah God,*
*reveal your power.*

The steps to the roof were damp from the evening dew.
Deborah wondered if she should carry Lucia, but feared she
might slip and fall. Although Lucia was nearly weightless,
Deborah wasn't large herself. She pulled Lucia's left arm over
her shoulder and held tightly to her hand. With her other arm,
she wrapped it around Lucia's waist and together they shuffled
up one step at a time.

The air was balmy and the night clear with only a slice of
the moon's face exposed. Lucia's breathing was labored. Half
way up, Deborah stopped to let Lucia rest.

"Are you okay? Do you want to go back down?"

"No, no. I must reach the top. How many more steps?"

"Only four, mistress. One step at a time and then we'll rest."

Lucia took another step, but she slipped and fell on one
knee. Deborah caught her and lifted her up, holding her tight.
There was no railing.

"Mistress, this is dangerous. I fear for you. This is too much
for you."

"I must see the stars and the Heavens before I die. Yes. Let's
keep going up."

Deborah bent over and lifted Lucia's right leg up to the next
step. "All right . . . now lift." There were three more steps to
the top. Deborah feared the worst. It could be fatal. She kept
a firm grip on Lucia. "This is the last step. Can you lift your
foot again?"

"Yes, I can do it." The moment she reached the roof, she
lifted her head up and gasped, "I can see the stars . . . Look,
Deborah, the stars."

Tears pooled in Deborah's eyes. She, too, lifted her eyes
to the Heavens. Then she knew why Lucia wanted to see the

stars. It was her step of faith. The roof-top had been furnished with a lounge where Alexander often spent twilight time to meditate. Along the edge, earthen pots with delicate shrubs and herbs for the kitchen formed a border. Carefully, Deborah eased Lucia onto the couch—her breathing was shallow and labored. Deborah knelt down and wrapped the robe tightly around her, pulling the collar up to cover her neck.

"Look . . . look." She was mesmerized at the expanse of the Heavens. Flung across the horizon, stars glittered as millions of lights ebbed and flowed with intense brilliance. Deborah, too, stared in awe. The stars seemed to dance. Words flowed into Deborah's heart like a stream of good news from God himself.

Before she could utter a word, Lucia cried out, "Oh God, who made the stars, the moon, and the Heavens, come to me. Come and sing to me your song of joy." Tears streamed down Lucia's face. She held her arms up to the Heavens. A new strength seemed to possess the frail body as her soul reached for the God of the Heavens and earth.

Deborah found herself singing, *"The Heavens declare the glory of God, the skies proclaim the work of his hands. Day after day they pour forth speech; night after night they display knowledge. There is no speech, or language where their voice is not heard. Their voice goes out into all the earth, their words to the ends of the world."* [17]

"I see him, your God who made the Heavens. He is a holy God and I am full of shame. Oh forgive me, Holy One, for following other gods. I see forgiveness in his eyes. He's calling me . . . can you hear, Deborah? Can you hear his voice?" Lucia's eyes were sparkling with a new brilliance. "Listen, Deborah, he is calling my name."

Deborah wept, yet smiled softly. "Out of respect we call him Yahweh. "His name is precious to all who worship him." His

---

[17] Ps. 19:1-4

name means, *I AM WHO I AM*."[18] She spoke the words in deep reverence. "Only *you* can hear his call in your spirit. He calls each one of us by name. Yahweh is calling you, Mistress Lucia."

"Yahweh, Such a beautiful name! Come and take me to yourself, Yahweh. I want to come to you."

Suddenly a meteorite burst through the atmosphere. It threw stardust across the night sky and disappeared into the distant horizon. Like a grand finale of fireworks, the Heavens proclaimed God's glory . . . and Lucia gasped at the display of splendor. As she surveyed the Heavens, her large round eyes reflected the brightness of the spectacle. She had found the God of the ages. Lucia lowered her arms. Her face was radiant. A peace washed over Lucia that transformed her entire countenance.

As Deborah gazed at Lucia, she began to pray quietly, finishing with a Psalm, *"May the words of my mouth and the meditation of my heart be pleasing in your sight, Yahweh, my Rock and my Redeemer."*[19] How gracious God was to accept Lucia as his own.

For a long time, Deborah stared into Lucia's eyes. She watched as peace descended upon her and calmed her fears. Malignant cells had taken so much from this woman's life. Doctors, spirits, wine or medicine couldn't diminish her pain—but God had. His presence washed over her body like the rays of the sun. Muscles relaxed down to her fingertips. Her spirit became tranquil. God was with her and in her. A smile lit Lucia's face. "Thank you, Deborah, for telling me about your God who brings all that I need in this life and the next. I'm ready to leave."

Time passed until finally Deborah knew Lucia was gone. Home at last. Deborah rested her head upon her mistress' breast

---

[18] Ex. 3:14 God reveals himself and his name to Moses. YHWH is only pronounceable in English as Yahweh. Calling God Hashem literally means "the name."

[19] Ps. 19:14

and silently wept. *"La mia bella mamma . . . m*y beautiful mother . . . I will miss you, but I'll see you soon. One day I, too, will be coming home."

Dawn began with a faint tinge of rosy pink on the distant horizon. Beyond the rooftops a rooster crowed waking Deborah from sleep. A noise down below startled her. Someone was in the villa. She lifted her head and realized she had fallen asleep resting beside Lucia's body. A fear rushed through her wondering what to do next. She would have to carry Lucia's body down the stairs alone. She had never prepared a dead body for burial.

A door slammed and Deborah could hear footsteps running throughout the house. Alexander's voice bellowed out like military orders. Deborah shivered anxiously.

"Lucia. Lucia, where are you?" Footsteps raced from one room to the other. "Lucia!" Alexander's urgent voice raised a pitch. Deborah could hear fear and anger. "Deborah, where are you? Where have you taken Lucia? What's happened? Answer me now. NOW!"

Alexander stood face to face with Deborah on the roof. "What have you done, you fool? Why have you brought Lucia up here in such a weak condition?" His face grew red.

"Mistress asked to see . . ."

Alexander slapped Deborah so forcefully she fell to the floor, her face searing with pain. The soldier bent down and listened for Lucia's breathing. "She's dead! You've killed her, you stupid Jew. You've killed my dear Lucia."

Deborah started to get up, but Alexander slapped her across the back of her head. She covered her head in protection. The force was so fierce she nearly blacked out. "Get up." Alexander yanked her arm and pulled her up to her feet. "Explain to me how this happened now. I can kill you, you know. You're my possession."

Deborah withered and trembled. Wrapping her arms around herself she said,

"Master, I am so sorry. I tried to discourage her from . . ."

"Sorry? You fool. You're a murderer." He pulled a knife from a belted sheath.

"Oh master, no! Please believe me. Mistress Lucia begged to come up and see the stars. She knew she was dying and wanted to see the stars . . ."

"The stars? You've been up here all night?" He raised the knife and Deborah fell at his feet begging for her life—pleading for forgiveness.

"Master, I loved her. I would have done nothing to . . ."

Alexander was shaking with rage. The dagger hung in mid-air. Deborah dropped her head to the ground. He had trusted her with everything in his household, even the care of his ailing wife. His knuckles blanched as his grip tightened. Deborah, who never once had given her master cause for concern, shivered beneath the blade.

"Get out of my house before I kill you."

"Yes, master." Deborah rose with head bowed. "My mistress was up here praying. She knew she was dying and begged to see the stars one last time."

"Praying," he bellowed. "Praying to whom? I see no gods up here."

"Praying to Jehovah God," the servant spoke softly yet with certainty.

"How dare you try to convert my wife to your pathetic Jewish god. He's nothing."

Suddenly there was a crack of thunder that seemed to shake the rooftop with its resonating force. The morning sky had turned menacing and huge drops of rain hit the rooftop like pellets of iron. Another flash of lightning was followed by a shudder of thunder that cut through the atmosphere. Alexander could feel the hair on his arms rise. Rain pelted the rooftop with such intensity that Deborah rushed without personal concern to cover Lucia's body with her own. Suddenly, Alexander felt a strange fear come over him. *Who is this God?*

He turned back to Deborah. "Get away from her!" With a single shove he pushed her aside and picked up Lucia's body in his arms. Deborah caught herself before falling down the stairs. She bowed her head and backed away from her master.

The rain quieted as quickly as it had begun. Deborah started down the stairs with Alexander following her when she suddenly stopped and turned.

"Master Alexander, I loved Lucia as my own mother." Tears streamed down her face. "I would never have done anything to harm her. I gave Lucia her last dying wish. She died in my arms." The servant looked into her master's eyes. "Good-bye, master Alexander." Within a few moments the servant girl had collected her belongings and was gone.

Alexander knew he could have killed this slave with one slash and no one would have known or cared. However, never once had she violated his wishes. How close he had come to killing this girl. He felt regret and confusion mingled with sorrow.

Downstairs, Alexander laid Lucia's body on her bed and eased himself gently down beside her. His whole world was unraveling and he could do nothing to stop its destruction.

## Chapter Nine

# GERASENES, SYRIA, 29 A.D.

W hen Democritus awoke, the sun was fully suspended in a seamless, cerulean sky. Birds sang as they flitted through the branches overhead. This had been the first time in ten years that he had slept a full night's sleep. There were no demons to stir the darkness of fear, no haunting demands, and no silent eyes peering into his empty soul. He had found a peace that filled his cup of wanting. That peace was given at a price he had yet to comprehend.

It was the fish that awakened him. The aroma of roasted white fish was irresistible, stimulating, arousing an outrageous hunger. The campfire that died during the night had been relit and crackled with new logs blazing. A rough spit had been driven into the ground and fresh fish were roasting over the fire. A flask of wine was sitting beside an oak.

Democritus sat up and blinked. He didn't want to miss a moment with Yeshua and was already disappointed he had slept longer than intended. Although his tortured body had been healed, rest had helped to restore his broken spirit. The Messiah was settling his soul, restoring memories of childhood laughter, dissipating the demonic ties that had kept him bound. He felt reborn.

In the distance, Democritus could see a fishing boat and recognized his new friends already at work. The boat's small, dark hulk seemed motionless in the calm waters while its dingy sail hung listless.

Democritus stood and stretched. He was startled as the garment he had been given unfolded around him. He had lived for years with nothing. Today he was wearing a royal robe; Yeshua's robe. He walked to the water's edge and peered down at his reflection. He was stunned. The man staring back was unrecognizable. Democritus was overwhelmed by the utter transformation in himself. What else was waiting for him down the road?

His life had changed in a single moment—the moment he met *Yeshua HaMashiach*, his Messiah. Still mesmerized at his own reflection, he touched his face where scars had been. His face was clear, his eyes lucid and sparkling. He raked his fingers carefully through his hair—no blood and crusted flesh, just unsoiled waves of hair that he brushed back.

"How can this really be?" he whispered to himself.

"Because you called and I answered." Yeshua had been standing by a tree. "You're a new man."

"Master." Democritus rose. "I am your servant. You are surely my Messiah who I have longed for my whole life—*Yeshua HaMashiach*."

"Democritus, come sit down and have breakfast with me. I have much to share with you." He nodded toward the boat. "They've already eaten."

As the men talked and ate, deposits of darkness began to fall away from Democritus' soul. He'd been held prisoner for ten years by spirits so evil and unconquerable, until the Messiah came near. Pure evil had reigned over his life for so long. Somewhere within, he'd longed for freedom. The demons fed him debilitating lies, tortured his emotions, controlled his heart through deceit, and convinced the man that his soul was already lost. They convinced him that without their presence he would die.

"I want to be with you forever." Democritus looked anxious. "I can't lose you."

"You won't lose me. I'll always be here for you, but first I must go up to Yerushalayim and then I'll return for you. Before that happens, I have some work for you to do."

The price of freedom was still yet to be paid; death had yet to be conquered and every step brought Yeshua closer to the cross. Without it Democritus would never find victory; death would claim him forever. Conquering death itself would break Satan's grip of power upon the human race. For Yeshua, the cross was his alone.

Yeshua stopped speaking and looked up along the crest of the hillside. Democritus followed his eye, and said, "Looks like we've got some angry pig farmers."

The mob came rushing down the slope toward them, gaining momentum as they descended. Leading the pack was the pig herder himself. Yeshua seemed unfazed as the crowd came closer. He stood and began to break up the fire from the morning breakfast. The crowd was aggressive. Yeshua poured handfuls of sand on the fire, smothering the flames. The crowds were cursing. He stamped out the scattering embers, then calmly looked into the faces of the people that had swarmed around him.

The swine herder who had fled had now returned with a crowd full of accusers. With irrational anger, he began to scream as he approached Yeshua.

"This man is a conjuror." He pointed at Yeshua. "He used his magic to destroy my entire herd of swine." The man was animated. "He killed them all . . . fed them some kind of poison that made them go mad."

Yeshua made no response; gave no defense. But he looked at the crowd with great sadness, staring silently at their faces. Only the brazen ones held his gaze.

The crowd began to jostle and shove. They moved in on Yeshua, but no one touched him. They wanted this man to go away.

Democritus shouted over the crowd. "Listen . . . this man is the promised Messiah of the Jews. He delivered me from demons."

An old man argued, "Messiah of the Jews? We're not Jews so leave us. And whoever he is, we don't need him. Anyone who destroys our livestock is not welcomed here."

The crowd was growing restless. Yeshua remained steady. A few rabble-rousers on the fringe picked up stones. A few held clubs. It was looking troublesome.

From the lake, Peter and John had noticed the crowd along the water's edge. Wasting no time, they dropped sail, picked up oars and rowed furiously to shore. As the fishermen jumped out and splashed ashore, they overheard Democritus speaking. They were startled by his bold persuasion.

"Drop your stones and clubs, men. Don't be so foolish. There'll be no killing today." He paused. "This man came at my request." Yeshua and Democritus glanced at each other.

"I am Diablo."

There was a stunned silence and many of them gasped.

"Yes, you all know who I am . . . the damage I've done in this town. I'm the possessed man chained up in those hills for ten years." They were listening. "Most of you thought I was just mad and so did I." He turned around. "This man, Yeshua, set me free."

"How do we know you're Diablo?" A man pushed through the crowd. "You don't look like him."

Democritus smiled. "Well, Simon, you don't look like the Simon I remember either. Remember stealing those melons from the market stall when we were ten? You got caught and I didn't." Simon gasped. Some in the crowd snickered.

"And you." Democritus singled out a man still holding a stone. "It was your men that chained me in the cave over the ridge. You had to. I was dangerous. Remember how many times I broke those chains? Madness didn't do it, demons did."

The man became agitated and his hands shook. Many were trying to make sense of it all.

"I'm here to tell you that this man, Yeshua, is the Messiah the world desperately needs. He's healed me; body, soul and spirit. I'm a new man as you can see with your own eyes. If he can do that for a disgusting crazy man, he can do it for you too, if you only ask."

"Shut up. Get out of here. We don't believe you or your Messiah."

Democritus turned to Yeshua. "They're the crazy ones. I can't believe this."

From somewhere at the side, a rock was hurled at them. It whizzed past Democritus' face and grazed his ear. Others were grabbing sticks and rocks. The mob was closing in. Peter and John surrounded Yeshua and Democritus.

Democritus turned to Yeshua. "I don't understand. Why would they reject truth that could set them free?"

"Because the darkness cannot comprehend the light. They're so used to darkness they're blind to the light. If they want deliverance, they will see the truth and live."

Yeshua spoke to the crowd and said, "We'll honor your request and leave." He then turned to Democritus and said, "Their hearts are as hard as the rocks they throw. But you must keep spreading the word throughout Decapolis. You must train to fight on a spiritual level. You've seen the dark side. You know how violent it can be. Some will believe and their salvation will be worth the fight. You must train both body and spirit."

As the crowds dispersed, the two brothers gathered their belongings and put them into the boat. Democritus was aware that he would be staying behind. Yet he never wanted to leave Yeshua's side.

Yeshua called out to him as the boat slid into the lake, "Democritus, I'll come back for you." He pointed to the dwindling crowd. "Some will believe. Go."

"I'll tell everyone I meet, Master." Democritus waved to them and then turned back to catch up with two stragglers headed home. One of them asked about Yeshua. Democritus began to tell the story of all that the Messiah had done for him.

Chapter Ten

# YERUSHALAYIM, OLD CITY QUARTER, 29 A.D.

Malchus sat hunched at a corner table of the dingy tavern in Yerushalayim's lower end. He had slipped in through an alley entrance where rubbish was thrown. He wore an inconspicuous coat that paled into the dirty walls like folds of stucco. He had stubbly facial hair and eyes black and round, glistening like pools of oil. Loose curls of dark hair surrounded his face giving him a sort of wildness. But his Roman facial structure stood in contrast to his Semitic coloring. He considered himself a half-breed; father Roman and mother Jewess. Reveling in self-contempt, he had convinced himself he was an offense to both cultures.

Malchus frequented inns and taverns. He was a loner. Seldom noticed, he seldom spoke. But sitting alone in the dark corners, he watched . . . and listened.

The room smelled rancid. Three brass oil lamps hung from the ceilings. The oil burned upward leaving black curling fingers that touched the ceiling with a sticky residue, then filtered across until it hit the walls. The dirt floor was crusted with spilled ale and food droppings, but deeply saturated with stories of battles and scoundrels that roamed the Mediterranean ports. That's why Malchus came and that's why he listened. His mind filed away details that perhaps could be useful sometime; useful in different circles to bring disdain of his enemies for a price, or perhaps honor for himself.

In the center of the room two rough tables were surrounded by eight or nine men, each so drunk that they thought it necessary to shout at one another as though it were a colony for the deaf. Malchus felt miserable. He hated the drinking holes where men gathered. But he was always there. It was a secret part of his life.

During the day, Malchus was servant to the Temple-appointed high priest, this year Caiaphas. He followed the well-padded priest around the palace quarters, scurrying after him, bowing to his demands, "yes sirs" to his every requirement no matter how trivial it might seem. Malchus lived a double life. Because he served the high priest, he was on the inside. He listened there, too. Besides the high priest, he listened to the scribes, scholars and politicians twist and transform the Torah to make God's laws fit into their comfortable world. When off duty, he slipped into the shadows of taverns, hiding from the indignity of his lowly position, but always dreaming that one day he would make men proud of him.

Malchus found great intrigue in the crookedness of men's ways to gain power. He watched what they did to gain it. He analyzed their schemes, picking flaws in them. Rome's strategy for new conquests was always amusing. They were conquering the world, for what? Like the buzzing of bees, Malchus kept hearing humming reports of increasing decadence of Rome's royal festivities. All news could be used in some way toward his personal gain.

Now the reports of a new soothsayer in Yerushalayim stirred Malchus to know more. He had seen this man from a distance. Apparently he did miracles and that troubled his boss, Caiaphas. Large gatherings followed him throughout Judea. Everywhere he went it was reported that he did amazing feats and challenged traditional religions. Apparently he was even known to raise someone from the dead.

Malchus mused at the thought of this prophet. *It has to be a hoax. Only God can raise the dead; he's just another zealot wanting attention.*

Malchus' hope was that sometime, someone would give him enough information that would ultimately change his life forever. Tonight was obviously not the night.

As the night closed in and men began to leave one after the other, Malchus decided to call it quits and head for his room. Just as he thought this, a man burst into the tavern with wild eyes. Looking small and dark, Malchus thought that the man looked similar to himself, but without the Roman chin. The man walked between the tables toward the counter, his multicolored robe brushing against the men still seated. A few eyes stared at him, then the men went on with their conversations. Malchus watched silently. He would stay for a few more minutes.

Iscariot was sweating profusely. Not only had he walked quickly from the other side of Yerushalayim to the tavern, but also, beneath his mass of dark hair, something was rumbling in his head. Malchus could see it in his face. Iscariot's eyes flicked around the room like a man under extreme pressure.

Malchus' pupils narrowed as he watched with intensity. He sensed fear in this man. The man was about to make a decision, or had already done so.

*No. He hasn't decided yet. He's too anxious, too unsettled to have made a decision about something. Something important.* Malchus leaned back against the plastered wall, disappearing all the more into the room's dark shadows.

"I'll take the strongest wine you got." Iscariot slapped down a leather coin pouch on the counter. The bartender eyed him suspiciously for a moment and then made a decision. He went into the back and came out with a jug.

"Black wine of Sharon. Black as ink! No water added."

"You're sure it's not diluted?" The guest was agitated, unnerved by something.

"You don't listen very well, man. No . . . water . . . added. You take this jug of black wine and it'll make you drunker than a monkey from Asia in one hour. I also have a hin[20] of barley wine, but you'll pay extra. It comes from Egypt."

"How much extra?"

"Black wine is five drachmas for the entire jug. The barley wine is eight drachmas. What's your choice?"

The man was jittery and slapped his hand on the leather pouch. He spread the contents on the counter and tallied the sum. "I'll take both for ten drachmas."

The bartender shouted, "You're a cheat. Trying to cut me out of a profit, huh? No way. Thirteen drachmas or nothing. I don't run this establishment just because of my pretty face."

The little man turned his head toward the door, smirked and said, "I don't see a queue waiting here. Ten drachmas for both or I'll go to the next tavern. I know old Zimri will cut me a deal." The bartender's face reddened and Iscariot shrugged.

"Twelve drachmas then. Nothing less," the bartender said.

Iscariot began to loosen up, taking pleasure in the haggling as though it were a game. His hand scooped up the scattered coins. "Ten or nothing. You lose the sale and your buddy Zimri next door will go home with ten drachmas extra for the night."

Malchus saw a smirk on the man's face as the customer began to pack up and walk out of the tavern.

"All right. Ten drachmas. But you are a cheat and schemer." The bartender pushed the two containers of foreign wines toward his customer.

---

[20] About six pints or three quarts

Iscariot threw down some coins on the counter, grabbed up his bounty and laughed as he walked toward the door. "Pleasure doing business with you, sir." He disappeared out the door.

The bartender collected the drachmas together, counted them and then shouted, "You filthy swine. You've only left me nine. Lousy swine." But Iscariot was long gone, laughing in the darkness.

Malchus stared at the doorway for a long moment. *Who was that man? He's ruthlessly clever.* He must find out. He slipped out the back door and followed the man into the night.

Malchus moved from shadow to shadow. The night was dark with the slivered moon clothed in a thin mist of cloud cover. His target was as shifty as himself. The man moved with stealth, peering down alleys and into shadows. He definitely had something on his mind . . . and he feared. Malchus could sense this man's fear ten yards away. He knew something. Something important. And he was keeping it to himself.

Iscariot turned down a side street, his footsteps light on the cobbles. He peered behind him with a sense that he was being followed. He saw nothing and kept walking. He stopped to take a swig of black wine. He shuddered as it rolled down his throat.

Malchus remained twenty paces behind. He followed him down one street, then another, then another. *He knows he's being followed. He's trying to lose me.* The thought hit Malchus again. *He's so much like me it's spooky. I can almost predict what he'll do next.*

Malchus decided to cut him off at the next street. Seeing the man turn right down a narrow cobbled street, he entered a parallel street, knowing that the two would meet at the next intersection. Malchus held his breath and ran. He kept his feet light as possible for the night was silent and still. He also knew that the man had stopped a couple of times to take a drink, and that would slow him down even more.

Breathlessly he reached the corner at the far end of the street. He stopped and gulped in large amounts of air, then deliberately calmed his heart rate by taking slow, even breaths. He peeked around the corner. He was right. The man was only half way up the lane. In fact, he had stopped as Malchus looked, and was swallowing another gulp of wine.

Iscariot looked behind him. The street was empty. His head felt a bit woozy. He took another swig, wiping his mouth with his sleeve, then walked to the end of the lane. Just as he came to the corner, he turned one last time to see if anyone was following. No one, or was there? As he turned back around, a man crashed into him, knocking him back against the wall. Iscariot's head banged against the stone and his hand dropped the jug of black wine. The jug made a loud crash, echoing between the buildings. Shards of pottery exploded across the paving stones. A dog barked at the sound. The wine splattered against the buildings while making dark stains on their clothing. The hin of Egyptian wine also dropped. But it was in a skin, and it plopped on the ground with no more than a soft gurgle of noise. Iscariot was dazed.

"I'm so sorry," Malchus said. "I should have looked where I was going. Are you okay?" Iscariot's face was flushed from the wine, but his anger made him boil. The black wine was gone.

"My apologies for this, sir." Malchus bent down, picked up the skin of wine and handed it to Iscariot. "Please let me pay you for your loss." Malchus pulled out his coin pouch quickly.

The man was still flustered and shook his robe to rid it of excess wine. When he heard the coins rattle he looked up.

"Would thirteen drachmas cover your loss? It probably was expensive wine. Here, let me give you fourteen for the trouble I've put you through." Iscariot looked surprised. The anger quickly faded and he reached out his hand to accept the payment for the damaged goods.

Malchus counted out the coins then slipped another coin in his hand. "Does that cover your losses, sir?"

"It was an accident," Iscariot mumbled. "I should have paid more attention. But thank you for your generosity. I just didn't anticipate running into someone this time of night."

"Nor I," Malchus lied. He gave a slight nod and said, "My name is Malchus."

Iscariot stared at him for a brief moment, but his head was reeling and his vision blurry.

"Uh, my name is Iscariot." He seemed wary.

"It's my pleasure, sir, to meet you. You must be a local. You seem to know your way around."

"Yes, but I must be on my way. Thank you . . . um, Malchus. Good night."

"Good night, Iscariot. I hope we'll meet up again."

"Perhaps." Iscariot turned the corner and was gone.

Malchus stood still a moment, wearing a cunning smile. He shook the remaining coins in his pouch and grinned. *Money. He loves the sound of money. I'll find out his plans.* Iscariot's face was now stamped in Malchus' mind.

# Chapter Eleven

# YERUSHALAYIM, LOWER QUARTER, ANNA'S HOUSE, FOUR MONTHS LATER, 30 A.D.

Anna lay tense in the night. The moon's face was frosted with a cold autumn lace. Silently it peered at her through the window, casting only the palest of light in the room. Sweat beaded on her forehead. She felt powerless, as if the earth were moving beneath her. She could not stop the season for birth. Her body was demanding attention, but she was scared and not prepared.

*Foolish girl. Why didn't I make plans for this? Why didn't I think this through?* She berated herself, nervously pressing her fist into the straw bedding. She was alone. She had no midwife to help her, no husband beside her, no mother to console her. She had not expected the baby to come so soon. Panic rose up like a lump in her throat.

Her self-condemnation had such a familiar ring to it. It was Papa's voice, Papa's words. "Foolish girl." That's what he called her. The harder she tried to please him, the more he demanded. She shook the memories from her head. Tears erupted.

Self-incrimination would not help her tonight. It would only intensify her pain and complicate what she had to do, deliver this baby. Instead, she called out, "God, be my helper tonight. Show me what to do."

*If I have another contraction, I'll need to get some help.* She must rely on God and the natural instincts of her body to bring life into this world. This baby had an agenda of its own.

An hour later another spasm gripped her stomach and squeezed. It hit so fast it took her breath, moving like a coiled python tightening around her swollen abdomen. It clenched so rigidly that she felt she might pass out. Growing tighter as it rolled down toward her groin, it finally snapped its tail against her arched back then grudgingly released its grip. Anna screamed. She began to pant and her heart beat wildly.

"God help me," she gasped as she struggled to sit up. It was hard for her to breathe. "How long will this take?" Her clothes were soaked with perspiration. Her jaws ached from clenching her teeth. Anna climbed out of bed and began to pace the room.

"Lord, what do I do?" Her mind scurried to few possibilities for help.

For a month now, Anna had prepared for everything else. Like a mother bird preparing her nest, she instinctively scrubbed the house from top to bottom. She'd gathered blankets for the winter and found some discarded furniture that would provide a homemade cradle for the infant. But she hadn't planned on the baby coming early. She had to find help . . . now. This baby was going to be born tonight. Uncertainty mingled with excitement and a new fear swept over her. She prayed.

"Lord, be my helper. Make my mind clear so that I can do the right thing. Most of all, Lord, keep the baby safe. Thank you." When she finished she knew what she had to do.

Anna shivered as she threw a cloak over her shoulders and slipped out the door into the night. The cobbled stones under her bare feet were cold and damp. She stared down the lane and quivered. No lights shined in the windows of houses nearby.

The world was asleep. Anna timidly approached the door of her neighbor. The house was dark. She hesitated, then a sense of urgency compelled her.

Anna knocked on the old woman's door. Nothing. She knocked harder. The noise echoed down the lane as if it were bouncing along the tops of the stones. Anna felt panic rise in her chest. Finally, the woman's croaking voice shouted back,

"Go away! Leave me alone! It's the middle of the night for goodness sake!"

"It's Anna from next door. Please. I need your help. I'm in labor. My baby's coming and I need someone to help me."

"I don't care. It's not my concern."

Anna had no other choice. She kept banging with her fist. "Please. I beg you, please. I need help to deliver my baby."

Anna was desperate. She looked around for any other options. Her breath exploded in puffs and she felt the pull of another contraction coming. Her damp clothes clung to her body, chilling her to the bone.

Anna heard several bangs and clunks behind the door. A minute later she saw a flicker through the cracks in the door. The woman opened it only a wedge. Her gray hair hung in two long braids and she was obviously irritated.

"Please help me deliver my baby. It's time. The baby won't wait any longer."

"Go to your mother. Let her help you." She started to shut the door. Anna put her hand against it.

"I have no mother. I have no one. Please. My water has broken. It can't wait. Please, will you help me?"

Somewhere in the woman's memory, a slim maternal emotion crept over her. She consented, but curiosity outweighed her sense of compassion. She had always wanted to see inside the harlot's house.

"Go back and get yourself ready. I'll be over. Do you have a fire going?"

"Yes . . . a few live embers."

"Get a pot and put some water on, then go lie down. I'll be over shortly."

"Thank you so much." Relief washed over Anna. She smiled weakly and walked back across the lane. As she put her hand on the door latch, another contraction hit causing her to slip. She fell on one knee. She groaned out in pain. The python's cinch was tighter than ever. It was time.

When the old woman arrived, she'd tied her hair back and put a cloak on over her nightgown. Upon entering the small dwelling, she peered without shame into corners, touching the fabric of Anna's life with a voyeuristic curiosity.

Her eyes, dulled by cataracts, surveyed the bed and seemed surprised at its simplistic form. She had expected the room to be dripping with exotic pillows and coverings from the east, with the smells of perfumes and incense wafting in the air. The room was nearly barren. Anna's cry jarred her thoughts to urgency.

"Ohhh! The pain; its unbearable!" she screamed. "I don't think the baby will wait any longer."

The old woman rolled up her sleeves and began to scrub her hands in preparation. After inspecting Anna, she announced, "Breathe deep, dearie. It's not time to push yet. This child can't come until we're satisfied it's the right time." Although old, the woman's instincts of midwifery were as natural as breathing. She took charge and coached Anna along the way. Anna knew God had sent this woman to help her birth this child.

The next hour passed like an eternal night. It was filled with agonizing pain and uncertainty. At times Anna felt as if she might pass out. But she reminded herself that God was overseer of both life and death. Fear gradually gave way to hope and promise. At a certain mysterious point in labor, the woman began to shout.

"Okay, dearie. PUSH!" She motioned. "Give it all ya got."

Urge gave way to instinct and the girl pushed with every ounce of strength she could muster. Tears squeezed from the corners of her eyes. Blood vessels burst. She went dizzy with exertion. Her screams were so loud that dogs began to bark down the lane. Blood spilled on the bedding. Anna's legs were raised as she gripped them.

"Don't stop, dearie. Come on, I see the crown. Come on, dearie."

In an instant when Anna's strength were at its limit . . . it happened. Anna pushed a life from one world into another. Suddenly, a tiny voice was heard and Anna wept.

"*Mazel tov!* Congratulations!"

"*Mazel tov!*" Anna cried and laughed all while gasping for breath.

Emerging into a new world of dark shadows, strange sounds and unfamiliar smells, a tiny new life cried her way into Yerushalayim.

The woman's fingers worked quickly to clear the infant's airways until a good strong cry pealed out. She immediately cut the umbilical cord and tied it off.

"This little princess has strong lungs, she does. Oh, what a beauty. Already with a crown of carroty locks." Anna lifted her head to look down between her legs to see her baby. She could only see a glimpse of the tiny peak of ginger hair. The woman washed the baby and wrapped her in a small blanket Anna had prepared. Any pain that Anna felt was completely overshadowed by the joy of this tiny new life now wrapped in her arms.

Miniature fingers of pink searched the air for something to grasp. Arms and legs kicked and stretched to discover a larger world of air and space. The baby's round eyes stared at her new surroundings, curious about the strange images and sounds that were different from the dark watery world of the womb. The infant looked into the eyes of her mother with a gaze that bonded with Anna's heart forever. The inexperienced mother blinked back tears to see clearly. The Lord had entrusted this tiny life into her hands for safekeeping. Anna felt so undeserving.

"I shall name you Charis, my tiny miracle. The love of God has rescued me from sin because of his great love and mercy. You are a gift of love in spite of my past sin." No heavier than a bag of sweet cane, the baby gazed adoringly into her mother's eyes.

The old woman half listened and a puzzled expression furrowed her brow.

Anna was so grateful. She smiled as the woman fussed over her. "I know you've been aware of all the comings and goings at this house. My life as a prostitute has brought dishonor in this community. For that I'm deeply ashamed. I've brought shame to this community, to myself and to God. But I have met *Yeshua HaMashiach* and he has forgiven my sin and now . . ." She was overwhelmed with emotion. "And now, God has allowed me to have this beautiful daughter. Thank you for helping to bring my baby into the world. I pray that Yeshua would bless you for your kindness."

"Kindness? I'm just a nobody. I'm just doing what I have to!" The woman looked momentarily puzzled. "Yeshua? Never heard of him." She wiped the baby's fingers. "And how can anybody forgive sins except God? And who can be certain that *he* does?" The woman continued cleaning. "Having your first baby brings a bit of emotion with it. That's all your emotion talking. I've had five children and outlived all but one. I'm nearly useless now."

"Not tonight. God used you to help me bring Charis into the world. What could be more valuable?"

The woman gave a low *"humph"* and went back to finish the cleanup. She would soon be finished here and wanted to get back home to her own bed. She was puzzled by Anna's comments.

*"Humph,"* she repeated. "So, who's the father?" Her meddlesome question stabbed Anna's heart with a fresh new emotion.

"I don't know," she spoke very softly, "but God does." Anna held the baby to her breast, guiding Charis to find nourishment from her. With pure innocence, the baby stared back through a pool of wonder. Anna felt she could gaze at her new daughter for a lifetime.

The woman finished tidying up and headed for the door. She turned back around and said, "Make sure you find the man. Make sure he pays dear for his moment of pleasure. Otherwise he's just a rotten person."

Anna refused to focus on her hurtful words. Instead, she said, "Tonight, the Lord blessed me through you. Thank you for coming to my rescue." The woman made no remarks. She shrugged and stared at Anna and the baby for a long moment.

"It was nothing. Get some rest. Night."

"Thank you *Bubeleh, Alaichem Shalom*. Thank you, dear friend. To you be peace."

The woman stopped still in the doorway at Anna's words of endearment. She had not been treated so kindly in years. Refusing to show tenderness, she brushed a tear from her cheek before it rolled into sight and then she was gone.

In the dim candlelight hour between birth and dawn, Anna nursed her daughter and sang a blessing over Charis. The melody was sweet.

"My dear daughter, *'Yahweh bless you and keep you;*

*Yahweh make His face shine on you and be gracious unto you;*

*Yahweh turn his face toward you and give you peace.*

*So they will put my name on the Israelites, and I will bless them'"*[21]

Charis eventually fell asleep on Anna's breast. The baby's heartbeat was strong and steady against her own. The young mother contemplated the mysteries of a gracious God who allowed an innocent life to be born in spite of her life of sin.

---

[21] Nu. 6:24-27

Together they slept until the sun cast its first rays of gold across the room.

## Alexander's Villa, Puteoli, Italy

Lucia was dead and buried. Alexander's loss had numbed him. He immersed himself in the affairs of Rome. The commander dulled his sorrows by long hours of discipline and work. With almost ruthless desperation, he forced his soldiers into the rigid structure of his own lifestyle. He weeded out the weak and rewarded the strong. His house was empty and his heart cold.

Lucia's sarcophagus was exquisitely detailed in red granite that gleamed in the Mediterranean sun. Alexander's sketches had been carried out to perfection. Each day when he returned from work, Alexander rode past his villa to a grove of Cyprus trees. There, standing majestically among the evergreen branches, was Lucia's tomb. He would stare into the stone face and try to remember her soft skin, her liquid eyes and glistening hair. But now her stone smile seemed to him unyielding and insincere. The inscription on the monument stated simply, "My dear Lucia, now in perpetual sleep." The question he struggled with was, "Is this all there is?"

The artisans of Rome focused on an earthly permanence with little thought of Heaven. The gods of Rome were there to provide men and women with the sensual pleasures of this world. In brief moments when Alexander allowed time to stand still, he pondered one of the Greek philosophers, was it Pliny or Socrates, he wasn't sure, who stated that life consisted of the now and no more. "I was not, and I became; I was, and am no more."[22]

---

[22] "The British Friend," William and Robert Smeal, vol. 42, page 228

*Does that mean that Lucia is no more? Has she gone into a non-existent state? Was her life of suffering and pain for nothing?* These thoughts always took him into a downward spiral of emptiness, and then he would drink himself into a stupor. He wondered about Anna. It had been eight months since he last saw her.

Chapter Twelve

# YERUSHALAYIM, LOWER QUARTER, MONTH OF SHEVAT, 30 A.D.

The days were bitterly cold, the desert nights colder still. Anna's breath lingered in front of her face like a mist. She wrapped her ankles and feet in rags to keep them from frostbite. She bound her hands with cloth strips leaving only the tips of her fingers exposed. Charis was bundled in layers to keep warm. Anna never left her out of sight. She gave her daughter as much nourishment as possible. She'd been a wonderful baby, seldom crying, and now tiny smiles lit her face.

Anna had used up all the coins that Alexander had thrown into her house on that tragic rainy morning. But Anna didn't doubt God's provisions. Those coins were a gift from God. She had no doubt. The stinging words Alexander had spit out regarding the cheapness of her God had long faded in her heart. She knew that her life and the life of Charis were firmly placed in the care of a loving God.

Each day when the winter sun rose to its highest, Anna would bundle Charis so that only her tiny face would show. Then taking her along, she would go out beyond the wall and collect wood for the fire. It was difficult having a sling with the baby in front of her while carrying a sling of wood over her back. But once the fire warmed the room, she knew it was worth it.

She had made soup of lentils for tonight. It was the end of her supply. Anna poured the last cup of dried lentils into the boiling water, sprinkling it with a touch of salt, then stirring. Over the past two months, Anna had lost much weight and it took more energy to do the things she used to do. She took a sip and savored the moment. She'd found that eating slowly helped her to feel fuller longer.

Anna had ceased to hope her own father might be compassionate. Before Charis was born, her father had disowned her for leaving prostitution. He was angry that she made only pennies and was further outraged that she had become so religious and fanatical. Now here she was, poor and alone, only streets away from her father's house. To him, she was dead. She remembered the day he'd disowned her.

"Papa, I just need a little money to buy some bread. Just a few pennies."

"You're a stupid girl for following this pretend messiah. You were making good money and now look at you. Why should I give you anything?" But his efforts at humiliation worked no longer. Anna spoke truth. She longed for her father's love, but she would never return to the life of a harlot.

"But Papa, I was selling my soul."

"So what? You've abandoned your father in his old age. Who cares about your soul? It means nothing. You had a good job and threw it all away. Look at you. You dress like a washerwoman. You're always tired. You're scrawny. No man would want you this way."

"Papa, I've given you everything you've asked and still you don't love me. You've taken everything from me, even my virginity. I can give no more. God accepts me just the way I am. He's forgiven my past and given me a reason to live."

"Then let your god take care of you."

Anna took another sip and it warmed her stomach.

She remembered her father's last words to her. "Get out of my house and don't ever come back. You or your baby. I want nothing to do with you again. I have no daughter. She's dead." Anna had then slipped out her father's door for the last time. She drew strength from God's comfort but wept for her father.

Anna sipped the last spoonful of soup and looked into the empty bowl. She still was hungry, but she had so much for which to be thankful. She and the baby were safe tonight. She had used every scrap of furniture to keep the fire burning, all but Charis' cradle. They were safe in God's care.

An unusually cold wind blew across Yerushalayim. The ground was frozen hard like iron. Families huddled in their homes around fires for warmth. They heated bricks, wrapped them in blankets and put them in their children's beds. But as darkness descended, a freezing rain fell. After midnight, Anna felt a chill rising and she began to cough. Rain had been seeping through the rafters and the earthen floor smelled of mold.

Alexander stood aboard the ship as it sailed into the port of Joppa. He still had a night's journey until he arrived at Yerushalayim. The commander had paced the deck in a circular motion, arms wrapped around his body for warmth.

*Why am I trying to find Anna? I'm such a fool. Why do I care so much for a woman whom I hardly know?* He thought of the child, and guessed that by now Anna had given birth or, something worse, it might have been stillborn.

*Our lives are of two different worlds. There can never be anything between us.*

He had sent a message to her but had never received a reply. He wondered if he was only fooling himself that she ever cared for him. Perhaps all this emotion was some cruel joke of her god. If indeed he was a god!

Tomorrow morning, he would be in Yerushalayim and resolve this cauldron of emotions once and for all. Maybe seeing her face-to-face one last time would quell his hungering love for her. Maybe seeing her with her child would satisfy his desire to know she was safe and moving forward with her life. Maybe seeing her would help him realize he never really loved her at all . . . that it was just passion and lust.

He paced the deck as darkness shrouded the harbor. Four torches were burning as the ship navigated into the narrow port. Rain had begun to fall making any travel treacherous. A horse would be saddled and ready when he got on shore.

The lentil soup had been finished three days ago. Her cupboards were bare and Anna could not find work no matter how hard she tried. The icy winds howled through Yerushalayim. Anna's hunger pains had been strong for the past three days, but by the fourth they began to subside. She felt somewhat better and decided she was fine just drinking water. Her main concern was for Charis. If the baby could not be nourished from her mother's milk, she would become weak and die.

*Father,* she sought for words from memory. *"Lord, you are my God; I will exalt you and praise your name, for in perfect faithfulness you have done marvelous things, things planned long ago . . . You have been a refuge for the poor, a refuge for the needy in his distress, a shelter from the storm, and a shade from the heat."*[23]

Anna opened her eyes. The baby was sleeping. She had grown, and at two months had already developed a tiny personality of her very own, a small giggle, a gentle smile. That was

---

[23] Is. 25:1-4a

Charis, God's plan. Her eyes were already a deepening emerald green and her curly red hair framed her face. Anna had no doubt of who her father was.

*God, I pray for Charis. You have not brought her into this world to die because of hunger. You are our shelter, our place of refuge. Father, in the name of Yeshua, I pray that you would provide for Charis. Amen.*

Outside, a freezing rain began to fall. It clattered like glass on the roof.

The stallion was as black as midnight. The whites of his eyes flashed as Alexander mounted, pulled the reins taut and spurred him onward into Judea. His muscles flexed with unrestrained power to run like the wind. Yerushalayim was their destination. By daybreak Alexander hoped he would see the horizon of the city of peace.

The night was unsettling. The bitter weather seemed to bring with it a sense of urgency. Alexander pushed the mount harder. Further inland, the ground felt hard and frozen. The horse's gallop grew louder as if it were racing across a sea of glass.

The storm deepened. Rain made the stallion's coat glisten. Alexander pushed the horse onward. Like training his men, he gave no room for weakness. Something else was pushing the soldier. What it was, he knew not. But in his heart, there was a sense of urgency and danger. He wanted to pray for help but dismissed the idea as hypocritical.

The sound of hoof-beats fell into rhythm with his pounding heart.

Charis began to whimper. The embers had finally died out while Anna had dozed. But there was nothing left to burn. She'd used Charis' makeshift cradle as fuel. Sitting on the damp earthen floor, Anna nursed Charis and gently rocked her. Anna's cough had worsened and pain tore through her lungs. In her heart she was praying.

*Lord, there is nothing left. My baby needs warmth and food. What should I do? Where do I go?* Rain fell like sheets of ice, its sound soothing yet fearsome. There were new leaks in the roof, and the floor was muddy with the bitter smell of mildew stinging her nose. *God, show me the way.* Tears whelmed up as she feared for her baby.

Anna listened to the silence. Doing nothing meant certain death. It was no longer days that concerned her, it was hours and minutes. Their need was urgent. Perhaps someone would take them in, if only for a few days. There must be at least one compassionate family in Yerushalayim. But she risked being stranded in the storm if she left the house. She stood, cradling Charis and pacing, struggling with uncertainty. She peered out the window and noticed that several homes had flickering lights in the windows. It was better to plead for help than wait for death. She would knock on every door she passed until someone took pity on them.

Once decided, Anna hurried. Gathering layers of material, Anna stood and bound her baby with the cloth. She then ripped off strips from the hem of her own tunic. The cold air rushed around her legs. Twisting the strips together, she wrapped them around Charis and tied them as tightly as possible without harming her. Her hands shook with weakness. Charis looked trustingly at her mother and gave a tiny smile.

Anna tore off another corner of her tunic. She would use it to cover the child's face from the storm. She kissed her forehead then covered it gently with the material.

"We're going to look for food and shelter, my child. God will provide." With the infant gathered tightly in her arms,

Anna opened the door of her house and stepped out into the storm. Instantly the wind whipped the door from her hands, flinging it back against the wall. It took her breath away. With her head down and the child's face covered, she pushed against the storm and moved toward the lighted windows. Rain felt like needles falling down upon her.

Anna hammered on every door she passed. One man bellowed for her to go away. A woman said she already had too many mouths to feed. As she moved up the street, she felt her strength weaken and her cry growing faint. She pleaded for someone to open a door, but her voice was frail and lost in the storm. She was determined to find food and shelter. She cried out along the streets. Poverty had tried to crush her spirit, but she refused to let it kill her daughter. She trudged up another street.

For a moment she considered turning around, but that would only be their grave. Her only hope was finding someone who would take them in. She prayed out, "Lord, you are the God who sees me. You rescued Hagar and her child in the desert; I know you can rescue us in this storm." Each door she knocked on echoed silence, while the storm howled back. Anna's fingers were numb and she feared she might drop the baby. She pushed on and moved toward the upper end of Yerushalayim. Would she find compassion there?

"Lord, you do not fail. Great is your faithfulness. Save my child." Charis whimpered slightly then quieted again. The mother pushed against the wall of wind and rain. After a while the baby's silence alarmed her. Anna lifted the blanket to make sure Charis was still breathing. Her eyes were closed, her face very red, but she was breathing. "Thank you, Father God."

Chapter Thirteen

# Road from Joppa to Yerushalayim, Month of Shevat, 30 A.D.

Alexander pushed the steed harder. Steam puffed from its nostrils as it traveled along the road. His ears lay back and muscles rippled as it chased an invisible ghost through the night.

*God, if there is one and you're listening, help me make it to Yerushalayim on time. Something is wrong.* He chided himself for his wavering thoughts. How odd to pray when one doesn't believe. *What is... is! Words cannot change what is. Prayers are only words of longing. They do nothing. They change nothing.* He remembered Lucia. But he was desperate and could not lose another woman in his life.

Anna pressed hard against the storm. Up ahead, she could see the market square. The stones were slick; twice she fell but had cradled the baby securely. She must have cut her knees for she felt blood oozing. She reached the square. The wide-open courtyard seemed colder than the lanes she had been traversing. There was no place to hide from the storm. Anna was uncertain where to turn next. Yerushalayim was without pity.

Anna moved to a wall along the south side of the square. Three stone steps led to a door. She banged with force but the rags that bound her cold and bleeding hands muffled her knocks against the wood. She called for help but her voice was nearly gone. She could only whisper.

"Lord, save Charis. Don't let her die."

Too weak to go any further, she crouched in the corner of the steps. It was the most protected area in the square. She noticed blood was seeping through the rags she'd wrapped around her feet, but felt no pain. Charis was safe in her arms and she was alive. Anna thanked the God of Heaven. As she cradled her baby and closed her eyes she whispered a text from the prophets. *"On this mountain he will destroy the shroud that enfolds all peoples, the sheet that covers all nations; he will swallow up death forever. The Sovereign Lord will wipe away the tears from all faces; he will remove his people's disgrace from all the earth. Yahweh has spoken."*[24]

She needed to sleep.

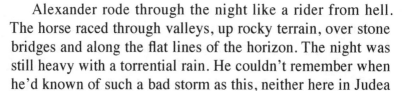

Alexander rode through the night like a rider from hell. The horse raced through valleys, up rocky terrain, over stone bridges and along the flat lines of the horizon. The night was still heavy with a torrential rain. He couldn't remember when he'd known of such a bad storm as this, neither here in Judea nor in Yerushalayim.

Alexander could feel the horse's exhaustion, and yet he drove him harder. "You can't stop now. Keep going." The soldier strained his eyes toward the horizon. Something dark

---

[24] Isa. 25:7-8

and solid lay across the landscape. The slant of the rain was blinding, but through it Alexander saw something. He pushed the horse harder almost into a flight of terror.

"Yerushalayim . . . keep moving . . . keep moving." The stallion's eyes were round and wide, the whites flashing wild. Ahead Alexander saw the walls of Yerushalayim rise up before him. He bellowed at the horse. It seemed to sense the nearness of the city and the urgency of the flight. Alexander's heart raced as he closed the gap.

"The gates. The city gate!" Alexander yelled. He pulled the reins slightly right, heading toward the wide arch of the northern gate. There was a glimmer of light at the entrance. As he drew nearer, the outline became a distinct group of old men bundled in rags, huddled around a blazing fire. They were beggars, their clothing drenched with rain. One man looked up and saw the rider.

"Messiah?" The old man questioned. Alexander pulled the reins back and slowed the horse to a canter.

"Move back old man. No Messiah tonight. Just a storm." Alexander leaned in close to the horse's ear. "You've done well. Good job." They trotted through the city gates, leaving the old man staring as he moved off into the shadows of the city.

An inner calm had settled over Anna. Somehow in this bleak empty place, God was going to take care of them. She knew it and that assurance calmed her spirit. She trusted God with her child. Charis would be saved. She lifted the covering and studied Charis' tiny face; so perfect, so innocent. She was protected by the warmth from Anna's body.

The storm still raged around them, wind sweeping through her clothing, but Anna had a peace in God that was unshake-able. He had not failed. Charis made a suckling noise as she stirred in her sleep.

For the first time since the food ran out, Anna had an overwhelming assurance that God was sending help. She smiled and closed her eyes a moment. Why had she worried? The God who made this magnificent universe would take care of them. He knew what was best. He saw them huddled there. They weren't alone. There was no need to fear. She looked down again at her baby. Charis was safe and contented within her mother's arms.

This growing peace coursed through Anna's body like a warm calming sensation. It soothed her. Here in this storm, she felt strengthened, comforted, watched over. She knew God would provide.

Anna glanced across the open square. The driving rain formed into a swirling mist creating whorls of wind and ice that were strangely beautiful. Mesmerized by this beauty, Anna began to see images of her past. Thousands of memories flickered before her until they slowed to the face of her beautiful Charis . . . and then her beloved Alex . . . and finally the face that changed her life, Yeshua. She knew salvation was near. God was sending someone to rescue both of them. From where she huddled, she felt sheltered from the storm. Unexpected warmth streamed through her limbs and radiated throughout her body. She was no longer numb with cold. She could even feel the baby's body relax as she snuggled closer into her arms.

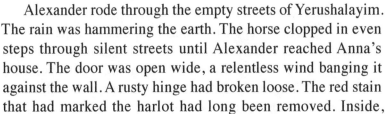

Alexander rode through the empty streets of Yerushalayim. The rain was hammering the earth. The horse clopped in even steps through silent streets until Alexander reached Anna's house. The door was open wide, a relentless wind banging it against the wall. A rusty hinge had broken loose. The red stain that had marked the harlot had long been removed. Inside, rain had turned the hardened ground into mud. Alexander dismounted and rushed through the house like a madman.

Suddenly a flashback hit him of the night he found Lucia dead. "NO! Not tonight! Anna can't die tonight!" The place was barren except for a few scraps of parchment. He'd touched the door latch, a shard of pottery, a piece of twine. These were all that remained of Anna's world but she was gone.

It was as if Anna had never lived here. There was not a stick of furniture, not a drop of food. The black charred remains of the fire was cold. He rushed out and called her name. He banged on the neighbor's door. When no one answered, he banged again with his fist. Finally, an old woman opened the door.

"What do you want? I've done nothing against Rome. I'm just an old woman and I've paid my taxes. Please leave me alone."

"I don't want your money. I need to find Anna now. Do you know where she is?" He towered over the old woman. "Tell me! Where is she? Did she have a baby? Are they alive?"

When the old woman realized she was not going to be beaten or clubbed, she spoke quickly. "Ah, you're the father. You've finally come, but it's probably too late. I haven't seen much of her lately. Earlier today, I heard her door banging in the storm, so she's gone, no doubt, and taken her baby with her."

The soldier turned and quickly mounted again. "Thank you, woman. I'll find her."

The woman began to close her door but stopped. She called out. "You're the baby's father. With your ginger hair and green eyes, she's yours without doubt. You abandoned her, you know. Left her to raise that tiny thing on her own. It's your fault. Typical man. Had your fling and abandoned her."

As Alexander began to head up the street, the woman shouted out, "She named the baby Charis, something to do with a gift from God, although I can't figure how'd you be a part of it." With that, she ducked inside and locked the door. The woman's words stung but were true.

Shaken by this news, Alexander was all the more determined to find Anna . . . and their baby Charis. The commander traced the streets of Yerushalayim against the harassing storm. The rain had turned to sleet. Glass-like shards struck everything in sight, spiking the earth like daggers. Driving wind whistled along narrow alleyways and through deserted streets spewing debris everywhere. The lonely hoof-beats clattered against stone, echoed against walls, drummed against time.

Alexander shouted Anna's name into the wind. He pounded on doors but no one had seen her: they shut their doors to the intrusion. He feared he was too late. Was she dead or alive? Did she have her baby with her? He tried to think back on what made him come to Yerushalayim. It was an impulsive decision. Was it his emptiness or more than that? A Roman officer wasn't given to soft whispery voices calling out to him. He certainly hadn't heard Zeus boom out a command. But somewhere in him, he felt he needed to be here *now*, to find Anna and her child.

The horse cantered into the open square. It was barren and sterile. There was no place of refuge here. The soldier surveyed the smooth white walls of stone. Behind them were the secluded homes of wealthy merchants and politicians who lived lavish lifestyles in private, their front doors protecting them from Yerushalayim's poor. He guided his horse along the perimeter of the square. Steps jutted out at equal distances along the wall. Each step led up to a huge wooden door that recessed into a deep limestone wall.

The freezing rain fell like spears of glass, striking Alexander's face, forcing the soldier to shield himself with his arm. He shivered for the first time. Alexander shouted Anna's name across the courtyard. He thought he heard a voice.

*Anna watched the spiraling vortex of wind and rain move in her direction. She reached out with her free hand. Hope grew. Ground mist swirled upward and billowed out as a figure of a man emerged from it and walked toward her. Anna blinked, hoping her eyes weren't betraying her. "You've come," she whispered. Anna wanted to run to him but she was too weak. The storm and lack of nourishment had taken its toll on her.*

*"You've come to save me and my baby."*

*Anna wept with gratitude. Charis remained secure and peaceful. She wiped her tears to clear her vision. She wanted to shout for joy but she was too frail to run to him . . . her body could not move. In his last few steps, the mist parted and Anna saw his face as clear as the noon day sun.*

*"I knew you'd come." Her voice was barely audible. "I've been waiting, expecting you. Here, see my baby." Anna pulled back the covering over Charis' face. "Isn't she the most beautiful daughter ever? She's perfect. I've named her Charis. She's my gift of love."*

*Anna wanted to stand but she was too weak. She looked helplessly up at him. "I don't seem to have much strength left. But my baby is strong and healthy."*

*He smiled. "I've come for you, Anna." His powerful arms reached down and lifted her up into his embrace. He caressed her brow and kissed her forehead. "I knew I'd find you here, Anna. You and your baby are safe now. I'm taking you away from all this. When she's older, I'll tell her about this night and your sacrificial love for her. And you, Anna, you have an important task ahead of you."*

*Tears blurred Anna's vision. "You came to rescue me. You really do love me."*

*"Yes, Anna. That's why I came back for you tonight." He held her gently. "I'm taking you home." His embrace was what she'd always longed for from her father but never got; from a loving husband she'd never had; a loyal friend she'd never found. Anna's deepest yearnings were immediately satisfied.*

In an instant, Anna was gone.

Tucked away in the cleft of a stone wall, a baby lay hidden from the storm. Charis slept peacefully in Anna's lifeless arms.

The cry was tiny against the harsh wind, yet so much alive. Alexander followed the sound to a set of steps where a crevice offered some protection from the storm. Anna lay huddled with a child wrapped tightly in her arms, looking so serene in the midst of this storm. Alex marveled. The baby was bright and seemed more hungry than hurting. Her eyes were the greenest Alex had ever seen. Her head was covered with red curls and his heart pounded with a thrill he had not expected, especially not on this terrible night. Yet there she was, a beauty to behold and wrapped in the arms of the woman he loved. Now he knew why he was led to Yerushalayim. This journey had a purpose to find his dear Anna and his beautiful daughter whom he had never met.

"Anna. It's me, Alex." He leaned in close and whispered her name. "I've come to take you home. I'm so glad I found you in time. I had a feeling I should look for you here. And your daughter . . . our daughter . . . will be safe with us now." Alex kissed Anna's cold cheek. "I'm so sorry for all the things I said in the past, Anna. Please forgive me. I've been such a fool."

Anna's face was serene and she seemed to be looking across the courtyard at something in particular. Alexander followed her gaze, yet he saw nothing but driving rain and mist that hugged the earth.

Alexander stared back at her. "Anna?" Her gaze was unblinking. "Anna. I'm here. Anna, wake up. It's me, Alex." The soldier put his face close to Anna but she had no breath. His body shuddered as fear rippled through him. He shook her shoulder. "Anna, you're freezing. Wake up. Please, Anna, wake up!"

Slowly a gut-wrenching truth stabbed his heart. "Anna, no. No! This can't be, after all the journey."

The soldier knelt, reeling back and forth as reality pressed against him; first Lucia and now Anna. He tried to hold her but her body remained rigid and lifeless. He hung his head as great sobs escaped from the weight of this loss. Pent up within him since childhood, Alexander, an officer of the Roman Guard, was overcome by grief so immense he could not contain it. The baby had quieted as she heard the sound of a human voice. Their eyes met, and she stared wonderingly.

Alexander realized that, in finding his daughter, the love he felt for Anna was like a deep ravine without a bottom. He carefully pulled her stiff arms away and lifted the baby into his. Anna's arms remained in the embrace she had held for so long, waiting for someone to come and rescue her daughter.

"My precious daughter, I've come to take you home."

Gently he carried the child, the horse following, toward the nearest inn. The inn keeper was able to locate a wet nurse who would care for the baby until Alexander returned. Torn between leaving a daughter he'd just found and returning to care for a woman he just lost, he rushed out into the storm to tend to Anna's body. He would bury her in the morning. As he lifted her frail body into his arms he choked back a sob and kissed her frozen cheek. The warmth of his breath on her cheek turned a single remaining tear into liquid. It ran down her face and was gone. Her suffering was over. He carried her into a stable and laid her in the soft hay. Even in death, Anna's arms refused to unburden her embrace. All she had lived for was conformed to embrace the one she loved.

Alexander buried his face in Anna's lifeless body and sobbed. "Anna. I loved you so much. But your God has taken you from me. I will love our child. I know this beautiful child is . . . yours and . . . mine. You have given me what no other could give. I will cherish this baby and raise her to please the gods. I will tell her of your great sacrifice to save her life."

The morning sky was mottled gray like pigeon feathers, the air iron cold. Before dawn, Alexander had visited Hermes' yard and roused him out of a deep sleep. Together, the two men walked between the bone boxes inspecting them for size and depth. A rough-hewn box lay at Alexander's feet that seemed less than adequate for Anna, but it would have to do. The two hoisted the box onto the back of a wagon. Few words were spoken as Alexander went through the functions of doing what needed to be done. Hermes kept spices and herbs on hand for those needing immediate burial. The horse and cart followed the rutted trail back into the city where Anna was laid gently into the tomb by the man with a broken heart and tortured soul.

"Your god didn't save you, Anna." His words were spoken from deep sadness. "You followed a god who was not a god at all."

The soldier brushed her raven hair away from her face. She looked serene, yet Alexander knew that she was no longer there. He surrounded her fragile body with fresh herbs and packets of spices. The white tunic that had been soiled in the mud as she pushed through the night's storm fell silent around her. The soldier unwrapped Anna's hands and feet and cleansed the dried blood from them. She had suffered to protect their daughter.

Hermes waited patiently beside the tomb, his eyes watching closely for the sign to seal the bone box. He would seal the box, then deliver it to rest among other sarcophagi on the Mount of Olives.

Alexander lingered. Sobs welled up in his chest and again he stuffed them back in. He looked at Hermes a moment.

"Just give me one more minute, Hermes. I need one moment alone with her."

Hermes nodded and slipped around a corner. Alexander knelt beside the bone box.

"Anna, I've lost you but gained a daughter. I'll raise her right and care for all her needs. I'll love her with enough love for both of us." He choked. "Anna, a light went out in my life when Lucia died. Now you are gone. How shall I deal with such pain? Every time I look into our daughter's eyes, I'll see you."

He reached into a pouch secured to his leather belt and pulled out the gold ring. The emperor's face and seal were prominent. He lifted her hand and held it in his. Her fingers looked as delicate as porcelain. He slipped the ring on her finger, and then gently folded her hands.

"Anna, this is my token of love. If there is a Heaven, you will find it. Sleep well, my love."

The big soldier sobbed again. Anna was gone. He wept for her. He wept for Lucia. He wept for the loss his daughter would have of never knowing her mother. He wept for an emptiness even a child couldn't fill. Then he wept for his empty soul.

When his emotions were utterly spent, the soldier felt weak. Never before in his life had he allowed emotion to overtake him like this. Finally, the soldier called Hermes back, and together they lifted the stone lid and placed it atop the bone box. Anna's face remained serene. Her hands were clasped together and the gold ring gleamed one last time before all went dark within the tomb. Anna's body lay silent in darkness beneath a slab of cold stone.

Chapter Fourteen

# MEDITERRANEAN SEA, 30 A.D.

Malchus paced the deck of the Alexandrian merchant ship, the *Aphrodite*, as it neared the port of Crete. The ship was weather-beaten. Patches of gray timber had begun to expose its true self in spite of repeated coatings of colored paint. *Aphrodite* had sailed through squalls, a northeaster and beneath a relentless blistering sun. Blotches of flesh-colored paint had peeled from her right arm as it stretched out with her index finger pointing the way from port to port. Her lusty face and bosom led the way around the island and headed toward land. The spray of brine splashed in rhythm against her cheeks while she pointed homeward unblinking.

The lonely passenger circled the main mast, walked to the bow, then back to the stern. The hull of the ship creaked and groaned as it swayed to the placid motion of the sea. The world was quiet on this brilliant sunny day, with only sounds of gentle splashes and a handful of screeching sea-gulls.

The weather had been calm, thus making the journey slower than expected. The dirty white sails looked listless. Such weather made Malchus either restless or lethargic. Today, he was restless. He knew why. He was in-between his two worlds. One world was as a servant to ecclesiastical Judaism of which he had no faith, the other a mover and shaker in the Roman Empire.

He had been sleuthing in the political marketplaces of Rome and it pressed on his soul. Sometimes he wondered if he was in league with darkness. But since he didn't believe in right or wrong, he chose power over weakness. If it would profit him, he knew he would do it. Being the offspring of a Roman soldier and godless Jewess, he had his pick of gods and goddesses to call upon. As a general rule, he called upon his own sense of desires and longings to make choices. Without spiritual moorings, Malchus simply went with the flow. Currently he was the servant of the High Priest Caiaphas in Judea. It was merely a job. Maybe next year he might be in Rome's court sipping wine and indulging in the orgies and festivals beside the imperial family.

Malchus eyed the sea-gulls and concluded that he was very much like them. He was the scavenger type, picking off the discarded morsels that others left behind. He had to use his limited resources well; that was his lot in life. He rubbed the stubble of beard on his chin, and suddenly felt fatigued.

Turning his back to the sea, he walked the length of the deck and disappeared down a flight of worn steps to the lower level. The lower deck reeked of sweat and fish as men worked to clean and salt their catch. The area was dark with only a couple of oil lanterns swinging from the ceilings. Black ribbons of smoke rose from the lamps, sometimes wafting to the right, sometimes to the left. He heard a sailor's raucous laughter, slurred by too much ale. A fat rodent scurried beneath his feet and hid under a sack of grain. He went to the furthest end of the ship and found a corner where he stretched out and tried to sleep. When sleep didn't come, he began scheming as to how he would uncover Iscariot's secret. Two weaknesses quickly came to his mind; money and wine. Bribing was an easy trade for Malchus.

*What scheme is Iscariot working on? And what plan does this little band of Jews have in mind? Who is this Jewish magician? Where did he come from? What is his agenda?* The gentle rocking of the ship eventually lulled him to sleep.

The Decapolis was a prosperous region of ten Greco-Roman cities, each built with the architectural elegance and splendor of Rome. The cities were a relief from the parched desert, with their elaborate aqueducts, crystalline pools and dazzling fountains that glittered in the harsh sun. Rome's paganism was absorbed into the fabric of its culture by carving gods of stone into the walls of temples, along colonnades and at ritual centers. The carved statues of Zeus, Astarte, Hercules, Demeter, Dionysus and other Grecian gods and goddesses rose up like pillars of the earth.

Pella was the birthplace of Alexander the Great and, so they believed, was the mother of conquerors and mighty warriors. Yet peace was fragile in Pella; war dominated its walls. It had been conquered by General Pompey in 63 B.C. and, ever since, was fortified by Roman garrisons on all sides. It was the strife within that claimed the city. And just like Rome, it thirsted for blood.

Pella was known for its palatial houses and luxurious public halls. But it had one feature that exceeded Rome's splendor, a theatre built in the creek-bed of the Wade Jirm. They would flood the stage for magnificent aquatic performances, and people came from throughout the Roman Empire to watch these sensational displays of art and form. [25]

---

[25] https://en.wikipedia.org/wiki/Pella,_Jordan

Democritus headed toward Pella. He heard that Yeshua had traveled into this territory months earlier. Moving deep into Syrian territory, away from where he met his Master, Democritus sensed an unsettling change. His skin prickled. It was early afternoon and the day was bright, yet something was gathering force. He tried to shake off the unease and move on. He was heading into unknown territory and was bound to feel the discomfort of change. In the distance, dark clouds were forming. A thunderstorm was moving in from the desert with erratic flashes of lightning. He was heading right into the storm.

The skies had grown dark in Pella and storm clouds gave a deep rumble as Ashen made his way down toward the creek-bed. He plodded alone and focused on a small path that led him to the river's edge. Another rumble brought fat drops of rain that sent people scampering in all directions. In the central Piazza, rain pelted the stony face of Hercules and sent rivulets down his massive torso. The goddess, Diana, was wind-whipped, and a branch had caught in her stony hair. In other parts of the city, gods lay safe from the storm, hidden in dark recesses of people's homes, lurking in their pockets, hiding in their cupboards, worshipped in their prayers. Ashen found his spot and set about building a fire. He would need its warmth tonight.

By the time Democritus had arrived in the city, its grandeur had been diminished by the intensity of the storm. Palm fronds rattled and shook; debris whirled into small cyclones. The magnificent structures were now gray and sullen. That prickly feeling chased down Democritus' back and into his gut. He hurried across the deserted Piazza in search of a small footpath that led down to the Wade Jirm. He was looking for one man. He'd been told there was one follower of Yeshua in Pella. Living here among the people of darkness, one bright-eyed man seemed undimmed by evil.

Ashen was sitting by a fire beneath an arch of the theatre. Shadows stretched into pools of darkness, and the fire appeared as a small flicker within the folds of a black night. Democritus followed the spring along the Civic Complex, keeping his eye on that single burning light. As he approached, Ashen looked up and nodded.

Ashen was in his late fifties, yet lean. His back hunched slightly and his hair showed wisps of silver. Still wet, it hung loosely and rested on his shoulders. His skin was tanned and the wrinkles around his eyes revealed a light-hearted wisdom. His eyes sparkled and caught Democritus off guard. Few middle easterners had nothing but jet black eyes, but his were blue like sapphires. Ashen had a story and Democritus had come to hear it. Democritus smiled and squatted by the fire. He took his finger and drew a curved line in the damp sand, then stared into Ashen's eyes.

In silence, the man drew a second curved line connecting the two. He whispered, "I am Ashen. Welcome in his name."

"I'm Democritus." The men were silent for a moment. "I follow him, too."

The old man put his finger to his lips. "We must be very careful. It's dangerous to speak of such things in this place. They're watching from everywhere . . . everywhere." He leaned in close. "I feel their presence tonight."

"I know. I see them assembling now." He studied the buildings surrounding them. Finally, Democritus settled down and crossed his legs. "How long have you lived in Pella?"

"Only a short time. They hunt me from place to place. When they find me they bring others and chase me out." His passion seemed undimmed by the battle. Democritus knew this man was a fellow warrior.

"Tell me what happened to you, Ashen." Democritus watched as the flames flickered between them. Raindrops sizzled as they touched the fire.

"I lived in Caesarea Philippi." He took his time. "Our Master hadn't traveled through that region before, but he didn't seem surprised at what he found," he mused. "I wasn't born with any ailment. When I was a child, my parents taught me to speak, read and write. But when I was five years old, something happened, a disease, and I found my world of sound fading. It happened slowly at first. One day I realized that I hadn't heard the singing of the birds for a long time. Their music had stopped."

Democritus didn't move. A gust of wind sent the flames upward. The coals burned more brightly. He studied the man's face.

"I asked my mother why the birds had stopped singing and together we realized that something was wrong, but no doctors could help. By the time I was six years old, I had lost all my ability to hear. I withdrew. I refused to speak because I couldn't hear my own voice. I was afraid of the silence. My mother tried to coax words out but when I spoke, they came out garbled. No one could understand me. Children mocked me as if I were an idiot. So I withdrew, living without sound. Eventually my voice dried up. I soon lost all communication with my world."

Democritus warmed his hands at the fire. The storm lashed the trees, tearing leaves from their branches and spewing them across the ground. Ashen closed his eyes for a moment. His story was well-rehearsed, as inquisitive neighbors had asked many questions. But Ashen relished reliving it. It was so profound, so life-changing. His eyes opened and he continued.

"I'm fifty-seven years old. My world of silence lasted for fifty years. No one would employ me except for farm labor. I wandered from city to city trying to get work, but people thought I was a lunatic because I couldn't hear or speak."

"I can understand." Democritus recalled his years of being a cave dweller and how the people feared him.

"I'd not heard of *him*, the Jewish prophet. But when he saw me, and looked into my eyes, he instantly knew everything about me." Ashen paused. "Somehow he read my heart."

Democritus smiled. "He does that kind of thing." The two men smiled, each reflecting upon their own encounter with the God-Man who read hearts and saw their needs. "Tell me how it happened."

Ashen leaned closer to the fire and spoke softly. "He put a finger into each of my ears. His touch was gentle but there was a strange fire that ran through them into me. It felt white hot." Ashen's eyes glistened in the fire light. "This prophet looked up to Heaven and sighed a heavy sigh."

"I don't understand. What kind of a sigh?"

"I felt like he was grieving over our human frailty. I felt he was experiencing my loss as his own, taking on my deafness as his own. Then he said, '*Ephphatha* – be opened.' It happened instantaneously."

From the night's gloom, Democritus saw shadows gathering. They crowded in the tree tops and whispered and hissed a name that grew louder. "Diablo. We know you, Diablo." Intuitively he stood and waved his hand at the darkness. He bellowed. "Be gone! Yeshua is our Master!" There was a quivering in the trees at the sound of that holy name. Reluctantly, a cloud of phantom wings flapped upward and dissipated from their presence to settle elsewhere in the city. The rain turned to a slow drizzle but the wind grew in intensity.

Ashen was startled at the outburst but understood. "I'm still blind and deaf to some things, but I sense their presence often. They've left us, haven't they?"

"Yes, for the moment." He sat back down. "Now back to your story . . . what did you hear first?"

"Yeshua's breath." He paused. "I knew I was in the presence of God Himself and I felt his breath on my face and heard it in my ears." Ashen was still amazed at the revelation. "I was so stunned I wanted to cry for joy, but my words had died and all

I could do was make a grunting sound. Something more was about to happen."

"You speak with perfect diction."

"I had forgotten how to pronounce a single syllable. It was as if my tongue had dried up in my mouth. All I could use it for was to moan and eat."

"What did Yeshua do then?" Democritus pulled his robe around him.

"He put his finger on the tip of his own tongue then placed it on mine. The taste was like honey. As he did this, words began to flow from my mouth like a song. My mind had suddenly remembered words and how to express them. The healing passed from his lips to mine, then my mind and heart were awakened again to speech. But now I knew words and concepts I'd never learned as a child. My mind gained knowledge miraculously."

Democritus remembered his own deliverance. "So the miracle was more than your hearing and speech, the miracle included knowledge deposited into your mind before you even spoke." Democritus smiled. *This was one of the reasons the Master wanted me to come to Pella. To hear Ashen's story. I am not alone.* Democritus leaned back against the wall. The contentment of knowing God's power over darkness once again overwhelmed this young warrior. He closed his eyes and quickly envisioned Yeshua's face.

Ashen's voice was almost a breath. "But there is a presence here that hates my story."

"It's the darkness of hell itself, Ashen. I, too, feel its power. But the gates of hell cannot rip away what Yeshua has given you." He lifted his face from the fire to Ashen.

"Keep telling your story. It sets people free." Democritus paused. "They can only threaten you with fear, but they cannot take your new life from you. One day I'll tell you my story." The two men locked eyes in agreement.

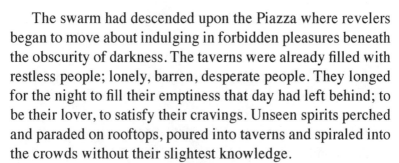

The swarm had descended upon the Piazza where revelers began to move about indulging in forbidden pleasures beneath the obscurity of darkness. The taverns were already filled with restless people; lonely, barren, desperate people. They longed for the night to fill their emptiness that day had left behind; to be their lover, to satisfy their cravings. Unseen spirits perched and paraded on rooftops, poured into taverns and spiraled into the crowds without their slightest knowledge.

*"Leave the fire and speak my name to the crowds."* Democritus looked across at his new friend but he seemed unaware of the voice.

"I believe God is speaking to me, Ashen."

"Then follow his instructions. I'm safe here. His hand is on me."

Democritus bid farewell and headed back up toward the Piazza.

Between a thin film of darkness in which to hide, the people of this great cultural city with its sophistication and grand architecture had descended into brawling wantonness. Men and women behaved without shame. Without a savior this city would destroy itself like Sodom and Gomorrah. No wonder Yeshua came. No wonder he called the warrior to "go to Decapolis."

In the distance, Democritus heard a girl screaming in terror. Her sounds of hysteria rose above the mayhem around him. Democritus followed her cries to an alley where the girl lay pinned to the ground surrounded by a gang of drunken thugs. She was only a child, and already they'd torn her clothes off her body as she kicked and clawed to free herself. Her face was bruised and bleeding. The men began to fight over who would have her first.

Democritus charged down the alleyway bellowing at the top of his voice. "Stop this evil! She's only a child!" He pushed the nearest man off the girl. Democritus was strong but he couldn't defend himself against four men at once. He'd surprised the men by his sudden attack and they momentarily scattered, but came rushing back.

"In the name of Yeshua, leave this child alone."

A second man leaped on top of the girl, pawing at her. Democritus rammed his fist into the man's face and pulled him away by his hair. "In the name of God, leave her alone." The man lashed back and Democritus rammed his fingers into the man's eyes.

A third attacker jumped Democritus from behind while another beat his fist into his stomach. Winded, he fought back using his feet to push his assailants away. From the side, he saw the girl struggling to get to her feet. "Run, run for your life," he called to her. The crowds grew, cheering and jeering for more action. Now it seemed as if the whole city had gathered to defeat the child's lone protector. "Run. Go quickly." The girl ran, naked and bleeding, stumbling into the shadows, leaving a trail of bloodied footprints on the cobblestones.

Two men pinned Democritus down while another man hammered his body with his fists. One blow caught his left eye and his senses whirled. Everything went dark for seconds. Then he was back again.

"Do you think you can defeat us, Diablo?" The words burst involuntarily from a fourth man's throat because the demonic predator had no vocal cords of its own. The sounds were guttural and violent. This man was the size of a beast and he stared down into Democritus' face without focus. He seemed to be in a trance-like state as voices hissed and screeched from his throat. The crowds backed away in fear.

"Diablo is dead. You know who I am and why I'm here. I come in the name of Yeshua."

"Shut up," the voice screamed. The beast of a man became animated and pulled a serrated dagger from his waistband. He leaned close and slid the blade across Democritus' neck until the flesh was torn.

Democritus didn't flinch. "I have no fear of death." He turned his attention to the man instead of speaking to his predator. "The God-Man Yeshua can set you free. These demons cannot stand in the face of Yeshua."

"Silence, you fool," the predator demanded. "Together we are still powerful."

"Your gods are weak, my God is strong. He has rescued me from the pit of hell and he can do that for you. What's your name?"

The man's eyes narrowed looking straight into Democritus' face. He opened his mouth to speak, but gagged instead. "I . . . I . . ." Democritus watched as if invisible hands were mangling the muscles within the windpipe, tightening the cords and squeezing off air, ". . . can't . . . breathe."

The weapon froze in his hand as the man's face blistered red. His eyes bulged, tears seeped, as they stared into an unfathomable horror.

The two men holding Democritus against the ground got nervous. "Kill him, Jarad. Kill him."

Democritus watched helplessly as life was snatched away from Jarad. Democritus cried out against the invisible enemies, but he was too late.

The man fell limp on top of Democritus. The men let go and Democritus gasped for air and rolled the body off. The blood-smeared knife fell to the ground.

"You thought you could save the man, didn't you, Diablo," the distorted voice belched out from the twisted vocal cords of the dead corpse. "You failed." In an instant the corpse jolted off the ground and suddenly dropped as the demonic entity was snatched away from earth's atmosphere and thrown into the Abyss.

The crowds were terrified and turned to Democritus. "Leave us. Look at what you've brought upon us."

The warrior said, "Turn to Yeshua, before greater judgment comes upon you."

As the crowds swelled, the unbridled violence grew. The men were now carrying stones. "Not again," Democritus moaned. They began to stone the witness. As stone after stone struck him, Democritus shouted, "Turn to Yeshua, the Messiah. He will forgive you if you repent." He stumbled down the alleyway as a barrage of stones struck him in the back.

"Get rid of your idols and demons. Far greater is the power of Israel's Messiah, Yeshua, than any demonic force you could ever call up from the pit of hell. Leave your life of sin and turn to him . . ." Then a rock struck the back of his skull and all went dark.

Democritus had lost the thread between day and night. He heard voices and felt his body being shoved and pushed, but nothing made sense. His thoughts were jumbled. Another burst of pain and he reeled into oblivion again.

"Eh, there's a meat wagon. Take a hold of his feet, we got his arms." Three men dragged the foreigner's body through the alleyway to the end. The meat monger's rubbish wagon was full of gristle, fat and bones.

"Okay? Ready? Heave." Democritus' body was flung on top of bones and fat cut from pigs and sheep. There was a crack as Democritus' arm was twisted backward, broken and caught beneath his body. His mind mercifully succumbed to darkness. The driver forced the donkey into a plodding gait.

Democritus was carried out of Pella. He was deposited with all the refuse at the riverside. Unconscious, he lay there through the night. Deep in the darkness, he would emerge from his numbness to realize that an animal's snout was pushing past his body to devour the fat and grizzle surrounding him. They licked his blood clean but left him unharmed. By morning the jackals were gone, and so was the gristle and blood. The salt from the animal's saliva had begun to cleanse Democritus' wounds, but his body was badly beaten. He had been left as refuse by the River Jabbok.

When he awoke, the sun was high. His body ached. His head throbbed. He stood and immediately fell. With his last ounce of strength he crawled into the river where he pushed through the reeds until he could cover himself in the cleansing water. He crawled to the bank and collapsed, his mind weaving in and out of consciousness.

Democritus had made some miscalculations in his battle strategy. The truth was he had none; no plan, no direction, but lots of boldness. However reckless his efforts were, the truth of Yeshua *was* proclaimed to people lost in darkness. He stood firm for Yeshua but no one was converted, no fruit was borne, no one turned from sin. He came away alone, just as he had entered. Broken and defeated, Democritus realized he was still training for battles yet to be played out. He prayed for strength to face evil if he should survive this torturous hour. He had to deal with today and, so far, God had spared him. Tomorrow had not yet been created; it was still full of promise.

## Chapter Fifteen

# RIVER JABBOK, 30 A.D.

Democritus stumbled along the banks of the River
Jabbok until it joined the Jordan, his face badly mis-
shapen and his left eye swollen shut. He lapsed in and
out of consciousness for hours at a time. Only when the evening
cooled could he recover enough to continue away from Pella.
His left arm was useless, dangling against his side with brutal
pain. His radius had splintered and protruded just above the
wrist and the wound kept hemorrhaging. With shaking hands,
he tore strips from the hem of his tunic to make a sling for
his arm.

He looked down at the dirty crimson robe Yeshua had
placed on his shoulders. He shuddered. *I'm not worthy to wear
his robe. I'm so ashamed.* Although the burning passion of a
warrior still beat in his breast, Democritus was defeated. He
could see the enemy, warn the people, but he didn't have the
experience to conquer darkness. He must find Yeshua.

Pleading with God he cried out, "Lord, I've failed you in
my very first mission. This city is full of darkness, but I couldn't
help a single person see the light of God. Forgive me, Master. I
need your help." Remembering Yeshua's compassionate face

caused him to weep. "I can't stand alone. I need you, Yeshua. I need you desperately."

He staggered. Pain tore through his body and a wave of nausea swept over him. He thought he saw the shadow of a man coming toward him. "It's you, Yeshua, you've come." He reached out but the image faded. "I need you, *HaMashiach*." Democritus wavered. Just as consciousness began to fade, he heard a voice. *"Democritus, I am with you. You were never alone. You must learn to trust me in battle. I will teach you how to fight with the power of my Spirit."*

"Thank you, Yeshua, thank you," he whispered. Democritus' legs gave way and he sank to the ground. Light faded into an eclipse of darkness, then he passed out. His body lay nearly hidden on a bed of broken reeds along the Jordan. Death was just waiting for a final gasp. But he was not alone.

---

## Yerushalayim, City Gate

Artamos sat at the city gate for almost thirty-seven years. He'd earned his place of honor among the beggars and thieves by virtue of longevity. The soldier had seen beggars come and go. Most died by the gate because of the cruel winters or starvation. Few returned to their families. Artamos' family had tried for years to help him back to sanity, but he no longer recognized them. The worn soldier could not distinguish a family member from a stranger.

Artamos had survived all these years because his mind had wandered so far from reality that living as a beggar seemed the most natural thing to do. He learned survival techniques; how to make a shelter during the winter, how to build a good fire with flint and how to keep himself company. He learned how to joke with himself and make himself laugh.

Artamos collected cast-off clothing from others. He was not concerned how he looked as long as he kept warm. His gray hair had wisps of white. His untamed beard left only his nose and blue eyes visible. His clothing had become his home, a hiding place from the cruel world. Layer upon layer of clothing insulated him from others. When necessary his body could shrink into the shell of rags and his mind retreat into a confusion of fantasy where no one could find him.

Artamos watched with monotony as the caravan of foreign traders left the city gate. He scratched at his beard as the colorful entourage passed by. Their mixture of strange languages and foreign dialects mingled with faintly familiar smells of an eastern world Artamos once knew. As a Roman commander, he had once traveled throughout the Mediterranean ports. But his mind had grown dull and his memory of foreign lands had faded. His focus was on one person coming into Yerushalayim.

Flies buzzed in circular motion as the camels jangled beneath the arch. The beasts lumbered slowly past the beggars. Artamos watched as the long spindly legs with oversized hoofs passed in front of him. Their goods sold and transactions complete, they were leaving Yerushalayim.

Artamos tried hard to remember his military campaigns for Caesar. Try as he would, his memories stopped at the point of his last assignment. The horror of it had blocked out anything good that had happened before. A shudder rolled over his hunched back and shoulders. He suddenly felt cold in the middle of the day. He trembled.

The dust kicked up by the beasts billowed in his face. His eyes watered, and he let the tears stream down his dirty face into his beard. He could not remember anything good in his life. Herod's demands had robbed him of everything. If only the Messiah would come.

"Ah, he's awake," a dark Egyptian shouted as Democritus opened his one good eye. The sky was jostling above him as he lay on a stretcher.

"Where am I?" He was frightened. "What's happening to me?"

"Ah yes, perhaps we made a good decision." The man's face appeared only inches from his face; his beady eyes glistened in anticipation of a profitable return for his efforts. "They said you weren't worth the effort, but I thought there still might be some life in you yet." His accent was as thick as gruel; a rusty turban wrapped around his head like a spool of cotton.

"Who are you?"

"Me? I am your new master, that's who I am. I am Dedelion, named after a notorious soothsayer of the 4th dynasty. You can call me Dede . . . Master Dede." His skin was oily. He grinned, revealing a mouth full of yellowed teeth.

"My Master is Yeshua."

"Not anymore. I found you nearly dead by the river. I considered leaving you there, but then thought better of it. You could bring me some profit. You're my *heka*, my lucky piece."

"You're a slave trader?" Democritus' mind reeled with the thought. *How could this happen?*

"I trade in everything I find. Listen, if I left you back there, you'd be dead by now. You owe me your life. I've got to have a fair return for my efforts." As he laughed, Democritus watched his jowls shake. He tried to lift his head, but the pain was too much.

*I'm a prisoner . . . again.* Democritus was stunned at the thought. For only a short time he'd been free. Now he was helplessly at the mercy of slave traders. Four black faces glistening with sweat were at each corner of the stretcher. His new master walked beside him for a while wearing a big grin. Democritus turned his head away and closed his eyes. *Yeshua, where are you? I need you. I cannot make it on my own.* He listened but heard nothing.

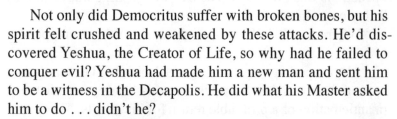

Not only did Democritus suffer with broken bones, but his spirit felt crushed and weakened by these attacks. He'd discovered Yeshua, the Creator of Life, so why had he failed to conquer evil? Yeshua had made him a new man and sent him to be a witness in the Decapolis. He did what his Master asked him to do . . . didn't he?

Democritus whispered a prayer. "Master, did I do something wrong? Why couldn't I defeat those demonic forces in Pella? Why am I here, a slave once again?" he groaned. But there was only silence in response to his prayers. There seemed no answer, no voice to guide him. He closed his eyes and finally succumbed to his captive state . . . until Yeshua's voice would speak once again. He knew Yeshua would not fail him: his only doubt was . . . had he failed Yeshua? What more should he have done?

In spite of Democritus' failures, Yeshua was offering the Good News to the gentile world. Democritus felt utterly defeated, yet seeds of salvation were sown in Pella. Yeshua would soon turn his face toward Yerushalayim to surrender his body to a hideous and torturous death. Many of his disciples would look upon his broken body and believe that he, too, had failed in his ministry. Soon, atonement would be paid providing salvation and God's holy power would descend upon his followers around the world. They would reap the harvest.

## Chapter Sixteen

# DESERT ROAD FROM SYRIA TO YERUSHALAYIM, 30 A.D.

S till overwhelmed by his new shackles, Democritus
had sensed that God had heard his prayer. He was still
bruised and broken but he surrendered his anxiety to
God and closed his eyes. No demons came near his resting
thoughts. Soon he was lulled to sleep by the swaying movement
of his bearers. His life had been spared and somehow God was
involved in this rescue. He would trust God for the outcome.

By nightfall, the caravan had stopped and fires were built.
They had found a grove of date palms and a bubbling stream
between the folds of sand. Five tents were erected and the
camels and donkeys along with a herd of goats were tethered
to stakes in the ground. Democritus' stretcher was now on the
ground and he peered through his one good eye to see what
company he was with. He was surprised that the caravan was so
big. There must have been thirty or forty traders, with perhaps
fifteen slaves. The camels were laden with everything imaginable. Democritus saw everything from brass jugs to baskets of
spices and jugs of wine, and then there were the slaves, soon to
be auctioned to the highest bidder. What great city lay ahead?

Above, the sky was a canvas of black. Only a slender crescent of moonlight had slipped through the envelop of darkness, but the canvas was covered with star clusters as far as the eye could see.

Several campfires were lit and food was being prepared. The smell of rich spices floated across the desert floor. Someone was baking barley bread. The smell was intoxicating for Democritus. He had not eaten for days.

Soon the food was passed around. A sauce made of ground dates, figs and raisins mixed with vinegar was used in which to dip the hot bread. Warm goat's milk was available, and the meal was finished with honey cakes baked with sesame.

Lying flat, Democritus stared into the night sky and considered his life. Although badly wounded, he was still alive. Therefore, God's purpose for him was not yet complete. His life was spared for a reason he had yet to discover. He would trust God to use him in whatever way he saw fit. If he should die tomorrow, he was ready.

Before dawn, the caravan had packed camp and was on its way. Although he still lay on the stretcher, Democritus' mind was clear and he felt stronger. He was satisfied with good food. He used this time to pray. He was speaking to Yeshua and sensed that he was listening. Yeshua had heard his call from the cave. He'd hear his prayers in the wilderness. Now, they communed as he was carried forward toward the unknown.

"Move along. We've no time to waste."

Somewhere behind him a whip cracked in the air. Two days had passed and Democritus was stronger. He trudged in the sand chained with several other slaves who were going to the market. He had been fed well and his wounds had been treated. The swelling in his face had gone down bringing a semblance of humanness to his features. His arm was obviously severely broken and useless, and the makeshift sling offered little support. He guessed his arm would never be fully reliable again.

The relentless sun beat down on the travelers. Within the cave, Democritus' skin was pallid; now his tender skin was darker and blistering under the desert sun. He mused at such contrasts in his life. Perhaps Yeshua would not recognize him if he did find him. *Foolish thoughts! He would recognize my heart no matter what my looks might be. I of all people should know that.*

"Where are we headed?" he finally asked another prisoner in front of him.

"Into Judea, to Yerushalayim. They have many rich Jews there."

Democritus' heart skipped a beat. Suddenly he lifted his head and looked forward to the rest of his journey. *If I can't find Yeshua, perhaps he will find me.*

The sun was past midday and Democritus was sure he saw something up ahead. Was it just a mirage? In the distance, movement appeared on the crest of a sand dune then slowly disappeared down into its shadows. Like a snake slithering across the crest of a dune, another caravan was approaching them in a long wavering line. His group chattered away. They had noticed it too.

As the sun was setting on the ledge of the earth's surface, images became distinct. The two caravans of traders would camp in the next cradle of sand. There they would exchange stories and learn what the selling prices were and the expectations for bartering their goods, including Democritus.

The campfires were low and the excited voices had died down between the two camps. Democritus lay on his side trying to sleep, but beside him a huddled group of men from the other camp were deep in conversation. They had been drinking sweet watery wine for an hour. One man spit into the fire and spoke in hushed tones to Democritus' master, Dede.

"There's a traveling magician in Yerushalayim that's causing quite a stir."

"Nothing would surprise me in Yerushalayim," Dede said.

"This man is unique. They say that his miracles are beyond what any other man has ever done. It seems that all of Judea is following after him."

"The Jews are always waiting for someone to deliver them."

"They hate the imperial Roman rule," a third man spoke.

"Who doesn't? Each people should be allowed to rule their own. But that's never going to happen in a thousand years. Nations are always trying to conquer each other."

Democritus curled up tighter causing his chains to rattle.

"Well," the first man continued, "this man claims to have raised the dead and heal lepers. He's caused blind men to see and the deaf to speak."

"Perhaps I should meet him." Dede picked his teeth with a thin chicken bone he kept on a string around his neck. "Magicians always bring crowds and crowds bring money."

"He says that the Temple is going to be destroyed and he will rebuild it in three days." They all laughed. Democritus heard the fire sizzle as someone spat into it again. He knew they were speaking of Yeshua.

"That would be a wonder. I want to be around when that happens."

"But I heard there's a plot from within his own followers." Democritus felt a sudden chill wash over him.

"Interesting. What kind of plot?" Dede replied.

The man's voice was hushed. "One of his own."

"A traitor?"

"Yes, one of his closest followers."

"I've known some nasty villains, but the worst kind is one who would betray his closest friend." Dede paused then said, "Who's after him?"

"The Jewish Temple priests. Apparently they have a quarrel with him."

"The Temple priests?" He paused in bewilderment. "What gives them authority to take legal issues into hand?"

"They hate him and fear him. They've just taken it upon themselves it appears. But there's enough unrest that this could really happen."

"And where did you get your information?"

"Ah. Intriguing, isn't it?" He leaned closer and his voice lowered. "A tavern in Yerushalayim called The House of Kedron."

"Men gossip more than women in a tavern. But it's seldom reliable," Dede grumbled.

"Perhaps. This servant works for the Temple priest himself. He said he'd befriended this follower of the magician. Learned some things and was certain they were reliable. Said he'd been trying to tease out more information about his plans, and it was just a matter of time."

"What's in it for your friend?"

"Either fame or money. There isn't much else, is there?"

"Power." Dede rubbed his bristly chin and seemed thoughtful.

"You're right. It could be power he's after," he mused. "I guess if you're in those circles, power could be a formidable tool."

"And the traitor?"

"I haven't a clue. But apparently he seems obsessed with the idea."

Democritus grew restless as the conversation continued. Yeshua was in danger. The two men noticed him stirring. Suddenly they changed into a Syrian dialect that Democritus found impossible to understand. However, he had heard enough to fear for his Master. He prayed into the night for wisdom to make sense of it all. He must find Yeshua. With that, he fell into a restless sleep until dawn.

The following afternoon, Democritus' eyes widened and his heart jumped with joy. They were approaching Yerushalayim and he could see the magnificent walls surrounding the Temple Mount, shining in the waning sunlight. "Yeshua," he whispered, "I'm coming to you." As they drew closer, he saw the city walls twist around the old city at angular turns conforming to the rocky terrain.

The caravan trudged wearily through the gate into the city limits. Beggars littered the entrance, hoping for scraps of food that might fall from the travelers. One man scurried to grab some rubbish a camel driver tossed. He dashed between the lumbering animals but was not quick enough. A hoof crushed his left leg into the sand. The man gave a chilling scream and the rider cursed.

"Get out of the way you beggin' fool!" He cursed in Egyptian, then Syrian, then muttered some Arabic slang. He waved his hands excitedly, then carried on, unconcerned about the beggar's suffering.

Democritus looked back over his shoulder. He could do nothing because of his chains, but he grieved at the suffering and hardness of the human condition. He remembered his former chains.

The slaves were herded into a stall where they would stay until the auction the following morning. By day break, the guards had scrubbed and oiled the slaves. They wore new tunics as they stood on display before the crowds of wealthy merchants. Democritus refused to give up the tattered remains of his robe. He tucked it away into a sack.

The auction was held not far from the Temple Mount, on a road where worshippers traveled. It began at the Pool of Siloam and ended on the southern slope near the Temple. Each slave was taken up the stone steps built in a pyramid fashion.[26] One by one they would step onto the platform as the bidding began. With chains and manacles, Democritus waited his turn. In the merchants' eyes, he was worth almost nothing. His useless arm determined his value. He had little worth except for domestic service. Dede stood at the podium and the bartering began.

"Twenty pieces of silver. Who'll give me twenty?"

"He's nearly worthless, only half a man. I'll give you five pieces of silver if his brain is sharp."

"He's brilliant," Dede said. "Great thinker. He can calculate your expense account with his good mind and right hand. He's worth more than five, who'll give me ten?"

There was silence.

"His arm is a minor problem. He'll heal soon. He fought a lion and killed him. He's as strong as an ox." The crowds looked skeptical and the twitch in Democritus' face became apparent to the onlookers.

"Six and no more," the same man offered. "He'll eat more than he's worth."

Dede slapped him on the back causing Democritus' muscles to ripple in the sun. He hung his head, then remembered that he belonged to Yeshua. He looked up and peered through the crowds, wondering if he might see him.

"You're robbing me blind. But he's yours for six pieces of silver." He nodded to the bidder. "Take his chains off." He motioned to a ruddy Egyptian nearby. "Collect the money." The trade master looked Democritus in the eyes and squinted. "You'd better work hard, slave. I don't want to see you again. You cost me much and brought very little."

"My Master is Yeshua." Democritus said in defiance. "He values me."

---

[26] http://news.discovery.com/history/archaeology/mysterious-2000-year-old-podium-found-in-jerusalem-150901.htm

"You should be killed for that, but I no longer own you. Get out of my sight," he said with a scowl. "I should have left you for the birds." He clenched his teeth then turned back to the crowds. A black burly man stood on the platform next, chains and manacles holding him in place.

"Now here is a man worth his weight in gold. Look at him. He's a statue of perfection. Thirty pieces of silver. Who'll give me thirty?"

Democritus' new master was tall and lean with weak eyes that strained to see. He was pale and had slender shoulders. With delicate yet determined hands, he checked Democritus over, pushing and prodding as if he were inspecting a cabbage.

Finally satisfied he said, "Carry these documents for me." He shoved a bundle of ledgers at Democritus. He grabbed them and thrust them under his good arm. "What do they call you?"

"Democritus. My name is Democritus."

"Strange. That's a Roman name. You're not Roman."

"No. I'm from Gadara. My master gave me that name. It means a judge of the people."

"I'm your master now and I'll decide what I want from you. Your name is insignificant. It means nothing. Certainly you're no judge. Not as long as I own you."

"My apology sir. I don't presume to be a judge. I was simply explaining my name." Democritus bowed his head in submission. Then he added, "I am a follower of the Jewish Messiah, Yeshua. He gave me my name."

The man stopped dead still. His face turned red and a large vein throbbed on his forehead. Democritus drew back several steps. The man was quick like a hawk. Democritus didn't see it coming until it was too late. The slap across his face made his vision blur. He quickly recovered and stood straight. He was baffled at his master's reaction, but he would not withdraw his statement.

"Yeshua! Don't *ever* speak that name in front of me again. That crusader has caused havoc to my profession. Tax collectors are hated as it is, but because of his brazen opinions, the poor are getting richer and we're losing profit. He's nothing but smoke and mirrors." Once again, Democritus wondered what his future held.

The man glared in silence at Democritus. "Get moving."

"Yes sir."

They walked along several lanes toward the upper quarters of the city. The homes were well built with lush landscaping. They made one more turn and stopped in front of a large dwelling. The stone house had ornamental gates that opened onto an arched entry. The door was dark with black scrolled hinges and a latch. Against the wall, a climbing bougainvillea hung in full coppery bloom. His master unlocked the door and proceeded in with Democritus in tow.

The room was luxurious with polished furniture crafted from exotic African hardwood. A tapestry hung on one wall depicting a scene of Rome's colossal buildings. The furnishings were of Grecian design upholstered in various textures of silk. Democritus was speechless as he surveyed the huge room. At the far end, a carved stone fireplace rose up to the beamed ceiling.

The master took the scrolls from the slave and led him to a small room with a straw mattress on the floor, a square table and one chair. On the table was a clay oil lamp.

"This will be your quarters. You'll eat, sleep and work in this room." He unrolled one document on the table. "So you can do ledgers?"

"Yes, master. I can read and write and do numbers."

"Good. I collect the taxes from the Jewish sector in the lower district. Your job is to record the taxes required by Rome beside each name, plus the percentage of interest for late payment. I collect the money, give you the information and you record every penny into the ledger. You'll balance the ledgers every day and I'll review them for accuracy." He studied Democritus' face. "Is that clear?"

Democritus nodded.

"The late fees are recorded in a separate column." He started to turn but then stopped. "They all pay late fees. It's a symptom of the Jewish resistance to Roman rule."

"You charge them late fees whether they're late or not?"

The tax collector stared at the slave. "Certainly. They hate Caesar and they despise tax collectors. It's the least we can get out of them for their arrogance."

This news disturbed Democritus. He sat down at the table and opened the ledger. His master stood over his shoulder and pointed to one account.

"See this man, Joseph, son of Etham? His taxes for Rome were twenty-five drachmas for six months. I added an extra five drachmas for late fees." He ran his finger down the list to another entry. There on a similar line was the amount of the payment, the date due, the date paid and the last column was the late fee payment.

"I'm sorry. I guess I'm confused. Residents must be aware of the dates for payment. Don't they question a late fee if they know they've paid on time?" Democritus studied the ledger with a growing unease.

"We call it a surcharge. Most of them are too ignorant to know the difference."

"But *you* know. Isn't this stealing from the poor . . ." Democritus nodded toward the opulent decor ". . . to pay for . . . all this?"

"How dare you judge me, you insolent fool! You're calling me a thief? You think you're *my* judge, do you?" He struck him across the back of his head. Momentarily, Democritus was blinded from the impact. His head was still bruised from the beating in Pella. "The money is none of your business. Your responsibility is simply to enter the information and forget everything you wrote. Do you understand?"

Democritus bowed low. "I want to please you, master. I want to help make your work successful." He raised himself and looked the man in the eyes. "But I can't be dishonest, sir." He tried to reason. "Here, see? This man actually paid early and he was still overcharged five, sorry, seven drachmas."

The tax collector was enraged. "You'll record what I tell you or you'll be beaten and thrown into prison."

Democritus rubbed his wrists, so recently freed from a lifetime of chains. Why was he sabotaging his newly given freedom all because of a little dishonesty? Was it worth it? He instantly remembered Yeshua's face. "Master, I respect your authority over me. I will work hard for you. But I've committed no crime worthy of prison. I'm an honest man. I can't cheat someone knowingly. I couldn't be a part of it." Democritus stepped back from the tax collector. "I'll do any other work you wish."

"You *will* do exactly as I command."

"I cannot be unfair. Yeshua . . ."

The tax collector cursed and screamed. He picked up an ornamental vase and threw it at Democritus, who moved to one side just in time. Democritus could hardly believe this was happening. The tax collector bellowed a name. "Theudas, get in here. Now!"

Democritus moved back against the wall. Suddenly a tall heavily built man walked in the door. In his hand he held a leather whip. He seemed anxious to use it.

"Yes, master?"

"Take this slave out back and give him thirty lashes minus one. Take your time. Then tie him up and take him to the authorities. He's insolent and refuses to obey my commands. You know how I hate that. Have him thrown in prison until I decide what to do with him."

"Yes, master." Theudas took two steps toward Democritus and grabbed his left arm. Democritus let out a scream as the pain seared through his body. Theudas dragged him by his broken arm outside the house. He nearly fainted from the pain. Theudas tore his clothes from him and shoved his face against the wall. Democritus laid his cheek against the stones and prayed. *Yeshua, you are the only good thing that's ever happened in my life. Take me home, Lord. I can't bear this.*

As Theudas slashed the leather whip across Democritus' body, he prayed that death would take him home before the night was over. By the twentieth lash, Democritus dropped unconscious to the ground.

When he awoke later that night, he found himself locked in a prison cell. Democritus lay naked on the stone floor with his face toward the wall. His body was stiff with congealed blood. His back, buttocks and legs were bloodied with open gashes. The back of his head had lacerations matting his hair against his skull. He tasted blood. A soldier had thrown the sack that contained his tattered robe beside him. He tried to lift his arm to open the sack. It seemed as heavy as a stone and it took every ounce of effort to move. Eventually, he was able to cover himself with his Master's robe, but he was too weak to move from where he lay.

After a long silence Democritus realized someone else was in the cell with him. He couldn't turn his head to look so he called out. "Is someone there?" There was a growl and a man cursed.

"Don't think you get a cell to yourself, slave. I don't like you here." His voice rumbled like distant thunder. "I don't like stinking slaves around me." Democritus groaned in despair. All he could do was pray.

He closed his eyes. *Yeshua, take me home. I've failed every battle that's come my way.* He lay there on the stony floor, blood seeping from his wounds. From a corner, a rat appeared and scurried across the cell. It sniffed at Democritus and scuttled toward some straw. There was a whisk and a sudden squealing of a writhing rat.

"I hate vermin." The squealing continued until suddenly the man shouted, "Go to hell." He threw the rat against the wall. The squealing stopped and the rat dropped to the floor dead. Its bloodied body was crushed.

Democritus' cellmate hissed in the darkening chamber, "The same will happen to you if you get in my face."

Democritus held his breath for a moment then whispered in a low voice, "I'll not make trouble, sir. You can see I'm too weak to even stand. I'm a follower of Yeshua. I seek only to do what is right and truthful."

"A lot of good he's done you."

Night brought rods of deep shadows that stretched across the cell. Down the long corridor, wall torches flickered brighter as darkness approached. Night brought a relief from the heat of the day and the prison walls were cool and damp. A guard had walked the length of the prison to inspect each cell. His armor and sword clattered in the silence. Satisfied that all was okay for the night he returned to a front table where another guard was waiting. Their voices were hushed, and soon Democritus allowed sleep to come close as he lay exhausted from his suffering. It seemed that even here in this lonely dark prison, God's presence brought solace to his soul. He closed his eyes and slept.

Sometime before dawn broke across the sky, Democritus awoke just briefly. He felt a presence standing over him. Democritus felt his body being lifted into the air, arms and legs dangling helplessly. Then with a hideous roar, his body was flung across the cell toward death, the last words he heard came from the beast's breath, "Go . . . to . . . hell!"

"Guards. Guards!" the murderer called out. "We've got a problem here. There's another dead body in my cell. I can't sleep with a corpse next to me."

Two guards hurried down the corridor where they found the crumpled body of Democritus. One guard groaned and shook his head. Democritus' skull was crushed. Blood dripped down the wall and pooled between the stones.

The soldiers opened the prison cell and removed the broken body of the man some knew as Diablo, others as a mere slave. But to Yeshua, the man was known as a judge of righteousness; Democritus. They carried his body wrapped in a tattered robe up to the Mount of Olives. On the edge of the gravesite, a few spaces were left for common people. He was buried there alongside other tombs in an unmarked bone box before dawn. A guard scrubbed the wall and rinsed out the cell. Finally, he threw fresh straw across the floor where Democritus had lain.

Streaks of murky gray light filtered in through the window's iron grid. The torch's flames were weak as the oil slowly burned away what was left of the night. Barabbas stretched out in his freshly scrubbed cell. A jackal howled outside in the graveyard. Barabbas reveled in destruction. Sometimes the power he wielded over losers made him giddy. Tonight, he grinned. He eventually closed his eyes and fell into a mindless sleep, his conscience as seared as a piece of spent coal.

Chapter Seventeen

# YERUSHALAYIM, CITY GATE, 33 A.D.

"Here you are Az, yesterday's bread for you and your mates." The baker tossed several loaves at Artamos' feet. He grabbed them with speed. No one knew Artamos' real name. The most intense thing about the beggar was his azure blue eyes. So *Azure*, or *Az*, became his preferred title among the hierarchy of vagrants outside Yerushalayim.

Today, Az sat in his usual place against the north gate entrance. He scratched his back against the rough stones. He was watching out over the landscape as he had done for years. He was waiting for the Messiah to come.

"Where are you, child? You've made me wait so long," he mumbled. "Herod is dead. He can't get you, child. He's gone to hell. He can't come back and get you." The confused man looked down at his clothing absentmindedly. He wore three robes, one red, the next striped yellow and black, and the top layer a patchwork of blue. All were faded and filthy. He mused for half an hour over nothing, then brushed his clothing as though he had just dropped some crumbs. He muttered to himself and laughed.

Az spent the next hour watching a spider crawl across the sand in his direction. It crawled onto his outer robe and paused, then proceeded up his sleeve. Az watched as the spider traveled up to his shoulder. Staring passively at the insect for a few minutes, he suddenly grabbed and held it between his dirty fingernails. The creature wiggled and squirmed trying to escape. Artamos was very apologetic. "Too bad, you greedy thing. I'm sorry but I can't let you eat up all my crumbs."

With a single motion, he popped the spider into his mouth and swallowed dryly. He let it slide down his throat and waited until the tickling stopped before he looked out onto the horizon again.

"Good bye." He felt sad for a few moments. "You failed, just like me, you failed." Then he refocused on the horizon. "Where are you, Messiah?"

Sleep overcame Artamos in the heat of the day. He didn't see the stream of people moving along the horizon, inching toward the city. Some of the beggars were startled as the throng got closer. Onlookers joined in quickly. A crowd was coming their way. Some were dancing and waving branches in the air. Children ran in circles holding streamers of brightly colored ribbons as if to celebrate some important event. The beggars mumbled to each other wondering what was coming. It was a remarkable sight. As the crowd approached the city gate their singing and laughter swelled. Finally, Artamos stirred. He bobbed his head awake.

"What's that noise? What's goin' on?"

"Dunno," a blind man replied. "Sounds like a party."

"I wasn't invited," Az grumped. "Can't be much without me there."

"You ain't dressed for a party," another beggar sniffed. "Gotta have some better threads than them you got on."

"Who cares what I have on? You ain't my tailor." Az spit, then stared at the crowd as it grew closer. He put his hand up to his forehead to shield his eyes from the sun's glare.

"Is that you, Messiah?" Artamos whispered. Like a growing sunrise, the crowd filled the landscape as it approached, dancing and singing the songs of King David. In the center of the crowd a man rode on a donkey. He was their focus of celebration.

"Who's that?" Artamos wondered. "Where's his horse?"

"There ain't no horse, just a donkey," a skinny beggar answered.

"No leader comes on a donkey." Artamos shook his head as he stared. "Caesar comes in a chariot, Herod rode a white stallion, no one comes on a donkey but a servant."

The crowd arrived at the gate. The man on the donkey did not look like a conquering king. Sadness filled his eyes. He was searching for someone nearby. He raised his hand to shade his eyes.

Artamos raised himself, mesmerized by the sight. The sun's glare was dazzling. He cupped his hand over his eyes to see more clearly and squinted to focus. He wanted to see the man's face.

A diaphanous cloud passed in front of the sun and, for a moment, everything was clear. The man had focused his gaze upon Artamos . . . and Artamos stared back into his eyes.

The old soldier felt a chill run through him. The man's robe was the color of unbleached linen. His hair was dark and features striking, but his shoulders seemed weighed down. Artamos studied the man's eyes; dark like chestnut. The old soldier was awestruck. He couldn't turn away. There was something significant about this man.

Staring at Yeshua, Artamos' world reeled backward to his former life; before the massacres, before his imprisonment. Memories of beauty flooded his mind. He remembered his wife, Claudia, and their two children. He saw them running in the green fields. He heard them laughing. He whispered their names gently, "Claudia . . . Demas . . . Janus, where are you? I . . . love you so much." His eyes were riveted to the man on the donkey. He stumbled to his feet.

"Come soon, Mess . . .," but he didn't finish the words; he was stopped by the man's piercing stare. For the first time in years he remembered good things; a life that offered hope, laughter, purpose.

Yeshua's eyes called to him. The sound of the throngs dimmed in the beggar's ears as he searched the face of the rider. Suddenly, the man was directly in front of him, the donkey's footsteps soft in the sand. Time stood still for Artamos and he could not steal his eyes from the man's gaze. They were compassionate, forgiving, comforting; even hopeful. Yet there was also sadness in his eyes. Artamos did not recognize him.

"Artamos, follow me." The man spoke someone's name. He called someone to follow. Az did not recognize his own name. The words echoed like a chiming bell, so unmistakable, so irrefutable.

"Artamos, follow me." Az took a step forward, then wavered. The crowds pushed and shoved through the gate, their voices echoing beneath the stone arch. Yeshua's eyes kept pleading for Artamos to follow. He stretched out his hand and beckoned him to follow with the others.

So many people. Someone shoved the beggar back against the wall. Singing and laughter filled the air as the donkey moved past him into the city. Yeshua's face disappeared in the sea of people, beneath the shadows of the stone arch. Artamos strained to hear Yeshua's final words.

"Oh Yerushalayim, Yerushalayim . . ." Yeshua's voice was a lament but it was quickly swallowed up by the crowd's cheers and clapping.

"Hail the King! Hail the King of Israel!"

Hundreds pushed and shoved through the gates until there was nothing left but billowing dust from the feet of the followers. Artamos looked to the ground. He spied a loaf of bread that had dropped from someone in the crowd. He stared at it for only a second, then lunged for it. Two others grabbed it at the same time. The three men tore and yanked the bread until they each ended up with only scraps covered in dust and sand.

Az settled back into his corner and greedily covered his scraps in the folds of his robes. It was not until dark that he ate the few bites. He was used to the grit of sand between his teeth.

The darkening sky brought a flood of deep sadness. He remembered the night of horror. The nightmare roared into view and Artamos began to whimper. "Messiah, please come," he groaned. "Will I ever find you?" His soul was parched.

## Chapter Eighteen

# YERUSHALAYIM, 13TH OF NISSAN, 33 A.D.

M alchus had followed Iscariot's movements spo-
radically for several months now. Something was
brewing. His only conclusion was that it had to do
with Yeshua, Iscariot's leader and friend. The strange man was
tight-lipped, a loner like himself. But so far Malchus had not
succeeded in getting into the mind of Iscariot to discover his
conspiracy. He made it his business to watch his movements
but they were always unpredictable. Like the twitching tail of
a tiger, Iscariot never stayed still.

At times his devotion to Yeshua seemed sincere, almost
to the point of servitude, yet something was hanging there.
Something wasn't right. Malchus knew because Iscariot was
too much like himself. He felt he could almost taste his thoughts.

It was a warm muggy evening. Everything felt suffocating.
The sun had washed the western sky with an orange glow. The
days were stretching longer as spring advanced. There was a
faint floral scent in the air. Passover was approaching. People
were busy preparing. Malchus walked across the western side
of the Temple courtyard where the high priest chambers were
situated. His leather sandals tap-tapped a lonely echo across the

stone floor. Two swallows swooped down into the courtyard then quickly disappeared into a crevice in the wall.

Malchus was the servant of Joseph Caiaphas, the high priest of Yerushalayim. Caiaphas, who controlled the Temple treasury and was considered the chief religious authority in the land, also ruled the Temple authorities. He was a powerful man.

Malchus was on duty and must prepare a bath for Joseph Caiaphas. He hated helping the man clean himself. He detested having to trim his graying beard and cut his thinning hair. He hated groveling for someone else.

*I despise that swine. Why should I clean the dirt from between his toes? He's arrogant and nasty.* He walked in between the columns of the Temple. Shadows lengthened deep within the walls, an immediate coolness washing over him. The swallows were somewhere inside the tomb-like chamber above Malchus' head. He turned south then headed forward.

More columns, and only the flickering light of oil lamps hanging above him offered an ambient light. Burning incense gave an ethereal presence to his surroundings. Somewhere up ahead Malchus heard hushed voices in the shadows. The tones were dark and menacing. He stopped dead still. The voices paused also. They waited to hear footsteps, but Malchus knew how to disappear into shadows. After an unnervingly long pause, the voices resumed their secret discussion. Malchus forgot to breathe. He slipped off his sandals and moved closer.

He heard a strange dialect speak quickly with determination. The slurred endings of some words reminded him of one man, one man that drank a lot, the disciple, Iscariot. *The Temple ground is a strange place to hatch a plot.* Malchus was intrigued. Iscariot was discussing something with the high priest and a group of guards. Malchus realized what was going on.

*This man is a traitor.* Malchus felt his blood warm as if he had just downed a pint of ale. Then he shivered. *He's plotting to deliver his master into his enemy's hands. He . . . wants . . . him . . . killed.*

Malchus' head thumped with adrenaline. *What kind of follower would do that? Turning him in was one thing, having him killed was pure treachery. Surely Iscariot would not want to be an accomplice to murder, especially this magician. His followers could riot.*

Then it hit him; this could be *his* good fortune. Stunned by his own impeccably good timing, he listened silently, hiding within the shadows of layered curtains. He moved close enough to the high priest's chamber to see the faint flicker of lamps through the curtains. He saw their shadows but not their faces. Malchus knew exactly who was in the room.

The man was bargaining, a plot emerging. It was betrayal of the darkest kind. Malchus was exhilarated with this inside information. It was perfect. This unplanned opportunity was a gift. Malchus stayed in the shadows and listened as this follower explained that he wanted to expose Yeshua as a fraud. And better yet, he would betray his friend for a miserly thirty pieces of silver, hardly enough to buy a mule. The token gift was mockery.

*I would have asked for twice that amount,* Malchus thought. *Get the most out of the trade. Maybe Iscariot has other motives.* He had arranged to meet Yeshua at an appointed time tonight in the Garden of Olives.

*Tonight!* Malchus had wondered why it took Iscariot so long to act on something. Betrayal grows in the heart from a seed of hatred. Iscariot had let the seed of wickedness blossom. The chief priest agreed to arrest Yeshua with a band of guards. The traitor would give a signal to identify Yeshua to the authorities, a kiss. All soldiers would be armed and ready to kill if he resisted.

Malchus could hardly control his excitement. He would witness the capture of this hunted man. But he, too, could hatch a plan. It came to him in a flash. He would let Iscariot lead him to the magician, then suddenly intercept the capture and claim the prize.

No, he and Iscariot were not the same. Malchus realized that he was the more ruthless of the two. He had no loyalty to consider, no honor to lose. It took him all of ten seconds to make a decision. He would cash in on this deal and let Iscariot pay the price. Malchus must ready himself.

The servant moved like a panther from behind the columns and out into the courtyard. The sky was darkening, streaks of blood red hung on the ridge of the horizon. He reasoned with himself that he was doing what was right. All he wanted was honor. He was tired of being treated with disrespect, tired of being regarded merely as a servant. Tonight he would be honored for the capture of Yeshua, the despised Jew that the world hated. His name would go down in history as parents would tell their children throughout the centuries of Malchus, the man who brought the false messiah to his knees.

After securing an eight-inch dagger from beneath his straw mattress and sliding it beneath his waistband, he headed back toward the high priest's chambers. Suddenly his task to prepare the bath seemed so simple. He rushed to the chambers and began heating the water while his mind plotted a glorious interception.

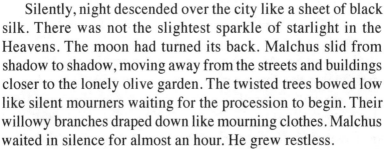

Silently, night descended over the city like a sheet of black silk. There was not the slightest sparkle of starlight in the Heavens. The moon had turned its back. Malchus slid from shadow to shadow, moving away from the streets and buildings closer to the lonely olive garden. The twisted trees bowed low like silent mourners waiting for the procession to begin. Their willowy branches draped down like mourning clothes. Malchus waited in silence for almost an hour. He grew restless.

Suddenly, beyond him, there was movement from deep within the garden. *Have I missed the arrest?* Malchus heard voices in the distance. He crouched near to the ground and moved beneath low hanging branches. The words became more distinct as Malchus approached. A voice spoke slowly, the tone filled with disappointment and resignation.

"Wake up, my friends. It's time to go! Here comes my betrayer. He's already on his way." A cold chill washed over Malchus as he heard the voice of the victim. *He knows. He already knows the plot. He's letting himself be caught, but why? Does he know that I'm here also?* The sadness in the teacher's voice troubled Malchus, but he didn't know why.

Everything suddenly became a blur of sound and fury. From behind him and to his right, footsteps of ten, twenty or more soldiers marched quickly toward the voices. Malchus peered into the blackness. He saw torches bobbing in disjointed rhythm toward him. He crouched low. He heard the clanking of metal against metal and the grinding of heavy footsteps as the crowd marched fearlessly into the bowels of the garden. He waited in the darkness.

Malchus was surprised to see so many religious leaders crowding behind the troops; religious leaders using military guards to commit an illegal arrest. They moved like a pack of wolves. Malchus sensed tension in the air like a prickly storm. He fingered the dagger in his belt. Excitement stirred in his chest. He remained in the shadows until the detachment of soldiers stopped directly in front of him. He felt the heat of their breath as they passed within inches of his hiding place. The hair rose on his neck. He was so close.

Impulsively, Malchus stepped out from the shadows and merged into the flowing mob. Torches flickering in the dead of night created distorted shadows of armies leaping over trees devouring everything in its path. Malchus' shadow had slipped in undetected. He recognized faces and it seemed like all of Yerushalayim had joined in the conquest. Malchus moved closer to the front. No one had spotted him yet. Too focused to notice him, Iscariot led the way.

Suddenly, from the deep shadows, the hunted Messiah stepped into the clearing. The soldiers were so startled that they moved back in surprise. Upon seeing the face of Yeshua appear out of the darkness, some were so shocked they collapsed to the ground. Their torches flickered fiery flashes of light in the man's face but he remained calm and sad. There was something regal about his movements and the look in his eyes. He seemed to be offering himself, like a lamb to the slaughterer. His hands were empty and open. There was no fear in his face, only sorrow. Malchus edged closer to the front. He found himself standing next to Iscariot. He felt a tremor run through his body. His eyes darted in every direction.

Iscariot took a deep breath and stepped up to Yeshua. "Master," Iscariot said in a thick mocking tone. The charade was over. Yeshua's eyes locked onto his betrayer. He was waiting for Iscariot. Iscariot stepped forward and gave Yeshua a stiff embrace and a kiss on both cheeks. The sadness in Yeshua's eyes haunted Malchus.

"You betray me with a kiss?" Yeshua's hands clasped Iscariot's arms and held him fast. His stare breached Iscariot's heart and looked Satan in the eyes. Then he let him go. The soft whisper was directed to Iscariot, but Malchus could hear. Now the deed was done and the betrayer stepped back into the crowd. Malchus watched the scene unfold before him. The soldiers took the kiss as their cue, stepped up and surrounded Yeshua. Malchus bolted forward and pushed past two soldiers. He slid the dagger from his waistband, and lunged toward Yeshua.

As Malchus screamed out, "He's mine," another man emerged from behind his Master. With one quick move Simon slashed a sword across Malchus' face. The blade missed its intended mark, slicing off Malchus' ear.

The dagger in Malchus' hand fell to the ground with a dull thud. Blood spurted everywhere. Screaming in pain and stunned by the blow, Malchus writhed and sank to the ground, his sounds swallowed by pumping blood. A circle of soldiers stared at the writhing man.

The great loss of blood caused Malchus' vision to dim. He could not even die like a martyr, only losing his right ear, forever shamed, marred for life. No one moved. The soldiers stood transfixed with spears raised toward Yeshua. The man with the sword stood dazed at what he had done. Iscariot stood in the shadows already shamed by his deed. Malchus lay writhing, covered in blood.

Yeshua spoke, "Simon, put away your sword," then stepped fearlessly toward the raised spears. The spears followed his movements, their tips touching his chest. He moved toward Malchus. The spears parted to let him pass. He knelt down and lifted Malchus' head. Blood was pumping profusely. A main artery had been severed and his mind was fading fast. Malchus quickly sagged while Yeshua held him firm.

The hunted man reached down and picked up the severed ear from the ground. Dirt covered the bloodied flesh. His movements were gentle like a skilled physician interested in the patient's greatest good. The soldiers stood like stone, not a muscle twitching. Their eyes followed his hands, curious as to what he might do. Yeshua looked into Malchus' eyes. They burned into the servant's heart and Malchus saw something he could not comprehend. He then took the broken flesh and pressed it gently against the open gash, holding it for a moment. Malchus felt a heat like the morning sun move from the man's hand to the side of his face. Heat radiated throughout Malchus' body. It melded flesh to flesh. The searing pain yielded to the man's touch and dissipated with immediate relief. [27]

Yeshua's touch felt like the touch of a father, the warmth of a mother, the comfort of a friend. Malchus wanted this moment to last forever. Yeshua's gaze penetrated his soul and shame caused him to look the other way. His ear was healed without

---

[27] Lu.22:51

the slightest disfigurement. This man was more than Malchus had bargained for.

Malchus started to speak, "Who are . . .," but the militia moved in with their spears. Yeshua stood and looked toward the soldiers. He willingly held out his hands that had just restored a servant's ear. They were open in surrender. A soldier grabbed Yeshua's hands and tied them with a cord. Then Yeshua spoke. His words tumbled into the night air with the steel conviction of reason.

"Why do you come as an army with swords and clubs?" His words cradled human submission in the palm of a divine hand. "Haven't I been here day after day and you could have taken me at any moment? Haven't I preached in the Temple, mingled with the people and made no attempt to hide? Now you come with swords and clubs in the dark. Take me where you planned. I'm ready."[28] He had taken control without the slightest effort.

Malchus was struck with absolute awe. A profound miracle had just happened before the crowd's eyes. But they failed to see who he was. They'd already condemned him. Their hearts were hardened like stone. Malchus, too, had already sentenced Yeshua before giving him a chance to defend himself. He gingerly touched his ear. No pain, no blood, no scar; perfect healing. *Did this really happen or is it a dream?*

The prisoner stood alone in the shadows of the Temple courtyard, bound with cords around his wrists. His followers abandoned him, every single one.[29] His face was serene, but his eyes were pools of sorrow mingled with divine loss. His gaze was unmatched by any human grief. Two Roman soldiers

---

[28] Lu. 22:52-53 "But this is your hour -- when darkness reigns."

[29] Is.53:3-4, Prophesied 700 years before the birth of Yeshua.

guarded the prisoner, tethered to a stake like an animal waiting for slaughter.

Malchus hid in the corner of the courtyard, deep in darkness, staring at the surreal scene. He shuddered. The world had abandoned Yeshua. All his friends had fled except the man with the sword who stood outside near a fire with a handful of servants. His sword was missing.

Heated conversation erupted around the fire. Shadowed faces rose and fell before the flames. The lone follower of Yeshua was at odds with an observant woman. She accused him of belonging to the band of Yeshua's followers. He raised his voice in protest. His eyes darted around him in defense. He pulled back from the crowd. Suddenly he heard a rooster crow, and the man turned his head at the sound. He shuddered as though it were an omen from hell. His face paled as he turned toward his friend. Yeshua had also heard the sound, and their eyes locked.[30] The man trembled, then grabbed his robes and ran into the dark, his voice wailing in sobs of remorse. Yes, the whole world had abandoned Yeshua.

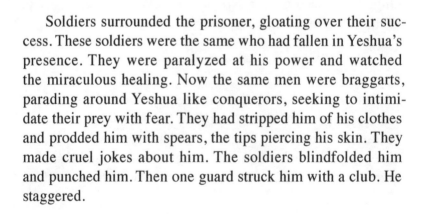

Soldiers surrounded the prisoner, gloating over their success. These soldiers were the same who had fallen in Yeshua's presence. They were paralyzed at his power and watched the miraculous healing. Now the same men were braggarts, parading around Yeshua like conquerors, seeking to intimidate their prey with fear. They had stripped him of his clothes and prodded him with spears, the tips piercing his skin. They made cruel jokes about him. The soldiers blindfolded him and punched him. Then one guard struck him with a club. He staggered.

---

[30] Lu.22:61

"Prophesy, mighty messiah. Tell us which one hit you. Surely you can do that."

They circled him with laughter and spit in his face, but he remained calm and silent. They plucked out his beard and shredded his back into ribbons of flesh and blood with a whip. The thorns they shoved on his head were laced with the poison of shame. They pierced through to his skull. His own blood blinded his earthly vision but crystallized his view of human need.

---

This arrest was illegal. The Jewish high priest had no authority to make such an arrest. Yeshua had committed no crime that warranted this action, either with the Roman or Jewish laws. He knew it and his tormentors knew it. For years he had slipped through their fingers like an elusive shadow. He would mingle in a crowd, heal the sick, raise the dead and then he was gone. He stood before them unarmed on many occasions and yet they could not snare him. They were powerless to capture him. Tonight Yeshua gave the commands. He surrendered.

Malchus' eyes widened in realization. *Yeshua surrendered his life! He put his life in the hands of evil!*[31] Deeper within the Temple grounds there was the clinking of coins thrown across the floor. Iscariot had thrown the blood money back into the Temple, cursed and fled. Tonight darkness reigned.

Malchus touched his ear then walked quickly to his own darkened quarters. He did not light a lamp. He lay down on his back with eyes wide, waiting sleeplessly until dawn. Terror filled his heart. What had he done?

---

[31] Lu.22:53 "But this is your hour—when darkness reigns."

## Chapter Nineteen

# YERUSHALAYIM, FRIDAY, 15 NISSAN, 33 A.D.

T he morning began with a blistering heat. Cobbled streets sizzled. Merchants were irritable and impatient. Inside the Temple courtyard, a pen of young lambs huddled together bleating for their mothers while buyers haggled over pennies that determined their fate. Flies droned in the hot air, hovering over fermenting straw and droppings left by the Passover lambs. Families bought herbs, oil, flat bread, and their chosen sacrifice. Tonight, lamb's blood would flow from the Temple altars down into the streets as families offered up sacrifices in hopes of having their sins absolved.

By noon, when the sun should be at its zenith, the skies blackened. The air grew curiously silent and heavy, closing in like a suffocating blanket. An ominous darkness settled over Yerushalayim. People became confused and disoriented. A bolt of ragged lightning rippled through the sky. Teeth-jarring claps of thunder resonated across the hillsides. But this was no storm of earthly dimension. Eternity was staking its claims.

Storm clouds crowded in close to the earth, strangely polarized on the notorious hill shaped like a bony skull where men were crucified. Golgotha's black sockets stared out into the

Judean hillside. In spite of the lightning and thunder, the skies remained stubbornly tearless. It seemed as if the whole of creation concentrated solely on a gaunt figure that hung suspended from two jagged beams in that place of the dead. God was offering his sacrifice.

For thirty-seven years from Herod's reign to Pilate's palace, Yeshua had been hunted. Finally snagged, his death would create a rift in the world where before only evil reigned. His sacrifice would cover human sin and offer life eternal to all who sought it . . . like an innocent lamb. Yeshua was fully cognizant of his purpose. He had surrendered to the cross.

The convict looked ordinary, a typical Jew. But unlike others, Yeshua hung there in silence. There was no usual plea-bargaining with the soldiers. In fact, no complaints came from his lips. No bitterness. Not a flash of self-pity. There was no sign of fear in his face, only sadness, deep unfathomable sadness. He was not like a man who had run from death his whole life. On the contrary, he was offering himself up to the Father.

The prisoner groaned as he shifted his weight the slightest degree, causing shockwaves of pain to ripple through his body. His face grew ashen. A ring of toxic thorns pierced his forehead, woven as a crown by some fool of a soldier.[32] Yet he wore it regally. Blood mixed with sweat and dust trickled into the crevices of his eyes. Instinctively he blinked to relieve the burning sensation. His bludgeoned face was distorted. The whites of his eyes blistered red with tiny blood vessels. His handful of followers could not recognize him except for the fluttering sign Pilate insisted be nailed above his head; "Yeshua, King of the Jews." Meant as mockery and judgment, the words declared his rightful reign.

The man's back had been stripped into ribbons of raw flesh and left to fester. Pus crowded the infected wounds.

---

[32] The crown of thorns might have been made from *Euphorbia Milii* with thorns up to 30mm long. Member of the Euphorbia family.

Long splinters sliced deep into these swollen gashes caused nerve endings to twitch in uncontrollable spasms. Flies incessantly harassed the man's face and torso. Spiked to a crossbeam, hoisted high and dropped into earth's socket, Yeshua surrendered to the merciless heat without complaint. His body instinctively recoiled from death's grip, but his will embraced it. Yeshua's final hour of human agony had begun. Would what appeared to be his darkest hour be his finest moment of glory?

For this man, death had been ever-present, lurking in the shadows, waiting just outside the door to snatch his glory. From the moment of his birth, evil clawed to reach him, but it had not been his time. He was hidden from soldiers, smuggled into Egypt under the cover of darkness. As an infant, the boy was shunted from place to place, despised like a child with leprosy. As an adult, his life took on a self-sacrificing nature that got up the nose of religious bigots. Yeshua! His name became the slang of the day, mere graffiti on the walls of latrines and stables. He was rejected like an unwanted gift. Yet he wore human suffering like a regal robe. And today a princely peace graced his battered countenance. His humiliation on earth was now drawing to an end.

Beneath the core of earth's rumbling, another sound grew. Yeshua alone heard its swelling tide; the sound of darkness so intense, so evil, it defied human reason. The sound rose in crescendos of throbs and screeches. Unseen hordes of demons soared through earth's atmosphere, descending upon the hill of Calvary. They flapped their fibrous wings as they settled upon the rocks, in the trees, upon the heads of people, for the long awaited death. Delirious with satisfaction, they screeched blasphemies until the deed was complete. Their claws clicked with nervous delight. They had never been so close to him and he had never before appeared so powerless to them as now.

Searching the sea of faces, Yeshua lowered his eyes and sighed with resignation. He saw the demons hovering, whispering with glee. He heard their curses and sneers. But his focus looked beyond them; beyond the hellish powers to the masses of broken humanity.

From deep within, Yeshua heard the cry of the human spirit. Crying as one voice, yet echoing billions of human woes, the cry spanned from the beginning of sin to the end of time. Yeshua sensed the anguish of the slaughtered innocents, the aborted millions, the malformed, the hated, the hunted, and the milieu of humans trapped in despair. Because of his overwhelming compassion for humanity's blight, Yeshua relinquished his life to the clutches of death.

Throughout his brief years, Yeshua had healed broken bodies, restored eyesight and raised the dead. But today he offered no visible deliverance for others or himself. Today the thirty-seven-year-old Jew looked as if he had aged a lifetime with sunken cheeks, drooping eyes and skin the color of death. Gray streaks already crowded his temples and peppered his beard. Yeshua had tasted the cup of human suffering and now would taste human death. Alone.

Until today, the growing crowd of followers had pushed and prodded, wanting him to pick up the gauntlet and lead Israel[33] into freedom. Now today, the day of Passover, the self-proclaimed Savior of the world looked the part of a pitiful failure. Eyes locked onto him with a morbid fascination, eager to watch death take its prey, curiously wondering if he would try to save himself.

As death drew nearer, the cloud of demons swarmed in closer for the kill. They paraded in front of the cross. Yellow eyes blinked and peered at the crucifix. Some brazenly perched on the crossbeam, murmuring curses, snickering at the emaciated sacrifice. Their heads bobbed up and down, moved back and forth, impatient for the moment in history when humanity would be totally theirs. It was inevitable. How easy it seemed to convince the Messiah to give up his reign. He had fallen

---

[33] http://www.letusreason.org/Biblexp63.htm

right into their laps. Their master would now become god. They would reign with Satan. They waited and watched.

The hot wind whipped circles of dust into the convict's face, his lips blistered and bleeding. His facial muscles twitched with excruciating pain, yet he showed no sign of bitterness. Unexpectedly, the prisoner let out a low unearthly wail that brought chills, unnerving even the soldiers. The demons screeched with delight. The onlookers stepped back and watched as the hairs on their arms bristled.

Yeshua moved his lips, trying to form them into words. His tongue was thick and stuck to the roof of his mouth, making it difficult to swallow. When the words came, they exploded in short breaths. Yet every word was profound. Before him were soldiers, beggars, a handful of women, a few stragglers and a convict on either side. They each heard the words, but most missed their significance. From his bruised lips came words of forgiveness and eternal hope.

"Father . . . forgive . . . them . . ." The words hung in the air for only a moment, then like arrows, pierced the hearts of the small crowd before him. His words struck deep, either burning like fire, or hardening the soul.

Roman soldiers stood nearby, curious to see how this man would die. A handful of isolated men hung back in the distance. They had followed Yeshua, believed in him until today. Now they, too, were uncertain. Doubts had sprung up as they beheld a dying leader. One by one they stepped back from the circle. They moved away like frightened children, but the fire had struck a flame in their hungry hearts. They would lock themselves away, waiting for some answers.

Joseph of the Sanhedrin stood alone, hidden in the shadows, overwhelmed by the evil that had taken place against this innocent man. He'd talked with him, put his faith in him, believed him. Joseph's stomach churned at the sight of such human anguish. He knew this man was innocent. He was alone in his defense of Yeshua in the Sanhedrin; alone in his conviction.

He stood by helplessly as the world turned its back and walked away from the cross. What could he offer? Nothing but a grave?

Earth's atmosphere was recoiling. Lightning struck a point in the earth that sizzled with an unmatched brilliance, then darkness returned. Demons danced and squealed as they flew into the lightning. Moving into an ecstatic frenzy, they knew nothing of the fire springing up within the human soul.

Yeshua was very weak. His body sagged as the pierced flesh ripped and muscles tore away from his bones. He closed his eyes in exhaustion, but his ears remained attentive to sounds around him. He heard robes rustling as the Pharisees scurried past and the tinkling bells worn by the Temple priests. Yeshua heard their muffled coughs and clicking tongues as they covered their mouths as they hurried by. Their hearts were uncompromised by Yeshua's words.

Yeshua heard the sound of weeping. With great effort he lifted his head and peered into the shadows. A dam of emotion burst from his mother's heart. He remembered her lullabies as a child, her prayers of Kiddush after she lit the candles on Shabbat, *Blessed are you, Lord, our God, sovereign of the universe* . . . He could never forget her voice. His mother's suffering opened a chasm of human sorrow. He felt the unholy despair of loneliness . . . and Yeshua embraced it.

"Father . . . Father . . . Why? Why have you forsaken me? Why?"[34]

Startled, Mary looked up, her eyes red and swollen. She moved closer and studied her son's face with a questioning look. She, too, questioned the Father.

*Why have they done this?* her eyes pleaded. *Who are you really, my son?* Tears splashed without shame. Her confusion cut at Yeshua like a knife. He knew that her pain would never entirely go away. Not in this lifetime. How can a mother watch

---

[34] Ps.22:1, 5-8,14-18, 31

her firstborn be executed before her very eyes and then forget? That image would be etched behind her eyes for a lifetime.

*Mother!* His eyes embraced Mary with compassion.

*Such a wicked world!* Mary choked with uncontrollable sobs.

*That's why I'm here, Mother . . . that's why I was born.* Yeshua wept for her.

Suddenly, Mary gasped. She clutched at her chest as a pain shot through her heart. She began to fall.[35]

John was nearby. In an instant, he reached out and caught Mary as she collapsed. As he held her steady, Yeshua spoke to his friend in a raspy voice. "John, take Mary as your mother."

Full of deep emotion he spoke to his mother. "Mary, here is your son. John will love you as I have." John nodded in agreement, then kissed Mary's cheek and held her firm as they wept together. Dreadful, heart-wrenching moments passed between the three of them.

Joseph of the Sanhedrin drew closer. He'd just heard Yeshua's cry of abandonment. He was stunned! *What is he saying?* Yeshua had just recited a verse from the ancient Davidic Psalm. As a scholar of the Torah, Joseph knew every verse from memory. He'd always questioned the meaning of these verses written a thousand years earlier. *Why is Yeshua quoting an obscure verse as he is about to die?* The Psalm described the suffering of someone as he was nailed to a cross and his clothes divided among his enemies. Joseph was stunned. *He called God his Father.* Trembling, Joseph fell on his knees and worshipped his Master. *Ancient scripture had just been fulfilled.* Joseph was a living witness.

Yeshua's rib cage heaved as he strained to inhale. His exhausted frame was becoming too weak to breathe. His body tingled and constricted for lack of oxygen. Lightheadedness

---

[35] Lu. 2:34, 35 . . . "This child is destined to cause the falling and rising of many in Israel, and to be a sign that will be spoken against, so that the thoughts of many hearts will be revealed. And a sword will pierce your own soul too."

caused black distorted shapes to block his vision. Yeshua blinked to clear his sight. He wanted to look upon those for whom he was dying—to look upon those whom he loved even in death.

A dark voice snickered in his mind. *Give up, ma-a-a-ster,* the sing-songy voice mocked. *There's no point in hanging on to this ridiculous cross. Why fight it? It's over. You've lost. I reign now. You chose death, remember . . . of which I'm the master.* Demons moved in closer to listen. Their eyes blinked and wings rustled in a restless frenzy.

Yeshua managed to swallow. A soldier prodded his mouth with a rag on a spear. It was soaked in wine. The smell made him gag.

"Open your mouth. It'll dull your pain." Yeshua turned his head away. Nothing could dull the pain of human tragedy. Nothing could mute his chosen sorrows. The cries of humanity rose up in anguish. Millions of voices echoed. He heard them all. He felt them all . . . abandoned children, rape victims, war crimes, Hiroshima, the Holocaust, Islamic terrorists and centuries of countless atrocities. Like windows into his creation, his heart viewed the history of human suffering, wave upon wave, all guilty of sin. Every heart a murderer. Every lustful thought adultery.

The challenge to surrender pushed at him. The demons grew restless. They jeered. Yeshua could simply submit to death. It would be so easy to . . . just give up. The pain was excruciating . . . unbearable . . . unimaginable.

Death would be such a release. Why lengthen his suffering? Better yet, he could step down from the cross. It would be so simple. The power within him stirred. Nothing could hold him, not the cross, not these nails, not death itself. It was his choice. Recognizing the source of this questioning, Yeshua silently shook his head; his will demanded Satan's voice into silence. The demons froze, surprised at the weakened Messiah's power over their master. They hadn't counted on his authority to command anything at this point. They moved back in silence.

His body was now contorted from prolonged stretching of limbs. Yeshua's eyes grew heavy and a tear ran down into his beard. He must continue . . . for broken humanity. He inhaled a frail gasp and choked. Coughing made his muscles spasm. His pain became unthinkable. But his mind focused on those he forgave.

"Yes, Father, forgive them."

One of the guards, a Roman centurion, listened. Sparks of truth flickered in his soul. Yeshua's stare had locked onto his. His gaze gripped the soldier for an eternity of a second. The soldier's heart was completely exposed, standing naked before the cross. His world passed before him: each sin, each murder, each crime played back, scene by scene, recorded and reflected back through the lens of the grief-stricken Savior. Together they saw the horror of his life, but alone, Yeshua forgave. The soldier's powerful body shook with sobs releasing years of regret.

"Master, please forgive me. I've been so arrogant. You are the truth that I've never known. I've been fighting in the wrong army." The soldier looked up. "I'm so ashamed."

Surrendered to the nails of the cross, Messiah's eyes embraced the soldier with compassion and absolute forgiveness.

The centurion threw down his weapons. A declaration of loyalty passed from the soldier to his new Master, Yeshua. The fire within his soul flickered higher when suddenly he was grabbed from behind and whisked away.

Now only breaths away from death, Yeshua looked deep into the faces of his Roman executioners and pronounced a pardon. Like pearls dropped in a pig trough, the precious words fell on sin-hardened hearts . . . then dropped to the ground unheeded. Burning tears rolled down his sunken cheeks, mingled with the dust of humanity and life's pain. He could see the faces of millions, hardened by sin's cheap rides. Yeshua expended his remaining strength weeping. He wept for those who would never repent; those who would hear but never listen. He wept for his own people. He longed for the day when Israel would return to him and mourn for him as for the loss of an only son.

In his last breath, he pronounced a pardon for all humanity. "It is finished; the debt is paid in full. Father, into your hands I commit my spirit."

The clock of human history stood still as its Creator breathed his last. Judgment had been served and the guilt-bearer ceased to breathe. His lungs stopped their rhythm, filling quickly with sticky mucus. The rasping halted. His heart ceased to beat and within seconds his blood congealed and became contaminated. His head dropped onto his chest, yet his tears continued to fall . . . dropping from his beard . . . splashing to the ground.

The masterful hands of the Creator now hung limp in death. His voice which had called the stars by name and set the universe in motion could speak no more. His eyes, always filled with compassion, now closed in death . . . his body hung lifeless. Above, the skies were foreboding. In the unnatural darkness people trembled and cried out for God's mercy. At the horizon's edge, a blood-red moon slowly rose and filled the sky with a crimson stain that now covered the landscape.

A trembling soldier gasped, "The moon . . . has turned to blood." [36]

Standing at a distance, a priest wrapped his robes tightly around him. "I know what it is." His voice trembled. "Joel prophesied, *'I will show wonders in the Heavens and in the earth: blood, fire and billows of smoke. The sun will be turned to darkness, and the moon to blood, before the great and terrible day of Yahweh.' "*[37] The priest fled into the darkness. The curtain came down on human transgression. Now there was a Savior, a Forgiver, a Redeemer for all who would accept him

---

[36] NASA, Kepler's equations, www.bethlehemstar.net

[37] Joel 2:30,31

as God's sacrifice for their sins. The universe understood and bowed in worship. The sun hid its face and the moon bled, signs pronouncing the redemption of the world.[38] For six hours Yeshua had hung, suspended in suffering as the sins of the world were laid upon him for all time.

---

[38] Description of the Crucifixion under the reign of Tiberius by Roman historian, Senator Tacitus, *Annals*, written AD 116, Book 15, Chapter 44

Chapter Twenty

# YERUSHALAYIM, 15 NISSAN, 3:00 PM, 33 A.D.

As the Divine Sin-Bearer was slain for the iniquities of humanity, the Temple priests were offering up *Qorbanot,*[39] a sacrificial lamb for each Jewish family in Yerushalayim. The high priest obeyed the Levitical observance because God declared that, "*. . . it is the blood that makes atonement for one's life.*"[40] They continued offering *Qorbanot* throughout the strange mid-day darkness. When the skies grew blood-red, a crimson stain washed across the Temple walls and marbled columns of the courtyard. Inside, the only light was the flickering of torches and the glow of incense offerings. The priest repeated the same prayers of contrition, droning on and on, hour after hour, until the last family brought their sacrifice before the altar of God.

An eight-year-old boy, a couple's firstborn, held a white lamb without blemish in his arms. The lamb made no attempt to squirm out of the boy's embrace. The child, however, began to tremble at the realization of what was to happen as he looked up at his father

---

[39] To sacrifice, Hebrew root, Qof-Reish-Beit, "to draw near."

[40] Lev. 17:11

for reassurance. Holding the lamb tenderly, he stroked his coat and kissed its head. Reluctantly, he knelt down, letting the lamb stand alone on the polished floor. Its innocent stare waited and watched. The lamb knew only kindness from his young master.

Troughs were filled with animal blood that ran from the Temple out into a gutter, then along the city streets, finally gushing into a basin outside the gates. The high priest stood at the altar before the Holy of Holies, his hands slick with blood. The smell of death lingered, while the great incense burners offered a pungent aroma of spices to conceal burning wool, roasting flesh and congealed blood.

The weary priest muttered a final prayer. The family had stepped back, leaving the lamb alone before its executioner. Its innocent eyes blinked and waited. Suddenly thunder rumbled and shook the Temple foundations. The marbled floors trembled and a web of veins ripped open. The priest clutched the curtain to hold himself steady. For fear of their lives, the family dashed out into the open away from the shaking columns and buckling floor. The lamb stood alone. Losing his grip, the priest fell then staggered back to his feet. The earth quaked again causing the pillars to rock. Dust filtered down from the rafters. Fissures tore through the marbled walls. The priest grabbed at a column for support, smearing blood down its spine. Another violent spasm rumbled below ground. The bowl toppled, causing the sacrificial blood to spill across the Temple floor. The lamb stood still as the river of blood washed past him out into the courtyard.

In front of the priest was the majestic veil of separation that shielded common sinners from viewing the pure holiness of God. It was the one spot on earth where the invisible God, whose name could not be uttered, chose to commune with humanity's brokenness. The sixty-foot-long fabric was as thick as the palm of a man's hand. The intricate veil began to separate from the Temple ceiling.[41]

---

[41] www.the-tabernacle-place.com; Mt. 27:51

The priest cried out in horror and buried his face in his hands. His heart throbbed, fearing certain death. "Blind me, Holy One, *Hashem*. I cannot look upon You." As Moses shielded his face from God's glory, the priest trembled and covered his face. There was a heavy rushing sound. The enormous weight of the material caused it to tear away into two parts. While the ground shuddered, the fabric popped and snapped separating the squares. Threads burst apart and woolen fragments drifted to the floor in soft piles.

Sweat beaded on the priest's forehead and his skin turned pallid. *It took 300 priests to hang the veil . . . what power on earth could tear it like that?* He gasped in horror. With one final rip, the fabric rippled and twisted, and plunged to the floor. Dust billowed into the air. As though the hand of God had reached down onto the human stage, God Himself had torn the curtain that had purposely separated the most holy presence of God from human eyes. Now there was no division. Could a holy God dwell with sinful humans?

Slowly, the old priest slid down the pillar and sat on the floor as his body drained of its strength. Before him was the Holy of Holies. It was empty and desolate. The priest's face twisted into a puzzled expression. *Where had God been all this time? Had he not heard my numerous prayers? Had he not received the sin sacrifices? Were all those animals slain for nothing?* A sense of deep disappointment swept over him. *Has God deceived me? Or have I just seen God?*[42]

From the shadows of the great Temple columns, the young lamb took cautious steps around the rubble. His tag-of-a-tail wagged as he looked for his young master. He moved past the broken priest and out into the street. He was free to frolic.

---

[42] Mt.27:50-51a; Acts 17:24; Heb.4:14-16

A swirling mist swept across the hillside while the thinning crowds shivered as they wrapped their cloaks tightly around them. Clouds billowed over the face of the moon, and the sky had turned into splattering rain. It was as though myriads of stars and limitless galaxies turned their heads and wept. Creation had no tenderness for humanity. Within moments, the Heavens broke open and threw down torrents of rain across the city, hills and valleys. Shards of ragged lightning blasted the hillsides and blistered lone trees. Skull Hill, the place of the dead, looked ghost white as ribbons of lightning split open the sky.

Yeshua's body hung limp as rain pummeled the earth and beat upon his broken form—his tangled hair lay plastered against his face. As the rain washed away the sweat and grime, wounds became more pronounced and ugly, turning deep purple as the settling of blood pooled in his lower extremities. Mud splashed up against his legs. Skin sagged upon his bones. From Yeshua's lifeless body, streams of sacrificial blood had flowed freely from his wounded side, his hands and feet, opening a fountain for sinners to come and bathe in its cleansing stream. On that day, the blood of God ran deep through the streets of Yerushalayim.[43]

Within the bowels of the earth, the prince of darkness stirred. His presence had settled over the landscape like a shroud. Hordes of demons swarmed high into the air, jubilant at their presumed victory and screeching their triumphal chorus. The human race, the crown jewel of creation, betrayed its own Creator and eliminated the Son. Now evil reigned.

No grave had been prepared for the convict's body. Because Yeshua had nothing of his own, a stranger, Joseph of the

---

[43] Ps. 22

Sanhedrin, offered an unused tomb carved into the hillside. As the storm continued to lash the earth, Joseph and Nicodemus, two closeted followers, quickly took Yeshua's body to the narrow tomb. They had wrapped him in a clean linen cloth. Both men, refusing to openly acknowledge the Messiah in life, came to his rescue in death, convinced of his deity. No former disciples offered to bury him.

Inside the tomb, the smell was musty and oppressive. Outside, the rains slashed the earth. Shuffling in backwards, the men carried the limp body into the court of the tomb which was nine feet square. Already the linen cloth was muddy and stained with blood. Once the body was laid out and cleaned, they quickly tore strips of cloth and began to wrap it, limb by limb. They put layers of aloe and myrrh between the cloths in a hasty embalming fashion. No words were spoken, only the heavy breathing of the men was heard as they worked quickly, each grieving in his own thoughts of failure and regret.

Rolling the great stone against the opening of the sepulcher, the men withdrew as Pilate's quaternion of four soldiers sealed the tomb. If the seal were broken the charge was punishable by death. The soldiers rotated their watch of the tomb, three guarding while the fourth slept, anticipating that the disciples might plan to snatch the body and say that Yeshua had risen from the dead. Silently, Mary Magdalene and Mary, the wife of Cleopas, stood at a distance watching how their beloved Yeshua was laid in the tomb. They were numb from the horror. Together they walked to the tomb and stood beside it.

"Why? Why?" Mary questioned in a flood of emotion. "He brought nothing but hope to this world." She wiped her eyes. "He loved the rich and poor—he even loved his enemies and they killed him for that."

"Let's go. It's finished. He's no longer with us," Mary Magdalene said.

Chapter Twenty-One

# YERUSHALAYIM, FRIDAY, NINTH HOUR, 15 NISSAN, 33 A.D.

D arkness lay like a mantle across the city and throughout the land; it seeped into the country lanes and lodged in the crevices of rocky hillsides. The Temple was empty and silent. A trail of blood had dried dark crimson across the polished floor. Flies hovered in circles. Near the Holy of Holies, a discarded ceremonial robe had been thrown in a heap. Just outside, a young lamb wandered through the courtyard until he found a pile of hay. There he curled up and slept. The sacrifices were finished.

In the garden, the grave of Yeshua was sealed shut with Rome's ribbon and imperial wax stamp. Three soldiers in full combat armor stood guard, surrounding the tomb. The Mount of Olives lay just beyond the city wall where hundreds of bone boxes and sarcophagi covered the ancient hillside. Now the Prince of Life lay with the dead. Yeshua lay blemished with other men's sins—the sins of the human race—the sinless one covered in sin, humanity's only hope, defeated by death. Creation seemed doomed for destruction. All looked hopeless.

Sometime during the strange darkness, the storm settled and the rains slowed to a drizzle. It seemed as though the sky had finally exhausted its rage against humanity, against earth's crust. The fight had ended; God's Son sentenced. But while people cowered, nature stirred.

The bedrock beneath the Dead Sea had been troubled with seismic activity for days. Slabs of bedrock had shifted and slid, shooting jolting tremors from earth's lowest point straight to the heart of the city, the Temple Mount. The Temple had suffered severe damage to its foundations only an hour earlier. The residents in the city were terrified. This phenomenon, together with the loss of daylight and the eerie darkened sky, caused residents to cower in their homes and pray. What was going to happen?[44]

Suddenly, the sea became agitated with heated streams bubbling to the surface. The seabed had broken open from an earthquake with a magnitude of great intensity.[45] The pressure exploded, sending funnels of toxic gases up to the surface. Thunderous jets of water shot high into the air, dropping back down creating huge tsunami-like waves pounding to the shore in ever-increasing succession. The flood waters rose further inland washing away plants and shrubs and swirling into a soup of destruction.

Another tremor jolted harder, and rocks split in two, tumbling down from the hillside of the Mount of Olives into the valley below. Fissures opened in the limestone layers leaving fine gaps in the hardened soil. Weathered and worn tombs began

---

[44] Thallus, circa 52 AD; Julius Africanus quotes Thallus in his 3rd book on history, "On the whole world there presses a most fearful darkness; and the rocks were rent by an earthquake, and many places in Judea and other districts were thrown down . . . as appeared to me without reason, an eclipse of the sun."

[45] These are the Jerusalem earthquakes of April 3 at the crucifixion of Christ (Matt. 27:51), and April 5 at the resurrection of Christ (Matt. 28:2) http://www.academia. edu/2474489/Jerusalem_Earthquake_of_33_A.D._Evidence_Within_Laminated_ Mud_Of_the_Dead_Sea

to shake, propelling pieces of stone into the air. Some crumbled to dust. Slabs of carved stone broke apart and fell away. The graveyard became animated as stones splintered and screeched while slabs fractured and broke in pieces. Some bone boxes ruptured exposing dusty bones, empty grave clothes. Other tombs held scribbled parchment texts that blew away as dust. Many tombs remained cracked and ruined, but deathly still as they'd always been. The wind swirled across the hilltop. Threatening clouds rolled across the horizon. Creation was still groaning.

On the edge of the graveyard another bone box had broken open. It was crude and had been placed on the hillside with haste. There was nothing ornate about it, just simple lines and irregular edges. Its rough-hewn lid had slipped sideways and toppled to the ground, shattering in pieces. Inside, the form of a woman stirred. Her face was exquisite; skin flawless like silk with raven hair. She appeared to be sleeping but suddenly inhaled, caught her breath and gasped. Her deep blue eyes fluttered open and she stared up into the overcast sky. With caution she sat up and viewed her surroundings. She seemed puzzled. She had not been bound in grave clothes. She wore only a ragged tunic that had been torn along the hem. It was caked with dried mud. Her confusion quickly vanished as she pushed away cobwebs and rose, stepping gracefully out of the box. Then Anna remembered.

Scattered across the graveyard some tombs lay silent. Not even the earthquake troubled them. But other bone boxes broke open, a once dead body now stirring with an irrepressible life force. It took moments for these resurrected people to get their bearings and realize they had returned to earth. As each rose, puzzlement quickly gave way to understanding. They possessed no fear of their future because they knew where they'd been. All around, life was stirring, humming, singing, as people rose from death's grip.

Anna moved with purpose toward the city. Others were doing the same. Anna wore only the dingy ragged tunic. Her feet were bare, but one thing was different. On her left hand she noticed she was wearing a gold ring. She couldn't remember anything about it. Quickly moving down the hillside, she enjoyed the sensation of cool blades of grass between her toes. She felt a thrill growing because she was certain this was her Master's doing and his ways were wonderful and exciting. Although she didn't know what lay in the future, she knew he was in charge.

As a storm brewed, deep darkness had covered the land from the third to the ninth hour while rain pelted the ground. The rains finally stopped, leaving behind a cloud cover that settled close to the earth. A soft breeze swept in as the resurrected witnesses found their way toward the holy city. In many homes, lanterns were lit as people groped in the abnormal darkness. Unknowingly, they were lighting the way for the visitors who arrived in Yerushalayim. Anna lifted her face to the breeze as it touched her cheek and gently lifted her hair. Excitement grew as she realized this was part of God's final redemption for mankind. She was humbled to be participating in something so significant.

———————◦———————

A child's coffin sat in the shadows beneath an olive tree. Its length was no more than three feet long. A worn text had been cut into the soft stone, telling of the death of a child. For thirty-seven years the box had sat in the shadows. The moss that nestled around its edges had been removed along with weeds and debris. Someone was still mourning. Three stones lay on top.

The quake had not disturbed the small bone box. Dried infant bones had lain encased in the tiny tomb. Now something was happening. Within the box there was life. Bones grew and lengthened, muscle and sinew developed, covering bone with flawless human flesh. Tightly wrapped limbs were growing and pushing, throbbing to be released. Muscle formed over muscle, feature after feature. The tiny box suddenly exploded sending stone fragments into the air. Adam awoke with his arms and legs flailing as the bone box shattered into a million pieces. Coughing and choking from the dust and debris, the boy finally caught his breath, stood up and stared, dazed at this new world he found around him. Stretching for the first time as an adult, he was amazed at his own height. His skin was bronzed, smooth and muscular. His grin was innocent and winsome. He appeared to be full grown and full of life. He began to worship.

*"Praise you God of all Gods. You are God alone. Your plans are so mysterious, so amazing and full of wonder and I get to be a part of it."* Adam began to sing. *"You lifted me out of the slimy pit, out of the mud and the mire. You set my feet on a rock and gave me a firm place to stand. You put a new song in my mouth, a hymn of praise to our God. Many will see and fear and put their trust in Yahweh . . . Many, Yahweh my God, are the wonders you have done. The things you planned for us no one can recount to you; were I to speak and tell of them; they would be too many to declare."*[46]

Adam was delighted by his new surroundings, yet entirely surprised. Eternity was filled with one surprise after another; always wonderful, always new. Adam didn't know his future but he knew it was good and mysterious. Back here on earth, the Father had only good things in store, even if that meant suffering or death. No matter what he was called to do, he would do it gladly as a witness to God's resurrection power.

The grown boy stood six feet tall with broad shoulders and muscular biceps. In spite of his size, his countenance still had traces of a baby's face, innocent and unpredictable. He held an infant's burial garment in one hand and combed his fingers through tousled sandy hair with the other. Apart from this garment, he stood there naked. Like a baby, his skin was flawless

---

[46] Ps. 40:2-5

with the exception of a ragged scar on his chest. At the nap of his neck a small heart-shaped mark appeared. Adam stepped from the pile of lime dust and moved away from the tombs. He took long strides enjoying the rhythm of his gait. He would follow the others.

On the outskirts of the graveyard another bone box stirred. Stone against stone creaked and groaned. The slab shuddered, spitting shards into the air. From beneath, a muscular hand grabbed the edge of the slab and pushed it off. It crashed to one side and broke in half. A man climbed out of the vault and looked around him. Standing tall with a dark complexion and strong muscular torso, he had broad shoulders and warm Mediterranean features. His square jaw and high cheekbones displayed a fearless confidence. His head was covered with black curls. A once crimson robe hung loosely over his shoulders, its edges torn into tatters. His dark eyes danced with an irresistible fire. Democritus greeted others with a contagious enthusiasm as they rose to meet the future. Others, too, would be witnesses to the unstoppable power of the resurrection.

A fragrance of sweet pine, rosemary and spring blossoms swept across the hillside. It rushed along with the breeze as the witnesses moved with purpose toward the dark restless city.

Promise had given way to triumph by the Messiah, but few mortals realized the truth. Yeshua, the Lamb, had come to take away the sins of the world and many would be witnesses to Yeshua's power over sin and death. Yeshua's spirit was still alive, never to be extinguished. They were in Yerushalayim to proclaim hope to people trapped in their own desperate sin. They, too, had once been in shackles but were now set free. The stage was set for victory day.

For three days and three nights, the witnesses would remain silent behind closed doors, scattered in various homes among the faithful across the city landscape. There they prayed. There they prepared. They sensed a battle brewing. The enemy was not content to kill the Messiah. He would hunt every follower of Yeshua to destroy life itself. A storm of supernatural proportion was coming when the believers of Yeshua would defend their faith with their very lives. They were given no details. That would come soon enough. Instead, these witnesses were called to go on a sacred journey that would lead them through a path of suffering. Yeshua had paid the price through his suffering. He had left them an example that they should follow. By faith they waited for the rising Son. These witnesses were resolute. Nothing could deter them, not even death itself. They were living proof that Yeshua's offering had conquered death's grip. No more sacrifice.

Chapter Twenty-Two

# YERUSHALAYIM, FRIDAY, 5 PM, 15 NISSAN, 33 A.D.

Anna had arrived in Yerushalayim. There the collective pain of people was invasive, almost tangible. Anna had forgotten how immobilizing pain could be when it gripped the body. It had been an eternity since she had last felt a single tear, but as she had walked toward Yerushalayim, she sensed the almost agonizing power of pain all around her. These people were frightened and anxious, suffering from a sin disease with no known cure. Until now.

Anna's understanding of her resurrection was limited. She expected she would face grief and danger once again because she was back in this flawed world. But she was confident there was also hope: the hope that she had grasped at when she touched the feet of Yeshua, when she left her life of promiscuity, which had carried her through the birth of Charis and released her at death. That same hope that carried her through to her dying moments in Yerushalayim's square was now a part of her, a part of Anna. Her resurrected appearance would authenticate Yeshua and bring hope to many people still living behind the walls of despair.

A part of Anna remained here on earth. She'd left behind her treasured daughter, Charis, a confusing relationship with Alexander and her contemptible father. She hadn't signed up for this trip. She simply found herself in the embrace of the earth once again, dirt between her toes, inhaling earth's atmosphere and subject to the harshness of the human condition.

She knew that Yeshua, the Messiah, died to take away the sins of the world. But how it all would unfold was still a mystery. It waited there like a blossom in bud, yet to bloom, its edges a flush red. When the flower blossoms, creation would finally see its splendor and smell its fragrance. There were still many unknowns, many uncertainties. Would she see her baby again? Would her feelings for Alexander re-emerge? Would he accept her Messiah? Would she be safe from the attacks of the enemy? Many steps in this operation were blurred. Deliberately!

Yerushalayim was dark, silent and in mourning. Her inhabitants had fled into the recesses of their homes, others into the subterranean crevices of the city. Their orderly world had tumbled into disarray . . . and they were terrified.

In the lower quarters of Yerushalayim where houses had been poorly built, the temblors continued to rock and uproot these structures, leaving only doorways or partial rooftops standing. People ran from their homes hoping to find safety at a friend's house. The strange weather patterns caused people to feel disoriented. The questions that plagued their thoughts were heavy. *What will tomorrow bring? Is the earth becoming unstable? Has a curse been released blighting the human race?* Yerushalayim was a city full of panicky people. Making her way through faintly familiar streets, Anna turned a corner where a woman waited in the shadows. Quietly she approached Anna.

"You are Anna?" she nodded. "You must come with me. Quickly, follow me." The woman's head was covered in a pale blue veil bordered in gold. Only her brown eyes were showing and they looked serious. Anna accepted this interception as orchestrated by God. What else could it be? The two women weaved in and out through crooked streets, stopping as the tremors rattled the earth, then continued on in silence.

Down a narrow lane, deep within the shadows of high walls, the woman unlocked a dark paneled door and led Anna in. She immediately bolted the door behind her then directed her down a long corridor, up a staircase to a single room hidden at the back of the house.

"This is for you, Anna. I've had a dream that you were coming. I only know that I am to provide this room until God is ready to send you out. My name is Priscilla. All you need should be here. There's a platter of fruit and breads along with a jug of water. If you require anything else, feel free to ask. Shalom." She closed the door behind her and was gone without asking a single question.

---

Yeshua's followers were hiding from the Roman militia and the ruling religious parties, both enemies of Yeshua. For three days and nights the people lived in an in-between period. It was a stage of death when grieving and sorrow mingled with the fears and apprehensions of tomorrow's reality.

The small band of disciples stayed huddled in a room, each dwelling on questions of the heart. They were morose and silent, their eyes betraying sorrow and shame, each with a personal loss. The doors were locked. There was a sense of waiting, but for what they did not know. The light from a solitary clay lamp brought a surreal presence in the upper chamber. But this was no dream. Each disciple busied himself with plans for his future, writing down thoughts and agendas, scratching out hopes and dreams of what might have been. Each man was plagued with troubling questions; *How will I face tomorrow without him? What about all the plans I had? What about the life I left behind to follow Yeshua? Why do I feel so abandoned? Why did I abandon him?* None of them dared utter the questions aloud. Two of them were missing, the traitor and the betrayed. Tonight there were eleven men disillusioned with life, disappointed with trusting in a Messiah who apparently failed them badly and now was dead. They had been blindsided. Now an immense vacuum was felt in the pit of their stomachs. It crept into their hearts. They didn't want to live without him. How could they?

In the gloom near a rocky precipice, a dark shadow hung from a gnarled oak. A cold wind howled through the branches whispering despair. The body swayed lifelessly. Above the corpse, beady yellow eyes blinked and peered down at the ruined figure. Like a sea of restless shadows, the shapes shifted and changed, eyes staring, as the demons gloated over their prey. Two vultures swooped down and lighted on the branch bearing the corpse's weight.

Iscariot's head was bowed, his hair hung down in damp strands, the face bursting in a red-black flush from strangulation. The man's lifeless eyes looked wild. They stared in a numb terror mirroring the final flight of the soul into the Abyss of eternal damnation. A blackened tongue exploded from his gaping mouth.

Iscariot had walked away from the one who could forgive him, straight into the embrace of the gallows. An eternal regret of the plotted *kiss of betrayal* would forever haunt his damned soul. His name would become a byword for all future traitors in every tongue and tribe throughout the span of human history; שקמ, *O Ἰούδας, Judas, the Traitor.*

Across the city, in the darkness of his bedroom chamber, Malchus lay silent on his side, his hand cupped beneath his head, cradling his left ear. He had experienced a miracle, witnessed ruthless betrayal, listened to the trials, the complete mockery of justice. Then he watched the unrestrained torture, and finally from a safe distance he observed the magician die in the most gruesome manner conceivable. The earth seemed to respond in turmoil. The death made him retch.

*How could a man heal people like that and then die for nothing? Why didn't he try to save himself?* Most astonishing to Malchus was the man's unsurpassed compassion. *Why would he care about a scumbag like me?*

Malchus rolled over in the dark. Was this all a dream? The servant lay still without sleeping, his pupils dilated in search of the tiniest spark of light. Then the earth shook. His room jittered.

Earthquakes terrified Malchus. No one knew why the earth shook and broke open. Entire cities had been destroyed by quakes. He gripped the sides of his bed as it slid into the corner of the room banging the wall with a thud. His fingers were pinched between the bed and the wall. Another movement and the bed slid back across the floor. In the distance he heard someone scream.

"God help me!" he cried. Warm blood oozed over his fingertips. Panic gripped him and he felt he couldn't breathe. It seemed as though the air had been sucked out of the room. Malchus could feel a cold sweat roll over him. His hands trembled. He wiped the blood onto his robe. Was the earthquake and darkness an omen? In some way, the strangeness of the day seemed closely linked to the capture and death of the man they called Yeshua. Malchus questioned himself. *What have I done? What have I done?*

Artamos lay among the debris beside the city wall. A shower of dust and rubble had rained down over him as the skies had turned black like night. He heard screaming in the city, rumbling beneath the ground, stones tumbling, and somehow he knew this was real. Something terrible had happened. Something evil. He pulled the blue tattered robe over his head and huddled in the darkness. It began to rain, pelting the dust and forming rivulets of mud. Like a frightened child he croaked out a ragged tune.

*It's okay. It's okay. The child's gonna come, he's gonna come today. It's okay. It's okay. The child's gonna come, he's gonna come today.*

His eyes were round with fright. He trembled beneath the robe, trying to sing his way out of the nightmare like so many other times, but it didn't help. This terrible day had suddenly lost its light and he felt the presence of evil lurking near him, moving and breathing all around him. The world seemed to be falling apart. He heard screams everywhere while the earth's floor continued to rumble. The old criminal remembered his evil and felt its presence very near. Like a swarm of bats, they came. His song and jokes no longer helped him face this darkness, this evil presence.

Artamos felt something heavy hit his head, then throbbing pain, and his world suddenly went dark and silent. He fell to the ground in a heap.

"That'll take care of 'im for a while. Az was gettin' on me nerves." A seasoned beggar threw the club out into the bushes and dusted his hands. "Now mates, help me drag 'im to his corner." Two beggars pulled at Artamos' rags, dragging his limp body over against the wall.

"I wonder what got into 'im," one of them asked.

"I dunno. But it's supposed to be day, ain't it?" replied a beggar in a pile of rags. The two peered out into the day that was as black as night. Their fire had died to smoldering embers.

They began to shiver. A wind howled over the walls and moaned across the hillside. In the distance they heard stones splintering.

## Puteoli, Italy, Friday, 5:00 pm, Nissan, 33 AD

Alexander paced back and forth in his library. Shadows hung long across the paneled walls. They curved up and over the face of Socrates and slithered down the back wall. Alexander had returned early. It was the Jewish Passover and many Jews in Rome were preparing for the ritual. This Jewish celebration always left huge gaps in the work force and a number of small businesses simply shut their doors for the day. Alexander was wringing his hands, rubbing his knuckles and popping them, an increasing habit of his.

The day had been strange; the skies had turned a dark green hue. They looked gloomy as though a rainstorm was brewing, but it never did. Static had charged the air. Spikes of lightning shot down on the northern hills but no drops of rain could be squeezed from the green-hued billows. The air smelled of sulfur and everyone seemed edgy and restless. There was an ominous sense of foreboding, but Alexander had no idea what caused it. He wondered if Emperor Tiberius was aware of these unnatural things.

Alexander had been anticipating time with his daughter, Charis. She was now almost three years old and seemed so bright and inquisitive. Her smile brightened his days. He knew right away that she had the determination of her mother. But when Alexander arrived home he found that little Charis was very ill. With a flushed face, her eyes rolled as though she were in a delirium. She was hot and lethargic. Those were not good signs. His new servant, Abigail, had not been successful in cooling her body down and Alexander was out of his mind wondering what to do. He was angry that the servant girl had not taken better care of her.

"How long has she been this way?" His face reddened in anger.

"Since early this morning, master." She moved one step back.

"Have you put her in a bath of cold water?"

"I did early this morning, master. After that, I kept applying cold water to her forehead."

"That's not enough, you idiot. She could die! Get her into a bath now . . . NOW!" the soldier thundered as he kept pacing. "She could burn up with fever. She could go into convulsions and die." He walked out of the room. *If only Anna were here. She would know how to make her daughter better. Or Lucia. She would have known what to do.* He remembered Lucia's servant, Deborah. She always soothed Lucia when she was burning hot with fever. Then the memory came back.

A sudden burst of anger flashed in his eyes as he remembered Deborah taking Lucia up to the rooftop only to let her die. He smashed his fist into the mahogany door in front of him. The only damage was to his fist. "Deborah's god failed. And Anna's messiah failed, too." He cursed. "Those stubborn Jews and their invisible god." He shook his fist at the ceiling.

Alexander slammed the library doors and walked out past Zeus onto the balcony. The skies continued with a strange light show, lightning striking shadows and shapes behind dense green clouds. Suddenly thunder rolled and shook the ground so hard that it vibrated Alexander's teeth. In the house he heard little Charis scream. Frantically, he rushed toward her cry with no idea what to do.

"Someone in Heaven, listen to me!" he shouted. "Whoever has power over the life of my child, please, I beg you, please save her. I cannot bear to lose another woman in my life. I will follow you, whoever you are, if you but heal my daughter. Please don't let her die."

Hours passed. He didn't know if anyone heard him or not. Alexander sat beside his daughter until his eyelids drooped from exhaustion. The soldier slept fitfully, dreaming of the women he had loved. Lucia's face looked at him with her granite smile. Anna's face lay frozen like ice. Charis' face was swollen red with heat. He woke often, hearing Charis whimper.

While Alexander slept, Abigail bathed Charis in cool water every hour throughout the long night. By dawn, her fever broke and Alexander was relieved. He was grateful, but he wasn't sure whom or what really made the difference. He wondered if the gods had listened or if the water had cooled her body and reduced her fever. He dismissed the servant to her chambers. He forgot his promise, although Someone had listened.

Adam arrived at the city alone. He strode down a little crooked street where shops were close together on either side. Laundry hung over a window ledge and flapped silently in the breeze. A few potted plants sat precariously atop another ledge. He stopped at a corner, his eyes searching the doors and windows. Nothing was open. No one was stirring. He hesitated momentarily then turned down another street. Here, the street dipped down a slight incline. The cobbled road curved and twisted like the rough surface of an ancient lizard's back. The houses were a patchwork of crooked walls all in different shades of beige. Doors were rough-hewn planks with iron latches. Adam peered into the shadows. Where was he to go?

All seemed dark and asleep. But somewhere in the shadows a tiny light flickered from a window. He moved toward it. The coarse woven curtain had been pulled back slightly, with a flame coming from a clay oil lamp that sat just inside the window.

Adam stood at the front stoop of the house, then hesitated. No noise, just silence everywhere. He heard a dog bark in the distance. He looked in both directions. No other resurrected witnesses had followed. He was alone except for a tabby cat that padded silently toward him then stood waiting at the same door.

He put his hand up to knock when suddenly he felt a bit self-conscious. Looking down at himself, he remembered he was naked. Could he stand at the door of a stranger's house, buck-naked and ask to come in? What on earth was he thinking? The tabby wove between his ankles, her tail curling around his legs.

In his moment of hesitation, the door creaked open and the tabby slid through in a flash. Eyes peered through the opening. Adam suddenly remembered the infant burial cloth in his hand. He quickly put it in front of him, but it didn't cover much. The eyes looked him up and down then the door closed. Adam's face flushed. He glanced in every direction, wondering if the whole neighborhood was watching. Everything was dark. An owl hooted.

Within a moment the door creaked open again. This time a wrinkled hand stretched out holding a blanket.

"Here son. Wrap this around yourself and come in. But be quiet, everyone thinks it's night." Adam pulled the woolen blanket around his shoulders. Its texture prickled against his baby soft skin. He stepped inside.

The small room was dark and low, with walls dingy from the constant burning oil lamp in the center of the room and the cooking pot. The tabby had jumped up on a bed and curled up, apparently at home. Adam's host was a tiny shriveled woman dressed in black. She had silvery gray hair, and had obviously been waiting. Her shoulders bent low. She strained her neck to look up at Adam's face. When she did, her eyes met him with uncomplicated acceptance.

"I see you've already met Peaches." She nodded toward the tabby cat.

"Not formally. Hello, Peaches!" Peaches' attitude toward this naked stranger seemed even more accepting.

For a moment, Adam stood awkwardly in the center of the room, unsure of what to do. His head came close to the ceiling. Sora busied herself rearranging some furniture.

"I shoulda' known. I shoulda' known." As she tugged and pulled and fluffed and patted, she kept saying, "I shoulda' known." Finally, she stopped and looked up at Adam.

"The Lord told me you was comin' tonight. I've prepared a room for you here." She pointed to the corner where a small bed was tucked away. It appeared to be Peaches' bed, too.

"It's the best I can do, I'm afraid." The bed itself was a wooden frame with webbing that held a mattress stuffed with straw. She continued talking without a break. "He just didn't tell me you were so tall. I shoulda' known. They make 'em bigger these days." Her eyes twinkled.

"I've got some clothes here for ya." On a table sat a pile of folded colorless clothes. "They were my husband's and he, bless him, was much shorter than you."

Adam chuckled out-loud then thanked her for her kindness. He was grateful for anything. The last thing he was concerned about was his looks. He grinned at the old woman and gratefully accepted the clothes.

"Thank you for your kindness."

"Kindness? You call this kindness? Not on your nelly. The Lord had to push and prod me until I finally gave in." She sighed wearily. "He didn't give me the details, and he sure didn't tell me you'd come in your birthday suit, but never mind. I've had lads of my own, so I'm familiar with your plumbin'. Nothin's a surprise ya know for an old woman like me." She winked. "I've seen everything."

Adam blushed pink. "Still, it's a kind gesture to me. Thanks for listening to the Lord."

The woman seemed preoccupied. She had already started another task. She took some bread from a cupboard and put it on the table. Adam slipped into the shadows of his bedroom corner and put the clothes on. He pulled a long tunic over his head that hung down to his knees. He had also been given a sleeveless robe that hung only two inches longer than the shirt. His long gangly legs were hairless and white in contrast to his muted clothes. Peaches seemed unconcerned. The woman had also offered a couple pair of sandals.

"What's wrong? You don't like the sandals?"

"Nothing's wrong. I guess my feet are bigger than your husband's." He smiled big.

"Whose mistake, mine or the Almighty's?"

"Neither. He lets me run barefoot in Heaven all the time. Shoes are optional."

Sora smiled exposing a missing tooth. Adam grinned in response. They both began to laugh until tears ran down Sora's face.

"I had five lads. But they're all gone now." She checked over his clothing and smoothed out some creases in his shirt.

"You're well suited to the task of mothering."

"Just don't get too comfy here, pet. My income is limited and you're a big lad. It will take a lot to feed you. Besides, I think you gotta lot of work to do during your visit. Where'd you come from?"

Adam noticed the warmth in her eyes. "Paradise."

"Then why did you choose to come to a dirty place like this?"

Adam liked this old woman. She sat down in a wood-framed chair and waited for an answer.

"May I call you "mother?""

"Not so fast, pet. We've only just gotten acquainted."

"You're right . . . auntie. Too soon." He was tempted to give her a hug, but he resisted. "I didn't choose to come. I was sent."

Democritus found his way toward the outskirts of the city. He headed directly to the northern gate. Only minutes after awakening from his tomb, he had recalled the layout of the countryside. He knew there were safe places to hide just outside the city walls. Of course, most of his life had been spent in caves and tombs in Geresa, but at times he had escaped from his captors and ventured toward Yerushalayim, curious about city life. He knew the countryside like the back of his hand. Each vein and crease in the ground had led him to a secure hiding place where he was safe from his tormentors at least for a little while. But they always found him. They hunted him down like an animal, chained him and led him back to his cave in the earth.

Democritus was not used to the company of many people. He preferred solitude. It was not until Yeshua entered his life that he realized what he had missed. The comfort and joy that came from being in his presence was an experience he could not put into words. Yeshua's companionship was like sunlight on his face. He hadn't wanted him to leave.

Before he met Yeshua, Democritus had learned to mistrust people. His only companions were the voices inside his head, dark, troubling voices. Because of this and the fear others had of him, he lived in solitude for most of his adult life.

Democritus knew that this time it would be different. He understood that the intimate relationship he had with the Messiah would now transform whatever relationships he would have in the future. He was a witness, a spectator to the power of resurrection. Everything about him was transformed through Yeshua's power. He shook his head. He couldn't get over the drastic change—from a demented crazy man to a mighty soldier of Yeshua. His short experience in Heaven had offered so much joy in fellowship with others that he could never be content to isolate himself . . . forever. That was hell, the place of absolute aloneness. Hell was the absence of significant relationships. During this in-between time, however, Democritus needed *some* solitude. He needed to pray and prepare. He would soon be in the midst of a war unparalleled by any war he'd ever faced. He would be surrounded by people—everywhere.

Galilee was about sixty miles from Yerushalayim and the roads would be treacherous. There would be thieves along the way. Some of the road was mountainous and his journey would take about six days.

The warrior walked slowly down the steep hillside. The ground was rocky like scabs on the barren landscape. Democritus followed the path carefully. The rain had ceased and allowed the moon to offer some illumination across the hillside.

*Guide my feet on this journey, Yahweh. May I not be quick to take action. Give me wisdom to show grace where grace is needed and courage when I'm weak. "Contend, Lord, with those who contend with me. Fight against those who fight against me. Take up shield and buckler; arise and come to my aid. Brandish spear and javelin against those who pursue me. Say to my soul, 'I am your salvation.' "*[47]

He prayed silently as he searched for a recess in the hillside. In the distance, he heard the lone jangle of a sheep's bell and knew that a shepherd was out there somewhere tending his sheep.

*Lord, be ever present with me during this journey. I fear nothing except disappointing you. This earthly body is so prone to failure. Help me make wise choices. Help me never to forget your face.* A surge of warmth went through him as he contemplated the face of Yeshua.

Democritus knew he was to travel to Galilee. If he kept a steady pace he could make it in six days or less. The most logical plan would be to follow the Jordan River straight down to Galilee. He knew he would pass very close to Pella where the Lord had sent him before. He had failed in his mission there, but this time would be different. His heart still longed to go back and finish what he had started, this time with the power of the Holy Spirit. First, however, he must head to Galilee where others would be gathering to see the resurrected Yeshua.

---

[47] Ps. 35:1-3

## Chapter Twenty-Three

# YERUSHALAYIM, SUNDAY, NISSAN 5, 33 AD

The Sabbath was over. Early before dawn, Mary of Magdalene along with Mary the wife of Clopas, another disciple of Yeshua, headed toward the tomb. They spoke little as they walked. The hasty pre-Sabbath burial had not given Mary of Magdalene a moment to grieve for her Master. She had focused her attention on comforting Yeshua's mother. Now before daybreak she would find solace in being near his tomb. She'd held back her emotions for the sake of his mother. Now she could grieve. And pray. Prayer was all she had left. In her hands she held a cloth sack of spices she'd prepared. This was her meager offering of devotion. Her debt to Yeshua overpowered anything she could ever do to thank him. Clopas' wife walked with her, silent and forlorn. Her gift was her tears.

The women looked with caution into the darkness trying to see their way. Mary's future looked as black as this night. The ominous sense of death was present. But somewhere there was a sweet floral scent. It seemed to permeate the garden. The fragrance so startled her that Mary paused. It reminded her of the perfume she had lavished on Yeshua that day.

She remembered the words of Iscariot. *What a waste. It should have been sold and given to the poor*. But it was Yeshua's rebuke that brought her to this moment. "The poor you will always have with you, me you will not." Now he was gone, just as he said.

Mary remembered Yeshua's words. This seemed the right thing to do. She did it out of the joy she'd found in this new freedom. He accepted her gift.

*"Leave her alone . . . She has done a beautiful thing to me . . . She poured perfume on my body beforehand to prepare for my burial."*[48] She stood still as a thought pierced her mind. *He knew he was going to be killed! He knew all along!*

"He knew. Yeshua knew all that would happen, and he didn't run away," Mary called as she rushed ahead of her friend, pushing faster through the darkened branches toward the tomb. There was so much she didn't understand. Mist filtered through the trees, spiraling low to the ground. She wondered what would happen now. The women rushed toward the entrance of the tomb.

As they arrived a temblor shook the ground. Mary gasped. *What is happening?* A rolling wave of earth rose up against her feet and made her stumble. Dawn filtered in between the branches, gray, cold and chilling.

The Dead Sea ruptured once again, tectonic plates shifted, stirring water and brine into murky soup so violent it seethed. Temblors roared up toward the hill of Golgotha. Its force arced in all directions as it rippled through the earth. Tendrils of energy bolted across the Kidron Valley, at the same time throbbing through the city streets leaving further devastation.

The women arrived at the clearing and stopped short. Mary was staggered to find a guard of soldiers stationed at the tomb. Her hope for solace instantly unraveled. The tomb was not as they had left it either. Roman authorities had placed a wax seal

---

[48] Mark 14:6-8

across the entrance. If anyone tried to open the tomb, the wax imprint of an official Roman signet would be broken and the world would know the body had been stolen. The Pharisees along with Pilate had obviously taken Yeshua's words seriously.

Mary's emotions plunged into despair. She still held the bag of spices in her hand and had come to grieve. She felt robbed of everything. Before she had time to react, another temblor plunged the earth into turmoil. Both women staggered while the guards struggled to stand erect.

While the earth kept rolling, a brilliant funnel of light descended from the sky. Sparks of lightning shot out as it drew near the ground. Within the dazzling light there was an appearance of a magnificent being. This angelic presence was so encompassing it left nothing untouched. The imperial seal melted away, and the huge stone began to pivot and wobble like a coin on edge. It rotated in a wide arc until it finally slammed against the earth and cracked.

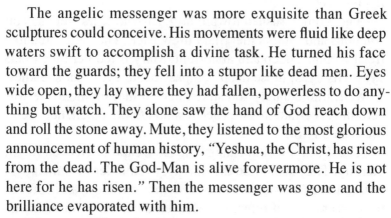

The angelic messenger was more exquisite than Greek sculptures could conceive. His movements were fluid like deep waters swift to accomplish a divine task. He turned his face toward the guards; they fell into a stupor like dead men. Eyes wide open, they lay where they had fallen, powerless to do anything but watch. They alone saw the hand of God reach down and roll the stone away. Mute, they listened to the most glorious announcement of human history, "Yeshua, the Christ, has risen from the dead. The God-Man is alive forevermore. He is not here for he has risen." Then the messenger was gone and the brilliance evaporated with him.

Imperceptible to human ears, a song arose across the landscape. The sound of a sweet melody began to swell with ever-increasing harmonies, complex and majestic. It was coming from the very rocks and stones surrounding the empty tomb.[49] The beautiful strains swelled into a great symphony of adoration which filled the hillside with song. A soft breeze swept through the trees causing leaves to flutter and clap their hands. The earth was giving praise to the risen Messiah.

Unable to move, the soldiers witnessed the faces of emotion the women experienced; instant confusion at the spectral visit, wonderment at his words, and uncertainty as they tried to grasp the message. The earth lay again in silent shadows as morning's dawn swept in. Mist swirled around their feet as the two women stood in bewilderment.

"What do we do now? Where do we go to find him? Who will believe *us*, unless we see him alive?" The two women stared at each other knowing what the other had seen. The guards were still paralyzed in chains of fear, their eyes focused straight ahead.

"Mary!" Yeshua stepped out from the recesses of the garden. He wore a simple white robe that touched his heels. The profile of his face was graced with peace, yet his hands and feet bore the jagged scars of humanity's rage. "Mary, don't be afraid. It's me, Yeshua."

The women rushed toward him. But the scars were so conspicuous and violent that Mary drew back. They appeared like fresh wounds, deep and abhorrent. Mary lifted her face to his eyes. His eyes, those deep compassionate eyes that she knew so well, immediately transfixed her. In that moment she was certain . . . certain this was her *Yeshua HaMashiach,* her friend, Messiah Savior.

These scars would change the landscape of Heaven for all eternity. They would be the one ugly reminder of humanity's fall and the Messiah's gift of redemption. Now and forever, these scars would remain in Heaven as an emblem of his triumph over death. Like the cross, his arms would be forever

---

[49] Lu. 19:40 "I tell you . . . if they keep quiet, the stones will cry out."

open wide drawing people into his embrace. The cross and scars were now an eternal part of Yeshua.

The God-Man turned his head toward the motionless guards. His eyes probed their souls. Their hearts were already stolen by their leaders. They would hide the truth of the resurrection with a bribe. No matter what they witnessed today they had already chosen denial. The father of lies had offered a pathetic price for the truth they alone had witnessed. Yeshua left them alone in their stupor and walked toward those who were seeking him.

"Yeshua, Master." The women fell at his feet in worship. The exotic fragrance of nard swelled into Mary Magdalene's senses and she remembered.

The first rays of morning burst over the landscape like the lamp of God lighting the way for the whole world to see. The women gazed upon his majestic splendor in speechless worship.

"Go tell my brothers to meet me in Galilee."

## Chapter Twenty-Four

# YERUSHALAYIM, UPPER CITY, 33 A.D.

Anna woke with a start at the sound of her own scream. Tears streamed down her cheeks. She had been thrashing in her bed when she awoke. "Where is she? Where's my baby? What have you done to her?" she cried out. Her dream broke through into the earthly night making her confused and shaking. A cold sweat rolled over her. She sat up and touched her face, surprised that she was crying. She had only been back on earth a mere couple of hours and already she was feeling pain, fear, danger and now tears.

"Ohhh," she sighed, putting her head in her hands. *This world is so sad. There is so much pain to deal with.* She had no need to dream in Heaven. Her mind did not need to create anything unreal to medicate her from reality. In Heaven, reality was so pure, so perfect. She needed nothing to refresh her thoughts, not even sleep. Heaven was more than she could have ever dreamed.

Now here on earth again, Anna knew that her return meant facing human suffering a second time. She also sensed another presence near her. It was the sinister presence of evil, barred from Heaven, but free to roam about the earth. Already she realized that evil could crowd her nights with dreams and push into her mind in waking moments. She couldn't control it, but she could control her responses.

Anna got up and wrapped a blanket around her shoulders. It was still dark. A single flame from a clay lamp flickered in the corner of the room. She glanced around her. The walls were paneled in rich wood tones. The aromatic smell of cedar soothed her senses. There were swags of deep-colored fabrics that hung from the ceiling and walls. The bed was hand-carved out of African hardwood, with bedding of deep purples and blues. Pillows of rich colors surrounded her on every side. A table stood nearby with a porcelain water jug and bowl, decorated with blue fluted patterns that twisted and curled.

Anna relaxed and let the tension of her dream drain from her mind. All of this was part of the human experience. She felt the cold and had no doubt she would experience physical pain. The enemy could not turn her heart to evil, but he could infiltrate other areas of her life. What about her relationships? What about the enemies of Yeshua? Her mission was to trust her Father no matter what. She might have to bear pain, rejection. She might have to face death again. But Yeshua would be with her and together they would declare the power of his resurrection.

There was a quiet knock at the door. "Please come in. I'm awake." Anna pulled the blanket around her as Priscilla opened the door and slipped inside. She smiled kindly at Anna.

"I heard you crying. Are you okay?" A furrow creased her brow. The woman's long tresses hung down. She wore a robe of blue that she had quickly wrapped around her. Her feet were bare.

"Yes, thank you. I had a frightening dream. It was about my little girl."

"Anna, I know nothing about you. I was told in a dream to wait for you at the city gate tonight. I saw your face in my dream. When you walked through, I recognized you and believed the dream was from God." She paused then pushed on. "It's been a terrible week-end. There's been an earthquake here in our city with many tremors, the skies have been black in the middle of the day and many strange things have happened. We're all afraid."

"I understand, Priscilla. I suppose our meeting was very strange when you saw a face from your dreams."

"Yes, but also comforting. As you might have guessed, I'm Roman. My husband is a centurion, appointed here three years ago." Priscilla moved across the room and sat beside Anna on the bed. "I've come to believe in the God of Abraham, the God of the Jews, the invisible God. In all my years searching through the confusion of the gods in Rome, I found no peace. Now I'm beginning to." She paused. "There was an appalling death on Friday. We have gruesome crucifixions here but this was far different." Priscilla's face paled and her voice lowered.

"Would you tell me about it?" Anna questioned.

"A man who has a following was seized a few days ago. He had done nothing wrong as far as the Roman law is concerned. Apparently the religious Jews had schemed to have him captured. I'd never met him, but those who had say he only did good. Supposedly he healed people young and old of incurable diseases; he even raised some from the dead." Priscilla's eyes were wide. "His teachings couldn't be faulted."

Anna had not heard the story from the earthly perspective. She only knew that Yeshua had gone through the torment of death on behalf of humanity. She could not see beyond the veil of what the Father had allowed her to comprehend. But she did know that Yeshua was alive. She knew that without doubt. She felt his presence very close although she had not yet seen him since her return.

"This is very important. Tell me more, Priscilla."

"My husband was witness to the entire crucifixion." She placed her hands over her face. When she lifted her head her eyes were wet. "He stood just a few feet away from the cross.

He could hear the words of the man who hung there. They were full of compassion. Phillip said he felt a heavy darkness all around him."

Priscilla stopped and looked directly at Anna. "You know what Phillip said about that night? He said that of all the bloody wars, slaughters and murders he's witnessed, he'd never felt such a heavy darkness until that day. He actually felt the presence of evil." Priscilla finally looked up at the ceiling. "My husband was a tough soldier. He thought he'd seen everything." She looked into Anna's eyes.

"Something happened that day that changed him."

"Your husband?" Anna questioned.

"Yes, Phillip. It was only three days ago, but he returned from that place a different man."

"How did he change?" Anna shifted and was sitting up straighter.

"His rage just evaporated. Rage gave him power as a soldier but it always frightened me. That's why he was good at his job. He could lash out at someone he didn't know. He could take his vengeance out on convicts for what he was struggling with inside. That's what he was doing that day, striking out at Yeshua because of his own rage. Something happened in his childhood that he's kept secret. It's tormented him in his dreams for years." Priscilla looked into Anna's eyes. "That's what made me rush in here so quickly. I'm used to my husband's dreams waking me in the night."

"Where is your husband now?"

"He's been arrested." Priscilla lowered her head. "It was reported to Pilate that he had failed his duties on watch that day." She wrung her hands. "He's also been charged with treason for surrendering his sword and becoming a follower of Yeshua. Even though he's dead."

"Oh Priscilla, Yeshua is alive. I know it. He's alive." Anna's eye's glistened with delight to tell the good news. "And perhaps they will drop the charges against your husband."

"How can this be? My husband saw him die, they prodded his body with a spear. He was dead. He couldn't have survived all the torture, the beating, the nails, the crown of thorns. My husband is used to such killings, but he couldn't look on him any longer. He saw them carry the body away to a tomb. He can't be alive."

"You would say the same about me, Priscilla. I too died, but here I am with you." Anna patted the side of the bed. "Here, come sit by me. I have a long story to tell you and it might take a while." Priscilla was hesitant but also curious. Finally, she scooted up against the headboard and sat next to Anna. Anna pulled the blanket around her shoulders and began to tell her story.

"I used to live in the lower end of Yerushalayim. Near the Serpent's Pool . . ."

---

The night drifted by as Anna's story unfolded. By dawn the oil had dried up in the clay lamp and the flame barely flickered. The sun touched the horizon and would soon blaze through the atmosphere like a streak of burnished gold. Birds woke and sang as the sun rose.

". . . and that's why I know he's alive. I've talked with him in prayer. Perhaps today he'll show up in the streets of Yerushalayim or down in Galilee. It's predicted by the ancient prophets."

Anna's fluid reciting of scripture rolled off her tongue in excitement. "Isaiah said, *'he was pierced for our transgressions, he was crushed for our iniquities; the punishment that brought us peace was upon him, and by his wounds we are healed . . . Yahweh has laid on him the iniquity of us all.'*" She studied Priscilla's eyes. *"After the suffering of his soul, he will see the light of life, and be satisfied; by his knowledge my righteous servant will justify many, and he will bear their iniquities."*[50]

Priscilla struggled to comprehend this story. "It seems too fantastic. I . . . I can't make sense of it . . . Yeshua's death . . . and you . . . and . . . no, Anna. I can't. This is too much for me to grasp."

Anna smiled. "That's okay, Priscilla. I know it's a lot to understand. God will help you. That's why I'm here. I'm living proof of the resurrection. There are many in Yerushalayim who knew me and knew of my death. The fact that I'm alive today is a testimony to Yeshua's resurrection. You'll see." Anna longed for Priscilla to understand and believe. Absentmindedly, she turned the gold ring around on her finger. "You'll see." But Priscilla's attention suddenly focused on the ring.

"Where did you get that ring, Anna?" Priscilla took Anna's hand and held it up to the morning light. She studied it closely and her face paled. "It has the image of Caesar on it. It's . . . his . . . royal seal." Her demeanor suddenly changed.

"It was on my finger when I arrived." Anna sensed a fear creep over Priscilla. Saw it in her face. Priscilla pulled away.

"What's wrong, Priscilla?"

"That's the royal seal of Caesar. No one has a seal like that unless they've been a part of Caesar's house or honored by Caesar. The seal belongs to him. Whoever has it is subject to Caesar and him alone."

Anna was confused over the ring's significance. It couldn't be that important. Caesar's face was on every coin in the land. Every drachma showed his face. But she knew the conversation was over; Satan had stolen the truth from Priscilla's heart. She had dismissed the incident by a wave of her hand and a smile.

"It can't mean much, Priscilla. I don't recognize it. If it bothers you I'll take it off." She slipped the ring off her finger and placed it on the side table. And that was the end of the

---

[50] Isa. 53, various excerpts

conversation. Priscilla stood and allowed her shocked expression to dissipate. She smiled and said, "Anna, I'm so glad you're here. Let's have some breakfast, then we'll go to the market. And I've got to find some clothes for you."

The sun streaked through the room in long shafts of morning light. They lit upon the royal blue pillows on the bed then glinted upon the gold ring. A warm breeze brushed Anna's face and she smiled.

"That sounds wonderful. I love shopping."

## Chapter Twenty-Five

# YERUSHALAYIM, UPPER CITY, 33 A.D.

The shriveled woman sat in the corner of the room waiting for her new guest to finish eating. The over-grown boy kept trying to speak with his mouth full.

"It wath a long time ago . . ."

"Okay. Enough. Eat and then talk. It's rude to talk with your mouth full."

Adam's grin was full of bread and cheese. He gulped down some goat's milk then stuffed another slab of bread in his mouth. The woman peered at him with incredulity.

"Listen, pet, I can tell that you're gonna cost me a bundle eatin' like that. I'll be out of food before mornin' if you don't slow down. And no one taught you any eatin' manners either. Got a lot of work ahead of us, don't we?" She shook her head in puzzlement then looked at Peaches who was preening herself like a princess.

Adam finally gulped the remainder of his food and milk, then burped loudly.

"Lord have mercy on you, laddie. My Peaches has better manners than you."

Adam looked a bit puzzled then said, "I guess I've grown up fast overnight. Sorry to be so offensive. Will you teach me how to behave?"

"Didn't your folks teach you anything?"

A memory flashed across Adam's face. Like a carver's knife, the image cut so deep it sliced at his heart. Adam blanched and his body began to shake. "I was only a baby when I was murdered. I never had much time to learn anything of this world."

Sora blinked in unbelief. "Say again? You was what?" She stood, spilling needles and twine on the floor. The tabby jumped off her lap and scurried across the room to hide underneath Adam's bed.

"Murdered. By Herod's soldiers."

Slowly he pulled loose the tie-string of his tunic and bared his chest. Sora moved closer, holding the lamp to examine his scarred skin. Adam's skin was as smooth as that of a baby. But between his upper ribs on his left side there was a red jagged scar almost like a bolt of lightning.

The woman's eyes blinked wide. "That can't be." She put her hand against the distorted flesh. Her face paled.

"Put your hand on my back, Sora." The woman hesitated, and finally touched his back. Beneath her fingers she felt the same uneven scar. She pulled her hand away quickly in numbing disbelief. Sora staggered for a moment then retreated to her chair.

"I don't . . . I don't understand what you're talkin' about, lad. It doesn't make any sense to me at all. How can you be murdered and sittin' here talkin' to me like this? If you'd been murdered, you'd be in a bone box dead as a door-nail." The old woman's mind couldn't fathom the reality of it all. She picked up her needles and twine, not accepting Adam's explanation . . . because she could not.

"Ok, now explain it plainly to me like I know nothing. I want it straight. No fooling this Sora. I can smell a lie a mile away. Now tell me what you're talkin' about and make it plain so this Sora can understand. And that Herod is long dead. He ain't goin' nowhere, 'cept where he belongs. And I ain't sayin' where that is."

Adam smiled patiently. Sora's bluster helped her deal with reality. Adam tried to focus. *Where do I begin? How do you explain a sunset to a blind man? Heaven to a mortal?* The passing from this life into the eternal and back again was beyond human words. It was beyond human understanding. Had anyone ever died and come back to tell about it? That was his job tonight, and he felt completely at a loss for words.

"Then you better relax," Adam said. "It's a long story."

"I ain't goin' nowhere. Now start explainin'." Peaches crept back out and sat listening with a distinctive intelligent stare. When she felt it was safe enough, she jumped up on Sora's lap and curled into a ball. Secure, she closed her eyes and purred.

"I was born in Beit Jala near Bethlehem during the reign of Herod the Great."

"Stop. That makes no sense at all. I told ya, he's long dead."

"Please just listen. You won't understand until I finish my story."

"I'm warning ya, you'll be out on your ear if ya waste my time tonight with nonsense." She paused. "Perhaps I'll get all my stitching out just in case. This little patch I'm working on won't do."

"Good idea," Adam said with a slight smile.

The old lady pulled out a basket with a folded wool blanket lying on top. Sifting through it, she found a ball of wool that rolled off the edge of the table. The cat's gaze watched it move across the floor. When it stopped, the feline jumped down, crouched low and hunched like a predator, eyes peering on the ball. Sora found the bone needle she was searching for and, as she grabbed it, yanked the ball of wool. Peaches attacked the ball with full force, skidding and crashing against the wall with the yarn clamped between her paws.

Adam let out a roar. Unfazed, Peaches looked at the man with questioning eyes then carried her oversized prize back across the room and crouched beneath the bed.

Adam began his story. The room was dark with only a tiny glow that rose from the lamp. Sora sat on a corner of her bed with twine and needle and began stitching a design on the blanket. Peaches clutched her possession under Adam's bed, purring as she kneaded the wool with her claws. Adam sat with his back against the wall.

With the streets silent, Adam's voice was soft as he began to tell the story from memory like all story tellers. Adam's story had never been told in the human world. It was his alone to tell.

"I remember my mother's face. She was crying. Her name was Rachel." Adam paused to comb his fingers through his hair. His words stumbled through his emotions. "I remember, she held me so tight it hurt. But she did it for a reason. She kept saying, 'Hush baby, I'm here.' She couldn't dare say what I wanted her to say. She couldn't say, 'It's going to be okay. I'll keep you safe,' because she knew she couldn't protect me from this evil man." Adam pulled his knees up to his chest and wrapped them with his arms. "I could smell her hair. It smelled like jasmine. Her eyes told me everything. Her tears were for me. I felt her strong love as she clutched me tightly. I kept staring up into her face."

Sora kept stitching, one stitch up, another down, up, down. Adam's words drifted softly on the night air. The walls moved closer to listen. The dim light focused on Adam's face, and the woman's breathing was light in anticipation of the rest of his story.

Adam's mind drifted further back. His voice was thick with emotion. "I remember my father, Ben-Asher, a big man. He was tall."

"With blond hair . . ." the woman finished.

"Yes, with blond hair . . . like me." Adam furrowed his brow in thought. "I remember my father praying over me, praying to the God of Israel."

*Shama Yisrael. Adonai eloheunu Adonai echad. Shalom.*

"My father had a solid faith. I could feel it in his arms when he held me. I could see it in his eyes and understand it in his smile." Something trickled down Adam's cheek. He reacted in surprise.

"What's this?" he said.

"Tears, love . We all have tears," Sora said.

"I'd forgotten how they felt. There are no tears in Heaven."

Without looking up Sora said, "What's troubling ya, pet?" She kept stitching a more elaborate design in the blanket. The template was hidden in her mind. The pattern was intricate with many colors woven through the piecework.

"My father tried to protect me. The man . . ." Adam trembled at this wave of emotions. He shuddered aloud. "All these emotions I've not felt since I was a baby. It's so strange to feel them once again . . . after seeing the face of God." He paused and took a deep breath. "My father believed I would bring blessing to the family. I was their only child. He used to pray for my future. He believed I would be a blessing to Jehovah God.

"My father, stood before the enemy. That mad soldier wanted to kill me. Who would kill a child? He slashed at my father with a bloody knife and cut his chest." Tears now streamed down his face without shame. "He tried to slash my father's throat." He paused to calm down. "I remember the blood. It was everywhere. It was all over his clothes. It splattered over me. I was afraid. Mother was screaming. I couldn't see the killer because my father's body was protecting me, but he was sagging, falling down. I felt my parents' fear and I could also feel the rage of the soldier.

"When I saw the killer's face, his eyes were so evil they scared me." Adam took deep breaths to calm his emotions. "I couldn't quit crying. The killer's face was in mine and I smelled his wretched breath . . . but his eyes were icy cold. The dagger in his hand was dripping with my father's blood. For only a second, a light flickered in his eyes and I wondered if he would change his mind." Emotion rose in Adam's throat and he stood to catch his breath. He had no idea he would get so emotional recounting the story.

"His eyes were filled with pure hatred. He raised the dagger and stabbed me, screaming out a curse as he did."

"Oh my poor child. The pain." Sora covered her face with both hands.

"The pain was there for only a couple seconds and then gone. So fast. I tried to scream but nothing came out. Then it was over." Adam leaned back against the wall. "The last thing I saw while breathing was the soldier's tortured face. Somehow I slipped from my skin and was lifted away from the evil. I saw my mother and father and a dead child tumbled in a corner. The soldier backed away.

"As I rose, all fear left. In spite of the tragic scene below, I felt joy, pure joy I'd never sensed before. The scene down below turned brown and colorless while before me was brilliance filled with unimaginable colors. The contrast was staggering. I still can't explain it. I had no sense of loss. Instead of loss, I felt *found*. I knew in that moment my brief life counted for something. I had been born to die." Adam repositioned himself. "I was created to be in God's embrace." He paused. "I wanted to stay there forever."

Sora had stopped stitching. Her hands went limp. She couldn't speak. Adam and Sora stared at each other in silence, one considering the possibility of life beyond the grave, the other comprehending the quantity of horror a human soul could carry.

"But . . . you're alive. You're here to tell the story. How . . . how . . . can . . . ." she stumbled through her words. "How can that be? It's impossible."

Adam smiled. "Nothing's impossible with God. Nothing."

"I don't understand. Please explain to me how you're here tonight."

Adam stretched his back and relaxed again.

"Being in God's arms is beyond human comprehension. I was held in God's presence. There's no evil, no fear, no malice, nothing can touch you." Adam contemplated his words.

"Untouchable from pain and sorrow." Sora spoke the words softly.

"Yes, it's what we all long for but never find here on earth. I was home."

"And where was this home?" Sora quizzed.

"I was in Paradise. I was at home with him, and wherever he is, is Paradise." Adam's face radiated. The curious woman stood. The room was awash with a glow in spite of the tiny quivering flame from the lamp. Waves of shimmering light splashed across the room. Sora walked closer and peered into Adam's eyes. A godly calm caught her gaze. She touched his cheek for a moment causing Adam to smile.

The woman finally sat down again and Peaches jumped on her lap.

Adam struggled to know how to continue. He had stared death in the face, felt it draw near and grab his heartbeat in its clutches. He'd also experienced the entrance into Paradise. No words in any language were adequate. Remembering back, it felt like life in slow motion, almost still images, until a jolt thrust him into a place where everything became clear, soothing and pure. It was God's embrace and it filled every human need he'd had or imagined.

Sora had never allowed her thoughts to wander into the stream of eternal wonder. Her sons had each died and all hope had withered on the vine. Now through Adam's eyes she had caught a glimpse of eternal bliss. Perhaps her sons had been ushered into Heaven's embrace. It would bring so much solace to believe they were there.

"My lads . . ."

". . . are safely home," Adam finished her thought.

A pool of tears filled the rims of her eyes then spilled down her cheeks in an unbroken motion. A dam of heartache had broken in her heart.

"You know?" she questioned.

Adam nodded with a confident smile. "I know of your pain, Sora. There's hope. All of your sons are content in the Father's presence. But let me tell you the rest of my story, then you'll understand where your sons are this moment." Adam waited for her response.

She nodded. "Please continue. I've been left with nothing but questions . . . so many questions. Keep goin.'"

"The peace we experience down here on earth is so thin, it's like a veil. Even for an infant, contentment is just a drop. At its best, earthly peace is always etched with pain. Our numbered days are unknown to us. We all face fears and heartache. My mother loved me so much, but in God's embrace I was complete. I wanted for nothing. His beautiful Presence was always in my vision. As far as I knew I was the focus of his undivided affection and he mine.

"In his Presence, I began to learn. There, I began to understand what life was all about. We talked as friend to friend. *Yeshua HaMashiach* explained the joy he took in creating my life. I grew in my understanding. I asked him questions about the beginning, the universe and how the Heavens were made. He told me the secrets of eternity, helped me understand the confines of time and space, allowed me to experience the limitless expanse of time without end . . . and his love." Adam's eyes glistened. "He let me see places beyond what the human mind can comprehend."

"So how did he make the universe?" Sora was in a daze.

Adam smiled. "That is for him alone to reveal in his time. These mysteries of God are too deep, too unfathomable for our human minds to grasp. Our words are too limited and, no matter what, we discover the ultimate secret is still with him to reveal."

Adam smiled and gave the woman a quick wink. "It's exciting to know there is more in store."

There was a hollow silence in the room. The flame of the lamp flickered. The two sat in silence and deep in thought. Finally, Sora breathed, releasing the room of its awestruck silence.

"What about my boys? They all died as babies." Sora asked with hesitation, "Are they still . . . babies?"

Adam spoke softly, "They are with the Father. They're perfect in every way. They're timeless." Adam smiled. "You've wept for years over the loss of your sons, but you've not wept alone. You remember Rachel, the grandmother of Ephraim and Manasseh who were banished from Judea? The prophet Jeremiah said she wept bitterly for them and could not be comforted."[51]

Adam leaned close and patted Sora's shoulder. "It might seem like you gave birth to sons in vain, because they died before they were grown. You must feel deprived of the satisfaction of seeing them grow up and prosper. That's the joy parents gain from the pain of bringing them into the world and caring for such helpless babies."

"Yes, I do feel cheated. They died at birth. They never had a chance to live this life." Sora paused in thought. "And I never had the joy of watching them grow, marry and give me grandchildren."

"But Rachel was consoled with the promise that her children were not lost forever. They would be brought back to Judea." Adam watched her eyes. "Sora, your hope is found in the reality that your sons are home in the Father's presence waiting for you."

Adam lifted his head and smiled at the withered woman. "Something happened in Heaven, the greatest event since the dawn of time."

---

[51] Je.31:15-25

"Please tell me. What happened?" Sora's eyes widened.

"In God's presence, all is timeless as he is. But in earth time, something most extraordinary happened that broke sin's power over our human condition."

"Spit it out lad. What happened?"

"The Messiah, Yeshua, announced his work on earth was finished. I heard the echo as Yeshua declared, 'IT IS FINISHED.'"

"What's finished?" Sora asked. Her mind was caught in a whirlwind.

"God's sacrifice." Adam closed his eyes to shut out the dimness of this world that cluttered his vision. He recalled Heaven's announcement that forgiveness had been proclaimed through the cross. Yeshua's life changed everything. He did just what he said, he came to set the captives free. His death alone opened the gates of Heaven for those who had waited by faith.

"It happened here in Yerushalayim only this week." Adam hoped the old woman understood. "Before today, all who died in faith entered Paradise where we waited for God's work to be completed. When Yeshua spoke those words, 'It . . . is . . . finished,' Paradise was filled with those who were living by faith when they died."

"You actually saw people you knew in Heaven?" She stitched a crimson thread through the blanket.

"Heaven is filled with knowledge so there's no having to guess who people are. And everyone is in the prime of life, full of beauty, rich in character, forever whole," Adam mused. "I think the differences are shown by how others bestow certain significance upon individuals. I recognized Daniel by his faith which seemed to embody him. I saw David in his royalty, together with his son, the son he never knew. So one day you, too, will walk with your sons."

Sora finally understood. "I've missed them so. Death seems so final. Now I understand." The old woman was suddenly released and weeping with joy.

Adam got up and walked over to the woman's bed. He sat down and put his arms around her. She seemed so small and frail. For a moment, a son longing to embrace a mother and a mother longing for the comfort of a son remained intertwined in silence. Adam whispered in her ear, "Your sons are waiting for you."

The night passed with images that sent the human mind spiraling in an explosion of wonder. Soon, morning weaved its threads of gold into the tiny room. Pale hues of dawn, orange and pink, plaited through the loom of the tiny window and tied a knot with the lamp's flickering flame.

Adam had comforted Sora whose greatest enemy had been grief. She began to let the skein of disappointment slip through her fingers. She discovered that all along God's plans had far exceeded any hopes or dreams she might have had for her children.

The woman snuffed out the spindly flame and pulled back the curtain, letting in the freshness of the morning. Peaches meowed at the door as the woman moved toward a cupboard.

"Out you go, Peaches." The cat was gone in a flash. The woman lifted a bowl of cold porridge from a cupboard and brought it near the embers. She stirred the fire and threw on some fresh coals. Soon the savory smells of hot porridge and warm goat's milk filled the room. Adam was ready to indulge again. The sense of *family* that had long ago been extinguished now began to warm the room. Sora hummed as she busied herself with breakfast. A fresh hope stirred away the sluggish lump in her soul . . . and she smiled.

"So, pet, what's your plan?"

"Breakfast, of course." He watched as the old woman poured steaming porridge into two clay bowls, then sprinkled dark brown sugar and golden currants on top. Her fingers were nimble. She dipped her hand into a clay jar, lifted a bunch of walnuts, then dropped them on top. Then she slid a bowl across the table toward him.

Adam seated himself on a three-legged stool and pulled himself closer to the table. Before a moment had passed, he whispered a prayer then smiled. Then they ate in contentment with the room growing silent. Adam thought about his future. It wasn't very clear. He knew he must search for his parents. *I have very little to prove I'm Adam. I have the infant grave clothes. But how would they believe such a tale? I guess I have to leave that in the Lord's hands. Only by grace could they receive the news.* Adam had looked at the tattered shroud. It had been made by his mother and his name was stitched in the corner. *She might think I stole it. She might think I'm a crazy man.* Of course, his return to an earthly shell was beyond any dream he could grasp. Heaven was contentment. He'd forgotten all the pain and suffering this world carried. His memories bore no pain or sorrow, until he stepped from the remains of the shattered bone box. *I must find my murderer, too.*

"A penny for your thoughts, pet." The woman smiled exposing her gap and grin.

"Mmmm. This food is wonderful."

"Come on lad, you were thinking about something deeper than gruel. Out with it."

"My mother . . . I was thinking about her. I can't fool you in the least, can I?" He laughed. "I was thinking about finding my parents. They must feel as you have . . . losing their only son. It has been so long. Seeing me would shock them slightly."

"No doubt," Sora said. "I'd say more than slightly."

"I have to believe that God has prepared them for my return. I hope they'll believe I'm their Adam." He pulled out the shroud. "See this? My mother stitched this for me when I was two years old. These initials in the corner are hers and here's my family name. *Adam, son of Ben-Asher.*"

The woman held the garment up to the warm sunlight. Then she took the blanket she had been working on throughout the night. She looked closely at her own stitching, then back at the infant shroud.

"I'd spot my shabby work anywhere. No doubt. If your mother stitched this, she was a fine seamstress, very fine." She looked thoughtful then said with slight hesitation, "Perhaps they have died."

Adam smiled. "I would have known," he said without the slightest pause. "My parents were waiting for the Messiah. They believed the ancient scriptures. I'm sure we'll meet them very soon."

The old woman shook her head in wonderment. She was amazed at his faith, simple yet profound. "You're such a bonnie lad, I'm so glad you came to my house."

"It was planned, long before I saw your lamp in the window." *I just need to figure what I'm supposed to be doing while I'm back here on earth,* he mused.

## Chapter Twenty-Six

# EAST YERUSHALAYIM, 33 A.D.

Democritus crawled out from the rocky crevice just beyond Yerushalayim's ancient walls. His body was stiff and it reminded him of the burden of pain in this human shell. He knew to accept hardship as a tool under the weight of the sculpture's chisel, but he knew little about his mission, only that he would do battle. He must ready himself for war. He must be his own trainer. Like a sparring gladiator, the warrior had drawn into solitude, exposing his human body to the harsh reality of earth's meanness. He would let self-deprivation harden his resolve through days of prayer and fasting. He stretched long then groaned.

Democritus' one earthly comfort was Yeshua's robe. It was stained and torn, and it no longer bore the purity it once had, graced upon the shoulders of Yeshua. But it reminded him of the man he once was and who redeemed him. His own blood had left stains now dark and coppery, a tapestry of battlefields. It reminded him of his own vain efforts to fight against spiritual powers. Within the tomb, mold had claimed a corner of the robe. This, too, reminded him of human frailty.

The warrior was cold, ferociously hungry and uncertain of tomorrow. But his heart told him something different. He had no direct instructions as to what he should do or where he should begin this passage of faith. That was why he needed to prepare for battle. His weapons were truth, faith, salvation; such things that required fortification. He knew that if he indulged in comfort, he would not be ready for what lay ahead. He well remembered the torment of demons. He had lived in their lair for nearly a lifetime.

Democritus needed water and nourishment. He headed toward a stream that ran into the Jordan during the spring. In summer it was a dry river bed, but this time of year it was a rushing stream. It was cold, swift and dangerous as the stony earth guzzled and gulped the surging waters from the melting snowy peaks of Mt. Nebo.

The journey down to the river took several hours. As he walked, he found a hedge of wild berries. He gathered figs that had fallen along the path. He passed an apple orchard and found fruit on the ground. When Democritus arrived at the river he knelt and splashed water on his face, then scooped up handfuls and drank. He stood and surveyed the mountain peak and the stream's origin. Melting snow still glistened its higher elevation.

Now alert, Democritus removed his robe, braced himself and waded in. It was ice cold. He waded in deeper to his waist then staggered, almost losing his balance. He spread his legs to steady himself. With one gulp of air he plunged beneath the surface and let the frigid water bury him. His body temperature plummeted, every nerve screaming out for relief. The rapids sucked him down then forward with the current. He let his body flow with the stream. He stayed submerged one minute, then two. His lungs screamed, needing air; he remained below. His limbs felt heavy, numb, aching for relief. Democritus released some air. His body drifted deeper, his chest scraping against the rocky floor, then he was shoved hard against a boulder. He could see a crimson stream escape from his broken skin where the boulder had cut his shoulder.

Democritus' muscles tightened due to the icy tempera-tures. As seconds passed, the soldier's body rebelled against the numbing pain, the pressure, the need to surface. Finally, when his instinct was to gasp, Democritus let his body rise to the surface.[52] He planted his feet onto the pebbly floor and pulled his head out of the water. He gasped and sputtered until he could inhale pure air. His body shook, his teeth chattered but he felt invigorated. He grabbed hold of an overhanging branch and scrambled onto the banks. He had a clearer perspective of why he was back here on earth.

"Lord, I am your warrior. Yours alone. I've seen your Magnificent Glory and nothing on this dusty earth scares me anymore. I have felt your Mighty Power and nothing compares. No force on earth, no armies, or demons, not even the Prince of the Power of the Air can turn this heart of mine from fighting for you and your kingdom. I am yours alone." Democritus had knelt on the stony shore. His body still wet and dripping, his knees cut and bleeding.

*I now understand the power of your Kingdom; I've lived in the presence of your Greatness.* Realizing he had drifted far down stream with the current, he walked back to where he had laid the robe. He reached down, picked it up and slipped it over his shoulders. *I now understand the price you've paid with your own blood. How can I do any less.*

Yeshua's robe was just a robe, but it bore the reminder of his Master's grace and courage. *I will fight every battle wearing your armor, living in the light of your countenance.* The sol-dier found a sturdy branch that he pruned using sharp stones to shape and fashion a staff. He then headed back downstream, moving toward the Sea of Galilee, hoping he would find the Messiah on its shores. It was there that Yeshua had called some to follow and many others to fish the depths of the human soul.

---

[52] wonderopolis.org/wonder/how-long-can-you-hold-your-breath-underwater

It seemed the most natural place to find the resurrected Messiah. Democritus began to run.

Priscilla smiled as she led Anna into the busy market stalls of Yerushalayim. Smells of hot bread and pastries wafted on the air. She bought some onions, a plucked chicken, three ripe tomatoes and a handful of spices. The warm smell of flatbread led her senses to a walking vendor. She bought enough for Anna and herself and some for tomorrow. Anna was relieved to see townspeople returning to normal once again.

Anna glided along the streets enjoying the bustle of sellers and buyers, haggling vendors and spendthrift shoppers. Back in this human shell, Anna felt a sense of her childhood desires return to her thoughts once again. Motherless, she'd often watched longingly as other children laughed and played in the streets under the gaze of adoring mothers. But Heaven had eased all longings as the Divine Presence became more than mother or father could ever be. He was her single contentment. She longed for nothing; needed nothing. Now back in this earthly body, salt had been rubbed into the wounds of human need. Mortal life offered mere ashes, sad memories, unfulfilled dreams.

Anna wondered how she was to live out this new life in her resurrected body. Then she thought of Charis, her precious daughter, and her heart leaped with excitement. She was sure that somewhere she would find her, maybe on a street in this neighborhood. All this passed through Anna's thoughts as Priscilla purchased a basketful of vegetables and returned to her side. Anna slipped her arm through Priscilla's and smiled in contentment at her new friend.

Within the first hour strangers had looked at Anna with a wary expression. She did not seem too concerned and even spoke to a few women, but they scurried away quickly, fear on their faces.

Anna mused aloud, "I recognize so many townspeople here. I imagine many must have heard of my death and were glad. I suppose seeing me is like seeing a ghost. I've been dead for two years." She smiled and looked at Priscilla. "It does sound strange, doesn't it?"

Priscilla was speechless, her complexion turning a shade paler. With a weak smile she pulled Anna along the row of stalls, ignoring her comment.

"Look over there at that stall. That merchant is supposed to have the finest silks and cotton from Egypt." Priscilla took Anna's hand and tugged her toward the stall where the cocky merchant was giving his sales pitch to a woman with stories from the East.

Anna said, "Oh yes, I remember him. You'd think that after so many years using the same stories people would be wiser." The merchant had convinced the woman to part with some of her money. Priscilla seemed unaware of Anna's connection with the merchant and she was eager to see what he offered today.

Priscilla pulled Anna closer to the stall. "I get most of my silks and linen from this man." Priscilla moved in beneath the man's canopy, away from the glaring sun. Hot air blew in dusty gusts toward their faces. Flies buzzed in rotating circles over the man's oily black hair.

Priscilla rummaged through the bolts of material. Green linen, purple silk, shimmering silver material from distant lands beckoned her. "You would look good in green, Anna. It would be striking against your lovely hair and soft complexion," she suggested.

The merchant finished counting his coins then stuffed them in his apron. He turned toward the women's voices. As his lips parted with his rehearsed sales pitch, he suddenly caught sight of Anna's face. He paled in shock and his mouth dropped.

Priscilla looked at him, then at Anna, then back at the merchant again. She saw recognition and confusion in the man's gaze.

A flood of memories reminded Anna of how deep the hatred was toward her in her past. She remembered the man's taunts and ugly hatred, but today her emotions held no fear or shame. Instead she gave him a forgiving smile. He stared, paralyzed and speechless. Anna suddenly realized that this shopping trip was more than finding clothes to wear. She was facing old enemies and forgiveness needed to be dispensed. Yeshua's sacrifice was for this man as well.

In a whisper she replied, "Priscilla, God's given me an opportunity to forgive this man." Then speaking aloud, "I love that color. I've always been fond of this shade of green." Turning back to the merchant. "How much will five lengths of this material cost?" The man's hand shook. "Sir, can you tell me . . ." The man continued to tremble wordlessly. Finally, he found his tongue.

"Take it. Just go, get out of here." Sweat dripped from his brow.

Anna smiled. "Thank you, sir, for your kindness."

"It's no kindness to give something to a witch. Just take whatever you want and leave. Don't ever come back. Go!"

Anna had to think quickly. She wanted to show forgiveness to this man while showing godliness toward Priscilla. If she had money of her own, she would have insisted on paying, but this was from Priscilla's purse. Priscilla seemed puzzled. Holding the green material in her arms, Anna leaned toward the trembling merchant and whispered, "I've been forgiven by Yeshua. I forgive you, too, for your judgment upon me." She turned to find Priscilla. But Priscilla was gone.

"Priscilla?" Anna saw the hem of her cloak as she darted around a corner. Anna rushed to catch up with her. From the direction she was going, Priscilla was heading home. One street away from the centurion's house, Anna found Priscilla huddled in a corner crying. Anna rushed to her.

"Priscilla. What's wrong? Are you all right? Have I done something wrong?"

The Roman woman looked up at the sound of Anna's voice. She wiped a sleeve across her wet face. A look of fear was masked by a trembling smile. "I'm sorry, Anna. I'm so confused. I'm ashamed that I left you there alone. Please forgive me."

"Priscilla, you have nothing for which to apologize. It must be confusing to have a stranger come to your home like I have . . . and back from the dead." Again the words made Priscilla shudder.

"Please, Anna. I'd rather not talk about it now. I just don't understand and my emotions are so confused. Let's go home and have a cup of tea. Then I can think more clearly. With my husband imprisoned, I can hardly focus on anything."

Anna slipped her arm around Priscilla's waist to comfort her. "Yes, let's head home." Anna's voice softened to a whisper. "I know what will help clear up the mystery though." Anna stopped and pulled Priscilla directly in front of her. "Look at me," Anna spoke softly. "Look into my eyes."

Priscilla looked tentatively into Anna's face. Anna smiled and wiped a tear from the woman's cheek. "I know my return is more than most people could comprehend. On top of that your husband has been imprisoned for believing in the One whom I believe in." Anna took a deep breath then continued. "I heard a woman in the market speaking with three others. She spoke of Yeshua, the same man that was crucified; the same man that your husband swore allegiance to. The woman said that Yeshua has risen and is alive. He wants his followers to meet him at Galilee in three days."

Anna studied Priscilla's eyes. "I see doubt . . . and I understand."

Priscilla pulled away, but Anna kept her focus. "The prophets foretold that the Messiah would come and suffer for our sins. Isaiah said he would be put to death but that he would conquer death and rise again. Yeshua fulfilled every prophecy referring to *HaMashiach*."

"I want to believe, but it seems so . . . so strange that anyone could rise from the dead." A web of disbelief wrapped itself across Priscilla's face. "I'm afraid. How could all this be?" She had accepted the Judaic laws and the belief in one God, but this new faith was too much. Uncertainty plagued her. It wasn't the news of Yeshua. It was the ring on Anna's finger. As a Roman citizen, she feared the implications of the ring. Fear had robbed Priscilla of faith.

A pasted smile moved into place on Priscilla's face. A pretense of faith swept across her countenance and the two women walked home arm in arm.

Priscilla said, "It's an amazing story. I think I understand now, Anna. When did you say Yeshua is meeting in Galilee? I'd like to go with you."

"Seeing Yeshua will take all doubt away, Priscilla. I'm sure you'll believe as I do when you see him. I only wish your husband could be there, too."

"Yes, I do too. I wonder what it would take for Caesar to release him." She turned to Anna as they entered the cool hallway of her home. "Tell me Anna, why are you wearing Caesar's ring again? I thought you decided not to wear it."

Anna smiled with a slight blush. "After you mentioned the ring this morning, a faint memory returned as to where it must have come from. A Roman man I once loved had tried to give me this ring." Anna touched it with a near tenderness. Priscilla kept smiling.

"I refused it," Anna continued. "He begged me to take the ring. I don't know how it came to be on my finger, but I thought, perhaps, I might see him again." Anna kept her head down as she spoke. Her voice was calm. "He, too, has something very precious of mine, actually of ours. He might consider sharing what he has with me. The value of this ring would be so small but it might make him consider." She wondered how Alexander would react to letting her see their daughter. Anna was convinced that little Charis must be with the soldier.

Anna remembered her last minutes on earth. She was alone. As her spirit slipped away, she saw a soldier bending over her still body gathering the tiny life into his arms. She knew Charis had not entered Heaven yet. She was still alive somewhere.

Anna was not about to discuss her daughter or Alexander with Priscilla yet; maybe along the road to Galilee, but not today. Priscilla was already confused as it was. She refocused on Priscilla's longing to see her husband. She understood her pain.

"There's one thing that might make a difference in the release of your husband."

"He's an innocent man, Anna. He would never leave his post. He would never turn from his orders. I know him. But the Roman authorities and Jewish rulers have colluded together against him. Only a miracle could release him. What could you know that would possibly change their minds?"

Anna wrapped her arms around Priscilla and pulled her tighter to her side. Priscilla stared down at the ring that touched her robe, her arm. "What do you have, Anna?"

"Yeshua! Yeshua's resurrection and appearance will convince the soldiers, all of Caesar's court, to release your husband. I believe Yeshua has the answers to your husband's release." Anna's eyes looked hopeful, but Priscilla showed a marbled stare. Anna's confidence swelled. "You will see, Priscilla. Many will see. We must set out tomorrow."

"Yes, we'll see," Priscilla said. "I'll prepare some things for the journey. You can start your sewing and I'll cook food for our trip." Her smile was suddenly calm and polished.

Rumor had spread throughout Yerushalayim that Yeshua had risen and planned to meet his followers in Galilee. The scoffers laughed in derision and the believers' hopes soared.

"It's a trick by his dim-witted disciples," the Temple priests mocked.

Roman authorities speculated on the increasing possibility of political disruption. Regardless of its validity, such a group of fanatical woolly-browed insurrectionists could cause major anarchy; especially if they were desperate.

The disciples, however, eagerly hoped Mary was right. In faith, they began their trip to Galilee, each recalling the thrilling hours on those very shores with Yeshua.

The words, "*IT IS FINISHED*," struck a chord in Adam's heart . . . God's perfect sacrifice was now complete. He had confidence that somewhere Yeshua would be found among the living. He had always felt his presence, had understood the need for a divine sacrifice and had joined in the chorus of his praises, but he longed to see his face and hear his voice. So overcome was Adam to see Yeshua that he'd lost his appetite, couldn't sleep and every muscle was tensed with anticipation.

Sora wondered if Adam was typical of most men, useless around the house. But since Adam had heard of Yeshua's return he seemed more incompetent than ever. He couldn't concentrate on a single task. Sora chuckled and went on with her daily routine. "Men," she said.

Sora agreed to go, and finally there was something practical Adam could do . . . pack. Adam stuffed clothing, bedding and food into sacks. He packed everything but Peaches for this journey. It would be a difficult trip for Sora and would take several days. But Adam's energy was boundless and he would make the journey as light as he could for her. He loved her dearly.

The sun was just streaking across the horizon as the two set out toward the region of Galilee. The tall sandy-haired baby-faced man trod brightly beside the bent old lady in black. Sora's heels kicked up the hem of her long skirt, stirring whirls of dust into the hot air. With a walking stick in one hand, she held tightly to Adam, the son of another mother.

Galilee sat like an opal on the leathery finger of Palestine. Its lake sparkled like a shimmering gem beckoning life. Only as travelers drew closer could they see lush greenery springing from its banks as though *all* life drew from this one pool.

Mary had spread the news everywhere. Yeshua had already made numerous appearances mostly near the Sea of Galilee. The message had traveled far and wide exceeding any limits she'd imagined. Not ten or eleven men and women, but scores who longed for a deep drink from the Pool of Life walked the dusty roads toward Galilee. People scattered from Syria's barren hilltops to Rome's marbled walls, many who had feasted at Yeshua's hillside banquets or shivered under his healing hand, trod the dusty path to find this victorious Restorer. The land of shadows was long and wide, but the Water of Life deep, sufficient enough to quench every parched tongue. Reeds, once bruised, rose tall and strong on the banks of the Sea of Galilee.

## Chapter Twenty-Seven

# 33 A.D., THIRTY-FIVE DAYS AFTER THE RESURRECTION

emocritus only knew to head toward Galilee. The news of Yeshua's resurrection had spread like a wildfire. While questions remained, those who longed to know the truth began to watch in anticipation of his re-appearing. They needed to see his scars, hear his voice and touch him once again. Yeshua had already appeared in various towns along the Galilean coast, from Magdala to Gennesaret, from Gergesa up the coast to Capernaum.[53] A large crowd had found him near the foothills of Mt. Tabor.

Democritus' natural inclination was to head toward the lakeshore which was a favorite place of the Messiah. This seemed a cherished spot for many of the followers. From here, Peter and John hauled in a miraculous catch from these waters. Here, Yeshua had commissioned Peter to lead his sheep. Here, Yeshua had walked on water. And it was here that the Messiah had come to Democritus and changed his life for eternity. Like himself, anyone who sought the Messiah would find him. He

---

[53] I Co. 15:6

was available to all people. Perhaps today his dear Yeshua would find him once again at the water's edge.

Democritus had reached the banks of the Sea of Galilee long before the crowds had gathered. He sat on a large rock that rose out of the water. He was deep in thought as he let his feet dangle while smooth laps of water curved around his ankles. He leaned forward and watched the reflection of his face. His image peered back joyfully, a face once distorted by demons' fingers. He touched the glassy surface. His reflection revealed his heart; the heart that Yeshua had set free.

Memories came back in ripples. Ripples of hope at Yeshua's glance, a ripple of sanity as the demons fled, a ripple of joy as acceptance replaced shame, a ripple of courage as Yeshua called him to come forth. Diablo was gone, never to return. These reflections reminded Democritus of whom he had become in light of Yeshua's suffering. With a quiet excitement the warrior waited patiently for his Master's approach.

Democritus' eyes drifted up at the sound of voices. He was listening for only one. News that the disciples had already seen him stirred his heart. He pulled his blistered feet from the lake and rose to face the crowds. Yeshua would be here soon.

A group of ten to fifteen men with several women came over the crest of a hill. They were in deep discussion with one another and hadn't noticed that they had reached their destination. They stopped at the shoreline and waited. At the same moment, a ribbon of heads bobbed up and down coming from another direction, their voices echoing off the water's sheer surface. Democritus pulled back within the shade of a huge spiraled acacia tree, letting the shadows linger over him.

Adam emerged from between two willows with the old woman well-seated on a donkey. The black-cloaked widow had found the journey beyond her ability to keep up, so Adam had found this pepper-gray donkey to carry Sora. Breaking out onto the lakeshore, Adam was followed by a long caravan of people. Features, faces and clothing exposed cultures angular to one another, but here, together on this lakeside, they were mirrored as one people waiting for the Ancient of Days.[54]

The expectant crowd grew to hundreds. Some disciples had already seen the Messiah, most had not. The shore was crowded with people. Latecomers slipped over the hill and sat on its crest.

Adam searched the sea of faces for Yeshua. He recalled the warm embrace of the Father the moment he entered Paradise. But to see Yeshua face to face was almost more than his human emotions could contain. This great assembly would forever change the course of human gatherings in Yeshua's name, for he would be in their midst. No more curtains of separation, no priestly mediators or sacrifices. No more intercessors, for Yeshua Himself would be the Great Intercessor.

Reports of Yeshua's appearance had only confirmed people's faith. Their excitement was tempered by the magnitude of the occasion: foreseen 740 years earlier, proclaimed to be Immanuel, God wrapped in human flesh, God's perfect Passover Lamb.[55]

Moses alone was permitted to see only a glimpse of God's glory. To see God in all his splendor would have killed even the most righteous human. Now the God-Man was here among them, just over the crest; any moment now he would appear for all the world to see, every tribe and nation. He came as God's Passover Lamb, taking upon himself the sins of the world. Today they would see and feel the wounds and know; they would hear his voice and believe; they would sacrifice everything to follow him to the ends of the earth.

---

[54] Dan. 7:9, 14, 22; Is. 43:13

[55] Is. 53

Adam wondered, too, if he might recognize his parents, Rachel and Ben-Asher. He knew earth-time ages both faces and bodies. But he doubted they'd be looking for him in this body. They would have no idea how Heaven had transformed him. Adam shielded his eyes from the sun's glare. He was certain that when he saw Yeshua, he would recognize him here on earth. He remembered his first encounter when God caught him in his warm embrace after he slipped from his mother's trembling hands.

Anna and Priscilla arrived in the midst of the swelling group of followers. Priscilla walked slowly into the crowd, anxious and uncertain. She kept peering behind her, looking from side to side. Anna leaned close and patted her hand. Priscilla smiled sweetly. But she was startled when she heard voices behind her speaking in Greek. As a Roman she had learned several languages, and today she recognized the dialects of different people all around her. These were Roman citizens without disguise. She pulled the veil close around her face so that none would discover her origins. She puzzled beneath the veil, *How have all these cultures learned of this man, Yeshua?* She heard voices from Gaul and Germania. She recognized rich black faces from Ethiopia dressed in colors of royal splendor. She saw Egyptian adornment and togas from Rome. Both rich and poor stood shoulder to shoulder . . . waiting. She was struck that Yeshua had touched so many cultures in such a short time.[56] *Can all these people really believe the story of Yeshua's resurrection?*

Priscilla glanced around for Roman militia but saw none. She leaned toward Anna. "Is he here yet?"

---

[56] Acts 2:5

"I don't see him, but the crowd keeps growing. There must be four or five hundred people. And they're from everywhere. I don't recognize a single face."

"Nor me," Priscilla replied. She gave a sideways glance at Anna who was searching the horizon for Yeshua. Priscilla eyed the ring and quickly turned her gaze away.

Adam had been surveying the crowd below. Suddenly he fixed his eyes on one spot. "Sora, I see him. He's moving down through the crowd. It's him, it's Yeshua."

The old woman's eyes were weak. She squinted against the sun's glare, studying the moving masses of people. She followed Adam's finger as he pointed. In this sea of faces, she saw a cluster of people surrounding a man. It was *Yeshua HaMashiach*. She knew it. There was a holy commotion surrounding the Messiah. As the crowd surrounded him, his response was astounding. When they paid him homage, he lifted *them* up; when they came broken, he *made them whole*. This man responded to each human need. He didn't give an oration to the masses, he was there for each individual, just like his years of ministry. Sora put her hand to her mouth in astonishment. "Oh, it's him. It's him. I know it's him. I feel it in my bones."

The resurrected Yeshua shunned no one who came near. His touch and message was exclusive for each person. He listened, he spoke and finally he breathed on them. From a distance, this act seemed to influence people in a profound way. Yeshua moved from one person to another. His attention was personal yet he'd come for the masses. He did not preach or declare war. He was not signing up recruits to fight or martyrs to kill and die in his name. He was not proclaiming war but a Kingdom. He was offering himself yet again with arms open wide.

Sora gazed at the man as he approached her. Yeshua was magnificent in appearance, yet so human. Sora noticed something royal about his stride. She gasped softly as she saw terrible wounds in his hands and feet. "It's him. He's the One I've been seeking all my life. I feel it in my soul." She spoke without taking her eyes off Yeshua.

"Lad, help me down off this foul beast." Adam lifted the withered woman down. As her feet touched the ground she knelt and bowed her head to the earth. She felt his touch. "Oh Master, you've arrived. My long awaited Messiah. Sorakin will do whatever you ask. I will follow you to the end of my life, be it days or years."

The black-cloaked woman appeared as a small bundle of cloth on the ground, waiting, listening for instructions. Silently, she heard her Master's voice. She nodded without lifting her head. The dirt was so close to her face, yet Yeshua's presence closer still . . . closer than life itself. Yeshua spoke and let out a long breath upon Sora. It was sweet and filled her with wisdom.

With a knowing look, Yeshua smiled at Adam and called him by name. His touch burned within him, Adam feeling the depth and breadth of Yeshua's love. Nothing compared. His touch was a father's touch; the friend of friends. Earth's affection dimmed. Yeshua's Spirit stirred in him as he was told all he needed to know about his journey back in human form. His life would now be a time of simple trust. Many uncertainties remained, but they were hidden beneath Yeshua's shadow and that was enough for Adam. It would be a life of faith, one day at a time.

Adam lowered his gaze as his knees touched the earth. Dust filtered into the breeze. Adam was relieved he did not know the future. He was certain it would be too much for him. Living by faith was much simpler. He would let Yeshua lead him just as a father leads his son. Yeshua's breath filled him with peace so pure that no deception could deter him from following. The

Spirit of God descended upon Adam and enveloped him. He was ready to follow *Yeshua HaMashiach* to the ends of the earth.

Democritus *felt* Holiness approach before Yeshua approached him at the water's edge. An excitement rose in his stomach, courage flowed through his veins as his Captain drew near. Already, Yeshua was speaking to him. The warrior knelt and lowered his head until it touched the dirt where he had just walked. Yeshua's words flowed through Democritus with certainty. He was given specific instructions without a word uttered aloud. Details were laid out, the burden was great, but Democritus would be given grace to fulfill Yeshua's design.

Democritus felt a holy touch upon his head. The power of God roared through him from his head to his feet. Then his Master whispered, "Well done, Democritus, well done. You have been faithful in small things, I will now give you greater tasks to do for me." With a smile, Yeshua said, "I see you still wear my robe well."

Yeshua lifted Democritus' head until their eyes met. Those eyes that had probed his soul as Diablo, those eyes that forgave, those eyes that were filled with compassion for a man no one else wanted. The soldier wept. The breath of Yeshua caused Democritus' world to become crystal clear.

A quiet hush fell as Yeshua moved among the people. They listened with their hearts. Hundreds upon hundreds saw him and believed. Such a stunning moment in the history of a people-yet-to-be! Yeshua was drawn to humanity. He could not resist loving them. He couldn't stay away. Not because of who they were, but because of who he was. Yeshua, his face full of light and hope, was drawn to these tender hearts. Yeshua's love was a regal love: no matter how broken their lives or shattered their dreams, his love conquered all.

The throngs bowed down in worship before Yeshua. Each head bowed until the shores and hillsides were covered like windblown lilies; faces humbled to the earth. His breath blew across the throngs like a rushing mighty wind, filling the people with power.

Anna's face touched the earth. She remembered Yeshua lifting her up from her shame once before, now she remained low, remembering his forgiveness. His hand rested upon her head and she wept. Words flowed into her mind like a rushing wind. She lost awareness of her surroundings as he spoke. Yeshua was speaking directly to her. She listened carefully. His words were precise directions she needed for the future. In spite of the great task she would be required to fulfill, his nearness filled her with comfort unlike any she had ever felt before.

She nodded and answered in whispered tones. Anna's face was radiant, tears profuse upon her cheeks. Yeshua accepted her heart's response and nothing more was needed. Yeshua's love was complete, absolute, all consuming. She felt embraced in his love. His breath upon her gave Anna the courage she needed to face tomorrow.

Anna was deep in adoration when suddenly someone jerked her arm and pulled her body upward. Rough hands yanked her to her feet. Bewildered, she looked at the faces of two thugs. At a distance Priscilla watched in silence, her head bowed in shame. As Anna was dragged away into the shadows, Yeshua saw the attack. Anna's feet kicked the air uselessly. A hand muffled her screams. Priscilla had disappeared.

As she was hauled away, Anna heard Yeshua's voice within. From the distance, she saw his stare. Yeshua's eyes were sad but his silent voice said, "Anna, it's okay. I'll be with you when the storm comes and the water rises." [57] This was the start of her journey. He would go through the fiery furnace with her. Anna saw his face, then all went black. The battle had begun.

---

[57]Ac. 22:4 "I persecuted the followers of this Way to their death, arresting both men and women and throwing them into pr

## Chapter Twenty-Eight

# ANTONIA FORTRESS, YERUSHALAYIM, 33 A.D.

C langing sounds throbbed in Anna's ears followed by searing flashes of light. She groaned. Her throat was dry. Another blade of light slashed her consciousness. Each burst left behind a residue of emergent light. Searing pain stabbed her temple and sliced down her neck. Anna was slowly regaining consciousness.

*Where am I? What happened to me?* The pain was hideous. She tried to stay under the spell of oblivion, but could not. She struggled to open her eyes but they were swollen and crusted shut. She willed herself to move.

*Move your hand, Anna. Open your eyes with your fingers.* She was bound with kelp rope that had pulled her feet back and connected to her wrists, then finally secured to something stationary. The only muscles she could control were her eyes. They fought against bruising and crusted mucus to open. She struggled to see.

*Open. Open. Lord, help me open these eyes.* Her right eyelashes parted and her pupil stared out into darkness. Everything was blurred. She saw the flicker of a flame somewhere in a cavernous darkness. S'

She closed her eye again and rested. Sounds and words came back to her. Someone was shouting words. "Traitor! Thief!"

*Where are those words coming from? Who's a traitor?* Panic rose up in her chest and she wanted to vomit. She gagged. It wasn't until then that she realized a foul-tasting rag had been stuffed in her mouth. She swallowed slowly, trying not to panic.

Time led her through a tunnel of dark and gray, of pain and throbbing sensations. She passed in and out of consciousness for long periods. She must have been hit or drugged. When consciousness re-emerged, she tried again to see through the slit of an eyelid. The light was dim and orange from a torch. The burning pitch left an acrid smell that stung her nose. She sensed she was in a dungeon or tunnel. The slightest sound echoed against stone walls. Her head had been pulled back so that she could not turn or swivel her neck.

Anna lay there, still and silent. She remembered Yeshua's face, and tears began to seep through her crusted eyelashes, melting the hardness. Tears swelled, rolling gently down her cheeks.

Suddenly, something stirred in the darkness. Listening, she sensed a presence nearby, an uneasy, restless nearness. Anna rested her head back against the cold earth. She listened. There was another sound but closer, and then a third. She had the strange feeling that something was staring at her, knowing it was very close and nervously intent on her. The tears had released her eyelids; they fluttered open. Everything was in dark shadows. She blinked several times to clear her vision, then wished she hadn't. Anna was not alone.

---

Adam's excitement was boundless. "So, the whole story makes sense now. Yeshua is the Messiah the world has been waiting for, the one the prophets foretold," said to Sora.

Adam pulled the donkey up a rocky incline as chunks of stone snapped away from the animal's hooves. The burden bearer was not happy being pulled and tugged against his will. He brayed noisily and shook his head.

Adam muscled the stubborn animal while slowly the three ascended the hill and stopped at the top. Below lay a smooth valley with the River Jordan twisting its way down the center. Green reeds and low lying vegetation drank from its banks. They stopped and stared in silence.

"Magnificent, Sora. What a sight. Isn't it beautiful?"

"Of course it is. Now move along. I've got things to do back in Yerushalayim and you're slowing my journey lollygagging like this."

"I didn't know you were in such a hurry, Sora. And by the way . . ." Adam stared directly at the old woman, ". . . I heard your prayer."

The woman scowled. "That wasn't for you. I was talking to my Messiah and it was none of your business."

"I didn't mean to listen. It just happened. But you called yourself another name. You called yourself Sorakin." His voice softened as he repeated the name.

"I did indeed." A flush washed over her pluck for a mere moment. "You see, the Lord has now given me another son. That fulfills my name, Sora, the mother of children, Sorakin." Then her shell closed around her. "And don't you go asking who that son is. Don't you dare!"

Adam's eyes pretended mock dismay. "Me? Why would I ask such a silly question as that . . . mum?" Adam squeezed the woman tight until she pushed him away.

"Don't go mushy on me, lad. Now, let's get moving. You're not the only child I have to worry about. Yeshua's given me the task of caring for someone, and she's waiting back in Yerushalayim."

"Did Yesh tell J ou specific things to do?" Adam led the donkey d path in a rapid descent.

286

"He certainly did. He asked me to do some very special things, and I must be there to take care of them." She flicked her hand to finish the chit-chat and move along.

"Well, Yeshua revealed some things to me, too, but not everything. I'm not too sure what to do next."

"Get me to Yerushalayim, you silly pet." Sorakin put on a pretend grouchy face. "He'll tell you when its time. Its faith, lad. Don't walk with a limp. Walk like you know where you're going even if you don't. Isn't that faith, trusting him to lead you?"

"Hmm. I guess that's right. Walk like I know where I'm going. Walking by faith." Adam shook his head in time with the donkey's footfalls. "Sorakin, who made you so smart?"

"Not smart, lad. I just practice listening."

---

## Caesar's Palace, Rome, 33 A.D.

Malchus, underling servant that he was, successfully slipped from the bonds of responsibility and fled to Rome, using the royal seal his mother had stolen for him from Artamos when he was born. The soldier had stolen her virginity; she stole the soldier's name. Over the years the seal had been Malchus' passport to and from Rome. Its inscription bore his father's name, *Artamos of Caesar Augustus, Commander of the Fourth Regiment of the New Roman Empire.* Emblazoned beneath was the Roman eagle. Malchus' father had given him nothing else in this world but breath, and sometimes he despised even that.

Malchus had fled Judea immediately after the earthquakes. They unnerved him. Then there was the strange darkness followed by the tomb raiders. Why would anybody want to break open a sarcophagus? He was scared. He'd heard that Iscariot had hung himself. What in the world was happening? Malchus needed *his* world to have some familiarity to it. He hated chaos.

And he wasn't about to wait around for another supernatural event to completely paralyze him. He was already drinking more than usual to calm his nerves.

He would take this news to Tiberius, using his father's seal to gain entrance. He had abandoned his post as servant and set sail for Rome immediately. He would head right to Tiberius' palace.

The servant paced back and forth, his leather sandals snapping against the emperor's marbled floors. He'd schemed up a message that he felt would delight the emperor's ears.

*Tiberius, my friend, I have news for you. Do you know of all the events taking place in Judea? Of course not . . . you're so busy with Rome and all the annexes you're planning. But Judea is in such a state of flux. The Jewish rebels are fighting back and they are making headway. They're ready to claim back what they think belongs to them, great and noble Caesar. Now is the time to squash the rebellion. And I can help you do it.*

Malchus continued to pace, flapping his arms in his imaginary discussion with the emperor. The upheaval in Yerushalayim had unsettled him to such an extent that he could no longer concentrate on servanthood tasks. His mind was now crammed with stories, rumors, earthquakes, empty tombs, suicides and the such that he felt he had enough material to convince the emperor to take drastic action quickly, strike while the iron's hot. Most importantly, Malchus was available as the go-between.

Malchus had used his charm and cunning in Roman affairs to win favor with the emperor. Tiberius was not really interested in merely ruling Rome. He had other passions that awaited him on the Isle of Capri—disgusting passions. The emperor used his governor, Sejanus, a Praetorian prefect, to rule in Rome, so why not use someone as well versed as Malchus in Judea? He could think of no one better.

Malchus smiled to himself. *Here I am, a mixed breed, standing in the emperor's corner of the world. I have news to tell him that he cannot resist. It will strengthen his power. Of course, nothing's free.* He put his right hand to his lips to suppress a broadening smile. *I'm chums with a man the world calls Pontifex Maximus, the chief interpreter of sacred law, Pater Exercituum, Father of the Armies, and Optimus Maximus Caesar, the title of all titles.* Malchus couldn't resist a grin.

Suddenly, he was jarred to attention. Towering double doors covered in gold filigree began to open toward him. He stumbled backward. There before him was a marbled hallway. A page called his name.

"Malchus, servant of Caiaphas, the High Priest, Governor Sejanus is ready to see you."

Malchus' face burned with anger. He hated the title of servant. Quickly regaining his composure, he swallowed his rage and nodded, then followed the page into the emperor's throne room. He'd wondered if Tiberius was in Rome. Sejanus used his position to belittle common people and Malchus was a great target, but considering the growing depravity of Tiberius, he was relieved Sejanus sat on the throne today.

Sejanus sat in the center of the massive room surrounded by the opulence of color, beauty and wealth. Walls were of polished red granite. Magnificent Doric columns of red-veined marble with fluted shafts stood supporting a mahogany ceiling. Sea-shell molding overlaid with gold ran around the top of the room. Gold cornices capped each column.

Distracted by such opulence, Malchus stumbled in protocol. He hesitated long enough to infuriate the emperor's governor.

"Your Excellency." Malchus bowed with such exaggerated humility that his head nearly touched the floor. He stayed in that humbled position waiting for the governor to speak. There was a long pause. Sejanus watched with disdain.

Malchus was sweating profusely. Surrounded by exotic slaves, a chained black panther from Africa, wines and a platter of rich food, Sejanus said nothing. All the servants waited in silence, ready for the signal to fulfill his wishes. They lived to do his bidding.

The governor took a sip of wine. After wiping his lips with linen he said, "Glad you could drop by and see me, Malchus. I hope your master, Caiaphas, gave you permission for this trip. I know funds are tight these days."

Malchus remained prostrate, nodding his head, waiting for the signal to rise.

"You can stand up now."

Between sweat, blood rush and humiliation of the highest order, Malchus lifted his head and smiled. "Absolutely, Your Excellency," Malchus gasped. "With threats of insurrection simmering, my master was anxious that you know all that is going on in Judea. I have a full report for Your Worship."

A portico on the left opened into a magnificent open-air garden. Three maidens carved in white marble poured jars of water into a pool. Surrounding the fountain were exotic palms, fruit trees and lush ferns. Birds flitted from branch to branch. A soft breeze blew across the throne room.

The panther raised his head and sniffed. Suddenly he became curious. He stood and glided in supple movements toward Malchus. His ears flattened, his shoulders hunched. Malchus wondered how long the chain was. Sejanus kept sipping wine. The sleek cat moved closer, picking up the human scent of fear. In a flash he bared his teeth, a growl rumbling from his throat. Sejanus was intrigued. None of his courtiers moved.

The animal was magnificent and ferocious. His golden eyes studied the man and then padded within a foot of Malchus' body. Malchus stiffened. The animal hunched lower and growled again. Suddenly it lunged upward with his claws extended, fangs bared and ready to slice Malchus to shreds in a single move. The animal's height was enormous, towering above Malchus' head.

Malchus let out a squeal of terror, certain he would be dragged away as meat for dinner. At full height, the chain caught the panther's neck in mid-air and he landed on his feet. Malchus was a nervous wreck. The cat padded back into the corner and plopped himself down on the cool floor. He turned his head and looked at the intruder for a moment, then closed his eyes and seemed as tame as an overgrown kitten.

Sejanus' smile was shrewd. He was as treacherous as Emperor Tiberius and could be entertained so easily. With a smile he turned to Malchus. "So, what news do you bring?"

Malchus had not expected the ruler of Rome to be indifferent toward international affairs. He'd come with information the governor would want to hear. Malchus was offering it freely, not wanting any favors . . . at least not immediately. Sooner or later he would ask Sejanus or Tiberius for something and he was certain he would get it. At the right moment, Malchus would ask for power and authority that the emperor's governor would gladly give to bring stability in Judea.

Chapter Twenty-Nine

# ANTONIA FORTRESS, YERUSHALAYIM, 33 A.D.

Anna lay shaking. Such terror was foreign to her. She'd forgotten what fear could do to the human psyche; paralyze, constrict the throat, triple the heart rate, pump the blood through the body like a fountain. All these things happened in a split second as she lay there in the dark. *Someone or something is very near.* Slowly, she opened her swollen eyes. What she saw staring at her made her scream. She shrieked into the dirty rag that was tied around her face and stuffed into her mouth, but no sound emerged.

Beady eyes stared back at her, unblinking. A huge rat had moved close and hissed like a possum. Its long tail, denuded of hair, flicked back and forth as it contemplated its next meal. Another sound emerged. Scurrying from the darkness a second rat moved into place. It stood on its haunches and bared its teeth.

As a child, Anna had always feared rats and spiders. She wanted to scream, but she couldn't, nor could she even run away to escape this. She was pinned to a wall and left alone with two huge hungry rats. Another rat moved in the shadows. Anna closed her eyes. It was no use. She felt the feet climb onto her leg and run up the side of her body. It sprang to her shoulder.

Her bloodshot eyes opened wide as she looked to the side. The creature stared unmoved at her face. Terrified, her body jolted into spasms, trying to shake the rats from her.

They closed in. She felt the sharp claws cling to and prickle her skin. The rat on her shoulder moved closer to her face. Its tail slid across her neck.

They were busy nibbling away at her and she could do nothing to shake the rodents from her. The only emotion she could express was fear and that brought tears. She cried. She closed her eyes, unable to look at the rodents. She also prayed.

*Lord, I'm here in this dungeon for a reason I don't understand. I see little value being eaten by rats, but I surrender back to you my very life . . . my very breath.* She remembered why she was here on earth. She kept her eyes closed, knowing the rats where still there, touching her face, her neck, her hair. They could chew her to pieces, but only if it was the will of the Father.

*Watch over sweet Charis. May she come to love you. Allow me to see her again and tell her the stories about you, Yeshua HaMashiach.*

Her prayer brought something intangible into the room. A holy calm washed over her. Without any logical reason, Anna relaxed. God was with her. The rodents' feet scurried. All three animals were moving across her body. She felt their tails moving, flicking as they busied themselves making clicking sounds with their teeth.

*Oh Yeshua, be my helper. I'm in the middle of a fire. Walk with me, Yeshua. Don't let the flames set me ablaze.*

Something popped. Anna's eyes opened. She couldn't see the rats any longer, but she could feel them. They were busy. Human instinct still brought chills, but the curious calm remained.

*What was that noise?* She heard another snap and her head jerked. Her head was free from the ties that held her against the wall. She turned to look sideways. The rats were startled by her sudden move. They stopped and watched for a moment. Anna remained still. The rats went back to chewing. Anna's body had been so bruised that if they had been chewing her fingers or toes she might not have known.

Another pop! What was happening? There was no new pain. Suddenly her hands were free. She dared not move them. Gradually it dawned on the prisoner that the rats were chewing away at her ropes. They had found kelp to be very tasty. Keeping her eyes closed and her focus on Yeshua, she gave thanks for his presence in . . . wherever she was at this moment.

A half hour passed and Anna was freed from all the restraints. Not a shred of kelp remained. She shifted her body from the long hours of stationary position. Her movement startled the rats and they scurried away into the shadows. With a great deal of pain and struggle, Anna lifted herself to a sitting position. Her head throbbed but she was free of the bonds. She opened her eyes, squinted into the shadows and thanked the Lord for rats. No, she wasn't free. But the bonds were gone and she was grateful.

Apparently, Anna was locked away in a dungeon. The only opening was a small door with bars on the window and a tiny hole in the wall about six inches from her head where the rats must have entered and exited.

Anna leaned against the damp wall. She thought of Charis and smiled. *Perhaps I'll see her soon.* For reasons unknown to her, she'd been taken into this foul dungeon and left to die. Anna fell into a sleep of exhaustion, yet comforted by hope. Perhaps God had other plans in mind.

## Rome, Caesar's Palace

Malchus cleared his throat in an attempt to regain control of his emotions. "Governor Sejanus, ruler for the great Emperor Tiberius, I've got urgent news from Judea that I know you'll want to hear. I've come a long way to deliver this information myself . . . at personal peril."

"Yes, like springing panthers," Sejanus said. He picked up some dates and chewed at them for a while, spitting out the pits into a bronze urn next to him.

"More wine!" he ordered, snapping his jeweled fingers that made the servants scurry.

Malchus marveled that this strange flamboyant actor could have such power over his world.

Sejanus suddenly became impatient. "Malchus, spit out your message and leave. I'm bored with you already. You're wasting my time."

"The news I bring is not good news, Your Excellency. It's serious news that troubles much of Judea. I felt it important that you know immediately. There are significant plans for insurrection." Malchus raised himself to the best of his limited stature. "The rest I must speak to you about in private."

"Talk to me in the morning. I'm too weary to consider anything serious today. You're dismissed."

Without another word, Malchus was ushered out. With a day wasted, he wandered through the streets of Rome until darkness fell. In Rome's shadows, Malchus felt ill at ease. He wondered what might come of his life. Instinctively he touched his ear.

## Antonia Fortress, Yerushalayim

Antonia Fortress sat on the northeastern side of the city, near the Temple. King Herod had built this seventy-five-foot tower and named it in honor of his friend, Marc Antony. It had several spacious apartments and baths for the Roman procurators and below, housed many of the Roman army that guarded the Jews inside the Temple court. Deep below ground were rancid dungeons where Rome's traitors and conspirators awaited trial. Imprisonment presumed guilt. Few who entered ever returned home. Prisoners waited at the whim of the emperor to bring them to Rome's great theatre. Fewer still knew of a secret tunnel that ran from the Fortress' tower to the Temple courtyard.

The prison headquarters was housed on the ground floor. It usually smelled of garlic and sweat. Today it reeked of booze. The jailer called himself Marc, his guards called him Captain. Finishing a jug of ale, he turned to see one of the guards climbing the stairs, huffing at each step.

"Captain, it's been two days since we put that woman in the cell down there," he panted. "I haven't heard a sound since we threw her in. What do you want us to do?"

"No one has touched her, have they?" Marc warned.

"She's a beauty, but unfortunately we roughed her up pretty badly. I told the men to leave her alone. Shame though." He paused. "What's her crime?"

"Yeah, she's a treat all right, but she's dangerous. She's a spy, working against Rome. She's used one of our guys, a commander, to get information about our military operations. As far as Caesar's concerned, that's grounds for treason."

"Hate to see such beauty wasted, you know, Captain?" The guard sniffed. "You got any proof of treason?"

"Sure do. I got it here in my hands. She can't get away from this tangible evidence."

The guard was curious but knew it was useless to probe. He'd been down that road before and it wasn't pretty. "So, what do you want me to do, Captain? She's probably dead, or nearly." He stood at the staircase with keys in his hands.

"Take a torch and check on her. If she's survived the rats and the pit, which I doubt, she'll be tried for treason. Don't spare any sympathy for her. And don't touch her, as badly as you might want to."

"Yes sir," the guard answered. He turned away, offering a hasty military salute and marched down the stone corridor toward a flickering torch on a stand.

———————◦———————

Anna awoke in dark shadows. Her cell was small and damp. It took a minute to remember where she was. She'd been through so much in such a short lifetime. Sleep had refreshed her, and she felt comforted at the knowledge that God's presence would remain even in this dungeon.

Anna pulled her knees up and hugged them, drawing warmth from her own body. She rested the side of her head on her knees and mused. God was so good. She recalled her flight to Heaven and the glory of him who had borne her home. An irresistible urge came to sing as a haunting melody rose in her mind. In the blackness, Anna's soft voice sang a song for an audience of One. The words brushed across the cold stones in a whisper. They caressed the silence, beckoning it to listen. She sang a melody that swept away tides of darkness and settled on the ground like something beautiful.

*"I will extol Yahweh at all times; his praise will always be on my lips. My soul will boast in Yahweh; let the afflicted hear and rejoice. Glorify Yahweh with me; let us exalt his name together. I sought Yahweh, and he answered me; he delivered me from all my fears. Those who look to him are radiant; their faces are never covered with shame."*[58] You are so good, so good to me. Tender joy melted the pain of the last couple of days. The darkness became as light although Anna could see nothing beyond her fingers. She felt bathed in comfort as though there was not a scratch on her, yet bruises and cuts still remained. She was at peace with God.

———————◦———————

The dungeons were a network of hallways and small dark cells, each monitored by a single guard. The guard sent by the

---

[58] Ps. 34:1-5

captain grabbed a torch from the corridor and headed into the darkness. Down the winding steps and into a long musty corridor lit only at intervals, he headed toward Anna's cell. His first prisoner was a man who sat motionless and stared at the dark walls. He hadn't spoken a word in two years. A second prisoner was constantly agitated, babbling nonsense hour after hour. The third prisoner lay on his side. He was young and muscular as if he'd trained for battle. He made no response to the guard's presence. Each prisoner seemed to be waiting for the inevitable terror to come.

The guard's leather belt squeaked, his scabbard scraped the walls, the keys in his hands rattled as he moved deep into the belly of the dungeon. As the torch stabbed the blackness, it revealed arches of stone, doors of iron and looming shadows that warped then disappeared as he approached. He hated this place. It smelled of death.

As he headed toward the end of the tunnel, he thought he saw a shadow moving toward him. He waved the torch and decided it was only his imagination. He shook off the gripping fear and kept moving into the tunnel when he heard a chilling hiss. A huge rat turned his way startled at his presence. Its eyes glimmered red. The rat was hunched, its fur bristling, and was slowly moving toward the soldier without fear. He swung the torch across the tunnel's arch. The rodent kept coming. "Get out!" he bellowed. "I'll kill you, you disease-ridden rat." He stomped his feet and flashed the flames in all directions. It kept moving toward him with others following. Twenty or thirty rats were steadily marching toward the soldier.

"Get away you filthy vermin." He cursed and swung the torch in a wide low arc. The red eyes continued moving closer with an unnerving stealth. In panic, he shoved the torch down toward the floor when suddenly it slipped from his grip and rolled away from him. Now, sensing his fear, the creatures swarmed toward him.

Beyond the threatening animals, the guard heard a strange sound coming from deep within the tunnel. It was musical and sounded as foreign as springtime in a cell. The flame on the floor sputtered. The singing continued. The torch flickered to a weak single flame. The rats moved closer. The song had a purity that compelled him. The prisoner's song expressed faith and comfort. The torch flickered once then fizzled to nothing. The darkness swallowed up the soldier and his advancing enemy. He panicked and became disoriented. He pulled his sword and swung from side to side. The rats climbed his legs. The guard screamed and turned to flee but rammed into the wall and stumbled. The rats scrambled up his back, ran down his tunic, bit his arms and neck. The soldier roiled onto the floor writhing and screaming insanely. In that dark hell, Anna's song beckoned hope and promise. Suddenly light emerged.

Two soldiers followed by the captain came running with torches. They rushed the rodents, plucking them off the man by their tails and slamming them against walls. The men helped the bloodied soldier to his feet as he panted for breath.

"T-this place is infested with these monsters," the guard stuttered, his face and neck bleeding. His fingers and legs had also been chewed. The soldiers helped the wounded guard make his way out of the tunnel.

"Listen . . .," one soldier said to the others.

"It's her, the woman. She's been singing in the dark," the bleeding soldier replied. "How can a dead woman sing like that down there in this pit, in the dark?"

The four soldiers stood in the middle of the shaft of blackness and listened.

The fluid sound of music drifted up from the darkness, *"Glorify Yahweh with me; let us exalt his name together. I sought Yahweh, and he answered me; he delivered me from all my fears."*[59]

---

[59] Ps. 34:2,3

"She's a witch. She's gotta be, to survive this pit and still sing. She sent the rats after me. It's a spell, I tell ya!"

## Rome, Caesar's Palace

The next morning in Caesar's palace, Malchus sat at a banquet table laden with fruit, breads and delicacies he'd never even heard of before. He indulged himself as he ate alone. Sejanus wasn't feeling too well and still lay in bed. Malchus was to report to his bedside when he finished eating.

*I could get used to this,* Malchus mused. *Do whatever you want without fear of reprisal.* He took in his surroundings as though drawing a blue-print in his mind. Settling deep within his conscience came a resolve to use whatever information he had to gain as much power as his world would allow. His father had done that, his mother too. The emperor was the supreme example of greed. Wasn't it natural to strive for greatness? Touching his smooth ear as he contemplated his discussion with Sejanus, he remembered Yeshua.

Malchus bathed after eating then entered the governor's chambers guided by his servant. The governor looked pale. His hair was damp and clung to his neck.

"I'm sorry, my brother. You're not well."

"I don't need your sympathy," a ruddy pique washed across the governor's face then dissipated, "and I'm not your brother."

Malchus replied, "I'm a Roman, your holiness. And I bow only to you in allegiance to Emperor Tiberius." Malchus was determined to stand strong against these charges. He hated being called a servant. He hated being identified with the Jews, at least when in Rome. "You are not well and I grieve."

"Someone is trying to kill me. I'm probably being poisoned." The governor was weak and short of breath, but not short of rage. "It runs in the emperor's family."

"What does, Your Excellency?"

"Poisoning, you fool."

"I can't imagine someone trying to poison you or the emperor." Malchus was truly shocked and did not have to pretend. "If I had an inkling who I'd track them down and destroy them with my sword."

Sejanus rolled onto his side. "I doubt that you're skilled enough with that dull sword of yours, Malchus. Words maybe, but not a sword. Anyway, I don't have the strength for this chit-chat. Now tell me why you've come so you can go. I'm already weary of you and don't want to be bothered with drivel."

"You won't find this information trivial, I assure you. But I will be brief." Malchus then told the governor in vivid detail about the strange happenings in Yerushalayim. He focused on the erratic behavior of the followers of Yeshua. He described the crucifixion and how he'd learned that someone had stolen the corpse of their fallen leader and was going to use its disappearance to stir up a rebellion against Rome.

"Coincidentally, many tombs surrounding the crucifixion mount had been opened and found empty. They are saying that people are rising from the dead." He laughed. "It's pure sacrilege and vandalism, people robbing tombs."

"Rising from the dead is a moot issue. Every religious leader promises to do that but they never get around to it. Promises, promises! No one has ever come back from the dead, except my mother's ghost. And I've banned her from my palace." Sejanus tried to laugh, but his face was so drawn his smile looked more like a sneer.

Malchus didn't laugh. This was serious business. He didn't like the emperor's leading ruler disregarding such news so lightly. "There's an army of followers ready to lay down their lives for this Jewish man, Yeshua."

"But he's dead." Sejanus' face became stormy.

"His followers believe otherwise. And there have been appearances. There is an impostor that says he is Yeshua. And they're meeting together by the hundreds. I believe there's going to be an insurrection and it could come soon."

"That little strip of dirt revolt against Rome? You've got to be joking. Why should I fear a handful of shepherds?"

"It's surprising what a little faith can do with a handful of people. But there's something more, Your Excellency." Malchus saved the best for last. "Someone has stolen a treasure of Caesar's. A gold ring was found on one of these followers with Caesar's seal from Emperor Antony's reign." Malchus studied the sick man's face. "It's priceless and belongs to Emperor Tiberius." Sejanus face was blank. "They are plundering your storehouses."

The governor's rage began to stir. It started from his neck and rose up until it reached his eyes. From behind his eyes, it exploded into the room.

Malchus moved back a pace.

The man rose from his bed, shouted for a servant to bring his robe, then paced in circles mumbling to himself. He coughed. Malchus was uncertain what the governor was planning.

Sejanus' hair was disheveled. A slave helped him slip on a robe. The governor stood still like a child while the slave tied the robe and smoothed it out. "Brush my hair," he said to the slave. The man obeyed.

"Has the thief been arrested?"

Malchus felt at last that his words were finally being taken seriously. He inhaled then continued. "A Roman centurion defected and has been arrested. His wife has turned the thief in to us. She found the ring on the woman's finger. They have arrested this woman who insists that she was raised from the dead. She says that the ring was on her finger when she climbed out of the tomb."

"Absurd. Who in their right mind would believe such a story? Where is she now?"

"Antonia Fortress in Yerushalayim. She's been beaten and imprisoned without food. She still insists that the ring was given to her by a Roman commander." He paused. "The ring had been in the family possessions of an Alexander of Puteoli.

From my research, the family was honored by the great Antony Augustus. But the strange thing is that the commander has not reported it stolen or even missing. This impostor insists that Alexander gave her the ring."

Sejanus paced across his chamber. "Then we need to contact Alexander and report to him that the ring has been found. We must discover what he knows about this whole charade. Can you find him for me?"

"Yes I can, Your Majesty. I will set out today."

Rome's puppet ruler looked pallid. He sat down on the side of his bed to catch his breath. "I'm sure I'm being poisoned. You must find Alexander."

"I will ride to Puteoli today."

"Who has the emperor's ring?" Sejanus asked.

Malchus knew he had touched the governor's greedy heart. "I have it, sir."

## Chapter Thirty

# ANTONIA FORTRESS, YERUSHALAYIM, 33 A.D.

T he rusted iron scraped as a key was inserted into the huge lock. A series of clicks and the door opened. A scurry of soldiers shoved in through the doorway with swords and torches.

Anna held her hand over her eyes. The flashing torches were blinding. She now had been in the dungeon for five days without food or care. The only water she got was from a damp corner where it seeped in from outside somewhere. It had created a little pool from which she scooped water in her hands to drink. She was certain the soldiers had not planned for her to survive this imprisonment. Anna was surprised, too, that she had lasted this long. She was so weak.

The soldiers looked at her in shock. She was still alive and freed from the ropes.

"You're a witch, that's what you are. The rats are even afraid of you."

Anna was pale and very thin. Her eyes were sunken and shadowed, but there was an obvious peace that replaced all her other features. "I'm no witch. I'm a follower of Yeshua and he's been with me through all this."

"Treason! Don't speak that name here. We have the emperor as our god. You are imprisoned because of treason against Caesar's house."

The soldiers grabbed her arms, lifting her frail body upright. She struggled to remain standing. The bruises on her face and body had turned pale and yellow, but they were still obvious. Without further word, two soldiers dragged her out into the corridor. She was too weak to walk so the soldiers dragged her down the hall and up the stairs. A cold wind whistled behind them and Anna shivered. Rough hands herded her toward a lit doorway.

Anna was pushed into a room where a chair faced a rough wooden table. Strong hands shoved her into the chair. A torch flickered in the corner. The smell of burning oil mingled with mildew stung the lining of Anna's nose.

The table before Anna was laden on one side with a stack of parchments weighted by a bust of Caesar, on the other side sat a platter with bread, cheese and fruit. A bottle of wine was corked and waiting. Anna's throat was parched, her stomach shrunken to a point of disinterest.

The soldiers were rough. A tear slipped down her cheek as the soldiers pushed her, forcing her to sit erect in spite of her exhaustion. She grieved at their hardness of heart but said nothing. She only looked into their faces with kindness as they tied her hands down at the sides. One soldier turned his head away.

The captain was tall and towered above all the guards by an extra three inches. He was also the heaviest, with his stomach hanging over his leather belt. He sat down opposite Anna with the table between them and slowly uncorked the bottle of wine. He poured it into a silver goblet, his eyes fastened to Anna's face. Putting the goblet down in front of her, he pulled the tray of food close. With a cruel grin he stabbed a block of cheese, cut a piece and popped it into his mouth without his lips touching the knife. He chewed away. His pupils narrowed like pinpoints.

"Would you like a sip of wine, my dear?"

"No thank you." Anna's voice was no more than a light sound. "Water will be fine."

"I offer you wine and you have the nerve to make your own request. How dare you, you cheap thief." Suddenly he grabbed the goblet and flung the wine in Anna's face. She gasped to catch her breath; instinctively her tongue licked the drops around her mouth. She could taste the salt from her tears.

"Now let's try this again. Would you like a thick piece of bread?"

Anna had lost all hunger for food after three days without eating. She couldn't live without water, but her stomach had gone into starvation mode, a form of self-preservation. She thirsted for water, yet she was so grateful for the muddy puddles that had kept her alive. The drops of wine had stirred her palate for more liquid.

The man ripped off a piece of dark bread and walked around the table toward Anna. "You must be so hungry, woman. Let me help you."

Anna turned her head away, knowing what he was thinking. He forced her head up and yanked her jaw, turning her to face him.

"Open your mouth and eat or I'll open it for you and you'll never close it again."

Anna's tears swept past her lips, but her eyes looked into the captain's face with courage. She opened her mouth, waiting for his rough fingers to touch her face.

"That's a good girl." He shoved the bread into her mouth, forcing it down her throat. "Such a pretty face but so greedy. My, my, little girl. Your manners are appalling."

The crusty bread immediately lodged in Anna's throat. She choked and gagged. Pieces flew out of her mouth. Her face reddened, desperate to catch her breath.

"Water . . . please . . . I need a drink." she managed to say.

"Ohhh, I love to see a beautiful creature like you beg. What would you like, sweetheart? I'll come a little closer so I can hear." He leaned close to her face, touching her skin with his mouth. "Please say it again."

Anna couldn't breathe. "Please . . ."

"Oh, something to drink. Perhaps some wine this time?"

The captain returned to the table and filled a goblet with red wine. Anna's face was turning purple. The man brought the cup toward her. He lifted it with a grin. "Here's to ya."

Again the captain tossed the cup at her, splattering her face and hair. She could not even sip the drops with her tongue since her mouth was packed with crust. Anna felt she might lose consciousness. Instinctively she pulled at her bonds, moving and writhing to shake the bread lose from her mouth. She was certain she was going to choke to death. Suddenly the captain stood and slapped her back, forcing the bread out of her throat. Her back would be tender for a while, but she could now breathe and was grateful to Yeshua for saving her life.

The jailer sat on the end of a table, folded his arms and studied the woman intently. He knew well enough that the taste of wine and bread crumbs would stir hunger in this starving woman. She would want some real food.

"I hope you've enjoyed your meal." He shifted. "Do you have anything to say?"

Anna's blue eyes begged the jailer for mercy. After several gulps of air, she tried to speak, "Why . . . am I here? Why have I been arrested?"

The jailer shouted. "Don't play dumb with me! You know why you've been arrested! Anyone who plunders a Jewish grave, takes on a false identity, then steals property from Caesar's treasures must anticipate retribution from Rome!"

Slowly Anna realized what it might be. *The ring.* She looked down at her left hand. It was gone. For the first time it became clear. She had been betrayed.

"Aha! You've just incriminated yourself. In my book you're guilty, but we'll let Governor Sejanus decide himself."

"The ring . . ." Anna was desperate to explain. "I had a ring and it's gone."

"Oh, no fear. We've sent it back to Rome."

Anna's face lit up. "Then that clears it up. The ring has gone back to Alexander and . . ."

The jailer's face turned white. "You, whoever you are, will be tried for treason against Caesar's house. Stealing one of Caesar's treasures is punishable by death. There are also the charges of tomb raiding and fraud. You could be spying on our military plans."

"But I can explain. If you allow me to get a letter to Alexander of Puteoli he'll confirm that he gave me that ring as a gift."

"Commander Alexander of Puteoli? Commander Alexander?" The captain looked shocked. Anna nodded her head yes.

"May the gods strike you blind. There is no way . . ."

"There is only one God, invisible and overall . . ."

A guard beside her turned and slapped her across the face. It burned but courage rose in her countenance. "I am a Jew . . . and believe . . ."

"I don't care what you believe. It means nothing to me what you believe. The gods of Rome have made her powerful and wealthy. The puny god of the Jews has only brought you barren dusty land. You're under Roman rule. You are subservient to our commands, our gods and our laws. You will be tried before Emperor Tiberius."

Beaten and battered, Anna remembered Yeshua's eyes as he witnessed her betrayal. He had promised to be with her and indeed he was. Three men twice her size had tried to defeat her faith. "My God is Yeshua. He alone is Lord."

In a moment of rage, the guards picked her up, still tied to the chair, and carried her down the long corridor, removed the ropes and threw her inside the filthy cell.

Anna was beaten and left to rot. The only word she spoke was in reverence, "Yeshua." She never complained or cried out. She remained silent and calm for the next two days and nights. By the next morning, in spite of her darkened room, Anna roused, crawled on her stomach to the corner and drank deeply from the muddy water. It tasted wonderful. She knew that Yeshua was by her side comforting her in the darkness and that he wept over her suffering.

# Chapter Thirty-One

# Puteoli, Italy, 33 A.D.

Alexander was livid. He was in such a rage that he grabbed whatever was nearest him and threw it out the window into the garden. He'd decapitated a statue of Venus after being notified that Anna's tomb had been ransacked and plundered. Whoever had done this had even taken her bones. Not a shred of memory was left untainted, not a strand of hair was found in the tomb. *Who would do such a sacrilegious thing?*

Alexander went outside, picked up the two-foot idol and apologized to it. Losing its head made it shorter. He carried the two pieces back inside, angry at what he'd done. Venus had been carved out of white marble.

Alexander had been informed that a woman was wearing the family's ring and calling herself Anna. *How could someone be so brazen? She'll never get away with this.* Now someone was coming to confirm the story. Alexander would have to think about losing Anna all over again. He'd have to drag out those painful memories, explain that the ring, his ring . . . he had been rejected by a Jewess, the mother of his daughter, Charis.

Alexander looked at the statue. *It's too bad they can't mend themselves.* He hadn't gotten over his reason for this violence, but he didn't want his household to see the damage he'd done to a god, and he certainly didn't want Charis to see. She understood more than he anticipated anyway.

"Papà, why do you have so many gods in the house?" Charis had asked one day in absolute innocence.

Alexander had struggled to come up with a clear answer. He finally said, "Charis, it's because each one of them has different powers and they can help us in different ways. Like Zeus, he brings the storms so the fields will stay green. And Diana, she . . . brings . . . families." He'd just lied to his own daughter. How many times had Lucia prayed to Diana for a child and all she got was a malignant lump that grew in her stomach?

Charis pondered that for a while then came back with another question, "Isn't there one god that can fix everything?"

Alexander shook his head slowly. He was amazed at his daughter's perception on spiritual issues. *She must get this curious inclination from her mother.*

"But Papà, that means they can't do everything," Charis pointed out. The father nodded again.

"They all do something different."

Then she threw another question his way. "Why don't they answer you? I hear you ask them questions, but they never speak."

"Well, Charis, these idols are just stone images of the real gods. They can't speak." Alexander thought the answer sounded plausible enough for a little girl.

"So why do you talk to them then, if they're not real?"

"I guess . . . well . . ." Alexander scratched his head. "It is rather silly isn't it?"

Charis smiled. She was now three years old and filled with many questions. "Papà, if these aren't the real gods, then where do the real ones live?" The cherub-like smile looked expectantly at her father for an answer. He had none, at least for this subject. It angered him. He should have an answer for the question that matters most; "Who fixes everything?"

Now today, Charis would find Venus broken, headless. Venus' placid smile didn't change in spite of being separated from her body. It didn't seem to matter to her one way or the other.

Quickly, Alexander gathered the remains and took them out to the fields. He'd bury them then get a new statue to replace this one. Something about the act seemed so undeniably silly, yet that was all he knew. The answer certainly was not Anna's invisible god. He had offered nothing but poverty and death which made Alexander remember why he'd thrown Venus out the window in the first place. And now some stranger is coming from Rome to discuss this crime.

Alexander looked at Venus half buried in the ground. Her marbled legs lay exposed, looking so human and so dead. Anger grew again. If Charis ever saw this, it would scare her badly. He picked up a big rock and with both hands threw it down on Venus. It felt good.

*I hate these gods who play with our lives like we're just pieces on some glorious board game. They take pleasure in watching us struggle with life. None of them offer hope.* He picked up another large stone and slammed it against the image. Venus made no complaint as Alexander broke her to pieces and smashed her nearly to powder.

As he walked away, he whispered, "Sorry," just in case he might be wrong. He could use a good bottle of vintage wine to start this day. *I'll replace Venus with a nice indoor fern.*

"Papà," Charis called from the patio. "Come for some breakfast."

"Coming, love, I'll be right there." Wiping the dirt from his hands, he headed back toward the kitchen.

Charis wrapped her arms around his leg and said, "What were you doing out there, Papà?"

He was thoughtful. "I was planting some seeds."

"What kind of seeds?" Her emerald eyes glistened, her face full of wonder just like her mother.

"Seeds of doubt, sweetheart, seeds of doubt." He swept her up in his arms and carried her to the kitchen where something smelled very delicious.

"What are seeds of doubt?" little Charis asked with innocent eyes. She was still wrapped in her father's big arms.

"Something I hope you never have growing in you." He knuckled her tummy until she giggled. "Now let's enjoy our breakfast and see what's in store for today. All right?"

"All right!" Grinning at each other, Alexander kissed her on the forehead.

The servant had laden the table with fruit and savory cakes with date-honey imported from Judea. They were still warm. The two-member family sat at the table with both reaching for the honey cakes at the same time.

In front of the villa, there was the sound of horse hooves, gravel crunching under foot, then pounding at the front door. The servants looked startled. Unexpected guests were rare out here in the country. A male servant scurried to answer the door.

Alexander groaned. A courier had already brought a message from the emperor: *"Expect my representative soon. He comes bearing news of unrest in Yerushalayim and he is in possession of a family treasure belonging to you. Greet him as you would greet me.*

*Signed,*

*Governor Sejanus"*

The thought of having any household members of the emperor in his home was distasteful. His representative would probably be some idiot with similar propensities for evil. Alexander did not feel like dealing with some stranger about the atrocities of Yerushalayim. It brought back too many memories of Anna . . . his loss . . . his daughter's loss. He didn't need a moron telling him what he'd lost or how to fight a war, either.

The governor's representative strode into Alexander's entryway with dramatic flair. Instantly, Alexander knew this was no soldier. He had no spine. The man was an enigma, a mélange of cultures not belonging anywhere. He didn't like the guy, especially because he came in the emperor's name. The man seemed ambitious, but nothing more.

## Pella, Greek City of Syria, 33 A.D.

Democritus arrived at Pella's open gates and paused to look back from where he'd climbed. The sky was a vault of untouched blue across the horizon. In the distance, he could see the lower elevations, low lying Judean hills on the valley floor, a humble monument to his faith in his Messiah.

The soldier turned toward the city. The grandeur of Rome's architecture had brushed across Pella's hillside with limestone and marbled buildings, a small amphitheater, a library fronted by colonnades and bath houses. A deep pool beneath a blazing sun shimmered as it divided into small tributaries that found their way down the thirsty hillside.

The inhabitants of Pella embraced Rome's pantheistic religion of multiple gods. Diana, Hermes, Apollo and Aphrodite were stationed within the circumference of the walled city. Their presence dominated the town and people lived under their control. Today seemed, however, a specimen of nature's magnificence. It seemed impossible that anything could shadow its crystal clarity.

For the first time, Democritus walked across the enemy's threshold with a genuine confidence in his defenses. He wore Yeshua's tattered cloak only as a reminder that he was covered in Yeshua's blood-bought armor. The calluses on his feet and knees assured him of his finite humanity. He felt Yeshua's Spirit burning within him. The passion in his heart convinced him of Yeshua's victory over death. That was all that mattered.

The city's entrance was serene as Democritus stepped through the gates. The air was dry, the sun brilliant. Unprepared for his arrival, all remained calm and pristine as the soldier strode toward the pool. He lowered his head while scooping a handful of water and drank. A sparrow mimicked him. People strolled across the paved walkways in deep discussion. Two boys ran, bobbing a small, leather, bean-filled ball, their laughter echoing against the courtyard walls. Lush ferns waved as the children ran past.

But the calm was short-lived. Within minutes the warrior's presence was felt. A tremor rumbled from shadowed corners and behind the eyes of the stone guardians of the city. The spirit world shuddered. Democritus had disturbed the darkness. Shadows now flickered against the buildings. Fast and furious, they fanned the air from their gathering grounds and swarmed down, surrounding Democritus like a wall. Yeshua's lone warrior stood in the center of the battlefield prepared to fight for victory.

The fighter followed a serpentine cobbled lane that led to a crowded hill. Following him, shadows followed restlessly against the walls, fearful to let him out of their sight. As he approached the summit, he discovered a large crowd which appeared to be women gathering around a twenty-foot image of Diana, the goddess of fertility.

The stone image was magnificent in detail. Smooth graceful lines of the woman's robe draped down to her ankles. Her face was serene, stone eyes looking out over the valley below, seeing nothing. A quiver hung from her back and her hair was tied with bands of ribbon that accented her sculptured profile. One arm stretched outward, beckoning people to her. Her beauty was striking, her smile sensuous and her bosom full. Her perfect image was alluring to all who saw her.

Behind Diana's eyes, something moved and watched. The warrior stared at the image and then at the wailing women gathered round her. They were desperate, begging for a child from the benevolence of Diana. The darkness was palpable.

Demonic eyes followed his every move, resisted his force, demanding he leave.

A holy rage rose in Democritus. The Spirit of the Lord rushed upon the warrior.[60] He pointed to the statue. "In the name of Yeshua, get out," he commanded. "Get out of Pella and be gone to the Abyss." There was a violent reaction and a loud crack as fissures spread across Diana's face and webbed down her neck. The integrity of the statue had been compromised. Although she remained standing, her beauty was instantly diminished. She looked more like a child's broken doll.

The worshippers were terrified and became frantic. Their voices rose louder and pleaded to Diana with greater urgency. A second crack formed from the crown of her head and travelled down one side of her face. Fragments broke loose and began to rain down on the women, yet they refused to move. They screamed all the more, pleading, chanting, begging for Diana to give them a child.

Democritus shouted, "Move away everyone! Your lives are in danger. This could fall and kill you." He rushed toward them, pushing some and pulling others by the arms. The left side of Diana's face, eye, cheek and mouth fell away, rubble tumbled to the ground and landed in the middle of the women. Its eye stared up to the sky, without sight or understanding.

Previously, women had lain prostrate, pleading for help from the stone face. They begged and wailed, willing to do whatever it took to become fertile and bear children. Gifts of desperation littered the ground; decaying fruit, wilted flowers, scattered coins left untouched. Now they stood back, shocked and confused.

Democritus recognized the delusion. These women believed a stone idol could produce a human child. Diana's secret seemed hideous to Democritus, to human reason. She

---

[60] I Sa. 10:10

seemed to laugh and say, "They're mine. They're all mine. I control their darkness."

Democritus remembered his own blindness, his own demons. It only took a single cry of help before his mind could accept the Messiah, one brief moment of hope. Democritus noticed one woman still pleading with the nearly faceless Diana for help. He walked toward her.

This middle-aged woman lay prostrate, her face in the dust. Her arms were outstretched offering several coins. She was slender and graceful, yet before the idol she was self-loathing. Democritus watched and prayed. Finally, she raised her head but didn't look up, tears streaming down her cheeks. The warrior moved closer. Ugly scars webbed across her face and arms. She pleaded wearily, "Oh Diana, I beg you again to make me as fertile as the Valley of Gihon. Give me a child. I'll do anything you ask, just give me a child."

Democritus knew. *That's how it begins. The human spirit cries out in desperation and darkness offers a promise of life it cannot deliver. If no one brings them the truth, they only have a lie to believe in.*

"Have mercy, Diana," she pled to the broken pillar of stone. "My husband has abandoned me, Diana. I'm a barren branch."

Before Democritus could do anything, the woman rose to her feet, pulled out a knife and slashed the blade across her cheek. Fresh blood flowed over ancient scars. She smeared herself with blood, hoping that Diana would notice and fill her barren womb. The act seemed in vivid contrast to her noble features. The broken statue showed no mercy.

Democritus was stirred by the weight of this woman's blindness. He felt her hopelessness and remembered his own until Yeshua set him free. He moved close enough to talk to the woman and whispered, "There is One God who hears your plea. He wants to lift your burden and help carry your load." The woman was startled and confused.

"Yeshua, God's Son, cares more for you than these slabs . . . than Diana. He knows everything about you and paid a great price for your life."

"Yeshua?" Already hope shifted her weight of despair. "Yeshua. I've heard of him. He healed a deaf man." She hesitated for a moment and looked up at Diana. She now saw the disfigured statue and the fire began to diminish in her anguish.

"Let me help you." Democritus lifted her from the ground. "I know this great and mighty Savior, Yeshua. He set me free from these same evil spirits."

She turned to Democritus. "How can you help me? You don't have the power of the gods. You're just a man." She dropped the bloody knife on the ground. She was weak and her hands trembled.

Democritus kicked the knife away from where they stood. "Yes, I'm only a man, a very weak one at that. But Yeshua gave his life for mine. He restored my sanity and set me free from the darkness of demons. His spirit now lives in me and I can see the world through his eyes. I see your suffering." Democritus looked into the woman's face. "Yeshua is more than a man. He is God and has come to bring wholeness to your life and take away the suffering you've lived with for years. He came to set you free." He took hold of her arms so she would look at him. "Isn't that what you want? Isn't that what you're looking for? Isn't that what you need?"

The woman's body was trembling. "Yes . . . I've pleaded with every god or goddess I know to give me a child, but I get no answer. Nothing." She seemed to sense the presence of evil around them. Democritus did too. "Can you help me?" Evil spirits were distracting her. They swarmed between Democritus and the woman . . . then swept up into the sky. The woman saw the spirits and reached for Democritus. "I see those dark images. They're after me. Help me, please."

Before Democritus could answer, a large shadow moved into his line of vision. The great statue was leaning forward.

It was about to crash to the ground destroying everybody. The warrior pulled the woman back and shouted to the crowd, "Quickly, move back . . . everyone! Diana is falling!" Then he shouted, "Spirit of Diana, you have no power over these people. Your demons are impotent before the God of the Universe. I speak in the name of Yeshua, the resurrected Savior, the Great I AM. Get out! Leave this city! Cursed are you to the Abyss!"

There was a quivering in the atmosphere and the force that gave power to the idol lost all its strength. Slowly, the huge idol with its broken face leaned further forward. Democritus saw spirits tumble helplessly from the sky. "In the name of the Great I AM, be gone!" The weakened demons scrambled away limping like wounded grasshoppers.

Democritus pulled the believing woman away from the crowd. "Move quickly! Move, everyone!" Stone shattered and cracked. Diana's head suddenly twisted. Fragments of broken stone shot out and rained down on the people.

"Get away. It's going to fall. Move! Move!" Democritus pulled people and shoved them away. The idol's head broke free and tumbled down with a thud. It shook the ground and landed face up. People screamed and scattered. In their minds, it appeared alive and they feared the wrath of the false god. The head cracked and broke apart. Diana's single eye had been sheared off and lay there. The eye stared at them and the women screamed. Democritus walked over to the shattered rock and slapped his hand across its face.

"People, you don't have to fear any longer. This rock is as lifeless as the stone from the mountainside where it was quarried."

Pandemonium ensued as weak-willed women ran screaming as the rest of the statue finally shuddered, split and landed across an ornamental garden. Flowers and shrubs were uprooted and torn in shreds. Gusts of wind blew the debris into the air.

Before the mighty power of the God of Israel, the colossal image tumbled from the sky.[61] Once she stood as a pillar of divine authority over the city of Pella, now she lay as dust that the wind carried along while people coughed and rushed to their homes, terrified at the power of one man, a stranger and his God.

Democritus turned to the trembling woman. "What's your name?"

"Daphne." She struggled to speak.

"What have you just witnessed, Daphne?"

"I've seen the hand of God."

"You've seen the power of God break down one of Satan's strongholds. If you believe, you'll see other great victories in the name of Yeshua. Others will find hope because of your faith. They will find life because of you."

Daphne believed hope had found its way into her heart. Her face and arms were covered with dried blood and dust. But behind that, Democritus could see courage.

"Do you have some place we can go? This city is going to be dangerous soon." A crowd of men were shouting and moving up the hill.

"I do. A year ago my husband left me for a younger woman. He left me with nothing. I rent a room and it's very humble, but you'll be safe there." She motioned and he followed her down a street away from the angry voices. She led him into the shadowy lanes.

"I'm used to caves, so anything is fine."

The woman hurried. She headed along an alley that turned right. They came to a row of shops. Behind was a stone wall. Democritus followed Daphne down the narrow alley where a door was built into the back of a shop. Daphne unlocked the door and led Democritus into a sparsely furnished room.

---

[61] I Sa. 5:3 "Dagon (a god of the Philistines) had fallen face downward on the ground before the ark of the Lord!"

Democritus closed the door and latched it. He found a stool and propped it against the door. "Do many people know where you live?"

"Not many. I have very few friends. When my husband abandoned me, I was scorned by the people of Pella. I was barren so he had a right to leave me. I've failed him as a wife." She pointed to the scars on her face. "These marks let everyone know of my shameful barren state." She paused. "I'm a scourge in Pella."

"Daphne, you had no part in not being able to bear children. You've punished yourself without cause."

"But I failed my husband." She wept.

"You failed no one but yourself by believing a lie. Tell me more about these scars on your body. How often have you done this to yourself?"

"The first ones came from my husband. He cut my face to tell everyone I was barren. After that, I found myself compelled to do the same thing. Every time I passed Diana, I felt drawn to her. She calls to me. She told me to offer my blood in exchange for a . . . a . . . child." She buried her face in her hands. "But today I saw darkness in her eyes. Those dark creatures, what were they?"

"Those were spirits that came straight from hell, Daphne. Your eyes have been opened to truth. The image up there on the hill, which is no more, was a mere representation of evil; evil that has controlled you and others in this city for a lifetime. God has sent me to bring release, and you are the first fruit here of his love."

Daphne cleared her eyes and smiled. "I've felt despair for so long. It feels like a weight has been lifted from my soul." Daphne paused to listen. Someone was passing.

"Daphne, you are a delight to Yeshua. Let me tell you how he loves you and found you today."

Democritus set to work as he spoke. He found a basin and poured water from a jug that was on the floor. The rich household items were ornate and seemed out of place in this earthen-floored room. The soldier could feel the profound depth of Daphne's losses. The few possessions she had from her former life were mere distractions now in this place of survival. Democritus admired the woman's honesty in light of these discoveries.

Daphne's eyes followed the soldier in amazement. Democritus' words were extraordinary, and so was his heart. Now his actions astonished her all the more as he moved to where she sat and began to bathe her face with clean water. At first Daphne flinched and turned her head away.

"Let me clean these wounds," Democritus said. "That will lessen the scars." He used a cloth to gently wash the crusted gashes. "You belong to Yeshua. He cares about everything in your life." Daphne wept at his tenderness. No one had cared for her like this before. No heart had been found in Pella as gentle and pure as this mighty warrior.

Without warning, something heavy struck the door with a thud. The sound startled Daphne but she kept quiet. Her eyes told Democritus this was dangerous. A second thud strained the hinges and forced the door inward, pushing the legs of the stool into the ground. There was a commotion of men's voices. "They've found us," Daphne whispered as the voices and cursing increased. Panels of wood broke loose as the door splintered. They both stood and backed away to the far side of the room.

Chapter Thirty-Two

# THE DUNGEON, ANTONIA FORTRESS, YERUSHALAYIM, 33 A.D.

Anna had survived on water alone for days now, but time had lost significance in the eclipse of darkness. When sameness rules in earthly bodies, it suspends time in the mind, but not the heart. In the perpetual blackness, Anna worshiped. She recalled David's words, *". . . if I make my bed in the depths, you are there . . . If I say, 'Surely the darkness will hide me and the light become night around me,' even the darkness will not be dark to you; the night will shine like the day, for darkness is as light to you."*[62] As time floated past her, she often sang those words or talked in hushed whispers to Yahweh and prayed earnestly for her daughter, and for Alex.

Without food her body seemed more like a shadow, but God had provided water of which she drank regularly. It quenched her thirst and kept her alive. She didn't know the details, but she knew she was being kept alive for a purpose. She would wait for that flower to unfold. She believed it was for the sake

---

[62] Ps. 139:8b, 11-12

of Yeshua and also for the salvation of Charis, her daughter, and perhaps Alexander. She prayed he would surrender to Yeshua's love.

Dozing for a while, Anna was awakened by a new sound. The water bubbled quietly but behind that she heard a human voice. It was a papery whisper. With the room black, she listened for the direction of the sound. She slid toward it. The sound was persistent. She moved along the wall and listened. It sounded like a woman's voice. How could that be?

"Love, I've brought you some food."

Anna was certain she must be dreaming. There was no way a person could get into this dungeon cell without passing the guards.

"Love, listen. Come closer to the wall. I've got food for you."

Suddenly a thin fingertip touched Anna's shoulder and she nearly fainted. The fingertip clutched Anna's shoulder. "Here, love. There's a hole in the wall. Follow my arm."

Terror metered by hope drew Anna toward the fingers, then she slid her hand along the wrinkled arm until she touched the opening in the wall. A flicker of light sprung from the opening and two wide eyes peered at Anna. She nearly screamed, then pressed her hands over her mouth in absolute joy.

"Oh dear, you've given me quite a fright. Who are you and how did you find me?"

"I am Sorakin. Yeshua told me about you and told me I must bring food until you are strong enough to travel to Rome." The wrinkled eyes blinked as the torch flickered in her hand. "I discovered this tunnel from the Temple to where you are and . . ."

"Where am I? I don't know where I am and I understand there are charges against me."

"You're in the Antonia Fortress. That sly ole' Herod built this to try and impress God, but we know what counts with God, don't we love!"

"But how do you know all this?"

"Listen pet, I'm a nosy old woman. I can find out just about anything. I also listen to Yeshua's voice."

Up until recently it had not occurred to Anna that someone might have turned her in. *Who could have done it? Priscilla?* She'd wondered where Priscilla was when the soldiers carried her away. *I've been betrayed.* Anna suddenly felt sick. She had trusted her. God had used her. Why had she done this? *Her husband. Yes, Priscilla must have made a deal to trade her in exchange for her husband's release. Who could blame her? She feared for his safety as well as her own. I hope the Romans kept their promise.*

Sorakin handed Anna a small loaf of bread. Next came some fruit, a piece of cheese and finally a leather pouch of goat's milk. "You must drink the milk now so there will be no trace that I was here. I'll bring you food and drink every day until the Lord tells me to stop."

Anna wept for joy as she took the food. She ate with a thankful heart. She would save the fruit for last.

"God never fails, does he?"

"Never, my pet, never. But we sure botch up his plans often. Look what a mess we're in right now. The Romans are rounding up everyone who follows Yeshua. You'll be going to Rome soon. I wish I knew what to do." She paused. "All I've been told is to care for you, my daughter. By the way, what's your name?" The eyes blinked kindly.

"Anna. My name is Anna. And I think perhaps you can help me with something else too, if you will."

"What is it, dear?"

Anna's voice heightened with excitement. A plan was forming in her mind as she spoke. "I'll need two pieces of parchment and something to write with. It will be difficult in the dark, but if you bring your torch again, I might be able to do this."

"What do you plan to do?" The old woman's nosy nature was right on target.

"I must write a letter to Alexander of Puteoli. I was accused of stealing his ring which is a family heirloom, and he's the father of my daughter. I want to see her so badly. If you can help me get the letter to Alexander, I'm certain he'll believe what I say and have me released." She paused. "Sorakin, I did not steal that ring. Alexander offered it to me when I was alive, and I turned him down. He must have put it on my finger when he buried me."

Sorakin took in a long deep breath. *Uh oh! Here's another one of those people who died and came back again. Why do I get all the strange ones?* Considering Adam's long story, she settled back against the tunnel wall and said, "Go ahead, love, tell me your story. If I'm going to help, I should know your story. Tell me everything."

As Anna talked, Sorakin's cunning mind formed a clever web that would attach one strand from Anna's black dungeon to Adam, an innocent messenger. He would carry the final thread of truth to Caesar's household. *Hmmm. A great thought. Must of come from up yonder. Two can play Caesar's sneaky games.*

"Sorakin, are you listening?" The old woman nodded in the flickering shadows. "I'll need some parchment as soon as possible. Can you arrange that?"

"Certainly I can, love . . . and I've heard every word. I'll come by tomorrow at this time with more food, but it might take a while to round up your writin' material." She paused only for a second. "I must go. This torch won't last much longer." Sorakin winked a wrinkled eye.

Looking through the hand-sized hole in the wall, Anna watched the old woman turn and hobble up the damp tunnel until she disappeared.

---

Sorakin emerged from the small archway into the filtered recesses of the Temple grounds. A shadow remained motionless like a pillar between the columns. The obscure figure had been following Sorakin. For a bold second she stared directly at the shadow, willing him to show his face, then turned down the hill toward her meager dwelling. Adam would be expecting his dinner. Sorakin smiled as she walked out of the Temple courts.

Shoulders thudded hard against the door frame. Splinters were shooting in every direction. Daphne stood back in horror. Democritus stood in front of her for protection.

"This is happening because of me, Daphne. I've brought this on you."

"No. It's happening because I turned my back on Diana and her forces. You've simply opened my eyes. The demons are angry. They control most of this city."

Curses erupted between the thudding and cracking of soft wood. Through the slatted door Democritus could see men crashing against it with their bodies. It wouldn't hold for long. Already the hinges were coming loose.

"Is there a back way out?"

"No. I'm sorry. This room is all there is." Daphne's face had gone pale.

"We have no weapons and we have no escape route. But we have Yeshua's promise and his power," Democritus said with certainty.

"What is that?" Daphne's simple faith was open to truth wherever it could be found. Democritus gave a confident smile that reassured Daphne immediately.

"Yeshua said, '*And surely I am with you always, to the very end of the age*'[63] He is here with us."

By faith Daphne believed these words were true and waited for Democritus' instructions. Instead, he began to pray. His

---

[63] Mt. 28:20

prayer was like an iron rod that struck against Heaven's door seeking permission for entrance. The man prayed quietly but with persuasion and assurance. Daphne listened and agreed with everything he said. Then Democritus became so overcome with prayer that he went silent. Beads of sweat dripped from his forehead. He was pleading, seeking entrance into God's presence through Yeshua.

The men continued to slam their bodies against the door. Another plank splintered.

Daphne moved behind Democritus who was now kneeling with his head bowed, touching the earth. Sweat dropped from the warrior's forehead, falling to the ground like raindrops. Daphne knelt behind him. Her lips called out in silence, "Yeshua," and in that instant a power flowed through her unlike anything she'd ever known. She believed all things were possible.

Her hand touched the warrior's shoulder to steady herself, and suddenly the pair melded into one voice of faith. "Lord, you opened blind eyes, you can also blind these men."[64]

With a loud shudder, a flap of wind and dust swept through the room. The door flattened to the ground with three grizzly men piled on top. Their ruddy faces and bulky shoulders left no mistake of their intentions.

Democritus didn't move. He didn't look up. Daphne stayed behind him, the two a single shadow.

The men scrambled to their feet and shook their heads. They were dazed and disoriented. They looked around the room. It appeared empty.

"*Mafee hena*," the shortest man was astonished. "There's nobody here."

"*Ana ma fehempt*,"[65] a second man said scratching his head. "I don't understand."

---

[64] Opendoors.org

[65] Arabic

The men stood at the entrance of what appeared to be a completely empty room. There was a bed, a small table and one chair. Near the table was a jug and water basin. The basin had a cloth hanging over its edge, still soaking up water from the bottom of the bowl. In the center of the room, drops of water seemed to be dripping on the hard earthen floor. The men were puzzled. One of them looked at the ceiling. There was no lamp, no light and no movement in the room. Everything was in shadows.

In the center of the room two figures were hidden from the eyes of their enemy; Democritus and Daphne remained covered beneath the palm of God's hand.[66] They felt no fear.

With foolish expressions the three fighters walked out, trampling across the flattened door. They immediately headed toward a tavern and did not speak to each other until they had drunk as much ale as they could afford. Only then did they dare to wonder.

---

[66] Brother Andrew: "seeing eyes made blind" OpenDoors.org

# Chapter Thirty-Three

# PUTEOLI, ITALY, 33 A.D.

Malchus loved the fact that someone was waiting on him. He was born for this. He loved playing the role of Caesar's messenger. The commander's servants fussed over him, bowing, removing his cloak and sandals, then guiding him into the atrium of the villa. He quickly helped himself to the fruit that was spread on the table then settled into a chair nearby, expecting the servants to offer drink and other delicacies that he deserved as an elite; the emissary of the conquering ruler of the world.

As Alexander entered the room, his face easily betrayed his annoyance with the little man. "What's so important that you've come all the way to Puteoli to discuss with me?"

"I come in the name of Emperor Tiberius . . ."

"Yes, I know who the emperor of Rome is. He's busy as usual, involved in some perverse deeds on the Isle of Capri. And what does the emperor want from me that his governor can't tell me in person? I run his armies. And who did you say you were?"

Malchus ignored the barb. He leaned back and said with an air of self-importance, "The governor is planning a three-fold attack against Judea."

The soldier did not show interest. Malchus plowed on with the plan. "First, he wants to send in troops to break up a band of religious fanatics."

"What band?" Alexander's eyes looked over Malchus' head at a distant point on the wall.

"Why, the followers of this Yeshua. I thought you knew."

"But he's dead. The whole world knows that. Certainly Rome can't be afraid of a dead leader."

"That's the point. His followers have stolen his body and made claims that he rose from the dead. His tomb was empty and the guards can't remember a thing. This has stirred up more followers than ever. Multitudes are following him. This magic *resurrection* story has seemed to entice them to believe. The band is growing by the hundreds, perhaps thousands, and they're not just Jews, but Greeks and even Romans." Malchus paused to watch the soldier's eyes dilate.

"Now there are people who claim to have died and risen like their leader. It's troubling the emperor greatly. And Governor Sejanus is not a well man. He thinks he's being poisoned."

Alexander scrutinized the man sitting in his home. He was annoyed by his effeminate gestures and trite comments. He groaned aloud. "And what are the other two parts of the plan Sejanus has, assuming that he successfully rounds up all the followers, which I have some serious doubts about . . . as a soldier myself?" Something wasn't right about this unknown messenger from Rome.

"He plans to put all tomb raiders on trial in the Stadium. There will be a mass execution of all found guilty of tomb raiding. His final step is to expel every Jew in Rome who follows Yeshua."

"Impossible. First, this band can't be large enough to build an army, and as far as I know they don't hold public gatherings. This would require using a great amount of manpower to scour Judea. We have other fish that are bigger and more threatening than this Judean humbug."

"More than Judea." Malchus looked at his fingernails as he spoke. "They are moving into Syrian cities as we speak. In fact, these Yeshua followers are scattered all across the Mediterranean coastlands. The weapons they use are not swords and spears, but power to change minds and loyalties. This could easily explode into an insurrection against the Empire."

Alexander groaned inside as he focused on this misfit. "You must be joking. The whole thing seems preposterous. Why would a movement grow and threaten Rome *after* the man died? These followers were not a threat to Rome when the man was living. Why didn't he try to recruit an army back then? It doesn't make any sense at all." Alexander was getting red in the face. This whole story of Yeshua was closer to him than he would dare to admit and he didn't like this weasel telling him how to run his military campaign.

Malchus leaned closer to Alexander's chair. "Who knows what these Jews and religious fanatics are capable of doing. I suspect there is an infiltrator at the palace. Sejanus is not well and it looks like poison."

"Come now, that runs in the family. You can't blame everything on these Jewish peasants."

Malchus didn't reply. He withdrew a leather pouch and held it in his hand. "There's nothing these followers won't do to pretend Yeshua is still alive. They'll do anything to convince the world they're right." He motioned for Alexander to hold out his hand. Then with a practiced flair he emptied the contents.

The soldier looked at the object, clutched it and slumped back into his chair.

Malchus smiled.

Alexander could face an army of men with courage, but the ocean of emotions that welled up within was too much for his broad shoulders. He slumped at the sight of the ring. Instantly, feelings of rejection, loss and betrayal consumed him. Malchus watched with victory as the great commander wilted like a leaf, and then knew he'd gotten to him.

"I know how personal this is to you, Alexander. I've taken liberty to have a scout follow up on this woman impostor. She claims to be . . ."

"I've heard," he said weakly. "She claims to be Anna, the mother of my child." Alexander's gaze went to the ring in his hand. He was feeling sick. To show weakness in front of this puny little man was too much.

"It's a terrible injustice that you've had to endure, the thing about her tomb being vandalized and desecrated. I know you must want justice and the criminal convicted."

"How would you know?" His voice was louder than he meant it to be.

"She might try to get in touch with you . . . this impostor. She's a desperate woman, and is being held in the Antonia Fortress until she can be transported to Rome." Malchus tried to make his voice tender, almost teary. "I know that you shouldn't have to deal with this impostor's mischief. It would be too much for you and your daughter." He watched the soldier's eyes. "I've got someone watching her right now. I'll make sure she doesn't bother you and that she arrives in Rome for trial."

The soldier's emotions had betrayed him. Instead of succumbing to them he stood, anger rising in his voice.

"I want this woman in Rome." He was almost shouting. "She must face Governor Sejanus and confess her crimes."

"That's just what I thought you would say, commander." Malchus leaned back in the lounge and took a sip of ale. "You are too important to have this thing clutter your life and hinder your career, not to mention puzzle your child." He shook his head. "Your daughter should never have to face the confusion of her own mother's identity. It's terrible enough for her to know she's dead, but to have an impostor announce that she's alive again?"

Alexander was too livid to notice the change in the messenger. He was caught up in the rage against such injustice done to him . . . and to his daughter. "How soon can she be sent before the Governor?"

"I'll make all the arrangements. We must pray to the gods that Emperor Tiberius will return to Rome."

"You've found that the gods of Rome answer your prayers?" Alexander couldn't help responding to this bigot's comments. Then he relaxed his shoulders. With a numbed expression Alexander asked Malchus, "What does Sejanus want me to do?"

# Chapter Thirty-Four

# UPPER YERUSHALAYIM, 33 A.D.

I t took Sorakin three days to find two scrolls of papyrus suitable for writing. It was expensive and rare. She had been uncertain how she would come up with pen and ink. They were also scarce. Then she thought of Adam. He could do it. Adam would have to get the materials from a scribe in the Temple. With Adam's winsome personality he would know how to convince an old scribe to give him a slightly imperfect scroll or two of precious papyrus, a pot of ink and a reed-pen.

Adam walked through the Temple courtyard into a small chamber where three scribes sat hunched over tables carefully transcribing portions of Yesha'yahu.[67] Most of the scribes were so intent they wouldn't hear the roar of thunder. One scribe was sensitive to any interruption, however. His hair was white and fell into ringlets. With steady bright eyes, he leaned over a parchment. He was dipping the reed-pen into the ink-horn when he caught sight of Adam strolling toward him.

"Shalom." Adam smiled and bowed respectfully.

"Shalom. Can I help you?"

---

[67] Yesha'yahu, "Isaiah" in Hebrew, meaning "YAHWEH is salvation"

Adam peered over the scribe's shoulder to see his work. The old man smiled. Unused to having visitors, the scribe leaned away from the parchment, not allowing a drop of ink to carelessly fall. One blotch or smudge would cost him a year's labor. He would have to redo the entire manuscript. On the floor was a basket with several slightly imperfect scrolls.

"The prophecies of Isaiah," Adam said.

"You can read?" The old man's eyes twinkled in mischief.

With his hands folded behind him, Adam leaned over the text and began to read what he knew by heart, *"The people walking in darkness have seen a great light; on those living in the land of the shadow of death a light has dawned."*[68]

The scribe was impressed. Adam looked at the last portion the scribe had been copying. The varnish was still glistening damp.

Adam read aloud, *"For to us a child is born, to us a son is given, and the government will be on his shoulders. And he will be called . . .,"* the scribe's voice chimed in with Adam's whispered reading, *". . . Wonderful Counselor, Mighty God, Everlasting Father, Prince of Peace."*[69]

The scribe was lost in the beauty of the text. His eyes seemed to sparkle even in shadow.

Adam uttered the holy name that came so easily from his lips. Both the old scribe and Adam whispered a name in unison, a name not transcribed, but was the fulfillment of Isaiah's vision.

*"Yeshua."* Their eyes locked, each burning with faith. Ten minutes later Adam carried out a reed-pen and an ink-horn of black varnish. Waving back to the scribe, he promised to return soon.

[68] Is. 9:2

[69] Is. 9:6

Sorakin moved slowly down the long throat of the tunnel toward the Antonia Fortress pit. She carried the torch in one hand and a sack that included food, papyrus and writing instruments in the other. She knew this would be a long night. She would be the torch bearer as Anna wrote two letters; one for Alexander's eyes, the other for Caesar. Sorakin prayed for safety of the letters and the messenger. She'd grown too fond of Adam to lose him.

She was feeling her age as she approached the small opening where Anna lay silent.

"Anna, love, I'm here. You must be quick because the torch won't last long."

"Thank you, dear Sorakin. You've done a worthy thing in providing these things for me. May the Lord bless you."

"We must be quick. I'm just Sorakin. Now be quick."

Anna took the materials and began writing the message to Alexander. She would tell him some things that only the two of them knew. She would tell him Yeshua is alive. She would ask about Charis. She wrote quickly for she had been forming the letter in her mind for days.

"Anna, love, we must hurry. I won't be able to see my way back through the tunnel without light."

Anna was on the second scroll. "Just two more words for the governor."

The old woman's hand was growing weak. The light shimmered against the walls and faltered briefly.

Anna blew on the ink for it to dry. The first parchment had been rolled tightly and tied with a cord. "That's for Alexander, the real document." She handed it through the opening and gave it to Sorakin. "This one is for the emperor, whichever one is reigning by the time it arrives." Anna started to roll it, but the torch in Sorakin's hand began to flicker.

"Anna, I must go. This is a long dark tunnel."

Anna handed the second scroll through the opening without tying it. "You must tie it yourself . . . here." Sorakin's small hand grabbed it when suddenly the torch flickered and died. Everything went black.

"Oh dearie me. I must find my way out of this hell hole." She groped the walls. Throwing the torch to one side, she clutched at her belongings in the dark.

"Sorakin, I'm so sorry. I will pray you make it home safely."

"Yeshua never said this would be easy. Pray that these scrolls make it safely home, Anna. God be with you."

Sorakin groped the wet stones to feel her way forward. One scroll was in a bag and another under her arm. The tunnel beneath the Temple Mount was damp and slick. She slipped as the ground began to rise. She took slow deliberate steps, her hands sliding along the stone walls and her feet moving sluggishly. She stopped and placed the scroll in the bag with the other one.

"Oh dearie me. What have I done? I got myself lost." Sorakin could feel sweat dripping from her brow. "This is worse than having a baby. Oh dear. At least I could see what was coming."

Suddenly Sorakin slipped. She fell forward. "Mercy, Lord. I need a little mercy." She pulled herself up on her elbows. She was winded and paused to catch her breath. She knew she must keep moving or else be buried here by tomorrow. She finally got to her feet. She had scraped her knees. Turning to look back the way she had come, it was as dark as pitch. Disoriented, Sorakin couldn't tell if she was coming or going.

"Sorakin, take one step at a time," she told herself. "I've done this my whole life, one step at a time. Always working in the dark."

She heard a scuffling noise. *Perhaps rats.* Sorakin stretched her hands in front of her and took several steps forward. The old woman heard more noise. She stopped and listened.

Someone was breathing close by. A chill ran up her spine.

"Who's there?" Sorakin's voice trembled. She realized too late she shouldn't have said a word. She gave her location away to someone who shared the same stale air as her. They, too, were in the dark.

There was a loud crack. Sorakin saw a blinding light and sank to the floor. Someone cursed. After a while the sounds began to fade. She let the blessed web of unconsciousness surround her.

When Sorakin awoke, her face was bruised and throbbing. But she was in one piece. "Help me, Yeshua, help me." Now too weak to stand, she began to crawl on shaky hands and bloody knees through the long tunnel, hopefully toward the entrance.

Sorakin collapsed repeatedly where she would lay for a while until more strength was summoned to move forward. At times she feared that she might die here before anyone found her. Then she remembered asking Yeshua for help. She knew he would.

She saw a glimmer of light up ahead. Gasping, the old woman crawled slowly across the damp floor. The light grew brighter. She was too exhausted to call out. At the entrance was a tall muscular man who stood searching into the darkness.

"Help me please!" Sorakin cried. Her voice was barely a whisper.

Suddenly the man reached down. Lifting the little woman into his arms, Adam carried her away from the darkness.

"They . . . didn't . . . get it." Her weak voice had a sound of victory. "They didn't . . . get it, Adam."

The giant lowered his head and kissed the wrinkled woman on her cheek. "You're a tough lady, dear Sorakin."

Her eyes closed in exhaustion.

Sorakin fell into unconsciousness as Adam carried her home. She was so small, yet feisty. Adam would need to stay nearby until she recovered. She would argue, but he would not leave her alone until she was strong enough. He would make sure she was well cared for, then he would set sail with the scroll safely packed in his bag. The other scroll had disappeared. No doubt it would find its way into the governor's hands.

A mysterious figure emerged from the tunnel with the coveted scroll. Night had descended in Yerushalayim. Like a flickering phantom, he moved silently through the city and out of town. His journey to Rome would be long but worth it. It mattered not to him what was on the scroll, for he couldn't read. His contact in Rome had a network of infiltrators embedded in this Judean sect. He'd gotten a tip from a prison guard and then one night he spied the old woman descending into the Fortress tunnel. It was his lucky day. Sliding the scroll into a leather bag that he slung over his shoulder, he moved toward the coast where he would find a fishing vessel that could give him a cheap passage. The man was quite certain he had left the old woman dead. There was no way she could survive his clubbing and the repulsive rodents that lay waiting for her flesh.

Anna tried to pray. She knew time had a way of taking the edge off of hope and she determined not to focus on that. God would have his way. The eternal dimension was always right. Anna nibbled on some bread Sorakin had brought. Sensing a need to pray for Sorakin, the rest of the night she talked to the Father about the well-being of the old woman. Daylight came and went, and Anna continued to pray and worship. Deep in touchable darkness, Anna was certain she saw a faint Heavenly radiance beside her.

*"Anna, you will go to Rome to appear before Emperor Tiberius' governor and all the people of Rome. Do not be afraid for I will be with you all the way."* Anna smiled in the

darkness and drifted into a peaceful sleep. She slept for hours undisturbed.

Suddenly blazing fire woke her. Shouts and curses and the clanking of keys stirred her mind awake. She was not afraid. She was ready.

# Chapter Thirty-Five

# PELLA, SYRIA, 33 A.D., THE
# MONTH OF SHEVAT

D ays had swiftly passed since Daphne had experienced
Yeshua's gracious protection upon her life. Daily, she
grew in her understanding as her teacher, Democritus,
told her how Yeshua had come in human flesh, fulfilling ancient
prophecies through his own suffering. There her aching heart
found solace. How else could the Creator really understand
human weakness and suffering? Yeshua understood it because
he walked as a man, felt pain as a man, was rejected by man,
yet he remained sinless. His teachings were profound, unlike
any other human instructor. He taught with authority.[70]

Daphne came from an influential Syrian family. While
her brothers were educated, it was unusual that women would
receive formal training. Yet Daphne's parents quickly realized her brilliant and inquisitive mind as she questioned her
instructors in the field of science and religion. As Democritus
instructed her in the teachings of Yeshua, her mind was finally
satisfied. *Yeshua is the perfect sacrifice. No one has willingly
suffered and offered himself up as a sacrifice for the sins of*

---

[70] Jn. 7:46; Lu. 4:32

*the human race. He came for men and women.* Daphne's faith
came because of Yeshua, not Democritus. He pointed the way,
but Yeshua gave her new life. The gashes from Daphne's own
knife wounds were slowly healing, but scars would remain. She
had learned that Yeshua, too, bore the nail scars in his hands
and feet and from the spear in his side. His scars would remain
for eternity to remind everyone of the price he paid for their
salvation. Daphne took comfort from this thought. Her scars
would be part of her story to help others believe.

The few remaining friends of Daphne were surprised to see
her no longer in anguish. The scars still cut across her face and
arms, but her radiance overshadowed them to the degree that
her real beauty was all that people saw. There was a peace that
centered in her being that changed her countenance. The goddess, Diana, never did that for her.

Today, Democritus sat under a large almond tree positioned
perhaps twenty steps from the pool. Its sprawling branches
were laced with early blossoms of a pink-flushed white, always
the first to bloom. It seemed a promise of new life. It was late
in the Hebrew month of Shevat. Before anything had poked
its head from the winter earth, the almond tree brought a con-
vergence of delicate signs that life could be stirred out of this
barren land.

The warrior sat like a giant beneath the arching branches.
Children had gathered round to listen to his stories. Democritus'
non-Jewish features gave him an acceptance among the people
of Pella in spite of the fact that he spoke so freely of Yeshua, the
Jewish Messiah. Pella's long history of Jewish oppression had
made them hate their neighbors. But the animosity was waning
as this emissary of peace brought promise to them. Several
women and men sat a distance away on the pretext of resting.

A young man was sitting cross-legged near Democritus.
He seemed disinterested when Democritus turned to him and
asked, "What do you think about this man, Yeshua?"

"He sounds like one of the myths we've heard about in our culture. All these enormous statues that mean nothing." He pointed in the distance to Apollo. "Yeshua is probably just another story that people want to believe."

"You're right. The stories make him sound like some Greek hero. Can I tell you about a prophet who lived in Yerushalayim about seven hundred years ago?" The young man shrugged and nodded. "His name was Isaiah and he saw many things that were going to happen to the Jews."

"He was a seer? That's what seers do, isn't it? They see into the future?"

"Yes, he was. He saw what God wanted him to see, and wrote it down. He prophesied that a man would be born who would not fulfill any of the traditional beliefs about a conquering king. Instead, Isaiah described him as a suffering king, one who would suffer for the sake of Judea and all of humanity, you and me. Many wouldn't believe his writings because they wanted a king to win their battles for them. They imprisoned Isaiah and killed him in a brutal manner. But his words lived on. Isaiah described in detail Yeshua's betrayal, crucifixion on a Roman cross, which was completely unknown at that time in history. He foretold how the suffering Messiah would be born, betrayed by his friends, crucified on a cross and rise from the dead."

"He was resurrected? That sounds like some Greek myth. I don't believe in myths. If you're dead, your dead. Nobody comes back to life." The youth got to his feet, caught up in the story.

"Right . . . and wrong. Nobody can come back from the dead, except the one who has power over death. Yeshua returned to life just as he, himself, had prophesied. He alone has power over death." He motioned for the man to sit back down. "Wait until you hear my story." Soon a group of six or seven young men gathered around, intent to know Democritus' story.

Across the city, three remaining sentinels—Hermes, Apollo and Aphrodite—stood as stone should stand, mindlessly gazing out over the valley. Demonic shadows still peered from behind the stone, in the rafters of houses and through the web of tree branches, waiting for their chance to snare this great enemy and tempt him to distraction. Now there were two to contend with, as this spiritual fire could soon destroy their stronghold.

The demonic forces must not lose their grip on these Syrian people. But they had been weakened by the warrior's presence and the influence that he'd created. To these demonic creatures, the Abyss seemed closer to them than ever. Democritus brought with him another Presence, a mighty, all powerful Presence before which the demons could only tremble. They flapped high into the skies when he came near. But, of course, this Presence was there, too. If they descended into the bowels of the earth, they would find him there. They could not hide from his gaze.

A swarm of weakened demons swirled into the sky seeking willing hosts. Below, four men staggered and slurred as they finished another round of ale at a local tavern. Dawn was just breaking. Their hearts were empty with nothing but ashes. Women had gathered there, too. In the absence of real love, the women had given their hearts to meaningless pleasures, hoping against hope that an ounce of purpose would be left for them. These men and women provided an opportunity for the presence of darkness to descend and claim their souls. With their minds confused and unguarded, darkness descended and quickly filled them with perverse longings.

## Yerushalayim, The Month of Shevat

Adam headed to the market to purchase supplies for the trip. Sorakin explained what it meant to haggle with the merchants. He first headed toward a fruit vendor where he stuttered and stammered trying to follow Sorakin's instructions. She said this was necessary to get a fair price. Adam tried to speak but his words never came out quick enough. He felt foolish when the merchants laughed. In defeat, he held out his hand with the coins and said, "What do I owe you?" With loud laughs the vendors helped themselves to the money and Adam realized he'd failed bigtime as a haggler. Shaking his head, he mumbled, "I don't think God intended for men to shop."

Adam bought a small block of goat cheese, five pomegranates, grapes, leavened bread and dried fish. As he gathered his purchases together, he had a strange sensation that someone was watching him. He turned around but saw no one looking at him. Adam shrugged and went back to his shopping. He bought some fig cakes and a small pot of date honey. He couldn't resist nibbling on one of the cakes, and finally ate the whole thing. He sampled another cake and decided to finish it off. Again, he had a feeling of being watched.

In the shadows, someone saw the tall young man move through the market stalls. She turned away when he looked up. As he went back to his shopping, she walked down a row of vendors in the opposite direction until she was behind him. Hidden beneath a vendor's canopy, she watched his movements, hand gestures and stride. There was something different about him— something strangely familiar. The observer moved closer and listened. His voice startled her. He sounded like her husband's brother. She shook her head in dismay. This can't be possible.

The streets were busy. Adam weaved in and out of the stalls, buying several items. He looked up again then moved quickly from stall to stall. His walk, his mannerisms were just like . . . Ben. Then suddenly he disappeared down a long lane and out of sight. She'd lost him. She saw hundreds of bobbing heads rushing back and forth, but he was gone. The lad was nowhere in sight. Her heart raced as a spell of dizziness washed over her.

*This can't be real. In this city of miracles, this is beyond impossible.* She rushed home to tell her husband, Ben-Asher. He'd think she finally lost touch with reality.

As Adam turned a corner, he found himself standing in front of the Dung Gate. Before him was a handful of wretched looking men crouched on the ground begging for food crumbs. They were as scrawny as any jackal could be. This corner of the city was their domain. Filthy rags hung on sticks to form cover from the cold. Discarded bones and raw garbage suggested these men ate whatever came their way.

Among the beggars sat one pathetic creature. He held out his hand begging for food. Adam surrendered some grapes to the dirty hand. The man immediately stuffed them in his mouth. Still chewing, the old man looked up for more when their eyes locked. Adam stood still. He couldn't move. Air to breath grew scarce. Adam felt light-headed. He leaned against the city wall to support himself. Those icy eyes were still there. Time had not erased them. And Adam's eternal glimpse had not released him from feeling fear and horror at those eyes.

Nothing else about the man looked familiar. Adam, however, could not ignore those eyes. The icy blue orbs bore right through him as they had some thirty years ago with a dagger in the soldier's hand. Those eyes were the last of humanity he'd seen before being drawn into the arms of the Father. Today, they stared back at him with no malice or awareness of reality, but the ice had not melted from the troubled heart.

*This is my murderer. This old man killed me. What's happening to me? Why do I feel these disturbing emotions?*

Strange feelings surged through Adam that surprised him. Until now, he was the happiest, joyful, grownup kid around. He loved life. In an instant, feelings of rage shot through his heart as he stared into those eyes. His hands trembled. A clammy shudder rippled over Adam's skin. He felt nauseous. He put his hand against the wall to steady himself. *What do I do with these emotions? How do I face this man knowing what he's done? Lord, show me.*

Artamos was busy looking for more food. He was thin and bony. Dirt clung to his skin like a cloak. As he chewed, his bristly beard bounced up and down to the motion of his jaws. Adam was amazed that this man could end up here on this scrap heap. What had happened to him?

As Adam was thinking this, another beggar spoke up. "You got any extra, mate? How about a fig?" At first Adam didn't even hear him.

"Hey, mate. Got any more food?"

"Sure, help yourself." He held out a date cake to the beggar. Still shaking, Adam knelt down beside Artamos who was busy chewing. He didn't look up when Adam squatted beside him. Adam studied his face thoroughly. A chill ran through his body. Suddenly, the old beggar turned toward Adam and jumped.

"Oh! Are you the Messiah? He's gonna come, the Messiah's gonna come."

"You're lost, aren't you, old man?" Adam's rage was tempered by a moment of pity. But pity is not forgiveness. Before him sat a man who had let sin destroy everything about him. Had Adam lived, he could not have brought more justice if he were to hack the man to death, an eye for an eye. Sin did its terrible deed upon the soldier, leaving him impotent to all that life could have offered. He damned himself before being sentenced by the Judge of All.

Another beggar next to Artamos offered information, "Old Az can't cause trouble anymore. Ain't nothin' left o' him." He spoke through gaped teeth. "He's as scared as a rabbit 'bout to be skinned. He lost his family, I s'pose. He keeps goin' on about em." The beggar wiped some drool from his face and went on. "Az keeps lookin' for some child. Is some baby Messiah s'posed to come?"

Adam slid down the wall and sat in the dirt. "He's already come." He spoke with flatness in his voice. The food tumbled around him and the beggars were quick to make lunch. A groan erupted in Adam's heart as he looked at the infant-slayer. The beggar seemed lost in a world of emptiness he'd made for himself.

*This world has so much pain.* So many emotions crowded his brain then flooded into his chest. Hatred! He hated those eyes which had looked at him and, without giving a second thought, tore life from him without hesitation. Those eyes looked upon his mother and father as their hopes and dreams fled. Adam did not know what to do with these human emotions. They were so heavy all of a sudden.

A familiar voice stirred in his mind. *Will you forgive him, Adam? Will you forgive the man who stole life from you? Will you forgive him for all the devastation he brought on your parents? Can you forgive a mass murderer?*

*No! I can't forgive him. I don't have the ability to forgive this man for what he's done to me and my parents. But I can't live with these ugly feelings either. God help me.* Adam was crying and didn't know how he could do what he must do. God was speaking and Adam struggled to listen.

*I understand 'forgiveness,' Adam. It originated in me. I've watched my creation rebel against me, watched them destroy themselves, but my love is stronger than any sin or sinner. Stronger than what this broken man has done to you. Through Yeshua, my forgiveness abounds.*

Adam immediately remembered words from the Torah describing God's forgiveness after humanity had scorned God with mockery. *"The Lord, the Lord, the compassionate and gracious God, slow to anger, abounding in love and faithfulness, maintaining love to thousands, and forgiving wickedness. . . ."*[71]

---

[71] Ex. 34:6-7a

In his human shell, Adam could not face the beggar sitting next to him. The old fool sat scraping his sores and scratching his scalp. He smelled worse than rotting food. He didn't have a clue that a child he murdered was sitting next to him. Yet Adam feared him. Adam hated his appearance. It made his skin crawl. He wanted to vomit.

*Adam, will you forgive him?*

*I can't. I don't know how to forgive him. How do I forgive a man who doesn't remember what he's done? He doesn't even know I'm alive! I don't want to forgive him. He's a mass- murderer. He doesn't deserve forgiveness.*

*That's right, Adam. He doesn't deserve forgiveness, no one does. But that's my choice, not yours. Even after looking upon my face and drawing you to myself, you still have choices to make. Yeshua was my only Son. Do you think I don't understand loss? Humanity hated my Son without cause. Herod's soldiers were not after you, they were after my Son. He was hunted . . . every day of his life. When he finally submitted to death it was his choice. I had to turn my back on my own Son. He took the place of mass-murderers, of all the senseless acts evil humanity has done since time began. Adam, Yeshua did this so that you could find forgiveness and have the power to forgive this man.*

*Lord, his eyes alone paralyze me. They bring back all the horror that destroyed my family. I can't do this alone.*

*Then let me help you. Forgiving Artamos will set you free. It's the way of the cross. You can forgive the unrepentant heart because I paid the price for this man's sins. When he asks, I'll set him free.*

Adam straightened his back. He glanced to his side, still unable to continue looking into the man's eyes. Flies hovered above him. *How could he have done it . . . slay babies?*

"Adam!"

Adam was so startled he jumped up. "Who called my name?" An audible voice clearly spoke his name. It was a deep, resonate, melodic voice. He looked around but saw no one. "Who called me? Where are you?" He stared at the old withered man, who mindlessly sat staring at nothing.

"Adam, have you forgotten my voice so soon?"

Adam closed his eyes in shame. "No, Adonai, please forgive me. I can never forget your voice. You are my life."

*Listen to me Adam. Give me your full attention now. This is very important. Human depravity is so dark it terrifies the natural senses, and yet every man or woman is capable of committing the vilest sins imaginable. It comes from the pit of hell. Whatever evil the mind can conceive my grace can forgive. It's possible because of my Son, Yeshua. He bridged that awful gap between evil men and a loving Redeemer. He made it possible for me to penetrate the blackest heart and offer forgiveness. You cannot forgive what I can forgive, for compassion and forgiveness belong to Me alone; but soon I'll give you my Spirit to forgive what is impossible with mankind. Trust me . . . I'll give you power to forgive Artamos.*

As the message sank into Adam's heart, the quiet voice of God began to fade. But an impression struck Adam with force; if the God of the universe forgives the sinner, any sinner, then he too must forgive. *Just give me the power to forgive this wretched man Artamos. I can't do it on my own.*

Struggling to face the creature, Adam turned to him. "Let's go get cleaned up. I want you to come home with me and have dinner." *Help me, Lord.*

The beggar's eyes grew wide. "Me?" He looked around him. "You want me to go with you? Are you the Messiah?"

Adam diverted his eyes. "No, I'm not. But I want to tell you all about him." He reached over, grabbed the rags and lifted the emaciated man, Artamos to his feet. Unable to stand on his own, he wheezed at each breath. *We're going to the pool, but first I need to buy you a new robe.* Artamos' shoulders were bent, his legs like bowed sticks. Adam was forced to wrap his arm around the stinking bag of bones, then led him into the market center. He cringed at the task. The crowds stared and quickly parted.

The two men went down to the Serpent's Pool. The day was waning and the sun lit the horizon like gold overlay. Many families were heading to their homes to eat and rest. Adam helped peel the layers of rags from the old man's bony frame and eased him into the pool. As he slipped into the water, Adam saw Artamos' back. It was streaked with long deep scars. They were a massive web from the top of his shoulders all the way down to his legs. Adam groaned inside. As water swirled around the man, he seemed to let go and surrender to the currents.

Artamos sank beneath the water, letting it wash away the filth from years of life's roadside traffic. As the old man washed he wept. His salty tears swirled into the pool as memories began to re-emerge. How quickly they flowed back into his mind. They'd never left . . . were just buried slightly below the surface. A lifetime ago, he remembered the blood of innocence swirl into the deep well in Beit Jala bringing sin's contamination. His tears could not wash away the memories of his own sin, the horrors he'd committed that were now inextricably a part of himself.

How could anyone forgive a mass-murderer? All battles the soldier had ever fought had paled into shadows compared to this one night of unleashed evil. The water pulled him down toward the darkness where the faces of babies, weeping mothers, the screams of innocence grew sharper. Death itself could not erase his wickedness. It defined it.

He stayed submerged for a long time, his hair swirling across the surface of the water. He felt someone pull his arm to lift him up. Not wanting to face tomorrow, he slipped away from the grasp. He was waking from his world of insanity and it was unbearable. He sunk deeper. His body felt clean and his heart wicked. No god would forgive him of all he had done; murder, rape, slaughter. There could be no god big enough to forgive such evil.

The murderer floated nearer the pool's center. Air escaped his lungs and he sank lower. He had carried a lifetime of evil memories like a millstone around his neck. Feeling the tug as the millstone pulled him down to the bottom, he sensed darkness coming near. *Just inhale water and go to sleep.* More bubbles escaped. Artamos' memories became more vivid. Would the memories die with him? Any second now, his lungs would instinctively scream for air and inhale. Water would rush into his lungs and plunge him into eternal sleep . . . or damnation.

Above him, the surface of the pool was like glass. Artamos saw distorted images of light and darkness. He inhaled. Water rushed into his lungs. His vision grew black and fear rose into his heart, a deep ugly fear. His limbs began to jerk. Death was not sleep—the memories were still inside. Suicide was a one way ticket to hell. From above, a body shot down into the pool toward him. A man took hold of Artamos beneath his arms and pulled him upward toward the surface. He pulled the limp body out of the pool and laid him down on the cobbled stones. Adam pounded on the man's chest until water gurgled out. Artamos choked then coughed. When the old man could finally breathe he begged, "Why?"

Adam dried Artamos without answering. He was angry and puzzled by his own actions. He dressed him in a pale blue robe he'd just purchased. He would cut his hair and have him shave his face, making him look somewhat human. Adam avoided Artamos' eyes.

"What were you trying to do down there?" Adam said with restraint. "I'm trying to help you."

"All I am is the scum of Yerushalayim. I shouldn't be allowed to live."

"Do you have any idea what your alternatives might be?" Adam asked in agitation.

"Haven't given it a thought," Artamos replied. "Just want out of this skin."

"You should, you wicked man. You can't run away from yourself in this life or the next."

He led him down the road toward home. "And leaping into eternity without God is unthinkable. There's only one way to be rid of your evil; repent to the God who made you. Whether you know it or not, someone has paid the price for your crimes, even though you don't deserve it. If you repent, Yeshua will cleanse your heart from your evil past . . . you will be forgiven . . . forever." Adam pulled him along. "I'll tell you more later."

Adam did not feel like speaking and Artamos was beginning to remember too much. Would Adam allow God to help him forgive the man who'd murdered him?

## Chapter Thirty-Six

# Antonia Fortress, Yerushalayim, 33 A.D., Month of Adar

An order came to the captain in the Antonia Fortress. Anna, the Jewess, must be sent to Rome to be tried before Caesar. This order was a command of the emperor's counsel, Sejanus, and confirmed by his commanding officer, Alexander of Puteoli.

The captain called his guards. "I want two men to bring out our female prisoner. The governor ordered that she be taken to Rome immediately."

One guard said, "I'm not going near that cell. Those rats spook me."

"You'll go if I order you to go. Either that or a sword to your head. And I need three of you to get the prisoner cart ready. I've got three other male prisoners traveling to Rome as well. Chain them in separate corners of the cart. We don't want her touched by them."

When Anna was delivered to the captain, he was shocked at her appearance. They forced her into a chair, guards standing on either side of her at attention.

"I swear woman, you're a mystery to me. You look healthier than I've ever seen you. What keeps you alive without water and food?" In spite of filthy clothes, her raven hair was lustrous. Her face was full. Her eyes glimmered with hope.

"Yeshua has provided for my every need." Her voice was quiet and sweet, without the slightest hint of sarcasm.

The captain struck the table with his fist. "Shut up about your messiah." His eye twitched. "Don't even breathe his name in my presence." His hand shook. "He's dead. Didn't you hear?"

Anna jumped from the loud bang on the table. Then, calmly she replied.

"I've seen him very much alive. We spoke together and he told me all about you." Anna wanted to say more but felt constrained to show respect. She looked down at her hands and waited. Her beauty was more radiant than ever.

"You must have conjured up some witch's brew. Maybe you've grown an appetite for rats." The soldiers laughed in unison, but the captain's nervousness could not be concealed.

"I'm ready to go."

"I suppose you think you're going to one of Caesar's revelries. He has many women and boys to entertain him." The captain grinned, exposing crooked teeth between a patchwork of prickly stubble. "You are going to meet our emperor's new messenger boy, Sejanus. He doesn't like tomb raiders. You will stand before all of Rome. Are you ready for that?"

"I'm ready. My conscience is free." Her eyes were clear without a shadow of doubt.

The captain walked behind Anna and whispered in her ear. "You cover your crime with religious words." His lips caressed her ear. "You perform secret rituals . . . drinking blood and eating someone's flesh."

Anna shook her head. "No, you're mistaken. We do nothing in secret. We celebrate . . . life."

"Shut up!" the captain shouted. His hands shook. "I know the things you do." His voice rose. "You're barbaric. You divide families, eat human flesh and refuse to worship Caesar."

Anna remained silent. The captain's arguments did not originate with him. These were stories that had been rumored and circulated around Yerushalayim and Rome's elite. *They've chosen not to believe, so the truth is hidden from them. If they looked, they would see and have life.* The prisoner calmed her anxious thoughts as the captain continued to buzz around her head, screaming abuse, throwing false accusations, shoving his odious face at her.

Anna turned her mind toward the hope of finding her daughter. A glimpse of Charis would satisfy her ache. *Oh, Yeshua, let me see my daughter before I fly home. Just one moment to tell her about you.* Anna's thoughts were interrupted as two guards grabbed her arms and pulled her up from the chair. She winced as they tied shackles on her wrists and ankles, then shoved her into a cage where three male prisoners were chained in the corners. The journey would take more than a month. Two oxen would pull the cart across land toward a waiting ship. The trip would be arduous. Anna prayed for strength.

Adam walked through the doorway of Sorakin's one room house. Behind him, a gaunt figure followed with his head down. He looked like a walking skeleton. Long bony legs moved stiffly into her tiny room.

"Sorakin, this man needs a meal, a good haircut and shave. I knew you could help fix him up." Adam's eyebrows raised in hope that Sorakin would agree. Sorakin didn't comment about the food Adam was to have bought.

"Where'd you get him?" Sorakin was dubious.

"Outside the Dung Gate. He's been waiting for the Messiah to come. He missed him and I need to tell him about Yeshua. But in the meantime, he could use some fattening up."

Artamos looked around the tiny room in bewilderment. So far, he hadn't said more than a handful of words. But little by little it seemed he was grasping at reality that had faded thirty years ago.

Adam realized he didn't know the man's name. He always thought of him as the baby-slayer. "What's your name, old man?"

"My name?" His pause was long. He frowned and wrinkled his nose. "Az, no, not Az. My name, my name? I can't remember my name." He looked up hopefully. "I'm Roman."

"You're a scrawny Roman, whatever else you are," Sorakin said and clambered through her cupboards for food and dishes. "You need something that will stick to your bones."

If Sorakin thought Adam had poor eating manners, she was in for a big surprise. The old man grabbed food before it touched the table. Adam sat down and bowed his head. When he looked up, Artamos was stuffing food in his mouth, both hands full of bread.

"Hey now, wait a minute." Adam yanked the bread from his hands. "You might have eaten like that on the streets, but not in here. Not in Sorakin's house. There's plenty of food for all of us here. You don't grab all the food. You eat what is given you like a man."

Artamos' eyes watered like a little child. He didn't know what to do with himself.

"Where did you say you found this man? He eats like an animal?" Sorakin shook her head as she handed Artamos a piece of bread. "I don't know, Adam. Since I've met you my whole life had been turned upside down. First you, then Anna, and now this man who doesn't know his own name."

"He's part of my past . . . God is showing me something through him. And he needs the Messiah desperately." They stared at Artamos who now held the bread but wasn't eating it. "Eat it man, it's yours." He lifted it slowly to his mouth, fearful that it might be snatched away again.

Adam watched from the corner of his eye. *Somehow God is going to help me forgive him.*

Outside, the night was dark with only a quarter moon hanging above. Clouds slid past the moon's thumb nail then spread toward the Mediterranean waters heading for Rome. A storm was brewing. When the meal was finished, Adam and Sorakin arranged the sleeping accommodations into a makeshift hotel. Sorakin noticed that Adam could not make eye contact with the withered man.

Something was terribly wrong. Fear seeped into her heart. *Who is this stranger Adam brought to my door? Why is Adam so troubled? I'll never sleep with so much drama in my tiny house.*

This new enemy, fear, had visited her once again and Sorakin's best way of dealing with it was action. It did her no good to sit and become paralyzed over something she didn't understand. She got to her feet, pulled the scrawny man into a chair and began to clip the frazzled crop of hair. Her fears subsided as she cut away all the stray and matted clumps until white curls began to crown his head. She pulled out her husband's old razor and soon had his face clean. Amazingly, Artamos began to look human.

Adam was impressed. "This man doesn't look so scary now. You've made a new man out of this beggar." Adam smiled. "I'll be sleeping at the foot of his bed. And besides, you have Peaches, a real tiger if there ever was one." Adam put some bedding on the floor.

Adam let Artamos sleep in his bed. He pulled the curtains around the bag of bones whose stomach was full for the first time in decades. Before he fell asleep, the man peered out the little window as the clouds swept past. He shuddered with some haunting memory. After a while, Adam could hear heavy breathing. He finally slept.

Sorakin couldn't hold it in any longer. "Who is this man and why did you bring him here? Do you think I can feed the world?"

"No, dear Sorakin. This man put me in my grave." Adam watched Sorakin's eyes grow round and moist.

"He's a murderer?" The woman pulled back against the wall.

"He's a mass-murderer. He was the Roman soldier that came into Beit Jala and Bethlehem and murdered every male baby he could find. I was one of them."

Sorakin's face paled. Her voice was raspy. "But . . . he looks so pathetic." A murderer was sleeping in her room and she had no ability to relate to this information.

"Sin has wasted him." Adam breathed and thought. "Sorakin, I need to ask you to do something for me. This man is broken. His ghosts must haunt him continually. And . . ."

Adam turned and looked out through the window, ". . . seeing him reminds me of my mother and father." He turned back. "I'm desperate to find my parents."

"Adam, you must first take the letter to Alexander of Puteoli." The old woman studied Adam's face. "Will you do that?"

"Yes, Yeshua has already prepared me for the trip." He hesitated. "While I'm gone, can you nurse this man back to health and try to find my parents?"

"You're going to leave me with a mass-murderer in my house, alone?"

"I know. I know. Tomorrow I'll take this man to the Temple. He's Roman, so I'll take him to the Gentile court. Maybe there he can begin to make his peace with God. He's a tormented soul but he's come a long way in a few short hours. What a mess . . ."

"Never mind. Spare me the details. How many more strays do you plan to bring into my cubby-hole of a house?" Sorakin asked.

"I don't quite know, Sorakin. But it seems to me that your cupboards never run dry. You always have enough for me, Anna, and for yourself. Perhaps God keeps stocking your cupboards when we're asleep."

# Chapter Thirty-Seven

# UPPER YERUSHALAYIM, 33 A.D.

Sorakin's house disappeared into the velvet folds of darkness. The night settled in silence as if the world had stopped breathing.

From deep within the stillness, a wild scream exploded, "Get . . . off . . . me. Get . . . away! Get away!"

Adam knee-jerked into a sitting position. Sorakin screeched with terror. Peaches' fur sprang up like a coil as she jumped onto Sorakin's bed. It was the old man. His bony arms and legs were flailing the air. With kicks and screams he fought an invisible enemy. His ghosts had returned to torment him. A demonic presence was felt and Adam began to pray.

"Get away. Get off me!" Artamos kicked the air and clawed himself.

Adam held Artamos down, pinning his arms at his side and talking calmly and slowly to him. "Old man, you're okay. You're safe. In the mighty name of Yeshua, we command all the forces of darkness to flee from you **now**!" There was a rustling of leathery wings, the flapping of angry spirits, an invisible force with which to be reckoned. They hovered close to the ceiling.

Artamos growled. "Babies. Babies' faces are all around me. H-e-l-p." His terror was real.

"God wants to free you, old man. Your past is haunting you and it needs to be erased." He turned to Sorakin. The room was dark with only a glint from the moon. "Can you pour a cup of water for him please?"

Sorakin nodded and responded immediately. Her hands trembled as she carried the cup.

"Take a drink and let yourself calm down." Artamos' hands shook uncontrollably. Adam had to hold the cup.

"Tell me about your nightmare. What was it about?"

"Babies' faces. I killed them all but they cry out to me every night. Crying, crying. Screaming into my mind." The man shook. "I'm going to hell for what I've done. I've seen it."

Adam cleared his throat. "What's your name?"

"My name is . . . is . . . Art . . . Artamos . . . captain in Caesar's army. We were deployed to Judea under King Herod's command." Moonlight had moved across the room and suddenly its light shone upon Artamos' face. Instinctively, Adam diverted his eyes from Artamos' stare.

After a pause Adam said, "And my name is Adam, the only son of the house of Ben-Asher." He exhaled. "I was born in Beit Jala." The old man stared at Adam without comprehension. "I was two years old when you came to Beit Jala."

There was a conscious flickering in the old man's expression. "No . . . you are wrong. I was ordered to leave no one alive. No one. I did what Herod told me to do. I did what he commanded . . . and it cost me everything."

"I remember you. I was one of those babies you murdered."

Artamos' face blanched. He shook his head like a child. It couldn't be true. He trembled. This was impossible. "NO . . . NO!" Artamos screamed. He covered his ears with his hands. The unseen demons crowded into a corner of the ceiling.

"It's true." Adam sat on the bed. Taking Artamos' hand and touching his chest, he said, "Feel this. You stabbed me with your dagger." He turned his back. "Feel this. See?"

Artamos trembled as he quickly pulled his hand away, shoving himself against the wall. "No, no. no. You're one of those ghosts who haunt me. Now you're here in my world. Help me, God. Help me. This isn't a dream anymore—it's a terrible nightmare. Oh, God, help me." His eyes suddenly turned wild as blood vessels burst. "God, please forgive me; even if you send me to hell, at least forgive me. I can't live with this evil any longer."

"I'm not one of your ghosts. I died that night, yet God raised me to life again so I could forgive you and tell you about *Yeshua HaMashiach*. I was resurrected at the Messiah's crucifixion. I came back for you . . . to forgive you of murder, Artamos. Look at me." In the blue-gray moonlight, Artamos turned his eyes toward Adam. A cold chill washed over Adam, then slowly . . . slowly, dissipated.

"No. This can't be real. My mind. I'm going crazy. My past will always haunt me. It will chase me into hell. I'm too evil to be forgiven. I've committed unforgivable sins."

"You were hunting down Yeshua, the Messiah, that night. You were not alone in your hunt. The Evil One has been hunting him for centuries. In each generation a man rises up to destroy the Prince of Peace. But no one can take the life of Yeshua without his permission. He gives it up of his own accord."[72]

"I don't understand." Artamos furrowed his brow. "I thought . . . I thought . . ."

"No, he was never really captured because no one could take his life from him."[73] Adam continued. "He's the Messiah you were looking for. He slipped Herod's reach and grew up in Nazareth. Satan pursued him every minute of his life, but could

---

[72] Jn.10:17 Yeshua discusses his authority over his life.

[73] Jn. 10:18 Yeshua surrenders his life under his own accord.

never catch him. Yeshua surrendered his life to a cruel death on a cross. In doing that he conquered and defeated death by rising from the grave. His death set me free. That's why he's the Messiah. There is no sin too great that he can't forgive."

In the shadows, demons grew agitated and swept through the room trying to induce fear in the huddled trio. Adam stood and spoke with authority. "Now you know the story, you sniveling agents of fear. Get out and be cast into the great Abyss for all eternity, in the name of the One and Only Yeshua, God's only Son. Be gone."

As though they were being dragged from the corner by a mighty hand, the dark swarm was pulled away, resisting by clawing the ceiling, flapping broken wings and screeching. Sorakin covered her ears and closed her eyes. Artamos was mystified. Adam stood strong.

Adam pulled a blanket around the butcher's shoulders. "Artamos, I'm one of those faces in your nightmares. I forgive you tonight. You are pardoned. You'll never see my face haunt you again." Adam had uttered the words that set both he and the old man free.

The old man touched Adam's face, trying to grasp the truth. He didn't understand it all, but enough to know that forgiveness was offered.

"I've asked for God's forgiveness a million times, but peace never comes. "

"Now you will find it. A fountain has been opened for cleansing of sin, even murder. The only true God heard every prayer you uttered. He sent Yeshua to pay the price for all that you did in Beit Jala and Bethlehem."

"You really know what happened that night?"

"Yes, Artamos. My parents were Rachel and Ben-Asher. Your face . . . your eyes . . . were the last thing I saw before I died."

Adam wrapped his arms around the old man and they wept together. As Adam's hand ran across the old man's back, he felt the jagged scars. It was a realization of the awfulness of sin. Adam was overcome with sorrow. *This is only a taste of how Yeshua felt as he hung there on the cross. He felt the scars on our backs and with his stripes we are healed.*

"I forgive you, Artamos."

Adam and Artamos stepped onto the white limestone courtyard of the Temple. They headed toward the Court of the Gentiles that surrounded the Temple. The sky was cloudless with the sun high above. Sorakin insisted on coming. From inside they could hear the Levites singing. Artamos peered through a gated passageway and watched as people offered up prayers to God.

"I can't go near. I'm evil," Artamos resisted.

"I know. That's why God came to us, because we could not go to him."

Crowds milled about while others moved with purpose. Adam squeezed past a group of men toward the entrance.

From another direction, an elderly couple followed a group of worshipers into the temple courtyard. Walking slowly and bent with age, the woman suddenly became animated. "Ben ... Ben ... look over there. It's him; the young man I told you about. Look, Ben. See him?" Rachel pulled her husband's arm in the man's direction.

"Calm down, Rachel. You're becoming hysterical." He lowered his voice. "Hush, we're at the Temple. Everyone is staring."

"It's him, Ben. He belongs to our family, I'm sure." She pulled away from her husband and rushed forward.

"Rachel. Stop!" Ben-Asher's voice was as loud as hers. They'd become a spectacle. It was then that he spotted him. "That young man looks like . . . so much like my brother's son."

"He walks just like you, Ben. Hurry, before we lose him."

"Rachel, no. I know what you saw in the village. But this will only break your heart again. Our Adam is gone. You know that, Rachel. Don't imagine something that will only let you down again."

Adam suddenly noticed an older couple staring at him. He was curious and moved closer. The man was a bit shy and looked away, but the woman grew excited, pulling her husband toward him. The man was tall with graying sandy colored hair whitened by the sun. Adam thought his mannerisms were so familiar, and stopped to wonder. Leaving Artamos and Sorakin behind, he then walked quickly toward the couple.

Ben-Asher became unsettled and pulled his wife close. As the man walked toward them, he whispered in a low tone, "Rachel, don't do this. It can't be Adam. You know that. It doesn't make sense. He died . . ." Ben grabbed both of Rachel's arms, forcing her to face him. "Listen, Rachel, listen to me. Our son is not coming back." He studied her eyes. "Please, finally, after all these years, accept the truth. Adam is dead. He died many years ago and we will never see him alive again."

Rachel pulled free of his grip. "It's Adam." She ran toward the man she believed was her resurrected son. "Adam . . . Adam . . ."

No other words needed to be spoken. Mother and son ran into each other's arms after a lifetime of separation. They held each other, Adam tall and strong, picking his mother up off the ground. The end of a lifetime of anguish for Rachel, the beginning of a mother's comfort for Adam. The whole Temple courtyard stopped in stunned silence.

Still in great doubt, Ben-Asher stood like a shy on-looker. Finally, Adam spoke, "How could you have known it was me?"

Rachel bubbled. "We found your tomb broken and empty. When Yeshua appeared in Galilee we knew the resurrection was true. We've been searching ever since." She looked up at her husband. "Your father has been trying to protect me from disappointment." She patted his hand. "But I knew. I just knew I'd find you. Thank you, Hashem."

Adam reached out and grabbed Ben-Asher in a strong embrace. The man hesitated, uncertain. "I know it's hard to believe. Let me show you my scars, father. You were there that night. You saw everything." Adam opened his cloak.

"How can this be? I don't understand . . . why would you claim to be my son if . . . you weren't." Ben-Asher broke out in a sweat. His hands trembled. "The Messiah . . . he heard my prayer that day. He listened to my anguish on the road to Yerushalayim." Ben-Asher grasped his son's arms. "Yeshua has done this. If he rose from the grave, then he can raise you, too." Ben-Asher shook his head. "It's you, Adam. My son. My only son." Holding Adam, he sobbed into his shoulder. "I buried you with a broken heart that day. Our lives have never been the same. Never." Ben-Asher stood back, studied his son's face, then turned to the crowd that was growing.

"This is my son. I have a son! I found him! He was dead and now he's alive!" he shouted. "My son is alive! He's alive!" Pointing to Adam he shouted, "This is my son!"

Rachel reached for Adam's hands. She touched his face and kissed his cheek. "It's you, isn't it. I could never forget my only son, my beautiful Adam. I didn't expect you to be so tall. You're taller than your dad. But you haven't lost your baby face."

"I'm still a kid at heart, yet God has given me some pretty big jobs to do." Together they laughed through tears. Adam reached into his robe, pulled out the burial shroud and held it up. With a half laugh, half cry, Rachel choked through the emotions that flooded her heart. Nothing could prepare her for this moment. Heaven's reunion had touched a corner of earth on the very mount where humanity and divinity intersected at the Cross. Rachel and Ben-Asher had their first glimpse of Heaven's jubilee.

"We couldn't have survived the loss without the comfort of discovering Yeshua. He brought sense to all the ancient scriptures." Ben-Asher's eyes glistened. "His presence kept us sane during those nights without you. God gave us courage in spite of that baby slayer."

Suddenly Adam remembered he'd left Artamos and Sorakin behind. He scanned the crowds. There, yards away, stood Artamos watching the reunion. He backed away into the shadows. Sorakin moved forward. She was needed now to help Rachel accept the whole story.

Rachel noticed Adam's distraction and followed his stare. There, against the limed wall, Artamos stood watching. That gaze froze her heart once again. She saw the riveting blue eyes of the butcher. Her eyes flickered for only a moment. She swayed and fell backward, falling into her husband's arms. He eased her down to the ground with an arm beneath her head.

Artamos was gone.

Sorakin arrived and knelt down beside Rachel. "Could such a great miracle happen in any place on earth other than here on this holy mountain?" She peered into the eyes of Ben-Asher. "Here, Abram offered his only son as an offering. Yeshua died and rose just outside the gate. Now God has returned a son of Israel to his parents and he wants the forgiven murderer reconciled." She stroked Rachel's hair. "God planned this reunion."

Rachel's eyes fluttered open as Sorakin talked away. "Your boy has forgiven that bag o' bones for killing him," she whispered in Rachel's ear. "Your son found that wretch of a man and forgave him." Sorakin smiled down at her. "My dear, if one child can forgive because of Yeshua, others can too . . . in time. We only have two choices, ya know. Either we forgive our enemies or we live by the rule of an eye for an eye. If we all followed that, it wouldn't take long for the whole world to become blind. One day Yeshua's love will give you the courage to forgive." She lifted Rachel up. "Until then my dear, let's go home and celebrate."

---

## Rome, Ostia Harbor, 33 A.D.

Cloaked in black, the figure slipped from the fishing boat that had docked in the Ostia Harbor. He smelled of dead fish and brine. Against the blackness of night, he followed a cobbled roadway, passing quickly through narrow streets from shop to shop. A storm had set in, making the streets slick. Turning up a narrow alley, he went through a small door in a wall. The parchment was secured in his leather satchel.

Malchus disliked both the smell and the man, but he gave a false smile because the parchment would bring him power. He took the scroll and tucked it away in a hidden compartment in the wall. The man stood with his hand held out. Malchus dropped three coins in his palm.

"That was not the bargain. I risked my life to bring you that scroll. Now give me what you promised or I'll slice your throat." He pulled out a double-edged dagger and flashed it in Malchus' face.

Reluctantly, Malchus dropped eight more coins in the man's hand. "We agreed on ten drachmas. I've given you eleven. Now get out of my sight."

The man walked out into the slanting rain and was lost in the night's shadows.

Malchus shut the door and locked it. He rubbed his hands together in anticipation of his presentation. Malchus didn't open the scroll. He was confident he'd secured something that would expose this traitor of Rome. The prisoner was traveling to Rome. She would be delivered to the prison chambers within the Forum Romanum Amphitheatre. His timing must be perfect. This letter could incriminate the entire movement of "resurrection" fanatics.

# Chapter Thirty-Eight

"**A** thousand roads lead men forever to Rome."[74] Rome's' splendor exalted humanity's great achievements of the day. Its artists, sculptors and architects elevated mankind into a godlike state. Yet this empire lacked a moral plumb-line to give guidance to its inhabitants. Across the shimmering Mediterranean Sea sat Yerushalayim, the beautiful city of God, his chosen piece of real estate for eternity. These two cities were diametrically opposed to one another. If the tyrant, Emperor Tiberius, could have looked across the water and caught a glimpse of Yeshua the Nazarene, civilization might have taken a better course. Tiberius was so close to the ultimate truth and yet so far away and desperately lost.

But for the city of Yerushalayim, *"They will live in the land I gave to my servant Jacob, the land where your ancestors lived. They and their children and their children's children will live there forever, and David my servant will be their prince forever. I will make a covenant of peace with them; it will be an everlasting covenant. I will establish them and increase their numbers, and I will put my sanctuary among them forever. My dwelling place will be with them; I will be their God, and they*

---

[74] Treatise on the Astrolabe (Prologue, ll. 39–40), 1391, Geoffrey Chaucer

*will be my people. Then the nations will know that I the Lord make Israel holy, when my sanctuary is among them forever."*[75]

Emperor Tiberius grew weary of political conquests and impatient with the troublesome Jews in Rome. He despised this new religion. Although he'd retired to the Isle of Capri to indulge his lusts for sexual perversions, he still ruled Rome through his Praetorian Guards, chiefly his deputy, Sejanus. When Sejanus spoke, it was the voice of Emperor Tiberius until the ruler's death. The enemies of Rome were the Jews and the followers of Yeshua. They were the resistance; Rome's fiercest enemies.

Those who swore allegiance to Yeshua interested Sejanus the most. They didn't fight back. They simply stood up for the truth that they knew and showed a determined courage. This infuriated Rome. As the message was proclaimed, Jews and Romans together put their trust in the irresistible Messiah. They were forced underground. Hunted like animals, they surrendered and were thrown into prison. These prison cells were infested with disease and human waste.

There, within the walls of the prison, the presence of *Yeshua HaMashiach* walked among them. Faith in him was contagious because it withstood the emperor's savagery. The more Rome persecuted them, the stronger they became. Their peace in the face of brutality was unrivaled.

Refusing to buckle against the emperor's demands for worship, they were known as the new "atheists" of Rome. In the name of Caesar, Sejanus set traps for these rebellious followers of Yeshua, the dead Messiah. Their only crime was simply being his disciples. Even though they obeyed the laws of Rome and paid taxes, they were traitors in the eyes of Rome. That was sufficient to have them roasted, spiked on a cross or torn apart by lions.

---

[75] Ez.37:25-28

The light of Yeshua first began its mission by reaching the Roman outposts like Pella.

## Pella, Greek Settlement on the Eastern Side of the River Jordan, 33 A.D.

Pella, of the Decapolis, once a citadel of darkness, now flickered with a slender thread of light. It brought a clarity never before seen in this pagan wilderness. For centuries, evil had bent and distorted the light to incite fear, demand blind devotion and poison its wells of understanding. This deep darkness was all it knew.

But a light had been shown upon this land. Yeshua had scattered seeds of faith throughout the Decapolis as he preached to the stunned multitudes proclaiming repentance, salvation and mercy. Everything they'd understood before was counterfeit.

Democritus was sent here as a warrior of truth. Soon faith was percolating underground just waiting to bubble up into a fountain of living water. Some Syrians had dreams of a Messiah while others had visions of a cross where the Messiah took his place to set them free. Unfamiliar with Israel's ancient prophecies written 730 years before, Isaiah's words unfolded like a flower; *"The people walking in darkness have seen a great light; on those living in the land of the shadow of death a light has dawned "*[76]

Daphne had matured as a leader in the city. She no longer pined over her barrenness; she was producing followers of Yeshua. Women sought her out. Others found refuge in her care. Daphne was known as someone who overcame the stranglehold of idolatry and the shame of barrenness. Eventually her backstreet room could not contain those who came for counsel.

---

[76] [75] Is. 9:2

Daphne chose to use the natural caverns in the lower part of the city as a dwelling for herself and her work. The walls of these caverns had once been used to write the stories of the ancient Greek gods. Even as men and women were being snatched from the fires of destruction, so too, Daphne boldly took the spoils of the Greeks and offered them up to the glory of God.

One day Pella would offer refuge for the believers of Yerushalayim. Looking only a few years ahead, the prophets had declared that in 70 A.D. Yerushalayim would be utterly destroyed . . . the enemies of God would not leave one stone upon another. The saints in Decapolis would provide a refuge for the growing followers of Yeshua. [77]

Democritus returned from God's presence with war flowing through his veins. He'd been sent back to fight for the saints and interrupt Satan's strategies. He was a warrior for Yeshua. Now there were others who would build spiritual communities here in Pella and throughout the Roman Empire.

In a dream, the warrior heard the voice of Yeshua speak. *"Democritus, I want you to go to Rome to be a witness for me before the corrupt rulers and the lost people of this city."*

The soldier's heart throbbed with confidence. He would go to Rome. He immediately made plans. In Rome thousands of saints, both Jew and Gentile, were being tortured and slaughtered as sport for proclaiming Yeshua. He needed to be there. Pella was just the training camp. If God's people were being imprisoned for their faith, then Democritus must be there to defend them. Once Yeshua's plans were clearly laid out in his mind, he made immediate preparations to travel to Rome.

---

Adam had set sail for Rome. His business was urgent. He must make it there before Anna was slaughtered or gang-raped

---

[77] [76] Josephus, *War of the Jews*

by Rome's violent forces. In Galilee, Yeshua had given Adam the task of finding a man named Commander Alexander of Puteoli.

Sorakin found Artamos in the Temple listening to the readings of scripture. She would feed him from her widow's cupboard that always seemed full. Soon they would go back to find his wife and children, then on to Beit Jala and Bethlehem. Sorakin couldn't remember when life had become so satisfying. She smiled as Artamos quietly followed her home.

Two months had passed before Democritus finally arrived in the great city. He was awed by its magnificent architecture even though it was stained by the darkness of idolatry. Shrines littered the roadsides. At each intersection, pagan temples were crowded with every image humans could conceive. They worshiped animal-human gods, beasts in human forms, flying creatures, clawing beasts and sensual images.

Democritus remembered a conversation he'd had with Daphne. She had explained that the demonic entities deceived her into believing a lie. When he passed the Temple of Diana he was deeply troubled in his spirit. He could not remain silent. He dismounted, climbed the temple steps and began to preach of Yeshua.

"Men and women of Rome, I have found a God above all gods. He is not just a stone image, but true in every sense of reality. His name is Yeshua." Instantly crowds gathered. The Romans warmed to rhetoric. Soon hundreds had congregated. Democritus preached Yeshua as the only forgiver of sin, the redeemer of broken lives. Never hearing such things, the crowds were intrigued and began to ask Democritus who this might be; where they could find him; what were his wishes. The warrior spoke of the ancient Hebrew prophets, how they had prophesied that a Messiah would come to deliver them from their own darkness. His name was Yeshua.

Commotion at the back of the crowd began to stir people. Shouts and screams arose as Caesar's horses broke through, scattering people everywhere. Democritus kept preaching.

As the dust rose and billowed, Democritus felt himself being snatched up and dragged from where he stood toward the center of the crowd. Ropes cinched around his waist restrained him before the crowd that had responded to his preaching. He stumbled to his feet and faced the guards.

"What is your business here?" the commanding officer shouted.

"I'm worshipping God, as many of these Romans are worshiping their gods. I'm telling them about Yeshua, the one true God who loves them." At that word, Commander Alexander spat in his face and shouted, "Arrest him!" to his soldiers. The crowds were agitated, shouting protest, some demanding this new truth, others pushing the soldiers to take this man away. Two soldiers quickly bound his hands. They strapped him to ropes that trailed from the reins of a large Spanish Andalusian, a hot-tempered beast, beautiful and proud.

Commander Alexander shouted, "It is declared today that any Jews found promoting this 'Yeshua rebellion' will be imprisoned by command of Emperor Tiberius." Suddenly the crowd grew silent for fear of their lives.

Democritus said, "But I'm not a Jew. I'm Greek."

Startled, Alexander snapped, "But you were preaching Yeshua, and that dead man has caused more trouble in this city than any other. Anyone proclaiming his name will be executed. The emperor will stamp out this Jewish religion once and for all." The horse turned restlessly. "Let this be a warning to everyone this day," Alexander raged. "We are actively hunting all of Yeshua's disciples. If you love your life, I'd suggest you be loyal to Rome alone and her gods."

He waved his hand as he reined in the horse. "Take him to the prison. He will be executed before the emperor's counsel, Sejanus."

Democritus replied, "I will gladly die for the sake of Yeshua. As you worship Diana, or Apollo, I worship the man who found me and set me free."

"Your wish will be granted today." Alexander's face boiled red as he ground his teeth. He pulled out a coiled whip from his saddle and struck Democritus across his back. The prisoner arched in pain but said nothing. Again and again the commander struck the man until his rage was worn out. The crowds had drawn back in surprise, unused to see a man in his position doing such a thing. Usually, such punishment was delegated to his soldiers.

"Get him out of here." Blood had stained the ground and the prisoner's back had deep gouges. But Democritus remained silent, joyful that he was counted worthy. Democritus was tethered and dragged through the streets of Rome. Struggling to keep up with the beast, the warrior ran until his legs gave way. Then the animal dragged his body toward the Amphitheater where others were awaiting their death sentence.

Democritus was grateful that he lived to face this day. Now surrounded by so much suffering, he fell on his face and prayed, "Thank you, Lord God Almighty, you who are the eternal one, we trust you alone. By your mighty power, you have begun to reign. May your name be proclaimed throughout the earth."

Back at the Temple of Diana, the crowds had quickly dispersed for fear of their lives. Yet they began to spread the story of the courageous soldier who wasn't afraid to suffer for his faith.

Commander Alexander was visibly shaken and, for a moment, seemed disoriented. Memories flashed back to his dead Anna who had believed in this same devilish religion and died for nothing . . . but had given him a gift of a beautiful child, sweet Charis. Alex squeezed his eyes shut, trying to rid his mind of the conflicting thoughts. But he had his beloved daughter Charis. Who planned out her life? What god decreed that she should be born after surviving that terrible winter storm?

Five weeks over land and sea finally brought the prisoners from Yerushalayim to the gates of Rome. Anna was relieved that the journey was over. She was now thrown into a dark bunker-like cell constructed of wood and iron. The place reeked of urine, vomit and human waste. Anna huddled into the far corner of her tiny space. The other three prisoners were put into separate cells, disappearing into the darkness of the prison. Mercifully, no one had touched her. If it weren't for their chains, she would most likely have been molested and maybe killed. She spent the first night in grateful prayer to Yeshua for his miraculous protection. He'd promised to go with her.

In the dim recesses of the prison complex, Anna heard someone speaking with great urgency. She peered between the bars but only saw deep shadows. *Who is he?* He warned the prisoners of dying without hope. A few men tried to silence him while others asked him to explain his words. Anna noticed that his message was compelling and urgent. The man was gifted at oratory, driven by passion. Then she heard one word that gave her courage, Yeshua.

*There is courage in that man's voice. He has no fear of suffering or death.* Anna grew hopeful that other believers were here.

Democritus knew his time on earth was short. Courage coursed through his veins. There was nothing to fear. He was not afraid and spoke often to the prisoners on either side of him. His voice was deep and low. Speaking of Yeshua as the only true God, his voice echoed through the long dark tunnels where the living sat among the dead corpses. Their only hope had lain in this man's words. Many prisoners lay among their own filth in utter despair. They had lost all desire to live. Democritus focused his message on these who had given up on life. Without Yeshua, they would die another death, eternally lost without hope, forever alone. Today they had a chance to turn to the one who died for them.

Other prisoners raged at the guards, claiming their innocence. They screamed and begged ceaselessly for pardon. Some tried to bribe the guards to no avail. Rome had rounded up many followers of Yeshua and the prison was filled with those of both Jewish and Gentile descent. These were the prisoners who waited and prayed in confidence. Yeshua had assured them of hope beyond this world. Although they feared the pain of torture, their last hope was Yeshua. They would willingly be a martyr for him. They huddled in prayer for their loved ones.

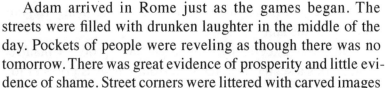

Adam arrived in Rome just as the games began. The streets were filled with drunken laughter in the middle of the day. Pockets of people were reveling as though there was no tomorrow. There was great evidence of prosperity and little evidence of shame. Street corners were littered with carved images whose sensual forms provoked cravings of the darkest kind.

Adam did not know where to look for Alexander. He headed for public buildings where a crowd might gather. Droves of people were crowding the streets, most going in a single direction. In the distance he heard the roar of cheers. He shoved through the crowds toward the Amphitheater.

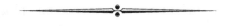

Malchus decided it was time. With a growing excitement in his stomach, he put the scroll under his outer robe and headed for the palace. His shadow had notified him that the traitor woman had arrived.

Malchus' presence was announced to the emperor's royal counsel, Sejanus. The deputy was making plans to head to the arena for the games. Non-stop games had proved an absolute success. There were many prisoners, mostly Jews, with many followers of Yeshua locked away awaiting death. The world would know who reigns.

Sejanus was impatient. He didn't have time for this pathetic man. He was a tiresome bore with nothing to do but whine. But the guard insisted his news was urgent. He said he had evidence that would completely uncover the insurrectionist plot in Judea. The games were the perfect place to expose these criminals. Reluctantly Sejanus agreed to listen to his babble.

Malchus entered the room and stood before the throne. He bowed and scraped. He wore a long crimson robe with a gold border. The scroll was in his hand.

"I hope you're not wasting my time, little man." Sejanus spoke with disdain.

"No, Your Excellency. I have physical proof of insurrection. Here's a secret message sent from a Jewess prisoner to a commander in your army. I intercepted it before it reached its intended destination. I'm quite confident this will expose their plot." Malchus kept his head bowed.

"Give it to me." Sejanus snatched the scroll from his hands. Malchus bowed his head but watched discretely as the deputy's eyes darted along each line. Malchus stood meekly, watching the emperor's counsel for a signal that he indeed had intercepted valuable information to expose this plot against the throne. As Sejanus' eyes widened, Malchus raised his head, smiling confidently. The most honored face that represented

Emperor Tiberius suddenly boiled red, and his eyes blackened with rage. His fists gripped the edges of the scroll nearly tearing it.

*Something's wrong.* Malchus shuddered inside.

Sejanus straightened his back and raised his shoulders. He glared at Malchus.

*What have I done? What . . . was . . . in that letter?* Malchus was certain he'd fooled the traitors, but had they fooled him instead? Worse still, had he made a fool of himself . . . again? He began to back away. The deputy stood, wild with fury. His hand shook with the scroll still in his grip. The words that provoked him were neatly written in Anna's careful hand:

*Hear, oh Emperor Tiberius, and you, his counsel, Sejanus, Yeshua Christus is Lord of all. There is no other God but him. He alone gives power and he alone takes it from men. He alone must be worshiped for he is King of Kings. You, Tiberius, are only a man bound by perverse passions that are driving you mad. You will die like those you've tortured at the Salto di Tiberio[78]. Your immoral iniquity will shame you in the annals of history. Take heed of God's warning and repent now while you still have breath.*

Sejanus' eyes lifted from the treasonous text and focused on the worm standing before him. "Guards, seize this man and throw him into the prison cells at the Amphitheater. He's made a mockery of me . . . of . . . the great Emperor Tiberius." In a screaming rage, spittle hit Malchus' face as he shrunk back in fear.

Malchus turned and ran, desperate to escape the counsel's rage. *I've just signed my own death warrant. What a fool I am. Why didn't I read that letter? I should have read it. It was supposed to go to Alexander.*

He'd been betrayed.

---

[78] Sheer 330 m high cliff on the Isle of Capri where Tiberius threw innocent children into the sea for his pleasure

Malchus dove between the guards, stumbled and slid across the marbled floor. One guard pinned him down but he slipped from his grasp and got to his feet again. A second guard grabbed at him and caught his robes. Malchus kept running, slipping out of the robes that tangled around his feet. He passed through the doorway and ran down the steps wearing nothing more than a loin cloth. Running along a paved pathway, he heard shouts from both sides. Others were coming. Malchus couldn't think anymore, he just ran straight ahead.

Suddenly he was struck by a blow. Someone tackled him from behind. He fell face first on the gravel and screamed out in pain. He tasted blood. When he was dragged back into Sejanus' presence, he was startled to find him burning the scroll in an incense burner. He wanted to scream. *What are you doing? What was in that letter? Why are you destroying it?*

"Get that man out of my sight. He dies today. Send him to the lions."

Malchus fainted.

"Squealing little weasel! I want to see him plead for his life." Sejanus turned to a guard. "Give him something to wear. I can't stand to see his scrawny body. He's disgusting." Sejanus headed for the arena in the great Amphitheater.

When Malchus woke, he realized he was in a prison. Above were the stands where people were joking and drinking, waiting for a great time. Not far away, he could hear the lions growling and roaring for meat. He heard dogs bark and snarl. The wooden stands above his head creaked and groaned as spectators continued to find their seats. Beer and urine trickled down on his head through the floor boards above. The smells of human filth mixed with his own blood made him vomit. He wretched until there was nothing left.

Shamed and bleeding, the pathetic little man sat with one arm chained tight. He never believed his life would end like this. He always thought he could pull himself up and gain power. But today he'd gone too far, presumed too much. In an instant his freedom was snatched, and his life lay crumbled before Caesar's throne.

Democritus was chained to another wall in the same cell. He sat silently as the soldiers dragged this man in and shoved him into a corner. He cried out and for that they beat him with punches and kicks. Instinctively, Democritus tugged on his chains to defend the man. He'd never seen him before but called out, "I'm so sorry for their mistreatment of you. I, too, have been imprisoned unfairly. God has given me peace in spite of these chains. Can I pray for you?"

"Pray? No god can deliver me from this. Don't speak to me. Just leave me alone."

Malchus turned his back and sobbed with self-pity. He hated who he really was, an illegitimate son of some deranged Roman and a Jewish prostitute who never had time for her son. He hated himself and he trembled at his future. He'd not prepared for life beyond this one. He hadn't given the after-life a second thought. He deserved nothing but punishment. He'd done nothing great, performed nothing holy and believed in nothing but himself. His life was a farce. Instinctively, he touched his ear.

"There's someone who will help you face death with hope. His name is Yeshua," Democritus said with quiet confidence.

Malchus shuddered at the mention of that name. His eyes were wild with fear. "That man died . . . even if he were alive, he wouldn't listen to me." His face had lost all color. "No one cares about my life. No one." Shaking violently, he curled into a fetal position.

## Chapter Thirty-Nine

# ROME, THE FORUM, 34 A.D.

Alexander arrived at the Forum, the great amphitheater. He climbed the steps toward the emperor's seats with his daughter. He wore a linen toga buckled at his waist by a leather belt. On his shoulders he wore ornamental armor engraved with battle scenes. He ducked beneath a wooden walkway that led him toward Caesar's box. Charis' tiny hand held on to his as her legs rushed to keep up with him. She cried and sniffled but did not resist. Alexander was angry. "Charis, hush. Hush! There is no more discussion."

But his anger was really directed toward Sejanus who insisted Alexander bring his daughter. "Romans always bring their children to the games. It's a family affair. The children love watching the sport. She needs to have her eyes opened to the real world. She needs to understand who the real enemies of Rome are."

"But she's only three years old. There's plenty of time for that. She should enjoy life, not be burdened with war and bloodshed. She's just a child." But Alexander knew the counsel's tone meant he had no choice.

Charis had to trot to keep up with her father. His hand was so big and hers so tiny. On one side of the rickety walkway, crowds roared and cheered as they passed each opening to the stadium. The noise scared her.

"Papà, is this a circus?"

Alexander's face was somber. "No sweetheart, it's not the circus. But you'll be safe. I won't let anything happen to you. I promise."

"But I don't want to go. I'm scared, Papà."

"Don't argue with me, Charis. We must go."

The child looked at her father's huge hand and then up at his face. "Okay, Papà. I won't cry anymore." Alexander reached down and lifted her up in his arms. She held him tight around his neck and squeezed her eyes shut.

"I've got you, Charis. You'll always be safe with me." Alexander turned toward the noise that had grown louder with every step. "Here we are, sweetheart." The crowd roared as Alexander entered the emperor's galley. He waved and sat quickly next to the emperor's empty seat. The crowd was already impatient for Sejanus to arrive. Charis buried her head in her father's curly hair as the spectators chanted his name, "Alexander the brave, Alexander the brave."

"Papà, hold me."

The sky was cloudless and the temperature quickly rose. As large groups of people gathered, a festive atmosphere erupted across the vast amphitheater. Romans streamed in from all directions, laughing and shouting to each other. Some families had brought baskets of food and were busy eating and drinking. Fruit, cheeses and dried meats were spread out, accompanied by plenty of cheap wine and strong ale. Children chased and played along the narrow rows of wooden seats. Down below the arena, sporadic fights broke out between nervous prisoners. By noon, the stadium was jammed with people waiting for the emperor's counsel to arrive.

Races began, scheduled to entertain the spectators until the main events started. Below in the grand elliptical arena, three bronzed chariots with their riders waited at the start line. Sunlight glinted from the tips of spears and gleaming armor. Each chariot and rider had a pair of stallions, trained and groomed for such a race. The restless horses snorted and tossed their manes.

Alexander sensed his daughter's fear. He regretted bringing her. He grunted a curse against Sejanus and Tiberius. Close by, something spooked a stallion and it reared, pulling against its restraints. The whites of its eyes flashed wild. Charis cried.

"Charis, my beautiful girl, don't be afraid." He smoothed the curls around her face. "This is a race, a game. One of these chariots will win. You're safe with me." She tightened herself in his arms. Feeling frustrated at his inability to comfort his daughter, Alexander refocused on revenge. This woman was below in a cell waiting her sentence. What she'd done was unthinkable, to desecrate Anna's tomb, rob it bare and impersonate the one he had given his heart to. He wanted this woman's crime made public and Sejanus was eager to make it happen. She must die for this.

Below in the maze of prison cells, terrified men and women awaited their destiny. No one ever got out alive. Chained to each other or against walls, they waited for their time to come. These prisoners knew Sejanus' penchant for mutilating prisoners before killing them. He was determined to win the people over to him. They wanted blood, and he was ready to become their appointed emperor.

Democritus spoke to one prisoner after another. He possessed a boldness unseen before in this cesspit of human need. He was sent to this place for this very thing, at this appointed time. If ever there were a time to offer hope it was now. He had returned to earth for this. He feared nothing because nothing could separate him from Yeshua's love. He was not ashamed of his faith because he knew its power. The emperor's games were scheduled for the next two days. Most of these prisoners would be dead by tomorrow. While others groaned or wept, Democritus was calm and confident.

The people grew impatient beneath the sun's blaze. The substitute emperor, Sejanus, was a master at agitating his audience. He chose the hottest times and the most grueling delays to stir people into a frenzy. The crowd had waited for more than an hour today. Emptying their flasks of beer, their impatience had escalated.

There was a flurry of movement and a blast of fanfare as Sejanus finally emerged from a tunnel accompanied by two guards. He wore a bronze breastplate and a richly ornamented robe in crimson velvet. Starting from his left, a sea of people rose to their feet, bobbing to catch a glimpse of their ruler. They clapped and cheered and waved. He looked jubilant. Sejanus stood in the center of his world and received their accolades. Alex's blood boiled.

"Let the games begin!" People roared and cheered.

Below, the three chariots and their riders waited at the starting line. The horses were nervous. Sejanus raised his hand accompanied by a roll of drums. The people hushed and waited for the signal. The moment his hand went down, spectators went wild and screamed, drums banged a thunderous roll and the horses shot forward. The center chariot moved ahead two lengths, pulled by an Arabian charger. Whips snapped while the chariots circled the arena twice. Dust plumed into the air. The charger was well ahead when suddenly it veered too close to the wall of the arena. The wheel spiked the wall, snapped it loose and flipped the chariot and rider upside down. The man's leg was caught in the spokes of the wheel. Helplessly, his body dragged lifelessly around the arena until it broke free. The crowd went wild.

Only two chariots remained. The inside chariot had gained speed; the two horses were neck to neck. One chariot careened around the corner and came back out, overshooting its lane. Unbalanced, the chariot swerved close and cut into the other horse's leg. It reared high, throwing the rider to the ground. The wounded horse slowed then finally fell, bringing the chariot down with it. The people roared as billows of dust rose in the midday sun. Revelers shouted for the winner while, below ground, men and women were preparing to die.

Sejanus rubbed his hands in delight and waved for the first prisoners to be brought out. They were poor Jews who would die for their indebtedness. They had committed no crimes. Democritus pleaded with them to turn to Yeshua. One woman begged, "God of Abraham . . . help me. I can't face this alone."

Democritus encouraged her with a loud voice, "Call upon *Yeshua HaMashiach*. He's the Messiah of your people and the world. He came to set you free." Red and swollen eyes stared at Democritus in desperation. Her lips began to move as the soldiers shoved her into the arena. Another soldier snapped a whip across the warrior's back, his body arching sharply against the barbed spikes.

The guards gave the first prisoner a head start before they opened one cage. A sleek panther sprang forward, propelled by a need to hunt and capture. The man screamed and tried to climb the walls. He leapt on top of the empty cage but the panther jumped across the entire span, taking the prisoner down with it. Within seconds the body lay lifeless as the cat clawed and dragged its prey off to the side. The Romans roared with sickening delight.

A second prisoner was released from one entrance and a pack of wild dogs from another. The man stood paralyzed against the wooden walls. The dogs snapped and growled as they spotted him. Suddenly, the man sprinted to his left, zigzagging in different directions. The dogs split up and came from every direction. He backed up but they came from behind. He was cornered. The dogs surrounded him, crouching low, their hair bristling. With bared teeth, they moved in for the kill. The throng rose up in excitement. They screamed wildly. Chanting in unison they cried, "Kill, kill, kill!" The man began to scream. When they were within three feet of him, they attacked as one. The cheers of the revelers drowned out the prisoner's screams.

Adam kept his head low and pushed through the crowd. "Sorry, an urgent message for the imperial commander," he kept repeating. In the chaos, slipping and squeezing between groups of revelers, Adam slid into the emperor's entrance. Two guards posted near the arena entrance half turned toward him. He moved into the shadows, tight against the wall. "Lord, send a distraction," he prayed. The roar of the crowd echoed from the stands along the corridor. If they discovered him before he got to Alexander, Anna would meet certain death. Somehow he had to slip past the guards to enter the emperor's grandstand box.

A prisoner, young and beautiful, stood in chains waiting under an arch. Before her was the vast floor of the Amphitheater, blotched and stained in crimson red. The Mediterranean sun had baked the earth with sweat and blood, as many bodies had been slaughtered for Sejanus' pleasure.

Sejanus leaned toward his commander. "Here's your chance for justice, Alex. This is your impostor."

Alexander looked at the woman and was stunned. "But . . . she . . ."

"I know, I know, she's so beautiful! But there are plenty more for the taking."

"No, it's just . . . she looks so much like the woman . . . like Anna. How could that be?" Alexander shook his head. "I buried her myself." His face turned white. He felt a growing unease in his stomach.

"People don't come back from the dead, Alexander. That can't be her. She's an impostor . . . unless she's a ghost. We'll find out soon enough." Sejanus gave a throaty laugh and slapped Alexander on the back. "No one, not even a ghost has survived Rome's power."

Anna appeared serene. A breeze blew strands of hair across her face, rippled her torn rags. Her shoulders were bare. Across her back were streaks of red seeping blood. When the iron shackles were removed, Anna raised herself and stood tall, her eyes focused straight ahead toward the emperor's box. She was looking for someone.

The spectators hushed in anticipation. Anna was so delicate yet so strong, unlike most of the prisoners. Pushed into the arena, she quickly caught her step and walked without hesitation, like a lamb, to the center where a ten-foot pole rose up from the ground. The woman did not wail or resist while her wrists were bound with rope and hoisted high until her toes barely touched the ground. She raised her head to the sky. She was going home. She heard her own limbs pop from their sockets as she swayed. Anna could feel her breath come out in short gasps as her rib cage stretched taut. When the guard finished and had staked the rope to the ground, he turned away, resisting her gaze.

"I forgive you, sir. Go in peace." Her voice was barely a whisper, but the guard heard every word. He looked shaken, his face went pale and he rushed back into the tunnel.

Anna had no fear of death. She knew its taste was for a moment, then she would be home. The torture would pass quickly, for the body and mind could only take a few moments before it would surrender to unconsciousness. But she grieved for her daughter. How would she understand love in a world full of perversions and violence? How would she know how much her mother loved her? How would she find her way in this life?

Anna felt faint as pain tore down her arms and along her rib cage. The sun bore down like a furnace on her skin. She blinked to clear her vision. Contorted and hung up like a piece of venison, the prisoner raised her eyes toward the sea of faces. Up in the grandstands, directly in her line of vision, was the emperor's box on the first tier. Sejanus sat there in all his pomp and glory. His senators, magistrates and vestal virgins flanked him on one side. To his right sat a military figure in uniform. Anna's heart leapt with excitement. She saw Alex, and within his arms was the small figure of Charis, her precious daughter. She was so beautiful, so innocent, so scared at all this violence. Anna's heart raced with hope. *Oh Father, you know the emotions I feel for my child. Keep me strong for her sake. If only I could hold her* . . . If only she could hold Charis for a moment and tell her she loved her. If only she could tell her that she'd died trying to keep her alive. If only she could tell her about the love of God and the stories of Yeshua. Her heart ached more than her body. With no concern for herself, she called out, "Charis, my baby, my beautiful daughter. I love you so much, Charis." But Anna's small breathless voice was caught up in the screams and laughter from the crowd, eager to see blood and gore.

The people cheered as two iron cages were rolled out from tunnels beneath the stadium. A young lion paced within the confines of a cage. The noise of the revelers agitated the animal and it rose up against the bars, pawing and roaring. It circled its cage until it spotted Anna, then suddenly crouched and growled. It was hungry and nervous. On the far side a second cage held another lion nearly twice the size of the first, whose hide was marked by old scars. Its roar was deeper, its paws larger. Both were much larger than Anna.

An officer of the prison guard walked across the arena floor and stood before Sejanus. Addressing the emperor's counsel, he saluted and waited for permission to read the charges against the Judean woman. The crowd loved the stories of crime and passion. They lusted to hear the stories of human pleasure lived out in spite of the high stakes against the imperial throne. Sejanus loved the attention of the masses. He lifted his hand until all was absolute silent, then waved—and the officer began reading out the charges.

*"In the name of Emperor Tiberius, to his counsel, Sejanus, and senators of Rome, this woman before you today is charged with treason against Rome, his holiness Emperor Tiberius and our great leader, Commander Alexander. She has been found in possession of a priceless heirloom from the Royal Treasury. She has desecrated and raided the tomb of Commander Alexander's betrothed, Anna of Judea, and is charged with impersonating this woman for personal profit. She claims to be a member of a Judean insurrectionist movement called The Way, who claims that Yeshua Christus is their long awaited Messiah and is the Son of God, the Most High."*

The crowds responded with boos and hisses. Shrill whistles screeched out approval from young men. Women and girls trilled their tongues to demand the death of this woman.

Sejanus raised his hand for silence. "Interesting . . ." He smiled at Alexander and tapped the arm of his chair in thought. "Very interesting. Do you have anything to add?"

"Yes, I do. She claims to have died and risen from the dead."

The people went crazy, wild. They stood and raised their arms in a gesture of stoning her. They laughed. They shouted names and threw garbage down into the arena. "Feed her to Max. He's hungry today," they chanted. "Feed her to Max."

Alex's emotions were torn in two directions. It sickened him to see the citizens of Rome behaving so badly toward this woman who looked so much like his Anna. He also struggled with the thought that she was an impostor. She'd been caught desecrating Anna's tomb for her own personal gain. What benefit was it to her? His emotions boiled.

Sejanus stood and shouted. "Who charges this woman with treason?"

Alexander stood, pumping his fist in the air. "I do. Guilty as charged."

Before the words had left his lips, he questioned his decision. She did not protest, but her eyes stared at him with such sadness that Alexander looked away. He raised his voice again but sounded less convincing. "She's an impostor and thief. She's stolen . . . a family heirloom." He looked at her again and their eyes finally met. *How could she be alive?* When she looked at Charis, he recognized the familiar gaze of the one he had loved. *She could not be Anna. Impossible.*

The crowd stamped their feet in a frenzy. "Feed her to Max . . . Feed her to Max."

Democritus stood chained to the inner wall of the amphitheater beside seven other prisoners. Scars and festering wounds across his shoulders rippled as his muscles flexed. Sweat and grime had rubbed into his cuts that were now swollen. The sound of rattling chains and scraping of iron cuffs brought flashbacks to Democritus. Then he remembered the first taste of freedom he'd found when Yeshua came. It was Yeshua, a friend of sinners, a man like no other who had freed him forever. These chains meant nothing, could hold nothing, could stop nothing. He was free no matter what the world said or did.

Malchus cowered beside the warrior, weak and trembling. His skin looked pale and sickly in the glaring sun. Already his forehead and arms were blistering. The servant of the high priest gagged a dry heave and sank, but the chains forced him to remain in place, gouging his wrists, evoking a curse.

"Don't be afraid. I know death, and if you put your trust in Yeshua, he'll give you courage to face it," Democritus encouraged.

"I don't want courage; I want to live. I'm not a soldier. I can't fight," his voice whined. "I'm afraid to die." He looked up at Democritus like a child begging for his father's help. His eyes were filled with terror. "There's got to be a way to stay alive. God help me."

Democritus' forehead smoothed. "That's what God's been waiting for you to say. If you put your trust in Yeshua, he'll walk with you through death and bring you safely home. Otherwise, eternal damnation will snatch you away."

"Yeshua is dead. He can't help me."

"I believe you're from Yerushalayim. I recognize your dialect." Democritus looked straight into Malchus' eyes. "Everyone in Judea has heard of Yeshua's resurrection. He's very much alive. I've seen him." Democritus shifted his weight. "To die without forgiveness is a far greater sentence than anything this world could do to us."

Malchus watched as the cages rolled closer to the woman at the stake. *Such a waste. A beautiful woman is about to be torn apart by the emperor's beasts.* He remembered his own crimes and burned with shame. Shame was a close companion throughout his life, except for one moment. He remembered the feeling of forgiveness and it was exhilarating. He remembered the look in Yeshua's eyes as he touched his severed ear and healed him. *Why did he do that? How could he?*

Democritus had stopped talking and watched the trainer approach the cage of the larger lion. The scarred cat hissed and flattened his ears. Standing on his haunches against the door, it roared as the trainer came closer. When he lifted the bolt, the animal suddenly reached out and swiped him, catching his head with his left paw, clawing his face. The man screamed and pulled back. But the lion shoved his other paw through the bars and grabbed him from the right. It tried to pull his head through the bars and into the cage.

The spectators were finally horrified at the gore. They reacted by throwing rocks at the cage to distract the animal. Within seconds, the man hung there lifeless until the lion let the body drop. The door swung open and Max stared out at his freedom.

Anna knew her death would be painful. Natural instinct quickened her heart, and she turned her face away, praying the attack would be swift and that she'd be found faithful.

The lion dragged the carcass away from its cage, seeking a place to feast. On the first level of seating, a group of youths taunted the animal by throwing apples. One struck the lion and it turned. With a lunge, it clawed the wooden walls only yards from the crowd. Screams erupted and the youths scattered. It was then that the animal spotted Anna, and its predator instincts took over. It crouched low and growled.

Democritus was ready. The lion was within twenty feet of Anna. She had little chance of survival unless . . . he looked at his chains and remembered . . . he'd broken chains before.

Yards away the lion moved with stealth. It was stalking its prey. Democritus hesitated for only a moment, then bellowed an unearthly howl. The lion was startled and confused. Democritus screamed again, "In the name of Yeshua I break these chains!" They snapped and broke like sticks. The onlookers shot up around the arena, row upon row, shocked and amazed at this scene below. They'd never seen such a performance. Sejanus saw the cat from the corner of his eye and he stood. Alexander stood with him . . . but his eyes remained on Anna.

In that split second, Adam had the distraction he needed to get to Alexander. The guards weren't expecting something from behind; they were hoping for blood down in the arena. Adam had only seconds. He slipped through the narrow opening and placed the scroll in Alexander's hand before anyone could stop him. He spoke quickly in his ear. "Commander, you're letting the mother of your daughter, Charis, be murdered before her very eyes. Stop this terrible slaughter and read Anna's letter. For Charis' sake, read it and stop this execution."

Alexander was startled and blocked Charis from the intruder's reach. The guards rushed the man, shoving him against a wall with their swords. Dazed, the commander held the scroll and stared down at the prisoner.

Adam yelled, "Stop this murder, Alexander. Stop them from killing Anna!" As he shouted, a soldier's sword sliced the flesh through Adam's ribs. As blood gushed, he felt light headed and staggered while resisting the soldiers. "Only you can stop this. If she dies, her blood is on your head!" he shouted.

Charis cried, "Papà. Stop! Stop them, Papà. This is wrong. Please don't kill that woman!"

Sejanus shouted. "What's going on here?" He waved his hand in a flurry. "Guards, get this man out of here!"

Adam cried out, "Save Anna, commander." Soldiers kept him pinned against the wall. He was sure his wound was not fatal. He had to return to Judea where his family was waiting, and Artamos would need someone to help him overcome his past. He was alive for the sake of others.

Democritus was agile. Before the guards could stop him, he ran forward and surprised the lion, luring him into the open. Bellowing, he swung the chains in fast moving arcs. He had to distract the animal from Anna. He leaped on its cage and taunted the animal. "Come on, Max. Come and get me!"

The lion sprung to the top of the cage where Democritus swung one chain across the animal's face, slashing it, blurring its vision. The animal shook its head and pawed at its face.

"Come on, Max, you killer. Come and get me. Come on . . ." Democritus swung the chains, rotating one then the other. The whirring sound and circular movement seemed to confuse the animal. It swatted at the moving targets, then backed off, but suddenly jumped through the flying chains at Democritus. The animal and man fell against the cage and rolled off the edge. The weight of the animal on top of him crushed his ribs. Claws slashed deep across Democritus' chest. His wounds were bleeding badly.

Alexander read the parchment.

*Dear Alexander, please believe that I am Anna. You offered your family signet ring to me on the hillside that day. I rejected your gift, not because I didn't love you, but because of my faith in Yeshua. I anguished over my love for you in spite of my sin. I know you doubt that there is a God who can love you. In spite of all we've been through and done, God was gracious to give us Charis. Isn't she proof enough? For her sake believe that I am Anna, the one you once loved. With my love, Anna*

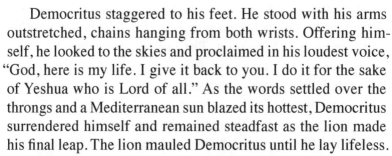

Democritus staggered to his feet. He stood with his arms outstretched, chains hanging from both wrists. Offering himself, he looked to the skies and proclaimed in his loudest voice, "God, here is my life. I give it back to you. I do it for the sake of Yeshua who is Lord of all." As the words settled over the throngs and a Mediterranean sun blazed its hottest, Democritus surrendered himself and remained steadfast as the lion made his final leap. The lion mauled Democritus until he lay lifeless.

This was an act of martyrdom in the name of Yeshua. It was done in the world's largest population center, the great city of Rome. Rome understood sport and torture, but not sacrifice.

The people clapped then chanted. They pleaded for the emperor's pardon of Anna. Now was the time for Sejanus to speak in the name of Emperor Tiberius. Someone was willing to die for this woman. Would the emperor concede?

Anna hung from the stake, exhausted and barely conscious. She knew death was coming and anticipated seeing God's face soon. The crowd had gone wild. Never before had Alexander seen such a thing. Could she truly be Anna? He could not comprehend it, but his heart said "yes."

Turning urgently toward Sejanus, Alexander stood and begged him to release the woman. "That's Anna! I know it is! I've made a big mistake. This is an innocent woman. I have proof." He held up the parchment. "I beg you to free this woman. She's committed no crime worthy of death."

The lion had pulled its prey to the side of the arena. Armed soldiers surrounded the animal and threw a net to capture it. The lion and its victim were dragged from sight.

Alexander said, "I beg you, Sejanus, she is not a traitor. Save her life for my sake and my child's. She is the mother of my daughter, Charis. I've made a terrible mistake."

Sejanus faced a dilemma. He was stunned. *What a strange religion, to have a man sacrifice his life for another.* Democritus was her savior. The crowd applauded the courageous act of the prisoner, a follower of Yeshua, the Jewish Messiah. Furthermore, his greatest military leader was pleading for this woman's life. What could he do?

A thought came to his mind. If he pardoned this woman, he would be hailed a great deliverer and perhaps seal his future as Emperor Sejanus. He would be divine in the eyes of the people. He longed to become emperor of the great Roman Empire. He was tired of being the emperor's messenger boy. He could not share his glory with that prisoner by letting him die in the woman's place.

Sejanus raised his fist, silencing the Amphitheater. The people waited. Finally, he smiled and shouted, "I, Sejanus, in the name of Emperor Tiberius, command you to release that woman." The crowd rose to its feet like a wave of the sea. The people roared like thunder, stomped the floors, clapped, screamed and hollered. Anna's eyes turned to the box where Alexander and Charis stood. Tears of gratitude rolled down her cheeks, yet her heart continued to pound.

A guard cut the ropes from her wrists. Her body collapsed to the ground. She tried to stand but couldn't. Alexander lifted Charis into his arms, pushed past the guards, telling them in no uncertain terms to let Adam go free. He ran out onto the floor of the arena. After letting Charis stand, Alexander knelt beside Anna and lifted her gently in his arms. She was trembling, as frail as a bird . . . yet so beautiful!

"Alex, my Alex, it's me, Anna." Tears washed her cheeks.

"I know it's you. I don't understand it but you're alive."

Anna let her cheek touch against her daughter's. "Charis, my sweet, sweet daughter, I've loved you from the day you were born. I fed you and sang over you. I've prayed God would allow us to be together again . . . and he has."

Shyly the girl reached out and tentatively touched her mother's hair. "You're just like Papà told me . . . only much prettier." Anna wept for joy.

Surrounding them on every side, the crowd exploded with cheers that a life was saved. They had witnessed martyrdom, love and forgiveness, a trademark of those who followed Yeshua. To die for a cause was something Rome had never seen, never understood until now. They went wild with enthusiasm.

Alexander stood with Anna in his arms. "Sweet Anna, I don't understand this god of yours, but he's been involved in setting you free. He brought you back to me. Will you teach me about this man, this God, Yeshua? I must know for certain who he is."

Anna gripped Alexander more tightly. "Yes, Alex, I will gladly tell you about *Yeshua HaMashiach*, my Lord and my God. I want Charis to know how much he loves her, too."

Charis looked up at her mother as she walked beside them. Shyly she held her mother's hand as they walked away from the screaming crowds. Anna did not know their future yet, but she knew she would find a place to be near enough to Charis to watch her grow up to know Yeshua.

# Epilogue

S ejanus shouted, "Let the games continue." Feeling secure in his future divine state, he grew excited. He would have Emperor Tiberius killed. He would be hailed as the great Emperor Sejanus. Next week he would have sculptors fashion his image in gold, then place it in Rome's bustling city center. He would subdue the followers of Yeshua. As Caesar, he could not allow this cult to grow. Already they were too powerful and their tentacles were spreading out into other parts of the world.

Soldiers led Malchus into the arena. Dust billowed as they dragged and pulled him.

Sejanus sneered with contempt. "This will be a real treat, getting rid of this weasel."

Malchus hobbled toward the center, following the same steps Democritus had taken toward the stake where Anna had hung. Democritus had offered himself as a martyr. How could anyone die for another? It was Democritus' faith that held him firm to his very last breath. Now it was Malchus' turn.

A lifetime of memories flashed through his mind, fast and all too familiar. Self-hatred occupied every scene. Who could love a mistake like him? He kept hobbling.

Malchus remembered the face of Yeshua. Who did he die for? A guard unlocked his shackles and shoved him against the stake. *No God is big enough to forgive all that I've done.*

The words of Democritus came to his mind: "To die without forgiveness is a far greater sentence than anything this world could do to us."

Malchus suddenly felt a strong presence beside him. He saw no one, but recognized a familiar loving presence, the one who stood near him in the Garden, the man Iscariot betrayed and Caiaphas despised. Yeshua, the man who healed his ear. The Savior Malchus had repeatedly scorned his entire life was now giving him one last chance. Could he really be loved by . . . God?

The young lion shot from its cage propelled by lust for killing. It had been spiked with spears and smelled blood, kept hungry, trained for attack. Malchus' legs gave way and he slumped. The air was thin and he couldn't breathe. Chains tore his wrists while his body weight dragged downward. "Help me." His cry was feeble but real. Nausea was so great he could easily choke to death on his own vomit if the beast didn't get to him soon.

His senses were skinned bare, his thoughts untamed and his shame so palpable as the world watched. The only place where he could listen was his throbbing heart. There, once again, he heard Yeshua's familiar voice. Malchus gulped in air.

*"Trust me."* Stumbling he staggered back to his feet. *"I died for you, Malchus. Give me a chance to take you home."* The lion left a trail of dust as it headed toward Malchus.

"Yes, Yeshua. Yes, take me, my sin, my shame, my wicked heart. I can't carry it any longer." The crowd screamed for blood.

Malchus had uttered the first prayer in his life. It was his only prayer. The muscular animal was ten feet from him and closing in. No more bargaining with God. In that final gasp, Malchus repented of a lifetime of hatred toward the God who made him. He surrendered a life of nothing and received an eternity of everything. Malchus regretted what he'd done against the One who now offered unconditional love; the love he'd sought his whole life. As death approached, Malchus heard

Yeshua's words, *"Malchus, I died for you. You were never a mistake. Give me your heart and I will bring you home."*

In an instant Malchus' past was erased. Courage surged through him like lightning. The cat had sprung the last final steps. Malchus didn't hear the crowd or see the lion leap, but a radiance washed across his countenance. He looked up. The last words the guards heard him utter were, "Yeshua, my Lord." Malchus died forgiven.

*"And everyone who calls on the name of Yahweh will be saved; for on Mount Zion and in Jerusalem there will be deliverance, as Yahweh has said, even among the survivors whom Yahweh calls."*[79]

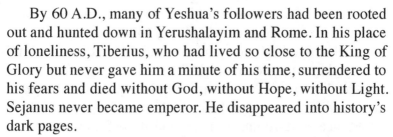

By 60 A.D., many of Yeshua's followers had been rooted out and hunted down in Yerushalayim and Rome. In his place of loneliness, Tiberius, who had lived so close to the King of Glory but never gave him a minute of his time, surrendered to his fears and died without God, without Hope, without Light. Sejanus never became emperor. He disappeared into history's dark pages.

Caligula waltzed into the vacuum after Tiberius, and the people worshiped him. He was more blood-thirsty than other emperors, using his military forces to hunt anyone who belonged to *The Way,* although he had made no specific ruling against Yeshua's followers. They were simply accused of being Yeshua's followers and condemned solely on that fact.

King Agrippa used his forces to round up followers and have them secretly killed. Many citizens of Yerushalayim would wake to find their neighbors murdered in the night. Authorities took no notice of any reports. Some families would simply vanish and never be heard from again. Children went missing.

---

[79] Joel 2:32

Within twelve months of the crucifixion, as many as two thousand followers became martyrs for Yeshua in Yerushalayim alone. The Cross was the central theme of their faith. *The blossom of martyrdom had come into full bloom.* The more the world struck down Yeshua's followers, the more they flourished. The roots of faith were watered in the blood of its saints.

Messianic Rabbi, Jonathan Cahn, a New York Times bestselling author, says: "In the world there are all kinds of revolutions throughout history: French revolution, American revolution, Communist revolution, Islamic revolution, the idea is that we're going to bring an answer, to change the world . . . but they never really change anything because the issue is ultimately 'sin.' We, (followers of Yeshua) are the true revolutionaries. Who has changed world history for the last 2,000 years? You look at the beginning and you had 12 believers, and ultimately, they changed the world."[80]

The disciples of Yeshua are called to spread the gospel to all the world, knowing in doing so, they will be persecuted and could face martyrdom. Jesus reminded his followers, ". . . *I have chosen you out of the world. That is why the world hates you . . . If they persecuted me, they will also persecute you . . . They will treat you this way because of my name, for they do not know the One who sent me.*"[81]

"Christians are the most persecuted religious group worldwide. Christians in more than 60 countries face persecution from their governments because of their faith in Yeshua. Today, in Middle Eastern countries, there is Christian genocide, wiping out the Light of Christ in an entire nation. In 41 of the 50

---

[80] Quote of Jonathan Cahn from WND Films "Global Jesus Revolution," Joel Richardson, copyright @2016

[81] Jn. 15:19-21

worst nations for persecution, Christians are being persecuted by Islamic extremists."[82]

Today there are over 2 billion disciples of Yeshua around the globe. For some believers, when comfort gives way to suffering, they quickly turn their back on him and allow their love to grow cold. Yeshua says, *". . . No one who puts his hand to the plow and looks back is fit for service in the kingdom of God."*[83] While scripture warns it also welcomes and embraces those who count the cost and surrender all to follow Yeshua. As terrorism increasingly targets Christians around the globe, there remains a growing stream of new disciples from countries where religious freedom is banned. Isaiah calls us to seek and find the Messiah. *"Seek Yahweh while he may be found; call on him while he is near."*[84]

---

[82] https://www.opendoorsusa.org/christian-persecution/world-watch-list/

[83] Lu. 9:62

[84] Is. 55:6